To Paula,

Incredible ostati a

Grave Purpose

The Adventures of Alan Shaw
Volume Three

Craig Hallam

Inspired
Quill

Published by Inspired Quill: April 2023

First Edition

Contact the author through their website: craighallam.wordpress.com

Chief Editor: Sara-Jayne Slack
Proofreader: Fiona Thomas
Cover Design: Deranged Doctor Designs
Additional thanks to: BB eBooks Thailand
Typeset in Garamond

Paperback ISBN: 978-1-913117-19-1
eBook ISBN: 978-1-913117-20-7
Print Edition

Printed in the United Kingdom
1 2 3 4 5 6 7 8 9 10

Inspired Quill Publishing, UK
Business Reg. No. 7592847
www.inspired-quill.com

Praise for Craig Hallam

*[*Old Haunts *is full of] Adventure, comedy, fiendish machines, dire plots and desperate heroism, with a charming side-order of subverting the action tropes. An excellent read.*

– Nimue Brown,
author of *Hopeless, Maine*

[In Greaveburn*], Hallam has crafted an engaging narrative with likable characters and a climax which makes a statement about human nature. However, one could argue the city itself is the real star of the story. Hallam's expert use of imagery helps us to imagine Greaveburn as a Gothic metropolis full of splendour.*

– S. Kinkade,
author of *God School*

Greaveburn *is such a rich literary tapestry it would be a shame not to dip our toes into it at least once more. Fans of George R. R. Martin's* Game of Thrones *and Mervyn Peake's* Gormenghast *are certain to enjoy getting to know Greaveburn and its residents.*

– Angharad Welsh,
Cotswold Style Magazine

[In Not Before Bed*], rest assured, there's something for everyone and each short story is unique as the last. Sheer brilliance this, one of the funniest horror collections I've ever read.*

– Nathan Robinson,
author of *Ketchup on Everything*

Hallam puts so much into his writing and certainly produces entertaining and believable characters as well as thrilling plot lines. If you like adventure, fantasy or the Steampunk genre then Alan Shaw *is a truly brilliant read.*

– Occasionally Adulting

As with the first in the series Old Haunts *swiftly got read [...] at work, at home, on the park bench, on other sofas, in the queue at the post office... because it was just too damn good to put down.* [Old Haunts] *is glorious unrepentant beautifully written pulp that drags you on with its wilful abandon.*

– Mark Hayes,
author of *A Scar of Avarice*

Dedication

This is for everyone who has joined Alan on his adventures; to all the friends he doesn't even know he has.

Contents

*Our fair metropolis sees a well-earned and long overdue
reward come to a local hero. Readers of The Illustrated
Times will be familiar with the name of Alan Shaw who,
as a boy, saved the future of the British Empire by
showing a fine moral compass that many would think
impossible of a lowly street urchin.*

*After many such honourable acts in support of Her
Majesty's Empire, Mister Shaw was thought lost in the
Indian Revolution. London wept for the hero and a statue
was raised in his honour in his once home of Covent
Garden. However, The Illustrated Times is pleased to
inform you, fair city of London, that our urchin hero has
returned home, alive and well. It seems that reports of
Mister Shaw's demise were exaggerated but somewhat
necessary to facilitate his work as a privateer for Her
Majesty on unfamiliar and unfriendly shores in ways that
boggle the imagination.*

*However, our hero returns to London under a cloud
of grief. His adopted father, Chief Inspector Jonathan
Carpenter of King Street metropolitan police station, was
murdered by the recent blight to the city known
colloquially as Mister Slay, a villain the likes of which
London had never seen. Instrumental in the justice
brought down on the head of this diabolical madman,
Shaw once again served our city, being gravely injured in*

the process as readers may remember from our July edition.

It is with great pride that we inform you that Mister Alan Shaw has been awarded special dispensation from the Metropolitan Police to function as an autonomous civilian consultant within the borders of our fair city.

Underneath is a photograph of a blonde man on crutches looking very uncomfortable before a statue bearing his likeness, accompanied by a beaming police officer who is clearly better at pretending. Beneath is the legend: *Alan Shaw, Protector of London, beside old friend Chief Inspector Humphrey Jennings.*

Alan Shaw and the Spectres of Sutton Hall

1

June, 1871
London, England

SOMEWHERE HIGH ABOVE, the moon made its lazy arc, but there would be no spotting it tonight. The smog had dropped, meeting the mist off the Thames and merging into a stifling pea-souper. The tap of a cane on flagstone resonated through the dense yellow vapour, its owner nothing but a vague shape in the gloom as it passed between pools of fizzing electric street lamps. As it grew closer, the hiss and release of the limping figure's respirator accompanied the cane's beat.

Curly stepped out from his alleyway, a rag tied across his face to keep at least some of the rotten-egg air at bay. He regarded the new arrival in their broad top hat pulled down low and thigh-length leather coat glistening with amber droplets. The cane's handle was a silver T; simple, functional, and probably worth a little something. This was a gentleman, for sure. Drawing a blade, eager for the relocation of a thick billfold into his own grimy pocket, Curly let what little light there was catch the metal so that the figure might see it. The gent drew to a stop a few feet away, the cane giving a final *clack* that echoed out into the night.

The respirator hissed, releasing a voice that sounded far away and reedy.

"What's your name, son?" The accent wasn't of a gentleman at all. It sounded more like Curly's own cheapside drawl, although the stranger's was a little diluted by reading and suchlike, if the thief was any judge.

"Does it matter?" Curly snarled.

"I suppose not. What is it you're after?"

"Whatever you've got, Gov."

"And suppose I don't give it to you."

Curly smiled behind his rag. From across the street, Two-fer stepped out of the fog as Beppo emerged from a shady alcove, both of Curly's boys sliding behind the victim who took half a glance back at them.

"I think you will," Curly growled.

It could have been a hiss of the respirator, but Curly swore he heard the victim give a tired sigh.

"Alright. Come and get it."

Blade first, Curly advanced.

The fog burst apart. Curly felt a whip of air and his hand lit up with pain as the knife clattered to the pavement. A shoulder barge slammed him to the ground, the air knocked bursting from his lungs in a pained cough. A *snick-snack* sound and Two-fer groaned briefly before keeling over. Beppo must have lasted longer because there was a slap of flesh on flesh and the stranger grunted. Then Beppo let out an almighty screech and folded double. Curly looked up as the stranger limped toward him.

Curly saw a wince of pain as the stranger crouched beside him, looking him up and down like his mother would have, with such disappointment.

"Go home and put some ice on it," the stranger said.

"On what?" Curly asked, instantly regretting it.

The stranger's fist slammed into his jaw and an already dim world went dark.

ALAN SHAW STOOD, letting his cane do most of the work, and rubbed some of the pain out of his thigh. Stepping over the thief, he carried on down the street at a leisurely pace, the mugging forgotten but for the lick of sweat beneath his shirt and a faint sting on his left cheek between the respirator's straps.

Coming to the end of the road, he stopped to listen. Even at this time of night, Regent Street was busy. Traffic hurtled through the fog, engines labouring and huffs of steam joining the pea-souper as drivers swerved to avoid collisions without actually slowing down. At a crossing, Alan gave a towering Mk I automaton a polite tap with his cane. Its klaxon sounded as the metal man stepped forward into the road, arms stretched wide, a pulsing light emitting from its single glass eye. Waiting for the screech of rubber to die away, Alan followed, giving the machine a reciprocated nod before limping off along the street. Cutting across Savile Row, he soon found his way to Hay Hill and a familiar red door.

Walking in without knocking, he began to shrug off his outer layers, coat and hat first, revealing a simple yet well-made suit and flash of blonde hair turning silver at the temples. He hung his revolver in its shoulder holster next and peeled off the respirator mask and wide filtration belt, rubbing his face where the mask had dug in, and set them down beside a row of others. Most of them were much better made than his own functional model, all filigree stitching and embossed leather. That was enough to set his nerves chiming. He could already hear chatter accompanied by the gramophone's scratch coming from the parlour. There would be a lot of people here tonight, most of them rich, over-educated, and all acting like they had eyeballs in their nostrils. It would take some expert avoidance if he was to survive.

Step one, locate the scotch.

Straightening his waistcoat and stretching his spine from the weight of his equipment, Alan considered leaving the cane.

"Pride and falls," he muttered to himself, sighing heavily and following the noise with cane in hand.

Lottie had decorated the hallway, as the rest of the house, with exquisite and subtle taste. The bottom half of the walls were dark red with the upper cream, an intricate border of plaster daisies between the two. The banister which Alan had used as a boy was still of dark wood but the metal spindles were painted cream to match the rest of the room. Moving down the hallway as stealthily as possible, he tried to make it past the parlour door and into the kitchen without being seen.

"Alan!"

His shoulders sagged. If he could just have had a drink in one hand, his cane in the other, he'd have been safe. Now he had one hand free and faced a room filled with hand-shakers. Turning into the parlour as if he meant to all along, he gave his adopted brother a weary wave. Simon broke off his conversation with a battleship moustache beneath which an elderly gentleman struggled to remain upright.

"I really didn't expect you to come," Simon said, slapping Alan on the shoulder. His glasses sparkled with the cheerful light of the eyes behind them. Alan couldn't help but notice that the parting in his brother's hair had moved from the centre to the side. He couldn't imagine that Lottie would approve of Simon covering up his bald patch. She was a practical person who didn't hold with such cheap vanity. This was a change purely for Simon's own pride.

Alan thought to mention it, but decided otherwise.

"Wouldn't miss it for the world," he said.

"Ah, sarcasm, just what the evening was missing."

Giving his brother a knowing smile, Simon slipped an arm around Alan's shoulder and propelled him into a parlour filled with egos and billfolds. Alan ignored them all, his attention aimed toward the dark edges of the room, searching for one face in particular that he never wanted to see. Alan's thigh pulsed with pain and he swung around, knowing exactly where he'd find the grinning spectre he sought. And there, certain as death, was Mister Slay.

In his dusty black suit the long-dead murderer turned his pale, grinning countenance to a chattering group beside him, laughing along with the conversation even though none of them could see him. Slay pretended to catch Alan's eye by accident and gave him an exaggerated wink.

Simon followed his brother's gaze, his brow furrowing at the empty spot at which Alan was aiming a scowl.

"What's wrong?" he asked, narrowing his eyes at his brother.

"Must have eaten a dodgy oyster or something."

Simon gave an unconvinced huff.

The next few minutes were a flurry of half-familiar facial hair and fancy hairdos. He spotted Lottie in the crowd and their eyes met for a brief greeting before the hostess was called to a conversation elsewhere. Alan shook some hands as Simon tottered off to get him a drink, only to stubbornly hold it for him when he returned.

"I can hold that myself," Alan muttered sidelong.

"But then how would you shake hands?"

"You're cruel, Simon. Have I ever told you that?"

"On multiple occasions. Lady Ottaway may I introduce my brother, Alan Shaw, Protector of London."

Rolling his eyes at Simon, Alan took a broad hand wrapped in lace. Lady Ottaway stood in excess of six feet, her silver hair well put together but without the pretentious faux-diamond slides and pins of the other hairstyles in the room. Her dress was stylishly subtle in black with only a silver filigree brooch for adornment. After the handshake, Simon finally handed Alan his drink and bustled away with a nod to them both. Alan had the distinct feeling that he'd just been dropped off with a babysitter.

Dipping fingers into his glass, he selected a chunk of ice and unceremoniously applied cold alcohol to the new graze on his cheek. That would be another to add to the collection of scars that surrounded his lined eyes, chin and knuckles, the tally card of his life. Content to stand in silence, he attempted to do so, but it seemed that Lady Ottaway was too polite for that.

"I hear that your investigation service has brought both honour and the reverse upon your reputation, Mister Shaw," she said without a hint of humour.

"If anyone ever says I care about my reputation, they're talking about someone else," Alan retorted as he sipped from his glass.

"I do so hate these gatherings," Lady Ottaway said with a hooded smile.

Alan clinked glasses with his new co-conspirator.

"Are you on a case at the moment, Mister Shaw?"

"Just Alan is fine, madam. I've been employed this evening, actually. An odd one. My favourite kind."

"London is wall-to-wall oddity. I imagine you're kept quite busy."

Alan nodded along. "I'm headed right back to work after this cattle market, in fact."

"So late at night? Something clandestine, I take it?"

Alan thought for a moment. To tell or not to tell. But no one had ever accused him of subtlety.

"A ghost hunt. For a gent who owns a big old house out Hackney way. Says he's tried to sell it but everyone who goes there gets spooked. He's at his wits end."

Lady Ottaway regarded him for a moment, trying to decide if he was joking. Alan replied with a shrug.

"It's what I do. What about yourself?"

"I mostly spend my family's money," she said. She waited for him to give some reaction, but Alan simply looked at her expectantly, waiting for her to continue. "Ill-gotten gains from the slave trade, I'm afraid. I'm trying to do my best with what I have to even the score. Do you believe in karma, Alan?"

"It follows me around whether I believe in it or not," he said.

"Well, I want to try to clean my family's slate, shall we say, before such things are totted up by the heavenly clerks. I rehabilitate orphans. Do you know the statistics for how many orphans live on London's streets? And how many are indoctrinated into the Gentleman's Consortium at a young age to perform criminal acts?"

"I have a fair idea." Alan polished off his drink despite having more than half a glass left.

"Well, I try to provide them with viable and legal opportunities, to teach them that crime doesn't pay."

Alan turned to her, his face carefully non-aggressive.

"The problem being, that it does," he said.

The lady's brow knotted with curiosity. "Surely you can't think that?"

"I'm not very good at saying things I don't mean, madam. But, from someone with personal experience, when you have nothing, anything is a step up. Those urchins aren't thinking about crime. They're thinking they can take a little from someone who has a lot and get a full belly in return. You could almost call it karma."

"That doesn't make it right."

"It doesn't make it wrong, either." Across the room, someone caught Alan's eye and he instantly regretted his casual glance in that direction. "Balls. Look busy."

Alan and Lady Ottaway closed like a book, trying to seem engrossed in conversation, but it was too late. The blustering form of an elderly gentleman stomped over to them, a string of military bunting across his chest.

"Shaw! Nice to see you out of your cave and mingling with your betters." The plump old fool gave a snort at his own joke, not seeming to mind when no one else joined in.

"I'm yet to shoot anyone today, Lyttleton," Alan grumbled.

Missing Alan's deadly serious tone, the brigadier whinnied another laugh and gave him a light punch on the arm.

"That's the spirit. Good man! That badge they gave you still burning a hole in your pocket is it? You should wear it on your chest, man. Be proud of your achievements." The little man puffed up like a rooster, rattling his own wind-chime jacket.

Alan felt the silver token in his pocket surely as a lycanthrope might.

"Being in the wrong place at the wrong time is nothing to brag about," he muttered.

"Poppycock. Saving the city once is bad luck, but twice is fate. Services to the crown, saboteurs foiled, madmen brought to justice—"

As Brigadier Lyttleton prattled on, Alan felt his attention drifting across the room to the grinning spectre who haunted the corner of his eye and Lyttleton's speech faded into the background for a moment as Slay hovered unseen, very much avoiding justice in his spectral form.

"–pride, man. If only everyone else with your beginnings worked as hard this city would be less of a cesspit," the brigadier finished.

Alan snapped his attention back from Mister Slay and made a non-committal sound.

"And who is this ravishing creature at your side?" the brigadier continued, seemingly unhindered by the need to breathe between great speeches. "I don't think I've had the pleasu—"

Lady Ottaway towered over the brigadier in height and character.

"Use such derogatory objectification toward me again, *sir*, and this creature will be more ravenous than ravishing."

Lyttleton recoiled as if the lady had spat boiling oil.

"M-madame, I meant no offense—"

"Then offend us no more. Be gone, little man," she commanded.

The brigadier looked to Alan for support and found none. With another whinny, he feigned interest in an adjacent conversation, and waddled away.

"Twerp," Lady Ottaway snarled after the little man.

Alan regarded the lady with a wry smile.

"You know, I really could shoot him," Alan offered. Lady Ottaway tittered, an intriguing contrast with the last few minutes. "I'm not saying it would be right—"

"It wouldn't be wrong, either," Lady Ottaway interjected, her voice quivering with laughter.

Alan wasn't so reserved and laughed so that Lyttleton might hear.

"Maybe another drink, instead," he said.

Taking their glasses in a pincer grip, he retreated to the back of the room where the liquor cabinet lay open and, laying his cane against the wall, set to work, taking great amusement in watching Brigadier Lyttleton shoot haunted glances toward the lady by the fireplace despite his new group of confidants.

"Alan!"

He knew that voice.

Helen Harrigan came out of the crowd like a bullet, arms flung wide. She enveloped him entirely, almost spilling the carafe in his hand. She planted a kiss on his cheek and wiped the red stain away with her sleeve just as quickly.

"You could have left that on," he said.

She gave him a playful tap on the chest. As always, Helen seemed lit with some internal light, some vibrancy that never dwindled, not since they were children, not even now little crow's-feet were starting to creep from the corners of her eyes.

"Now, now. You know Percy hates your flirtations," Helen whispered.

"You husband hates me breathing," he replied, decanting one scotch and one brandy.

"That's not true."

"He bloody shot me, Helen!"

"Oh, don't hold a grudge."

Alan looked at her with mock astonishment. She giggled.

"Forgiving is for people who are too lazy to hate long-term. Where is the weasel?" he said.

Helen waved a hand at the crowd.

"Good. Grab a drink and come meet someone you'll love," Alan said, and led on.

FOR THE REST of the evening Alan, Helen and Lady Ottaway chuckled and chattered between themselves, keeping the rest of the room at arm's length. Alan spotted the rakish Percy hovering around, his thin moustache twitching, but he didn't approach until the grandfather clock in the hall struck midnight and the room began to empty.

"Helen, dear, I think it's time we were away," Percy said.

At Percy's sneering tones, Alan was almost revisited by his last drink. In the shadow behind the door, Mister Slay licked his teeth. Percy being one of the few things they both agreed on.

Helen gave her husband a pat on the hand and turned to her friends.

"It really has been wonderful. Thank you so much." She threw her arms around them both as if she'd known Lady Ottaway as long as she'd known Alan.

"It's been a pleasure, my dear," Lady Ottaway replied. "I think I'll follow you out. I'm afraid that last drink has left me quite squiffy."

They all made a clumsy round of goodbyes and the Carpenter house fell quiet.

The fire dropped to embers as Alan sat rubbing his bad leg in the old wing-backed chair that had been his adoptive father's. Lottie swam into the room, straight of thought and radiant of face. Alan couldn't help but feel a pang of jealousy toward his brother but Lord knew that Simon deserved the comfort he and Lottie had built together.

"Are you staying with us tonight, Alan?" Lottie asked as she gathered a few glasses, never one to let their solitary maid do all the work.

"I don't think so. I have worked to do."

Alan drained the last of his scotch to steel himself for the inevitable pain of standing.

Lottie twitched toward him, wanting to help as Alan made it to his feet, but stopped herself.

"Does it never ease?" she asked.

He looked at her, letting his façade drop like he did with few others. He looked tired, the pain-wrinkles between his eyes deeper than the laughter lines beside them.

"Never."

"Perhaps we could—"

"Tried it. Whatever you're about to say, Lottie. Doctors, witch doctors, witches without doctorates. Chinese and Tibetan and Indian. Nothing shakes it."

"And Slay?"

Alan lowered his voice, checking the doorway in case Simon were to stroll in. Turning sorrowful eyes on his sister-in-law, he shook his head, just once.

Lottie sighed, dusting her hands on the apron that she had donned over her evening dress.

"I wish I could help."

"I've been beyond help for longer than you've known me," he said, making his way toward the coat rack in the hall and beginning to reassemble his equipment. Her face broke into a motherly smile as she followed him out.

"Where's Simon got to?" he asked.

"He lay down for a moment and went off straight away."

"Let him sleep, then. Don't clean too much or you'll wash the house away."

Lottie gave him a smile and forced him into a hug.

"Good night. And thank you for coming," she said. "I know how much you hate it. Be careful."

"You know me," he said as he stepped out into the street.

"Exactly," she muttered after him.

2

A THIN RAIN had begun to fall through the pea-souper, making London glisten urine yellow as Alan made his way to the Trafalgar monorail station. Admiral Nelson himself was far out of sight above the fog but the base of his pedestal and its lions loomed in the murk.

At the south side of the square, Alan's boots and cane rang on the steel steps up to the monorail platform where he found clear air and he tugged down his respirator mask for a lungful. As he regarded the moonlit swamp of his city's skyline, the platform beneath his feet began to hum and the whistle of brakes preceded the monorail shuttle's arrival. The driver gave Alan a brief nod before disappearing past and, as the carriage drew to a stop, a door slid up and over the huge brass and steel cylinder chassis. Thin leather upholstery made up every surface that could be sat, perched or leaned upon. Climbing aboard, Alan debated whether to sit and decided to hang from one of the overhead loops instead. Sometimes the effort of sitting and standing wasn't worth the intermediate rest. The door slid closed and, with a shudder, he was on his way.

The monorail streaked across London's north bank toward Victoria Park, soaring over rooftops and rattling windows. At every stop, the doors hushed open and closed to no one at all. The swaying caught Alan off guard, as it sometimes did, and he found his eyes eager to close.

He jerked awake, hurriedly glancing around the carriage. Falling asleep on a midnight monorail was a good way to get yourself filled with holes and your pockets emptied. Someone had entered the carriage in the how-long between his blinks. The crown of a head peeked over a chair back at the furthest end. A reveller, no doubt, as Alan could already hear soft snores floating down to him.

You and me both, he thought, and physically shook himself.

Victoria Park was the next stop. There, the monorail dove down to street level and Alan stepped out into a patch of night much different from the one he'd left. The heavy amber gas was absent here, but across the midnight park a thin mist hung in ghastly plaques between the trees. The fizz of tesla street lamps along Grove Road and Alan's breathing were the only sounds once the monorail rattled away.

He set off through the dark, unperturbed by the park's swarming shadows. Alan chose pain over lost pride, telling himself that it wasn't far enough a walk to justify a steam cab. Cursing himself, his damned leg, that long-ago blade and Mister Slay most of all, he arrived at his destination with a light coating of sweat on his brow. Beyond a low and gateless wall, a stark brick façade with wood-blinded eyes sat a little back from the road. One wing of the house was ivy-wrapped and in desperate need of a new roof, the other had fared a little better but sagged in pity for its companion's state. The house hadn't been lived in for a long time, that was obvious. But Alan wasn't looking for the living.

Mister Slay stepped up beside him as if he'd been only a step behind all along.

"Spooky," he rasped.

Alan didn't turn his head. He knew the pale countenance, the tall and lithe form of his companion all too well.

"That's rich, coming from you," Alan replied.

"What are you expecting to find in there?"

"Nothing but wind hooting through window frames and creaky old floors. If that place is haunted, I'll eat my hat. And if anyone knows about hauntings, it's me." Alan turned his gaze on Slay now, trying to burn a hole in the spectre's ear with the power of his mind.

Mister Slay smiled in the dark, never taking his eyes from the old mansion.

"Off we go then. You're not getting any younger," Slay said, and strode toward the house.

Alan ground his teeth and set off at speed, overtaking Slay in a hurried limp through the mansion's small yard and beating the grinning ghost to the front door. The black paint had given up trying to conceal the splintering rot beneath it, and a brass knob had long since been stolen. No way through. Wading through brambles, Alan circled the house. Thinking that he'd found a hole in the wall where he might get in, he realised that it was a dark patch of tar where a shed might have once stood against the wall. With a huff, he continued. The rear of the house was even worse. Nature had done everything it could to make the ground impassable, the house impossible to see. Weeds rivalled some of the smaller trees in height, and the taller foliage had taken to spreading wide and leaning in so that the moonlight struggled to break through.

Finally, he reached the back door, similarly barred and scarred. Alan searched the door frame for a moment, finding small humps of metal beneath his fingertips where nails had been driven into the woodwork.

"That's helpful," he muttered, giving the door's bottom panel a frustrated whack with his stick.

Pop and creak.

With furrowed eyebrows, he leant down. The bottom panel of the door had broken inward, falling completely in to reveal a square of deeper darkness.

"Must be rotten," Mister Slay chimed in.

"You're rotten. Be quiet," Alan snapped.

"Charming."

Alan took to his knees with a groan, putting his stick through the hole first, and crawling through after it with a little less finesse than he would have liked. Appearing inside, Mister Slay offered a hand from the darkness which Alan ignored. Not bothering to brush off his trousers, he took a look around. He stood in what might have once been a kitchen. Everything was stripped back to brick. A fireplace lay cold with iron fittings still inside. Doors lay halfway up walls, their wooden steps gone the same way as the doorknobs. In the centre of the room remained a table of sturdy ancient build. Alan ran his hand over the surface, collecting dust that he palmed off on his trousers.

Standing in that long-abandoned space, once filled with the life sounds of people but now quiet and lonely, Alan found himself touching the bare brick and dusty iron, feeling something close to a kinship with the beaten old shell of a mansion. He moved on, not wanting to waste his whole night on some fool's errand, even if it was keeping him fed. Climbing through the raised doorway with difficulty, a short corridor led him into wood-panelled living spaces.

With a *flickflickwhoomph* Alan sparked his little oil lighter to life.

As his eyes adjusted to the light, he let out a gasp. Stumbling back, his shoulder hit the wall as he fought to stay standing, hold his cane, keep his lighter lifted and draw his revolver on the pale shape that loomed out of the darkness. Short of the hammer striking home and lighting the house with the clatter of gunfire, Alan stopped dead and heaved a sigh.

Laughter tinkled down around him, followed by a rasping, sing-song voice as Slay stepped out of the dark beside the hanging white shape that had startled Alan, now evidently the narrow side of an armoire draped in a dirty sheet.

"Poor old Alan. He's had quite a fright. If you're afraid of a wardrobe, you shouldn't be out at night."

Alan's teeth ached and he realised he was grinding them. His heart hammered a rhythm that he felt as a stabbing pain behind one eye. Pushing himself from the wall, he limped toward Slay.

"That's it. Be gone, damn you. I've had enough," he snapped, staring right at the gaunt memory of a murderer. "I'm trying to work, dammit. Get back under your bridge."

Slay's face shifted from anger to amusement to polite resignation in a flash. With a slight bow and that infernal grin, he faded into the dark.

Now blissfully alone, Alan readjusted the lay of his coat, straightening his frame of mind along with it. With a final mutter, he felt as close to his old self as he was likely to get. He stalked across the room by the light of his little flame, past other half-covered shapes and straight to where old boards had been nailed over the window. With a grunt, he jammed the steel tip of his cane-cum-crowbar into the wood, and used the length of steel to prise the boards free. It was the work of a moment to send crystalline moonlight spilling into the room. Turning back, winded but triumphant, he instantly regretted what he'd done. Where he had been able to ignore half shapes in the dark, the moonlight now picked out every shadow, every white hooded item in the room; every lump, every potential ghost and imagined assailant. Dust motes danced in the silver luminescence, coalescing and breaking apart in ghostly eddies.

The night's cold breath had leaked in through the walls and the warmth of Simon's scotch faded into memory. As Alan moved through successive rooms, he tugged his coat a little tighter. That evening, he had walked the perilous streets of London and swam in socialite-infested waters. Both of those things were far more dangerous than a rickety old house. Still, icicles danced a Viennese waltz down his spine as he made his way onward.

Most of the rooms were barren. One held only a cobweb-smothered chandelier, its faux-crystal droplets stolen or lost. Others were impenetrable stacks of old furniture and bric-a-brac. The place was a hazard. Alan mused that a hastily dropped match would probably be an end to the place and his employer's problem to boot.

Completing his circuit of the lower floor, he came to the staircase without seeing any other spectres than the one he'd brought with him.

The stairs were a little wider than usual, but nothing spectacular. Tarnished brass tacks led upward, devoid of the carpet that had once laid between them, and a dark wood banister stretched up into an area bathed in moonlight from the landing window.

That little shiver ran down his spine again, something remembered from when he was a boy. It might have been a ghost story he'd once heard, the words carried away on the tide of time but the sand of fear remaining in his mind. It could have been the age-old monkey in him, still afraid of predators in the dark, begging to hide in a tree. Either way, he told himself that he'd faced worse than ghosts in his past and left them all in ruin. Still, his foot stalled on the bottom step.

Somewhere in the back of his mind, he felt Slay chuckle.

3

ACCOMPANIED BY THE tooth-grinding creak of the staircase, Alan climbed up toward the moonlit landing. There he found nothing but another strip of barren floorboards leading away in either direction. He rubbed the back of his neck, then pinched the bridge of his nose. He was ready for home now. This adventure had turned into a pointless ramble. He felt dirty all over, like he'd rolled on an old carpet, his nostrils tickling with dust, his eyelids and limbs heavy. And there was still a trip back home to be endured. He'd never been one to leave a job half done but that didn't mean he couldn't speed his way through a little.

Flipping a mental coin, he turned right. Every door along the hallway lay closed and he found himself ignoring one after another. If the ghosts didn't come to him then bugger them. He was half way down the hall, moving toward a T-junction which led toward the front and back of the most dilapidated wing when he heard it.

He was used to laughter in the dark; Mister Slay had made sure of that. He had also come across any number of creatures that could cackle and guffaw with the utmost wickedness. They would have almost been a comfort at this point, for those things he could usually anticipate. But the lyrical laughter that now floated around him; that was something he wasn't ready for.

Halfway through a step, he wobbled and froze, steadying himself with his cane. The floor creaked, and he winced against it.

He tried to turn about, slowly, quietly, so as not to disturb the old wood floors, to look back over his shoulder.

Nothing.

His mind raced through all possible explanations for a child's playful laughter to be emerging from an abandoned mansion in the middle of the night. It took a fraction of a second to come up empty handed.

"Well, I'll be damned," he muttered to himself.

When no more sounds materialised, he carried on down the hall, slower now. His head swung side-to-side like an old lantern, eyes keen and ears pricked. Nearing the end of the hall, he pushed his shoulder blades against one wall, sliding along it crabwise, to peer down one hallway and then the other.

Darkness and dust.

You've bloody spooked yourself.

Footsteps. Hurried. The pad of bare little feet on wood.

Alan snapped his head around. Down the hall, the way he'd come, a dark shape darted around the furthest corner. He threw his back against the wall again, one hand stuffed into his coat to search for his revolver, the other gripping white-knuckle to his cane. He suddenly realised that his eyes were too wide, his breath too frayed, and he forced himself to relax. He sagged, and breathed, and drew his hand away from his sidearm.

"Pull yourself together," he said, to exorcise the silence.

In the face of danger, Alan was a beacon of stubbornness. He'd faced worse than spooks and spectres, that was for sure.

This was his city and its shadows were old friends. Still, even by his very broad standards, ghost children were creepy as all hell.

With one hand, he patted the mouldering plaster behind him and spoke to the house in a voice that shook a little more than he liked:

"You have some secrets in you, old girl."

With caution masked as sneaking, he made his way back the way he'd come, back across the moonlit landing to the end of the hall where he'd seen the shadow dart. Near the end of the hall, he straightened his spine and stepped right out into the junction as bold as he could.

Nothing assailed him. No movement. No footfalls in the dark. Thankfully, no more laughter.

"Slay," he said, shocking himself when it came out as a whisper. "Is this you playing with me? If it is, I swear I'll lock myself in for a week and ignore you while I read. I'll borrow some of Simon's books so it's especially boring."

No answer.

So sank that theory. If it had been Slay, Alan was sure the bastard would have taken credit for it. He turned left, the way the shadow had gone, and edged his way toward the front of the building. Slashes of tesla lamplight from the street pierced through a boarded-up window, creating a dark portal edged with an uncertain glow at the end of the hall. A chill breeze drifted down toward him. He was certain that the night outside had been still. Cold, but still. As he took a footstep forward, he froze.

There, on the floorboards at the furthest end of the hall, a small cloud of particles lifted up, like a foot fall kicking up the dust. Alan felt his body tense, his breath hissed out of his nose as he fought to stay calm.

Another. Closer. Just the size of a little foot.

Another, and another. They picked up speed, hurtling toward him. The sound of running feet seemed to come from the walls, the ceiling. He could feel the thump on the floor beneath his own boots, but still there was no one to see.

He stumbled backward, making clumsy movements with his cane in the dark and his foot hit something behind. The floor caught him with a thump. Jarred from the fall, Alan's eyes widened as he saw what it was that had tripped him. Between his splayed feet, a music box, rolling to a stop where he'd kicked it.

He panted at it, eyes wide, certain that something was still to come.

Clink, plink.

Clink, tink, plink.

The music box only let out a few notes before Alan kicked the damned thing down the hall with a clatter.

Dragging himself to his feet, he moved back the way he'd come, very careful not to run. But as he turned the corner back toward the landing, in the mix of moonlight and shadow, toys covered the floorboards between him and the stairs where there had been none before; a leather ball, a small wooden horse, cubes embossed with letters, and a whip and top. And there it was again, at the other end of the hall, the way he'd first gone, the dark form of a child, silently watching him.

4

LEICESTER SQUARE BY daylight was a vast improvement on a Hackney ruin by night. Sat beneath the striped awning of a café which overlooked the square, Alan took a deep breath, and waited for Simon to say something.

"I can't believe it," was his brother's offering.

Alan sighed. "You know that there are weird things in the world, Simon. We've seen some of them together."

"Not that. I can't believe that you ran away." Simon shook his head, a bemused smile on his lips, the grey day reflected in the lenses of his spectacles.

"I did *not* run," Alan replied with leaden intent, shooting his brother a look. "I hobbled, at best."

Simon gave a stifled snort.

"You're not encouraging me to talk to you about these things," Alan said.

"Sorry, sorry. Drink your tea and we'll have a think."

Both brothers took a few sips as the London morning bustled around them. Chairs scraped from tables, the flap of waiters' shoes came and went and, across the square, the entirety of London life went this way and that; bonnet and boot heel, rag and rabble. Between it all passed one or two Mk

I automatons, head and shoulders above the crowd, looking a little worn and battered but still functioning in their simple tasks. But it was the Mark Vs that Alan was trying to spot, almost impossible to distinguish from the humans around them. If it weren't for the sun glinting from the odd exposed section of brass and steel hide beneath clothing and coats, Alan wouldn't know they were there at all, an idea which gave him another kind of shudder.

"So, the place is definitely haunted. At least we know that for certain," Simon offered. "The question now is how do you tell your client? I'm presuming that this Mister—"

"Sutton," Alan offered.

"—that he won't be particularly happy with your report. After all, who wants a house with a non-corporeal resident? Especially such an untidy one."

"The question is, how do I get rid of a ghost?" Alan waved to a waiter in an apron and spats who retrieved a metal teapot from the ornate heating unit inside the café before returning to refill their cups.

"In order to answer that, you would need to know what a ghost is," Simon offered. "There's been a little research, mostly by the Americans, perhaps unsurprisingly. But nothing certain ever comes of it, I'm afraid."

Alan thanked the waiter.

"My pleasure, Mister Shaw," he replied, as blasé as you like despite the strange conversation he had walked into. "Can I get you gentlemen anything else?"

"I don't suppose you know any exorcists, Charlie?" Alan asked.

"Not in my social circle I'm afraid, sir." Charlie gave the brothers a polite nod and made his hummingbird way from table to table.

"Good waiter, that," Alan said.

"He's heard us talk about worse. And so, were you serious about the exorcist? A priest perhaps?"

Leaving the saucer on the table, Alan sipped his tea, holding the delicate cup in a practical fist, unlike his brother's perfected pinky-raised drinking technique. "I don't know many priests. Not ones I'm allowed to talk to anymore, anyway. But I think it'd be better to give bad news tagged on to a solution than not."

"Not a bad idea. And that, I think, is why people call on you above other investigators. Some would report back and take the money, you always head for resolution."

"I'm a completionist."

Simon's eyebrows shot up. Alan gave him a bored look.

"You're not the only one who can read books. I read books. It's not as if I can do much else to pass my time."

"Evidently. How long before you need to present a solution to Mister Sutton?"

Alan checked the dials of his wristwatch. "About half an hour."

"Your vocabulary may have improved, but your timing is still rotten."

MAKING HIS EXCUSES, Simon headed off to his work at the British Museum, leaving Alan to sit alone for a while. Charlie came and went with another refill. The sun rose a little more, taking the chill out of the morning and washing the world in London Grey.

Alan knew that Simon would give him a little hell about retreating. He'd given himself enough since the early hours of that morning. But what else could he do? Automaton tigers:

shoot them. Mutated cult leaders: blow them up. Magical sceptres: steal them. Weave them together with enough quips to make it look effortless. Those things were very much in Alan's skill set. They were its entirety. But how could you shoot, explode or trick a ghost? There was the other factor as well, the elephant in the room, the Slay at the edge of sight; Alan wasn't what he used to be. The vibrant, athletic privateer that he'd been in his youth was as much a ghost as Sutton Hall's eternal resident.

As he was mulling that over with grinding teeth and a heavy feeling in his chest, Big Ben's fanfare rang out across the city, accompanied by a hundred little brothers, and the sticks-and-twine form of Alan's client cut his way out of the crowd.

Alan half stood and offered a hand to the scarecrow of a man.

"Mister Sutton."

Scrunched slightly at the shoulders with a twitching moustache, the gentleman had the habit of smacking his lips between speaking, as if signing on and off each sentence in Morse code.

"Mister Shaw," he replied with a *smacksmack.* "Would there be any of that tea going for myself?"

Alan gave Charlie a wave and the waiter bustled to work.

Both men took their seats, Mister Sutton's trousers riding up as he crossed his legs, revealing wrinkled socks over spur-like ankles.

"Wouldn't an interior table have provided a little more privacy?" the gentleman offered, tugging his morning coat a little tighter.

"I like to watch people," Alan replied as their tea arrived. "Thanks, Charlie."

"Indeed. I might conjecture that in your line of work,

observing people is most advantageous. All the same, I'd rather we weren't spotted conversing. But away from chit chat and to the matter at hand. I take it that you spent some time in my building last night. You have a similar look to the other sleepless visitors. And so, I can presume that you have a story to tell. However, I'm certain that it will be of a similar ilk to those who have come before you. Therefore, there is only one question that remains. How do I rid myself of a ghost, Mister Shaw?"

Alan, whose mouth had opened and closed several times throughout Mister Sutton's speech, took a second to reply. Sutton's moustache twitched at the delay.

"Frankly, that would be up to you," Alan decided as he said it aloud. "There are two ways we can go. Science or—" he thought in the split second about the word *magic*, and chose another "—religion."

"The swifter, Mister Shaw. The swifter."

Alan shrugged. Something about Sutton ground on his nerves. Maybe it was the disregard that the rich old bastard showed the ghost. It was a pest to him, a rat chewing wires, to be eradicated swiftly as possible. Alan couldn't shake the fact that it had been a boy, once. And children were too often thrown away. He thought of Lady Ottaway and wondered how she'd feel about the exorcism of a child's lasting impression on the world. He took a moment longer than he really needed to answer. Just to see that moustache twitch.

"They're much the same. Both involve books. It's the difference between clipboards and candles, when you get right down to it. If it helps, priests aren't exactly in my social circle," Alan replied. He caught a glimpse of Charlie's smile as he bustled past and struggled not to smile himself.

"Speed is of the essence, but so is silence, Mister Shaw. The last thing I need is a scandal leading to no one wanting to buy the house. Providing both will lead to higher monetary compensation, I assure you." Mister Sutton was on his feet and out across the square before Alan had time to reply, or Mister Sutton's piping hot tea had seen a single dip of his moustache.

"Well, that's just a waste," Alan muttered.

"You're not wrong, sir," Charlie said as he appeared to remove the untouched brew.

ALAN STAYED TO finish his tea and to sift through the favours he was owed. Some of the folks he knew around London would cause Mister Sutton's moustache to twitch right off of his face just by the sight of them. They might be able to help but would be counterproductive for a client who cared so much about appearances. It never ceased to amaze him how people wanted occult oddities to be fixed but were finicky about the how and the who. Frankly, he didn't know that many respectable-looking people. His mind wandered back to Simon who was pretty well respected and open-minded but useful only for insect-related enquiries, and briskly passed over Professor Anchorage who, he was pretty sure, was in the Mediterranean on another of his treasure hunts.

"Mister Shaw?" The voice was pure gravel, seeming to come from beyond a blocked nose.

Alan had long since learned to take a good look at anyone who used his name as a question. In a tatty long-coat and crusted boots, thinning hair slicked back with what looked like actual motor-oil, the ruffian was the kind of man you wanted to be facing at all times. An equally verminous woman leaned on his shoulder, a shorter jacket with the wink of gun-metal nestled beneath each armpit. They were either related, or unlucky enough to have found someone with the same face as their own.

THE WOMAN THAT Alan had mentally dubbed Ratessa, possibly Tessa for short, gave him a half-smile with half teeth.

"Mister Whitsun wants to see you," she said in the kind of voice made for whispering threats in dark alleys.

"Why doesn't he come see me himself? His legs broken?"

Ratso, possibly the brother, jumped in: "Why do you have to be a pain? Just come along."

"I might be busy," Alan replied with a shrug. "Lucky for you, I'm not."

Swigging down the last of his tea, he took a bank note from his pocket and tucked it under the saucer. Charlie cast a worried look toward him as he left.

"See you later, Charlie."

"I hope so, Mister Shaw," the waiter replied.

Alan gave him a jovial wink he didn't much feel.

THE RAT TWINS led the way although Alan already knew it: down to Dorset Street in Spitalfields and into a dog-chewed pub beneath the sign of the Blue Coat Boy. By the time they got there, his leg was aflame, his breath ragged, the palm of his cane-hand aching with the effort of holding on. The rat twins seemed not to notice, or care.

Inside the pub lay a crush of mismatched furniture and shadows, permeated with coughs, wheezes and the murmured voices of half-seen patrons. Alan was led through the pub, up the backstairs where plaster and walls were becoming estranged from each other, and past a series of rooms filled with stains and puddles of uncertain origin where filthy rag hammocks hung in the gloom. This was a well-trodden path, to the point that Alan barely paid attention to the hunched, the unconscious and the gurgling who slept it off in any spare corner. Where the tunnel of despair ended at the rear of the pub, another corridor, a bridge between this building and a warehouse beyond, led them to their final destination.

With the twins giving him self-satisfied snarls, Alan stepped into the headquarters of the Gentleman's Consortium, a high-brow name for the professional low-lives of London. The rotting, diseased surface of the headquarters peeled away as he stepped into a room that wouldn't look out of place in a gentleman's club. Clean floorboards scattered with rugs, albeit slightly worn, painted plaster, fizzing teslas along the long room's walls, and upholstered seats at the far end where a bureau lay open. Dick Whitsun sat at the end of the room in a high-backed leather chair which had seen a lot of bottom comforting, his legs crossed, hands dangling loosely from the arms and eyes closed.

"Say hello to Dick for me," Slay suggested from nowhere in sight.

"Give it a rest. He doesn't remember you. I already asked," Alan muttered.

"Just because I'm dead doesn't mean you can't hurt my feelings, Alan."

"Disturbing your nap?" Alan said louder, as he stalked across the room to take a chair opposite.

The scars on the Consortium leader's face rearranged into a smile, like opening a bag of knives.

"I was thinking," Whitsun said.

"I pity the poor sod you're thinking about," Alan replied,

rubbing the pain in his thigh without effect.

"You want something for that?" Dick finally opened his eyes. Dark, cold. But there was a smile buried deep when he looked at Alan.

Alan gritted his teeth but nodded. Dick thrust his chin at Ratso, who had been hovering. The thug left his sister picking something from her remaining teeth with a fingernail and disappeared.

"Won't be a mo," Dick said. "Been busy?"

"Not as busy as you, I bet. Three of your lads set on me last night. I figured you'd tell them to steer clear by now."

Dick laughed. "Why would I do that? Every time some young cully gets cocky, I put him on a street near you. It's only a matter of time before you send them back with an attitude change."

"You know, one day they'll actually get me. I'm not a lad anymore, Dick. And don't forget you're a year older than me, before you get smug."

Ratso returned with two glasses of amber liquid and a small bottle made of blue glass. Alan downed his scotch and regarded the bottle as Dick sipped his own drink.

"It's just laudanum. Not poison," the thief-master said. "Straight from the distillery, before they water it down, so you might want to take it easy—"

Sending the cork spinning across the room with a flick of his thumbnail, Alan took a swig. The honey hit his taste buds first, followed by the explosion of alcohol. As the bitter aftertaste tightened the muscles around his eyes, the opium crashed like a wave against his mind. The pain was still there. Nothing ever took it away. But Alan found himself caring about it a little less.

Dick watched his oldest friend's pupils slowly, slowly

widen, his face grow restful, and the rubbing of the affected thigh that had become such a constant habit slowed to a stop. Alan resituated himself in his chair, no longer nursing that damned leg in odd positions to give any kind of relief. To Dick, Alan seemed to pass back through time, returning to something of the savvy privateer he'd once been. Alan took a slow blink in the laudanum haze and smiled.

"Right," he said, his voice clear and confident.

"Christ almighty, Alan. That bottle could have floored an elephant."

Alan waved a hand at the comment. "What did you want me for? Ask me nicely and you might get it."

Dick shook his head, settling back in his chair.

"You're on a job. Sutton Hall. I want you to drop it," he said.

Alan raised an eyebrow. "Why?"

"Just tell the old crow that you can't do it. I'll even give you a few more notes for your trouble. Just go home, go to bed, sleep off that bloody bottle you just quaffed, and forget all about the house."

Alan felt it a little too late. The opium, still rising, had gone from the sensation of warm water on aching muscles to the verge of drowning him. He blinked rapidly, but he was falling into the well, the water rising up to meet him.

"I think—" he managed, and then was gone. The last thing he remembered was Dick's voice coming to him from beyond the well.

"Bloody hell. Just drop the damned job, will you?"

5

ALAN WOKE AT home, sprawled face down on his bed as if he'd landed there from a great height, fully dressed and with a head full of crumpled tin foil. He groaned, the sound rattling around his sparsely furnished bedroom. Tesla light from the street outside fizzed through the townhouse's upper window to light the bed, a lonely armoire and underfed bookcase at the back of the room, and two doors, one to the landing, the other to the bathroom. Arms filled with a familiar heaviness, Alan first rolled himself over to regard the ceiling, groaned once more for good measure and prepared for the inevitable hurdy-gurdy room spin when he sat up. He wasn't wrong. Walls last decorated to match a long-forgotten trend made carnival ride motions as he lurched upright. Pinching the bridge of his nose, Alan slowly came back to himself where he found Mister Slay's silhouette perched on the window seat.

"Just one minute of peace. That's all I ask for," Alan muttered, sliding his hands over his face and back through his hair, more to smooth his mind than his appearance.

"Poor old Alan, you've been out all day. Too much of the good stuff and you slept it all away." Slay gave his crow-like cackle. "Better check your pockets, old chum. If the Rat Twins

34

brought you home you're probably light of anything worth taking."

Half way through Slay's speech, Alan was already hurriedly patting down his coat. The ghost was right, something was missing. He shot to his feet as he searched, growing frantic. Alan stripped off his coat as his head danced a devil-may-care waltz and threw it to the bed then dug into his trouser pockets.

"Those rat-faced bastards. I can't believe it," he spat.

"Yes you can," Slay offered, twitching when he was ignored.

Alan's hand dipped into his waistcoat in a last-ditch effort, his body sagging as his hand came upon a leather wallet. He flipped it open to reveal his badge; a wide ring of silver embossed with "Scotland Yard. Civilian Specialist" encircling an inverted triangle intricately inscribed.

Alan Shaw.

Protector of London.

Scotland Yard hereby awards the named bearer with
restricted powers of policing within the metropolis of
London and her surrounding environs.

"And here's me thinking you didn't like that trinket," Slay offered. "You're losing it, old pal."

"I wish I could lose *you*," Alan snapped.

"You'd only miss me."

"Don't hold your damned breath."

"Couldn't if I wanted to."

Alan gnashed his teeth as he headed toward the bathroom, leaving Slay grinning on the windowsill. Leaning heavily on the small bathroom's sink, he regarded the cluster of dark circles that were his face. Lips cracked and pale, eyes sunken. The laudanum stupor provided peace, but no real rest. Splashing cold water from the tap gave a little relief but not as much as he'd hoped. Leaning on his good foot, he went through the motions of undressing and washing. The tap was steaming, now, and the hot vapour seemed to blow away the last few laudanum cobwebs. With rough flannel and extreme prejudice, he cleansed himself, working out any knotted muscles as he went, the ritual of an old warrior. The claw-footed bathtub was completely ignored. He'd tried that, only to realise that he couldn't get back out with a leg that wouldn't do as it was told. That particular embarrassment happened once, and once only.

With his bathing ritual almost complete, he had saved the worst for last. In the middle of his right thigh, a demon eye of dark scar tissue squinted up at him, purple veins creeping into the pale and pitted flesh that surrounded it, the muscle wasted. Next to its neighbour, the two might as well have been owned by entirely different people, one an octogenarian, the other barely into middle age. Setting his jaw against the inevitable, ever so gently, he began to clean. The flannel was wire wool, the hot water acidic but, with beads of sweat manifesting on his brow, he made it through cleaning the old scar. Then he stood for a long while, waiting for the pain to subside enough that he could walk, the sink taking most of his weight as he counted breaths.

Towel wrapped, he made his unhurried way back to his bedroom and plucked clean clothing from the armoire which held one good suit, a spare pair of trousers and a lot of the same shirt. The whole time he pottered, Slay stared out of the window. Eventually it was too much to bear.

"What are you even looking at?" Alan snapped.

Slay didn't even turn.

Enjoying the sensation of not using his cane for these brief trips, Alan came to the window. Leaning over Slay's shoulder, he looked down into the junction of Broad and Berwick Street, at a stretch of dark road lit in patches, a few parked steam cabs, and certainly nothing that would be of interest to the wraith. Except for the small figure standing just beyond the streetlamp's light, directly across from the house. Alan squinted, drawing it into focus: a child in short trousers, its head tilted up toward him, the cloth cap casting a dense shadow on all but the tiny point of a chin. The shape he'd seen in Sutton Hall.

With as much haste as he could muster, Alan darted away from the window, grabbing his cane from beside the door as he hurtled through it. He took the stairs crabwise, emitting all manner of colourful curses as the necessary combination of banister and cane drew him to something slightly short of a complete crawl. He fumbled at the front door and burst out onto the step, scanning the darkness for the small figure. There was nothing. Tottering down the step and out onto the pavement, he searched both ends of the street for any flash of shadow, the sound of little feet on the flagstones. Nothing. Nothing except the hum of the teslas and the distant clatter of the monorail over some nearby rooftop. That, and the pavement's cold creeping up through his socks.

"So that's how it is, is it?" he said to the night.

6

SIMON AND LOTTIE'S insistence that redecorating might make Alan's home more inviting had only solidified his decision to leave it unchanged. When his landlord had passed away and no living relatives could be found, Alan had been left owning a building filled with someone else's life. After donating what he could, he spread out his own meagre possessions from the single room he'd previously occupied. In the parlour, not a single piece of furniture matched and none of it complemented the room's ageing décor. Scattered on shelves and a solitary bookcase were artefacts of another life, placed in storage and retrieved years later to create a flea market, pea-on-a-drum aesthetic.

Slumped in the old armchair beside a fireplace close to burning out was another old relic, clothes crumpled and hair mussed from the bouts of fitful sleep he'd snatched as he waited out the last few hours before dawn. Alan watched the early morning light creep across the carpet's filigree designs, the room slowly filling with a peridot hue as the sunlight filtered through another sulphurous smog. His chest tightened at the very thought of the smell.

Adventure and mystery were bread and butter to Alan. The

artefacts around the room were a museum to the fact, his reputation a testimony. However, his approach to these things had changed since his younger years. He had once employed what could only be described as the piñata method; he shot, punched or blew up the source of the problem and answers tended to tumble out afterward. That had been then, and he was acutely aware that the *now* was very different. He would have to puzzle out this ghost problem the hard way.

Dick's last words kept coming back to him, half remembered and hazy.

"What do the Consortium want with a haunted house?"

Across the fireplace, in a twin chair, Slay cocked his head and shrugged.

"And what's really bugging me, is what kind of ghost follows you home?"

"Only the best kind," Slay chuckled.

"Shush."

Folding his arms in a huff, Slay muttered: "Why talk out loud if you don't want me to answer?"

Outside the window, the sound of rattling glass bottles and hissing pistons announced the automaton milkman's arrival. Someone shouted, possibly its human partner sat in the milk carriage. The tone implied some kind of reprimand. A bottle was set on the doorstep with a *chinkt*. Another yell and the carriage rattled away once more.

"I don't know what I'm doing," Alan said to the room at large. For once, the shadows didn't reply. "But I don't know how to do nothing." With a resigned sigh, he admitted: "I need help."

Even with such an opportunity to make a snide remark, Slay stayed silent.

Alan fortified his will for the task of standing and then

headed for the door, donning boots and respirator, holster and overcoat. After a brief smoothing of hair, he tugged down the respirator's mask, taking his first breath of filtered air, and stepped out into the day.

The fog cut his vision short only a few feet ahead, and the respirator filtered out everything but a faint metallic scent, but the sounds of London endured. Cabs roared and honked, the thunder of a thousand feet and clamouring voices rang out in the murk, and the ever-present clatter of rails changed pitch as they approached and then faded into the distance.

Alan joined the diffuse shapes on the street, heading south toward the river. Forms with wide skirts and high hats with nightmarish mechanical faces swam out of the fog and then disappeared. Shop doorbells jangled nearby, accompanied by a suck of clean air from their filtered interiors. Counting steps under his breath, Alan stopped where the butcher shop should be and made an exploratory move away from the roadside. Bare inches away from connecting with the shop's window, hanging fowl and sliced cattle on gleaming steel trays came into view. Alan finally spotted a figure hovering behind him in the window's reflection. Well-trained adrenaline responses kicked into action. He became aware of every sound, every movement of air that might be a blindside strike. Imperceptible in the fog, his hand crept toward his revolver, the other tightened on his cane. His mind raced. Would it be a rough voice that cut out at him? Or the haunting tinkle of a music box? Would he find wooden toys underfoot or a knife in his back?

Taking a breath if only to steady his shooting hand, he studied the figure through the corner of his eye. Wide of shoulder and waist, a cap tugged down over a face covered with a cheap rag mask, it certainly wasn't the shape of a child. A thug, then. As Alan registered it, the shape pulled back into the fog, not wanting to be seen, not realising it already had. The figure's swagger and shuffle, Alan recognised. Ratso. That meant Tessa wouldn't be far away.

Never one to pass up an opportunity, Slay's voice slithered out of the fog beside him:

"Alan's having quite the week. He's making lots of friends. I, for one, can't wait to see how he meets his grizzly end."

"One creepy sod at a time, please," Alan muttered and, pretending he hadn't seen Ratso at all, left his revolver where it lay as he shouldered the butcher's door and stepped inside.

A handlebar moustache, bowtie and apron combination smiled pleasantly as he entered. Without removing his respirator, eyes remaining fixed outside the window, Alan ordered a pound of bacon and received a paper-wrapped package.

Stepping back out onto the street, he caught sight of Ratso's unmistakable bulk tucked into an alcove only a few feet away. Alan smiled to himself under his mask. This was too easy. The fog meant Ratso had to stay close to keep sight of him, close enough that Alan couldn't help but spot him right back.

With a spring of mischievousness, Alan made off down the street at what he hoped would be a frustratingly slow pace for anyone who didn't need a cane, humming as he went. He kept that up all the way past Leicester Square and then on to Trafalgar, even letting his mind wander a little to the bacon by his side with a complementary cup of tea.

It was on the eastern side of Trafalgar Square, as he circled around the second grand fountain, that he decided to lose his shadow. Speeding up suddenly, he dropped the unsuspecting Ratso a little behind, a warning sting stabbing at his leg. He headed for the Strand, rapping on a crossing automaton with his cane. The machine's klaxon barked out into the murk, but more important was the warning light. As the automaton's eye pulsed, the fog flashed blinding white, and Alan took the opportunity to do a half-skip-run backward rather than across the road. Tucked back into the other roving forms in the fog, he waited. Sure enough, there came the thug in a hurry, not even bothering to look around before heading after the automaton's beacon.

"Sloppy work, Ratso," Alan snorted.

An ever-patient lion loomed out of the pea-souper as Alan escaped with as much haste as possible, skirting around the stone guardian's pedestal and south toward Whitehall. There the streets grew wider and the traffic lessened. The sound of gulls cut in above the din of the city and a blast of cool breeze stirred the fog as Alan made his way, occasionally checking over his shoulder but trying to enjoy the morning's little victory. It was swiftly spoiled.

"I know where you're going." Slay's hissed, accusatory. "He won't know anything."

Taking a little joy in Slay's discomfort, Alan didn't answer. Turning off the road, he crossed an open yard between stolid buildings and stepped carefully onto a slope down to Whitehall Stairs. High walls on either side hid the expensive homes from pedestrian view, ending only when the old stone stairs sank into the river itself beside row boats that bobbed on the tide. The boat's owners sat on the slope, chatting to each other, waiting for a fare to arrive so the bartering could begin. Finally, the sun showed itself, desperate and brief, beginning its daily work of banishing the fog. Alan stopped well short of the water at a gate of iron vines in one of the high walls where Slay lay in wait once more.

"You're doing this all wrong. You should go back to the house. Let Ratso find you. Then beat him. *Squeeeeeeze* him for answers. All this talking talking talking. This isn't what the young Alan would have done. He'd have this solved by blood and bullets before now," Slay said.

Pushing through both Slay and the gate, the apparition's lament faded. Alan stepped off the slope and into a walled garden. Hemmed on two sides by a wall and two sides by stern facades, the garden was nonetheless a breath of fresh air in London's arid landscape. Indeed, the fog seemed not to reach this oasis as it was so close to the expanse of the Thames. Alan tugged off his mask and took a breath, wondering if the mask digging into his cheeks or the stench of the river was the worse to deal with. Raised stone borders sprouted ferns and flowers in pink and purple while the pale bark of silver birches made good use of what little light there was. Alan made his way toward the broad side of a long and narrow three-storey home. As he reached out to rap on the dark wood door, Slay gave a rasping exhalation from somewhere beyond the gate, but said nothing.

7

I T WAS A minute or two before the door of the riverside
townhouse finally swung open on well-oiled hinges to reveal
a tall youth dressed in functional brown. Alan recognised the
collarless shirt and buckskin waistcoat as American in style,
which the fellow confirmed with his accent.

"Can I help you?" Not a single dose of manners in sight.
Alan took in the deep, cigarette-scratched voice and five-o-
clock shadow despite the time of day and realised the youth was
perhaps in his mid-twenties. Still, relatively a boy. And Alan
was regarded in turn, the youth's brow furrowing slightly when
he saw the paper-wrapped package that Alan was carrying.

Alan *humphed* as he regarded the hallway behind the
American. Nothing seemed out of place among the earthenware
pots on dark wood occasional tables that the house's owner had
scattered around the entrance to his home. Alan was almost
disappointed when he saw no signs of struggle or burglary. The
youth moved to block more of his view.

"Does Hogarth not answer his own door anymore?" Alan
asked.

The American's eyes narrowed. "Who's asking?"

With an internal shudder, Alan reached into his coat

pocket and held up the badge.

"It came with a certificate if you want to see that as well."

The youth *humphed* and stepped aside, closing the door behind Alan as he entered the hall. A small staircase curved its way from one floor to the other. A photograph stood on one of the occasional tables; five smiling African warriors with shields and spears, a Black man in the centre in trousers and waistcoat, grinning even wider than the rest.

"James is in the study. Follow me," the youth said with only a lick more courtesy than before.

"I know the way." And Alan set off into the house, feeling eyes on the back of his head like a cosh blow.

Through a parlour of rich carpet, plush seating and warm wooden panelling, Alan came to a sliding door left half open and gave a brief knock before pulling it wide enough to enter.

"Come on in," came the voice from inside, deep and well-spoken in an unhurried cadence.

Doctor James Hogarth stood off to one side of the room by a bookcase, a leather-bound tome open in one hand. Dressed in a quilted waistcoat and tie tugged down slightly at the collar, a curly mop of hair above a clean-shaven face made him look smart and yet casual, both the scholar and the poet. He made his way toward a leather inlaid desk before a wide fireplace over which hung the shield and spear of African make from the previous photograph, serving as the room's centrepiece. He didn't take his eyes from the print before him as he walked around.

"Good morning," Alan offered, and Hogarth finally looked up.

"Alan! I've not seen you in a while," Hogarth's face spread into the same infectious smile captured in the photograph. He scanned the empty air over Alan's shoulder. "Is your friend with you?"

"Don't worry, Slay won't come in here. He doesn't like you."

"Good riddance. The feeling's mutual," Hogarth replied. Setting down his book, he made his way toward Alan and shook his hand warmly. "It's good to see you, my friend. To what do I owe this pleasure?"

"I brought breakfast," Alan said, holding up the butcher's package.

"That looks like a packet of bribery to me," James said. "Lucky for you, I'm hungry." James flicked a switch on the desk and a faint buzz was heard somewhere else in the house. "Let's take a seat."

He gestured to a set of walnut tub chairs by the bay window that overlooked the Thames and joined Alan there.

"I almost didn't get in," Alan said.

"Ah, that would be Chester. He can be a little overprotective. I met him fresh off the airship. Nowhere to stay and a single valise to his name. Poor man needed work and I needed someone to keep an eye on the place. London's ruffians become bolder every year," James rattled off. "But I'm sure you didn't come to hear about my hiring policy—"

Alan gave James a half-smile. "Is that what they're calling it now?"

The gentleman's cheeks flushed as his Adam's apple rose and fell. Alan let his smile spread further and waggled his eyebrows. With a cough, James struggled back to his own smile, averting his eyes as he straightened his waistcoat unnecessarily. Chester stepped into the room.

"Chester, could you take Cooky the package on the desk? Alan will be eating breakfast with us."

The youth's eyes switched between Hogarth and Alan, care and curiosity. He gave a nod and strode back out.

"He seems nice," Alan said.

"Alright, stop it now," Hogarth said, shuffling himself closer to confidence in his chair, the flush fading in his cheeks. "If you're bribing me with bacon for information on Mister Slay, I'm afraid I've got nothing new. And I have been looking, I promise."

Alan waved the comment away.

"Don't worry, I know you've done everything you can. I think we've had enough favours go back and forth between us that we can stop keeping track now, don't you?"

Hogarth leant forward and pointed an accusatory finger at Alan. "You're a very sweet and wise man, do you know that?"

It was Alan's turn to feel heat rising in his face.

"Careful, Hogarth. I might start thinking you're not so smart," he said.

Alan recounted the story of his visit to Sutton's mansion, and his invitation to visit Dick afterward, making certain to mention the ghost boy on the street outside his home. By the time they were done, Chester returned with a gruff word address:

"Breakfast's ready. The fog's pretty much lifted so I put it on the balcony."

As he stood, Hogarth laid a hand on Chester's shoulder.

"Bring your own breakfast out there as well," he said.

Chester shot a look of worry toward James and then to Alan.

"You've no need to worry about me, son," Alan said.

Chester headed off while Hogarth led Alan up the stairs to the second floor and down to the narrow end of the house where a curved balcony stretched out over the river like the prow of a ship. The late summer sun had warmed the air, banishing the last of the fog and leaving the river sparkling. At the foot of Hogarth's home, where stone ended and the river began, a carpet of wild water lilies spread across the glistening water. An iron railing encircled the flagstone balcony, at the furthest end of which was a wicker table and chairs with plates and steaming teapot already in place.

"Those pump stations are a blessing," Hogarth remarked as they sat with their plates piled with bacon, eggs and spiced fried potatoes. "Some summers we had to keep all the windows and doors closed just to keep out the stench. It was unbearable."

Alan nodded as he ate. "I remember. That was the summer I first came to you about Slay."

Arriving with his own breakfast, Chester took a seat in silence, clasped his hands under some muttered words for a second, then went about his breakfast.

"And here I am again with another ghost to contend with," Alan said.

As Hogarth washed down some bacon with a sip of tea, he waggled his finger in the air.

"We had the same discussion with your existing companion. Ghosts do not haunt people, they haunt places."

"That ruins my next question, then. What kind of ghost would have Dick Whitsun all bunched up?"

"The answer remains the same: Not a ghost at all. Just as we discovered Mister Slay is not truly the after image of a life violently cut short but rather some symptom of the dark magic he was tampering with in his murderous blasphemies, so this spectral child must also be something else. Which implies that something rather more involved than a simple cleansing might be required. Perhaps a priest is what you need, rather than a shaman's grandson."

Chester, with a fork midway to his mouth, shot silent glances between them. Hogarth gave him a smile, but no explanation.

"You know that anthropology is only one part of my work, Chester. The other part encourages some strange conversations in this house. You'll get used to it," Hogarth said. He turned to Alan. "Chester is still getting to grips with some things that you and I take for granted."

"Still, an open mind is never a bad thing, eh?" Alan said.

Chester shot him a dark look while taking a violent mouthful of potatoes.

"I might suggest that I visit this place with you. Take a look for myself. On my recent visit to Benin I brought home some particularly potent dust that should work well for loosening the grip of a supernatural creature on the mortal realm, gifted to me by a priest there. He was a descendant of the same tribe as my grandfather and even remembered him as a boy." Hogarth's eyes focussed out across the river, somewhere in the direction of the South Bank timber yards but far, far beyond.

Chester cast the briefest look of worry toward Hogarth, but Alan caught it.

"Maybe you should sit this one out," Alan said, noting the tension drift away from Chester's face. "I appreciate the offer, but we don't know what this thing is or if it might decide it likes to haunt you more than me. I don't have anyone to stay safe for, unlike you. Just the dust will do. And idiot-proof the instructions for me."

Hogarth refocused on his friend and caught the look of agreement from Chester.

"I'm certain that any ghost or ghoul would think twice about entering my home. They'd get short shrift, I assure you. Still, whatever manner of thing that might take the form of a child to haunt an old house suggests a kind of adventure that you're more suited to than I. Perhaps you're right."

"Slay was pretty adamant about me not coming in as well. Don't suppose you have any spare rooms? I'm enjoying the peace and quiet," Alan said as he set his fork aside and wiped his mouth.

"Slay is still causing problems," Hogarth stated. "I wish I could help you. But whatever the stipulations of his curse, it's out of my realm of experience. I still extend the invitation for you to come along on my next visit to Africa. The shamans might be able to help." James lowered his voice, leaning forward with care in his eyes. "Of course, you know that you have to be willing to let Slay leave."

Alan's face fell to frustration, he gave an angry shrug.

"Of course I want rid of him. The bastard haunts me day and night."

Hogarth raised his hands in peace.

"I know, I know. I also know that you sometimes consider yourself worthy of haunting. Perhaps if you changed your low opinion of yourself, Mister Slay would have less of a hold, is all I meant."

"Thanks for the advice," Alan said, not quite able to hide the snap in his voice. He stood from the table as politely as possible. "I'll leave you to your day. If you could have the dust sent to me, I'm eager to get this thing over with."

Hogarth nodded. "Good luck. And thank you for breakfast, my friend."

Alan gave them both a nod and swiftly headed back through the house. Behind his back, James and Chester exchanged a worried look.

AS ALAN STEPPED back through the iron gate, he expected Slay to assault him immediately with snide remarks, but that wasn't who he found waiting for him.

"I'm not as easy to lose as my brother."

Tessa leant with one foot up against the wall, a cigarette between her fingers, looking almost like a regular person enjoying the sunshine rather than a thug with any number of blades about her person.

"Balls," Alan muttered. "The pied piper had fewer people following him than me."

"You're a fascinating person, aintcha?" Tessa quipped.

"I don't suppose you know why Dick's so mad over a haunted house do you?"

"Even if I did, I wouldn't tell ya."

Alan snorted.

"No one tells me anything," he said.

"You don't strike me as a listener anyway. Maybe you should work on that."

"I'm getting advice from some damned strange places today."

Tessa shrugged as Alan walked past her. After a while, she crushed out her cigarette and followed.

8

THE DAY PASSED slowly, Alan made sure of it. With Tessa in tow, he returned home and sat in his armchair by the empty hearth, in the perfect position so that she could see him from the other side of the street where the thug hadn't even bothered to conceal herself. He'd selected a book from the shelves, one the perfect weight for holding in a single hand, and settled to not read it. In his experience from growing up with Simon, there was nothing more boring than watching someone else read. He took sly glances out of the window, catching Tessa leaning against a lamppost, shifting her weight, crossing and uncrossing her arms and taking glances up and down the street with increasing frequency as the day slowly spooled out. He allowed himself a mischievous smile and continued to stare at the pages, turning them occasionally, while his mind remained on the old house he intended to return to that night.

He was striking off ideas on how to get there without being followed when there came a knock at the door. Rising with difficulty, he made his slow way there without his cane and, with one hand on the spare revolver he hung from the back of the door, he opened it.

There stood Chester, all buckskin and cheques with a

bowler hat perched atop his well-oiled hair.

"You know there's someone watching your house, right?" he said.

Alan peeked out from the door and gave Tessa a wave.

"You have no idea how glad I am that you can see her, too. When you've had a life like mine, you start to wonder."

"Doctor Hogarth sent me with this." Chester held out a leather drawstring pouch and an envelope. "There's instructions."

Alan took them with a nod, peeking inside at the thick red dust. Tugging the string closed again, he gave the young American a smile. The moment strung out. Chester, stood on the doorstep, his shoulders a little hunched against eyes from the street, hat tugged down low over his brow. Tessa, looking on from the street with eyes narrowed to the merest slits. Alan, holding the door jamb with one hand, pouch with the other, a look of curious expectation on his face.

"Was there—" he started.

"Nope. Nothin'." And with that, Chester took the step down to the street. Alan regarded his back for a second before going to close the door. He stopped when Chester's voice drifted back to him in a stage whisper. "You really mean this stuff, don't you? You and Jam—Mister Hogarth. The ghosts and weird stuff? You believe it all."

"No belief needed. One man's weird is another man's normal."

Chester nodded a little and made off down the street.

"Bye, then," Alan muttered as he closed the door.

THE LIGHT FELL over London, summoning the hum of street lamps that filled the air like cricket song. Tessa remained as dusk fell and the streetlamp winked on above her. After a while, Alan set his book aside with a feigned yawn and a plan in mind. He closed the curtains, making sure to give the thug a pleasant smile as he did so, and turned out the lights. Taking his coat and revolver from by the door, he made his pained way up the stairs and set them on the bed as he closed his bedroom curtains as well. Then he moved around the room for a while, his silhouette acting out getting ready for bed for his stalker's benefit. Lying on the bed fully clothed, he turned out the light, listening in the dark to the *tink* of the cooling bulb above and creak of the house settling around him.

A hissing voice came from the dark: "This isn't going to fool her."

"Stopped sulking, have you?"

Slay made no sound but Alan could sense the silent growl.

"She's too smart for this," the spectre said. "She'll be circling around the house, watching the front and back. She knows you can't move quickly."

Alan smiled in the dark.

He gave Tessa time to make a few passes front and back, letting her become frustrated, just as he would himself. Patience was painful. Then he rose, slipping on his holster and coat, and made for the stairs. Upward. The third floor of Forsythe's old building was unused but the maid Alan paid to come clean once a month still gave the barren space a cursory dust. Staying away from the curtainless window, Alan moved toward the centre of the open space in the dark, glad that there was nothing to fall over but wishing he had something to hold on to.

"You'll never be bloody satisfied, will you?" he chuckled to himself.

Putting his weight onto his good leg, he took his walking

stick by the pavement end and lifted it above him, hooking the metal tip through a ring in the ceiling. A hatch sprung open to reveal a square of darkness above. Lifting his cane into the gloom, he hooked the lower rung of a set of wooden ladders, pulling them down. Somewhere above a spring *gloing*ed but, with a shove, Alan clicked the ladder into place. Taking a long, slow breath, he regarded the rungs climbing into darkness. He took a second longer than necessary to readjust his coat and holster, check the lay of his waistcoat and clutch his cane securely in his hand. Then, with nothing else to put off the inevitable, he took the ladder upward, shoving with his good leg, using his arms as much as possible, gritting his teeth when his stricken leg had to take his weight for a second. By the time he reached where the summer heat had gathered in a stifling miasma in the attic, he was already sweating and had slipped out several curses.

"I may not be fast anymore, but I'm still stupid," he muttered as he sat on the attic hatch's lip to prepare himself for another stand.

"While I relish the sight of you in pain, I can't help but feel deeply saddened by this pathetic display," Slay's voice drifted out of the attic's impenetrable dark.

"Lucky for you, you never had the opportunity to grow old." Alan struggled to his feet. "You're bloody welcome."

With a spark, Alan's oil lighter came to life, casting a barely useful pool of light, but enough to make his way through the attic without bumping into the few boxes and chests that lurked there. At the other end of the room, where a wall marked his home's boundary, a knotted rope dangled from above. Slay gave a delighted crow.

"Alan's finally got it. He knows that there's no hope. I'll finally get to watch him twitch as he dangles from a rope."

"Keep dreaming, you creepy sod. I'm sticking around just for the pleasure of annoying you."

Tugging on the rope produced another ladder and Alan braced himself to climb. At the top, jaw aching from grinding his teeth, he drew back another hatch's bolt and threw it open. Night air fell like grace on his beaded brow as he fought his way onto the roof.

The vista of London's rooftops spread out around him, an old friend he hadn't seen in a long time. Star-scattered sky, moonlight on slate and the cold glow of tesla lamps from below made for an ethereal spectacle. Alan wiped his cheek, cutting off the trickle of a pained tear.

"Well, congratulations," Slay spat. "You're up here. Now what?"

Alan ignored him, moving toward the roof's edge and craning carefully over the brick parapet. Tessa appeared below in a side street where she would be able to see the back of the house, but she didn't look up to where he peeked at her. He couldn't make out her face but imagined it to be scrunched in annoyance. It made him feel better. Scanning the further edges of the street, the dark corners and yawning alley mouths, he spotted no other shapes lurking there, including the small one he was especially looking for. Straightening himself and feeling his spine pop in relief, he stalked off across the rooftop at a steady pace. When he reached a low wall that separated the houses below, he sat, swinging one leg then the other, and he was atop the neighbouring house. There were only seven more such hurdles between short jaunts of moonlit tile before he reached the end of the street.

"Best get to it," he said with a sigh.

Leaving Tessa circling his home, Alan made his stuttering and staggering way toward the end of the row where the roof of

St Luke's chapel rose across the street and the block of houses ended in an alleyway. Alan looked down first. The ground was lost to shadows, but he knew it was there, inevitably deadly from this height. He wasn't sure if he'd ever been aware of that before. Slay sat on the opposite parapet, feet swinging gaily.

"Jump it. Just like the old days. It'll be *easy*," he said, dragging out the last word, childlike, taunting.

Alan scowled at him.

"Get smart or get dead, Alan," he said under his breath.

Where the roofs extended in the shorter section of an L, the alleyway met a parallel street. There, by the light of the moon, he spotted a large, underlit skylight. Shooting Slay a snide smile, Alan headed that way. Making sure that Tessa hadn't somehow followed him, he regarded the crowd in the streets below as they bustled between little taverns, restaurants and theatres, leaned on walls with frothing glasses or chatted in groups. Several sources of drum and violin music contended with the voices of Londoners enjoying the summer evening. At the sight of those cellar-chilled beers, Alan's mouth suddenly felt very dry.

Turning back to the skylight, he peered inside. Small circular tables were scattered across immaculately smoothed and varnished floorboards surrounded by well-dressed diners half way through their meals. The tops of waiters' heads wove between them with trays held high and arms draped with white towels over shirt sleeves. A small horseshoe bar at the end of the room winked at him.

Unceremoniously, he rapped on the skylight with his cane. A host of shocked faces turned upward like so many hungry chicks. He waved to them and, producing his badge, pressed it to the glass.

After a short conversation between a waiter and a petite

man in a slim suit, a set of stepladders was produced and the skylight swung open.

"Much appreciated," Alan said, and made to climb down without giving the waiter time to react. Several hands reached up to help him as he lowered himself shakily into the restaurant. At the bottom, someone returned the cane that they had taken for him. Someone else was adjusting his coat. "That's bloody good service."

The *maitre d'*, shorter by a head and sporting a snappy moustache, addressed Alan compassionately in a French accent.

"Good sir. Are you alright? However did you get trapped up there?"

"You know how it is," Alan said, making the *maitre d'* follow him to the bar. "I was just out for a walk and got turned around."

The barkeep, frozen halfway through wiping the bar to watch the show, blinked slowly as Alan ordered a cold pint. As the *maitre d'* fluttered around him, Alan turned to the room of rapt faces. There was utter silence apart from the thin whine of a violin from the floor below. He raised his glass–

"Cheers."

–and downed the pint in one long, satisfying draught. Returning the glass with a bank note beside it, he made for the stairs. Down and down through three floors of curious diners with the stuttering *maitre d'* in tow, he finally reached the front door and paused before leaving.

"It's a nice place you have here. I don't suppose you have a table for one tomorrow night, do you?"

The slight Frenchman stuttered a response while summoning a pad and pen from his jacket.

Alan shared his name and made an exit.

9

SHOOTING GLANCES OVER his shoulder the whole way, Alan caught the monorail from Soho to Victoria Park and then a steam cab to the Sutton house, his series of climbs already making his thigh burn like a bundle of hot wire. He tested the weight of Hogarth's bag of tricks in his pocket. He'd had one fitful night's sleep and one bout of involuntary unconsciousness since he'd been here last. Stood once more across the street from that kicked dog of a house, it felt like it had been a week. But Alan lived in his own time zone, one where he gambled away the minutes and hours, a high-roller with nothing in the bank.

After an undergrowth shuffle and door panel crawl, Alan found himself inside the house's deserted kitchen. After tapping the end of Hogarth's envelope, feeling the note slide down inside, he tore off the topmost strip.

Dear Alan,

I hope this dust helps to solve your problem. Beginning with the highest room in the house, strew a small amount as you work your way toward the exit. The spirit will be systematically forced out of each area until it cannot return at all. Beware. As I said, this must be a particularly potent spirit. I'm certain that it won't be pleased with your interference.

Yours sincerely,
James

"Sounds easy enough," Alan said.

In the dark, Slay gave a non-verbal huff.

Alan snorted and made toward the parlour and the stairs beyond. The house seemed undisturbed since his last visit. Still, he moved slowly, checking every shadow as he slipped through the shrouded furniture and took advantage of the sturdy banister to make his way upstairs. On the landing he paused, listening. Somewhere outside the sound of tyres on road and the *phut-phut-phut* of an engine came and went. Tree branches whispered in the backyard. Otherwise, nothing. He checked the lay of his revolver, for all the good it would do, and set off along the corridor toward where the spirit had rushed him. No signs of any toys, but he was acutely aware of the sound of his own breathing, seeming to come in deafening rasps.

At the end of the hall he looked around. Thin shafts of light lanced through the boarded window. There were doors down there that he hadn't reached last time. Rooms that had to be cleansed. But no toys or hurried footfalls this time.

Alan addressed the darkness, the house, and whatever it was that might be listening.

"This is your last chance. You better start behaving or it's going to go badly for you."

He could feel his pulse tap-tapping in his throat, his hands twitching along with the power of it. But there was no sound.

"Your loss, kid."

The floorboards complained at him in great mournful

groans. The shifting half-light tricked the eye. The hairs on the back of his neck prickled. Sidling down the corridor with one hand on the dusty wall, Alan approached the corridor's end.

Thump

Jerking back his hand, Alan darted back from the wall, pulse rocketing, hand finding his revolver without consulting his brain. He shuddered out a sigh, eyes fixed on the mouldy wallpaper, before bringing himself to order. He froze, holding his breath to listen. Something had hit the wall with a solid thump, from the other side, right where his hand had been.

"You're still here, then," he said to the corridor.

Laughter in the dark. Multiple off-kilter, tinkling tones of children at play. Alan swung around, squinting into the shadows. Back the way he'd come, down the other end of the corridor entirely, a small dark shape stood, stock-still and shadow-wrapped.

"You're about to have a really bad night," Alan said, but he wasn't sure if he was talking to himself or the ghost. Dipping a hand into the pouch, he sprinkled a line in front of him. "Looks like you're stuck over there, sunshine." The shape didn't move. "That's right! Stay where you are while I get this done." Alan tried to sound confident as he turned back toward the boarded window and hurried to one of the doors there, still shooting glances over his shoulder as he went.

Noise erupted from around him. The clamour of storm-tossed wind chimes, screams from several sets of little lungs, what sounded like the clatter of pans and hoot of air in pipes. Dust rushed up from beneath his feet, filling the air, making him hack and cover his face with his coat sleeve. Although he could have used the last of his breath to say something useful or heroically amusing he chose to curse instead. Squinting against the onslaught he spotted Slay at the end of the hall, solid enough to block the light from the window behind, but he wasn't looking at Alan. Even in the dark, Alan could see that his dire companion was squinting at one of the doors, head cocked to listen. As if the night couldn't get more odd.

"There's something wrong, here," Slay said.

Alan stumbled forward and, through a cough, said:

"You're sharper than ever." But, of course, Slay was right. There was something off. "How did the little snot do all that with Hogarth's dust blocking the hall?"

Slay gave him a patronising smile. "Well done."

Alan ignored him and, without even trying the doorknob, applied his shoulder to the door. It slammed open, denting the wall behind it. Alan gave a manic grin. That lasted only a second before, despite his cane, his bad leg crumpled and he had to catch himself on the doorway. Screams erupted from inside the room, several little voices, but not the screams he'd heard before. Not angry, not scary. Finding his balance once more, Alan barrelled through the open doorway and saw the source of those shrieks. Dirty little urchin faces with wide eyes stared at him from out of the darkness.

10

THE ROOM'S WINDOWS had been boarded well, leaving the room in total darkness save for a small lantern almost out of oil which flickered in the middle of the room. In the cold light that leaked in behind him, crossed with the orange glow, the urchins' faces were made almost as unearthly as if they had been real ghosts. Harnessing his adrenaline into determination rather than anger, Alan made short work of the window's boards with the crowbar end of his cane and the street's light poured into the room. The urchins scuttled as one toward the room's furthest corner where shadows could still hide them. Finally, Alan could see what he'd stepped into. A bedroom. Mattresses lay on the floor, topped with blankets as dishevelled and moth eaten as the children who cowered atop them. Towers of cardboard boxes stood here and there, although he couldn't see what they contained. In one corner were piled the ancient toys that had been used to such ghastly effect on his first visit. Along the side of the room adjacent to the hall, copper pipes protruded from a hole in the floor like some complex wind instrument. Three large sets of wind chimes hung from the corner. And everything came together in his mind. He could have come up with something venomous to say but, as he looked from the ingenious set-up to the teary faces of the urchins, he found a little light still flickering in a cobwebbed corner of his heart.

He laughed. One hand on the wall, rubbing his ceasing leg with the other, he started a chuckle that rose to a laugh until he couldn't tell if his tears were pain or mirth.

"You clever little—," he started to say, but was cut short as he hit the ground with a grunt.

A hot pain flared behind both knees where something had struck him. The urchins screamed again. Something was on him, straddling his back and pummelling his shoulders and neck. He rolled sharply, leading with his elbow which connected with the assailant. He felt the weight roll aside, heard a gasp of pain. It was always a good sign when the thing you were fighting sounded hurt.

Now on his side, Alan fought his way to one knee, ready to use his cane to stand, but his attacker wasn't done. They came hurtling toward him and he caught the briefest glimpse of the youngster, wild and roaring, before their flying knee slammed under his chin, knocking him back all over again. Now Alan had his cane in both hands, forcing it upward as if warding off the chomping jaws of a lion. A flurry of glancing blows seemed to hit him everywhere, anywhere. There was no way to build an intelligent defence against it. But that had never been his forte anyway. Jerking his cane to the right, the already off-balance assailant flew away with a bark of pain. With his other foot, Alan kicked one of the box towers, sending it crashing down on his prone opponent. He struggled to his feet as fast as possible and, sweeping aside the boxes, grabbed the urchin's grubby shirt in one hand, raising the other for a final strike.

Her hands around Alan's wrist, the urchin stared up at him. Streaked with blood and dirt, hair rough cut at the shoulder, she regarded Alan with utter contempt. Her lip was bleeding, one cheek was scuffed.

Alan dropped her with a bump, collapsing back into a half recline on the ground.

"Bloody hell, kid," he coughed as they both laid back, catching their breath.

With Alan regarding the ceiling as aches blossomed across his body, the fight seemed thoroughly over and the other urchins became brave enough to move. Surrounding their champion, giving what aid they could, they muttered between themselves while shooting wary glances his way. One more appeared in the doorway, a young boy with a coal dust-coated but very alive face now that Alan could see him in the light. He gave another laugh.

"You need to go, old man. You better leave us alone or—"

Alan put up a hand to the champion, stopping her dead. He inspected her closer, now. She stood head and shoulders over the other children, maybe sixteen years old. The accent was pure Cheapside, like his own. But where he'd once been told his lineage might have been German, there was the far east in hers. In patchwork trousers and a work shirt two sizes too big, she was half-starved as they all were but, he rubbed the back of his head where a lump was forming, her soul had grit usually reserved for the likes of bare knuckle fighters and career sailors.

Alan reached into his coat pocket and pulled out Hogarth's dust bag and, taking a handful, threw it at them. The urchins squealed, some turned away. Their champion took most of the red cloud in the face, unflinching.

"Just making sure," Alan chuckled. "Are you going to help me up—"

He paused for a name. From behind a barrier of stern

uncertainty, she gave it.

"Connie."

With a sniff, the urchin stepped forward, lending her hand as Alan fought his way to sit on the edge of one of the mattresses. He gave her a grateful nod as he dusted himself down, but only made red streaks on his clothes.

"Bugger it."

"We know who you are," Connie commented. Her eyes were narrowed, her mouth tense. The champion's entire face was extremely mobile, giving away every emotion with an almost comical expression that would have seen her lose her trousers at the poker table. But she wasn't childish or naive. Quite the opposite. She wore her stern demeanour and astute scepticism for all to see, daring Alan to just try and fool her.

She dropped cross-legged on the mattress opposite him with a puff of dust and the other urchins gathered around the room, close enough to listen, far enough to get away if necessary. But Connie wasn't scared of him, that was for sure.

The other urchins were chuntering over something, like pigeons at a chunk of bread. The smallest boy, who Alan still thought of as the ghost, tapped on Connie's shoulder, offering up a tuft of old papers which she looked at and then looked at Alan. She thanked him. The ghost's name, it seemed, was Tully.

With her eyes cautiously scanning Alan's face for any signs of attack, Connie held out the bundle of papers to him.

"You're Alan Shaw, aren't you?"

Slowly, Alan reached out and took the papers. They were much read, crumpled and even a little soggy, but he could tell it had once been an issue of The Graphical Adventures of Alan Shaw. He thumbed through pages filled with pictures in small panels, speech at the top of each hanging over stylised images of a young adventurer and his friends in the Egyptian desert. Near the back of the issue, the story ended abruptly as several pages were missing.

"I used to be," he said. "Sometimes feels like I'm just wearing the name." He pulled out his badge to show them. Tully's face moved between awe and confusion.

"You got old," he said, leaning forward but still very much behind Connie.

"I noticed," Alan grumbled.

Tully gestured to the comic. "How does it end?"

"Still haven't found out." Alan handed back the tattered comic book.

Connie's stern face had dropped to what seemed like a more natural expression for her features, a smile. "I don't believe it," she whispered.

"I get that a lot. I take it you're the leader here, then? You put all this together? The pipes, the chimes, the toys and the noises? It's pretty clever. You had me totally fooled."

"We fooled everyone," Connie replied.

One of the urchins took something from a rough hessian sack in the corner and started to hand out small pieces. Connie took some as well and, breaking it in two, offered a little to Alan. With a nod of thanks, he took a bite. Stale as hell and dusty, the bread threw him back to other rooms like this where he'd huddled as a boy with children just like these, most of whom never made it to Connie's age, never mind his. The boy buried deep inside him even savoured the taste, that sensation of something, anything taking the edge off the hunger. Mouldy bliss.

Alan leaned in, ready to talk straight. "You had a good con going, but it's over. Dick must know you're here. He tried to get me to leave it alone. But even if I walk away, Sutton will just employ someone else. Someone less likely to keep your secret."

Together, Connie and Alan looked at the little mice nibbling at their stale old bread.

"You'd do that?" she asked.

"Urchins stick together, don't they?"

Connie nodded, her uncertainty evaporating. He held up a finger.

"There's a but. You have to tell me how you've pissed off Dick Whitsun."

The collective shuffling and gaze swapping of the other urchins was all he needed.

Connie's gaze hardened.

"You know what he does to urchins. Makes the young ones steal and the older ones—"

"Dollymops, mollies and cutthroats." For the first time, Alan regarded his knees. "I know."

"We don't want that. *I* don't want that. We want to grow up, just like you."

"No," Alan snapped. His eyes filled with an earnest fire. He rubbed a thumb over his badge where a shinier stripe had been created by the constant buffing. "Not like me, either. The stories tell a lot, but not all. What happened between them and what brought me here is a string of nightmares as bad as anything Dick has done. You have to be better, but you're not going to get a chance. Not with Dick on your backs. I bet me getting involved is all that stopped him burning this place down already. Because he knows—"

In the dark corners of the room the urchins leaned in, rapt and desperate. The gas lamp hissed, its light growing lower. Alan looked up at Connie's face. Eyes a little wide, mouth tensed into a pale line. He tried to remember what that expression was. He felt like he'd seen it before. It was her voice that made him realise:

"What does he know?"

Hope. Connie's face was a postcard from a place he'd never visited.

"That I'll stand in his way. I need to have a word with my old pal, Dick."

He gave her a conspiratorial smile.

11

CREAKING LIKE AN old gate, Alan rose to his feet, Connie tugging his hand and two other urchins shoving his legs like Lilliputians helping Gulliver.

"If this wasn't so embarrassing, it'd be funny," he said. "Now, you lot pack your things. You're all leaving before—"

Hobbling toward the window to adjust his clothing by the streetlight, he cut himself off.

"Balls."

Connie appeared at his side.

"Before that?" she asked. Alan gave a thoughtful grunt as he regarded the figure in the street below, hands plunged in the deep pockets of his coat. Dick Whitsun himself. Raising a hand to them, he beckoned.

"We should go down," Connie said.

"I should. You all need to be elsewhere."

Connie opened her mouth to protest, but Alan cut her short.

"I'm not telling you, but I am asking, and I hope you'll listen."

Begrudgingly, she moved away to corral the fearful mice in the room. Alan watched them for just a second as they scampered back and forth, stuffing blankets and their few items of clothing into sacks. He couldn't help but notice that the toys were left behind. Even the smallest children ignored them in favour of warmth.

"EVENING, OLD MATE," Dick said as Alan crossed the road toward the moonlit park. "I see you're still ignoring friendly advice."

"Never did know when I was on to a good thing," Alan retorted.

Dick scoffed.

"What're the chances you were just saying a fond farewell to those kids and heading home for a jug of laudanum?"

"About what you'd expect."

Alan set his face to steel as Dick gave a tired sigh.

"Just let me take the kids, Al. It'll solve a lot of problems all at once. You get paid, I get to go home, Sutton gets his house back and the kids get fed in the end. Everyone wins."

"And what if the kids don't see what you've got in store for them as winning?"

"They'll do as they're bloody well told and learn to feel lucky for the food I give them in exchange."

Alan shook his head and rubbed the knot turning to a boulder in his neck.

"You're no better than the workhouse, Dick. No better at all."

The Consortium's leader visibly snarled, his salt and pepper chin bristles forming peaks and troughs from his wrinkled grimace.

"You've known what I do with urchins for years, Al. Years. And you never cared before."

"I care now," Alan snapped. "And that puts you and me at odds."

Alan and his friend grew quiet. Somewhere in the park, a nocturnal beast rustled leaves. The air had lost its sunny day-warmth, leaving a night-sharp breeze.

"What would you have me do, High and Mighty? You think if I stopped that these kids would just turn into flower pickers and button sellers? They'd do just the same, only without what I offer. Safety. That's what you're trying to take down, if you fight me. The Gentleman's Consortium is what stops the ratbags of this city from tearing a hole in it. And it runs on a very simple rule. Dick Whitsun cannot be defied. Not by gutter runners like these, not by no one."

"Don't make me fight you," Alan said, all the energy draining from his voice. "Walk away. The kids didn't beat you. Let's just make a truce for the price of a few urchins. Because if you actually make me fight you, cripple or not, you know what'll happen. Someone's gonna die. One or the other, probably both."

Dick sucked his teeth.

"Not all of us were taken off the streets by a copper, Al. Some of us kept right on living out there. Alone. We had to make what we could out of nothing."

Alan could feel anger rising. An ancient anger and the strongest kind, anger at himself for letting himself be saved, bred from the guilt of betraying his street friends, for taking the easy way as they hadn't been able to, and for leaving the hellscape of London as soon as he'd been able.

"Careful, Dick. You're treading a line."

But Dick knew him too well, he might as well have been reading Alan's mind.

"Not all of us could grow up to be some big shot with your

stories."

"What do you mean by that?" Alan said, his eyes narrowing. If it had been anyone, anyone but Dick, they'd be staring down a barrel by now.

"You always were full of shit," Dick said without spite but full of cold, friendly honesty. "When we all escaped the workhouse. 'I know the way,' you said. And you didn't. Three good lads were caught because of it."

Alan could almost hear the clack of the looms echoing back from bare stone walls, feel the whip of air tug at his hair as the jenny sped above, finger-slicing fast. He could taste the bowls of oaty filth and the cold of the stone room that he and Dick had huddled in together. He looked at his friend's worn old face but saw the workhouse wretch beneath it. The lad he'd first made friends with, made plans with. The boy who ran by his side into a long-ago London night while angry whistles blew at their backs.

"I remember. It was raining," came Slay's voice from somewhere behind. The tone was enough to unnerve Alan. Sadness. He'd rather have Slay on a murderous rampage than that.

Dick's voice fell into the distance as Alan's head filled with too many memories. Everything came at once, one mistake leading to the memory of another, faces and voices mixed with muzzle flare and gunshot cracks, some real, some only flashes of old emotion boiled up.

Alan tugged aside the heavy curtain of memory to peer into the present once more.

"–Those who escaped did so because of me. Me, Al, and I never got no badge or statue or nothing. If we do this," the man on the surface of the boy said, "that means no more favours. I won't be covering for you any more when you get in too deep. This is us done."

Alan nodded. It was all he could do.

"But neither of us have to kill our oldest friend," he said.

Drawing his coat around him, Dick turned away with a scornful sniff.

"One thing you should know then, if these are to be our final words. Another rule of the Consortium." As Dick strode into the tree-lined park, his voice drifted back over his shoulder. "I can't take back orders that have already been given."

A scream lit the night like a phosphorus flare. Alan's head snapped around toward the house. Another yell, muffled.

He didn't even waste time cursing. Hobbling as fast as he could, extending his stride into the realms of agony, he limped back through the gate, the yard, circling around the house. A fist came around the corner like a steam cab and he was moving too fast to do anything about it. Tessa gave a snorting laugh as he reeled back, blinking the stars from his eyes.

"In a rush?" she asked.

In answer, he swung his cane in an underhand arc. She deftly blocked the blow before it hit her ribs, but it took both hands, which was what Alan was hoping. He let go of the cane, leaving Tessa holding it, bemused, and grabbed her by the forelock of her jacket. She slammed her into the wall once, twice, knocking the wind out of her and, as she doubled over, he slammed a fist into her temple, knocking her to the ground entirely.

Snatching his cane from her limp hands, he straightened to see Slay standing nearby, any lingering sadness from their shared memories washed away by murderous glee.

"Such savagery!" he squealed, but it was to Alan's back as he stalked away.

The hall's back door was open, something Alan had thought impossible. But as he stepped through he saw the splintered wood and broken nails where someone a lot fitter than himself had managed to break it open. Slay waited inside.

"You should have killed her." Alan walked right through him, into the furniture-choked parlour. "Just one more whack would have done it."

At the bottom stair, Alan ground his teeth. Slay called down to him from the upper landing as he scaled what might as well have been a wooden cliff.

"Won't you do anything for these mouldy little snots? Anything at all? You're angry enough. You've lost your oldest friend for them. You're in pain. I can smell it on you. You look like death. Like you're about to pass out. Rather Tessa dies than you. Who'll save them if she gets back up, comes up behind? Do you think she'll be so merciful?"

Panting, Alan turned down the corridor, his steam running low. He shoved right through Slay who made yummy noises in his throat.

"You've taken far too long to get up here, you know. They'll already be dead," he hissed.

Left at the junction, down another corridor whose end seemed to move away as swiftly as Alan could stamp toward it.

"Connie, dead. Little Tully, dead. Blood and rags. And what'll you do when you get in there? You'll get beaten, too. You got lucky with Tessa. It won't take dark magic or undead creatures or crashing airships to kill the mighty Alan Shaw. You're going to die beyond *that* door. In a dark room, alone, surrounded by the little bodies of the children you failed to save. Save the sweat and crawl home."

Alan might have had something clever to say, something cutting and poignant. It might have crossed his mind, but the sound of his pulse and rasp of his breath was too loud to hear it, buried as it was beneath a fog of pain. With every word from Slay his leg felt heavier, the cursed muscle bunched harder, a dark anchor that dragged him down, draining the little energy he had left. And so, instead of bursting through the door, revolver in hand, his shoulder hit the jamb and he doubled over, exhausted, and although he managed to draw his weapon, the fireworks in his vision wouldn't let him aim it, even if his weary arm would have been able to bring it to bear.

The fog in his vision, which pulsed in time with the pain behind his eyes, drew back to reveal a dire tableau. The urchins clustered at the room's corners. Ratso towered over them with Connie dangling from one outstretched hand like a mangy cat about to be thrown in the river. A raucous laugh exploded from the thug as he regarded Alan, crumpled and gasping.

"You come to save these little shits? Looks like it's you who needs saving," Ratso rumbled, and laughed again as Connie struggled valiantly in his grasp.

Alan growled. He knew how the urchins felt. He'd seen raging giants at their age, too. And he felt just as powerless as he had then. He caught Connie's eye. Tears streaked her face, but her eyes were hard, her mouth a sneer of injustice rather than fear.

"I'm done in, kid," he panted.

Her face collapsing into despair, Connie stopped her struggling. The thug laughed, the room seeming to rattle with it as he shook her some more. Those urchins who were able through their sobs, screamed.

Alan held Connie's gaze, making a connection as firm as hands clasping wrists. If he had anything left to give, it wasn't in strength or bullets, he knew. But that didn't mean he was weaponless.

"But I didn't come to save you," he panted. "Just didn't want to miss you kicking his arse."

Connie recognised that look. She'd seen it reflected back at her in shards of glass and rainwater puddles. Despite the old man's ailing limbs and depleted energy, despite the years that dragged him to the ground and some darkness that she felt in him rather than saw; some indomitable will still remained, something that they both shared. His was a glowing coal, growing cold, but it was enough to reignite her own.

Fatal acceptance and confusion fell away and grit rose up. Everything happened in fever dream flashes.

Connie twisted in the air like a cat. Dirty but effective, her knee connected with Ratso's chest. The air wheezed out of him and she dropped from his grasp. The thug stumbled back but found that his retreating leg had no knee left in it because Connie's boot had kicked it out. He fell to one knee and one hand but the hand wasn't there either. Making up for her complete lack of finesse with righteous savagery, Connie jammed the heel of her boot into Ratso's temple, slamming his head against the floorboards. The look of confusion on the thug's face slipped away with his consciousness.

She caught her breath with a speed that Alan coveted. Wiping her cheek with the back of her hand, she sniffed.

"I'm not crying," she said, her voice steady.

"Nothing wrong with a good cry," Alan groaned. "If I wasn't all dried up inside, I'd join you."

He shot a look out into the dark corridor. No sign of Slay. The wretched shadow had retreated for now.

"Who are you looking for?" Connie asked.

"No one. It's just us." Taking out his badge, he tossed it toward Tully, who sat wide-eyed and worryingly silent. "Go find the constabulary, Tully. Show them that. They'll come."

The little boy, slashes of clean skin on his dirty face, took the badge and left.

Resting his back against the door's jamb, Alan let out a pained sigh.

"Don't suppose any of you kids have something to drink, do you?"

12

I T WAS HARD to tell if it was the bed springs or his aching muscles that gave a pained creak. Either way, Alan gave a heartfelt swear as the sun lanced through the curtains he'd failed to close last night and hit him in the retinas. He rolled onto his back and buried his face in the crook of his elbow to let his mind wake up at its leisure. The last threads of the previous night wove together. Sending Tully for a copper, the ratchet of cuffs on the rat twins' wrists, a wriggling urchin on his knee as they were all bundled into the back of a barred cop-wagon not really big enough for the lot of them, Lady Ottaway answering the door of her Bloomsbury orphanage at such a late hour still fully dressed with a teacup in hand. Her look of pity as the urchins filed past her which turned from confusion at the copper's explanation and ended in an I-told-you-so smirk as Alan gave her a weary wave from the carriage. A copper shaking Alan awake as they reached his home. The fateful climb to his bedroom, and ultimate collapse into bed.

After dozing for a while, Alan only dragged himself out of bed when his stomach complained. His watch told him that it was closer to lunch than breakfast and so, with painstaking slowness, he dressed the bundle of knotted rope that he called a body. It was mid-shave that he heard a thump from downstairs. He stiffened, straining his ears, but there was no other sound. He wiped the foam from his face, grabbed his cane and made for the stairs. On the landing, he listened again.

Nothing but the sounds of the city whispering through the walls and wooden-framed windows.

Steadily, trying to avoid the stairs that creaked, he crept down and along the hall. The parlour lay undisturbed but, as he moved toward the half-open door of the kitchen, a shadow moved beyond.

"You're back then are you? Where did you skulk off to last night? Seeing me still breathing too much for you?" he said, bursting through the door, searching the corners for signs of Mister Slay. But there was only Connie, sitting at the small table in the kitchen's centre with hands folded, staring at him. She looked odd. Pale. It took Alan a minute to realise it was because she was clean.

Trying to hide his surprise, he moved past the urchins' champion from kettle to oven, collecting a pan from the hanging rack, and eggs from the humming refrigeration cabinet. All the while, he checked the back door, the kitchen window and even the kitchen's open hearth from the corner of his eye. There wasn't a hint of how the kid had gotten in.

"Lady Ottaway's nice," Connie said. "The others like her. She said they can stay if we don't mind sharing rooms." She gave a little snort of a laugh at that. "She has a toilet inside."

"You'll get used to it. I did," Alan said as he scraped scrambled eggs onto a plate and added pepper. Taking a seat across the table from Connie, he dug in. She watched him eat every morsel. He watched her watch him. "There's more in the pan. Don't let it go to waste."

She made certain that he knew she was in no rush but, in

the next few moments of silence, she retrieved the frying pan, put it on the table in front of her and began picking from it with her fingers. By the time Alan slid his empty plate aside, the kettle began to rattle and whistle.

"But you didn't come to talk to me about the marvels of modern plumbing," he said, tending to the kettle.

"The others were wondering what happens now, with the Gee-Cee. They'll find us eventually. And that toff will be taking his house back, I suppose."

"Dick won't be a problem. I had a word." The bolt just beneath his heart tightened for a second. He tried to ignore it as he slid a plain and practical mug next to Connie's frying pan and sat to sip from his own cracked version. "As for Sutton, I'll send him a note later. He won't care what went on as long as it isn't his problem anymore."

They sat in silence for a while, sipping their steaming tea. Connie wrapped her hands around her mug as if to warm them, a technique that Alan knew well.

"My brother and his wife are coming soon," he said, checking his wristwatch. "They like to come get on at me once a week."

Connie made to stand, to leave, but Alan held up a hand.

"No need to rush off, kid. I was just letting you know. I need to get the place ready. Drink your tea."

Once he'd thought to set a fresh kettle on the hob, he headed through to the parlour with Connie following, mug in hand. She watched him as he tore open the curtains with a groan.

When Slay's voice piped in his ear, Alan remained by the window, pretending to look out at the street.

"Are you just going to let her turn up unannounced like this?" the spectre asked.

"I wondered where you'd got to," Alan replied, his voice the faintest whisper so that Connie wouldn't hear. "She doesn't know any better. Lady Ottaway can teach her all that manners stuff. She'll be fine."

"And what if she keeps coming? What if she keeps following you around?"

"Are you worried she'll get hurt?" Alan said, mockingly.

Slay *humphed*. "Hardly."

He finally turned to see the sunlight glistening and bouncing from his trinkets laid haphazard on the shelves. Connie had floated toward them despite herself.

"Don't touch anything. Some of this stuff will literally have your fingers off," Alan said. He smiled when Connie nodded at him and, with both hands firmly gripping her mug, she leaned precariously on her tiptoes to look at a spent bullet in a small wooden box.

First teasing the fire into life, Alan dragged two chairs from their corners to rest near the warmth. It was almost cosy. Part of him hated it. The old carriage clock showed that he had a few minutes before Lottie and Simon would arrive. Just enough time for the kettle to re-boil and the tea to steep.

"You left her at the orphanage to get her off your hands. Send her away again," Slay offered.

Alan searched the corners of the room for Slay but he still couldn't spot the spook. For some reason he was remaining as a voice only this morning.

"What are you looking for?" Connie asked, her head cocked at him in curiosity.

"What?"

"You get this look. I noticed it last night. Like you're trying to find something. You just start looking around. Kind of frustrated, like you lost your wallet. Or you're expecting the tax man to turn up."

"She's on to you, old pal," Slay sneered. He gasped and a faint chuckle echoed out from wherever he was hiding. "You should tell her about me. That'll get rid of her."

"You live alone like me, you start to go a bit odd," Alan said, collapsing into his chair by the fire.

"You should get a cat," said Connie.

"There are enough strays in here already," Slay hissed.

Connie continued to move around the room, looking at the trinkets of another life, hands shoved deeply in pockets to show that she definitely wasn't going to touch them. She sighed a lot. Eventually, she made her way to the bookshelf at the furthest end of the room where Alan kept his copies of the Graphical Adventures of Alan Shaw. Contrary to what she expected, they were all in order. She slid one out and read the cover.

Alan Shaw and the Whistle of Death.

"They're brand new," she said.

"I don't need to read them, I was there," Alan said from the doorway.

"I know this one. The whistle was the groundsman summoning the wolves to eat people."

"You know more about my adventures than I do."

"Are they all true?"

"Yes." He took a deep breath before ploughing on. Offering conversation was such hard work, but he felt it needed to be said. "But it's not what's in them that's important, you know. Life's what happens between the adventures."

SHE TURNED TO where he slouched in his chair, the golden morning rays highlighting his wrinkles.

"Were there any you didn't tell?" she asked.

"No. Yes. Just one."

The jungles of India rose in his mind, the mountains, the eyes of a bandit woman unmatched in all his years, shifting to the eyes of a man, the light dying in them, the crumbling of ancient walls and a lonely road.

"You look sad," Connie said.

"You notice too much, kid."

"I want to have adventures like that, travel the world."

Alan nodded. He'd been the same, filled with dreams of America and adventures with cowboys when he was a boy.

"It's fun, exciting," he said. "But mostly full of regrets. You want my advice? Stay here. Make the people you love safe before anyone else. When something goes wrong you don't want to be so far away you can't make it back or it's too late to do anything about it."

Connie nodded as if she understood and slid the comic book back with reverence, making sure it was in the right order.

From beyond the window came the sound of hurrying feet. Nothing unusual for London, but Alan knew that specific sound very well. Flatfoot leather, running coppers. Connie's ears pricked up and she cast a haunted glance toward the window. It took a few seconds of darting eyes before she got control of herself, realising where she was. Safe. Or safer, at least.

"Scared little rabbit," Slay mocked.

Alan coughed angrily, and had to hide it in a fake flurry of other coughs when Connie looked at him. After a while, someone knocked at the door and Alan drifted out, muttering to himself.

"–like bloody Piccadilly. I know, shut up."

Connie's fingers trailed along the spines of Alan's adventures as she thought about the gaps and how they turned the privateer in the pictures to a limping old grump clattering cups in the kitchen. From the hall came the sound of an opening door, voices, and someone stepped into the parlour.

"Oh, you have another guest."

There stood a thin man in his fourth decade or so, slick hair and pince-nez glasses. From the utter lack of family resemblance, Connie assumed this to be Alan's adoptive brother. A woman came into the doorframe next, a simple drape-front skirt and blonde tresses piled neatly.

"A friend of yours, Alan?" Lottie asked, her tone implying genuine interest.

Alan pushed past them both.

"I haven't decided, yet," he said. Automatically he waved his hand from one person to the other, reciting names.

With that, the kettle whistle blew.

Lottie leapt to action. "I'll make it. You men sit down. Especially you, Alan."

"I can make tea in my own house, Lottie," he replied.

"But you don't have to. And there's nothing worse than watching you try to carry three cups with your cane in the other hand. You spill more than we drink. Perhaps Constance could help me?" Lottie asked, smiling at the urchin champion.

Simon and Alan exchanged knowing glances and took their positions by the fire as Connie drifted warily into the hallway.

"I didn't realise you'd have another guest," Simon said, trying to be polite.

"I'm as surprised as you. I don't know what to do with her. Maybe Lottie can fix her."

"In what way is she broken?"

"The usual ways. I gave her to Lady Ottaway but she came back," Alan said, his gaze falling on the doorway through which Connie had disappeared.

"Maybe she feels she has more in common with you."

"And you think I'm a good role model?" They looked at each other for a second too long, Simon breaking eye contact first. Alan nodded. "Exactly."

"But they see in you the possibility to change their fate," Simon added. "They don't need to know that you're a miserable old sod."

Alan barked a laugh.

"HOW DO YOU take your tea, Constance?" Lottie asked, as if she'd known Connie for years and yet this little tidbit had slipped her mind. "You look like you could use a cup."

"It's just Connie, Miss. Chun-hee, really. But it sounds like Connie so that's what people call me. And I don't mind."

Lottie nodded as she filled their cups.

"My mother used to say that the way someone takes their tea says something about their character," she continued.

"I don't really remember much that my mother said," Connie confided, heartbreakingly matter-of-fact. Silence spooled out until the kettle sang.

"The works it is, then." Lottie said, sliding a tea with milk and sugar toward Connie with a wink. "If you don't mind me asking, were you very young when she passed?"

Connie's delivery was cold, practised, brief: "I had my fifth birthday just before we left Hanseong. They both died on the ship. Mama was already ill, Papa they killed when they found us in the hold. I hid under Mama and ran away onto the docks when they went to bring ropes to wrap them up. The Gee Cee picked me up. They scour the docks for runaways."

Connie went on, staring down into the steam, explaining Sutton Hall and Alan's involvement in broad strokes. As Connie finished her story, she finally took a sip of her lukewarm tea and looked up. Lottie's teacup was still full, no longer steaming. She had given every ounce of her attention to the full story, not even breaking off for a sip.

"That's quite a tale," Lottie said, finally sipping her tea.

"It's how things go," Connie replied.

In silence, they drank their tea, and when they were done, Lottie made another, tossing the cups for Simon and Alan that were never delivered.

"You and your friends orchestrated quite the ruse," Lottie said as she waited for the kettle and began the brewing all over again.

"We had to find a way to stay alive. Smart is sometimes better than strong. And it was fun. I like tea like this."

Lottie smiled.

"You're very brave," she said. Connie looked up at her and Lottie answered the unspoken question. "Some people do wild things and are called brave because they succeed. But bravery comes in a lot of forms. What you did, taking responsibility for the lives of those little ones using nothing but your wits, that's very, very brave."

"Lady Ottaway is brave," Connie said, brushing off the compliment.

"She is. But a different kind again. So what brings you back here, to the house of a man who I can only describe as a bad influence. Although I love him dearly, of course."

"He started out just like me. And he had adventures."

"That's true. But truth is more of a spectrum." Lottie waited until the young woman looked up at her. Through the concerned eyebrows of a friend, she said: "Just be aware that the boy in those stories isn't the man sitting in the living room, Connie."

Connie nodded. "I can see that, now."

"WHAT ARE YOU boys talking about?" Lottie asked, standing in the parlour doorway with a mug in each hand. Behind her, Connie held a pair of cups and saucers.

Lottie handed Simon a robust old mug and Alan another, reserving the only pair of cup and saucer that Alan owned for Connie and herself. Connie was quiet, resting the cup and saucer on her knee as she perched on the footstool beside the fire.

"We were discussing how long it takes to make a cuppa," Alan snarked.

"Don't listen to him. Alan was just finishing off his ghost story," Simon said with a laugh. He leaned toward Connie with a wink. "Brilliantly clever."

Connie looked up at him through her eyelashes with an apologetic smile.

"One thing still bugs me," Alan said. "I can figure out how you smuggled Tully around to look like a ghost, how you put the toys out, and the noises you made between the lot of you. But I can't figure out how you made the footsteps in the dust."

Connie furrowed her brow.

"I—we didn't make any footsteps."

Alan turned his eyes to his brother and sister-in-law, Simon with his eyes a little wider than usual, Lottie with her eyebrows high. The distant sounds of London beyond the window filtered into an uneasy silence. After a few moments, Simon sipped his tea, coughed politely, and broke back in to conversation.

"Anyway, you're better off without that scoundrel Whitsun hanging around, too, Alan. He's been a no-good cad ever since we were boys."

"Simon," Alan snapped. "Give it a rest."

Simon cleared his throat, but did as he was told. After

another moment of silence whereby everyone avoided each other's eye line, Simon clapped his hands, dispelling the shadows.

"To lighter subjects! Have I told you about the current study we're undertaking regarding the migratory pattern of Painted Ladies?"

Alan made a quip about the Covent Garden lasses he'd known as a boy heading to Africa for the winter, and the mood lightened somewhat. Connie broke a smile and drank her tea the way she liked it.

ALAN GAVE ONE last wave to Simon and Lottie and closed the door. In the living room, Connie stared out of the window.

"Lottie asked me what I want to do when I grow up—" she said.

"No one in their right mind grows up," Alan quipped, but she ignored him.

"I thought I knew, but I've changed my mind."

Alan looked at her, carefully blank faced "Oh?"

She smiled at him. "Lottie told me something that I think I understand, now. I need to be good at what *I'm* good at, not what someone else is."

"That makes a lot of sense," he said with an earnest nod. "No point hanging around the ruins of someone else's life, kid."

"I best be going," she said, heading for the door. "Lady Ottaway will wonder where I've been."

"Hold on." Alan removed himself to the other end of the parlour and returned a few minutes later with two envelopes and a pound note in his hand.

"I can't get around as quick as I used to. How about you

run a couple of errands for me? One of them is where you're already heading."

Connie moved toward him gingerly, but as she tried to take the envelope from him, Alan kept hold of one end.

"How do I know you'll deliver them and not just do a runner with the money?"

"I suppose you don't," she said with a smile. Alan let go with a smirk of his own. He made to follow her to the door but she held up a hand to stop him. "I know the way. You should sit down, old man."

Connie left the doorway and, seconds later, Alan heard the front door close. He sighed heavily, wiping a hand down his face, and came up staring at the bookcase but seeing the past.

"You did the right thing," Slay said, appearing in the opposite chair, legs crossed and relaxed.

"Wipe that smirk off your face. I did it to stop the kid ruining her life, not because you said so. Don't forget, Slay, you're a passenger and that's it."

With a steadying sigh, Alan headed toward the stairs' agonising climb, leaving the spectre alone by a fire that didn't warm him.

Dear Mister Sutton,

I write to report my findings from Sutton Hall. After consulting with an expert on the subject of the supernatural, I can now confirm that your hall is haunted by the ghost of a small boy. When and how he died remains a mystery although the upper floors of the house are the most affected. My expert suggests that this ghost is impossible to get rid of completely. Anything done by priests, scientists or mystics would likely be painting over the cracks. And the amount of interest that might generate from the newssheets would make the house unsellable afterward. I have contacted a lady in my acquaintance on your behalf as she is particularly interested in supernatural phenomena and would likely purchase the house as-is for a reasonable discount. Regards the remaining payment for my services, please give it to the messenger who hands you this letter.

Yours,
Alan Shaw

Dear Lady Ottaway,

Thank you for taking in the urchins from Sutton Hall. I'm sure you know what they got up to and how clever the little blighters are, so good luck to you. I'm sure you'll handle them as well as you did the brigadier. I assure you that the Gentleman's Consortium will be no trouble to you as I have made arrangements.

I'd like to give you some information that you might find interesting. I expect that Sutton Hall will not only be up for sale after my investigation, but it will probably be going cheap. I'm certain that you could fill the house with your own little monsters. When you receive this letter, there should also be an envelope addressed from Mister Sutton. It's for you.

Lastly, if you've received not only my letter but Mister Sutton's package, then it's fair to assume that Connie is about as trustworthy as urchins get. She'd make a decent assistant, I think. If you end up buying Sutton Hall, she already knows all the nooks and crannies.

Yours,
Alan Shaw

Alan Shaw and the Shattered Soul

1

August, 1871
London, England

WITH ITS SMALL tables, wobbly chairs and dusty lighting, the Britannia Theatre was only a minor slip of the imagination from the tavern it had so recently been. Alan sat in the pit before a newly built stage curtained with deep green material and gold tassels all lit by gas light. Tesla connections were slow to arrive in this part of the city and so the stage lighting was still all gas lamps and cleverly-placed mirrors. Most of the theatre's tables sat empty. Still, there were excited whispers in the gloom, anticipation for the wonders about to be seen laced with the fear of what might follow the audience home.

"I hope this is worth the trip to Hoxton, Hogarth," Alan said. His neck might have been made of rubber for all he swung it around to check out the figures in the dark around them.

Doctor James Hogarth sat cross-legged and patient beside him.

"Why? Did you have somewhere else to be tonight?" the anthropologist asked.

Alan clammed up with a *humph*.

"I've sent a note ahead to Madame Masque," Hogarth continued. "Hopefully she'll agree to meet us."

"I bet that's not the name on her birth certificate," Alan quipped.

"There is a certain element of showmanship to the occult circuit," Hogarth sighed. "The roster of talent for this kind of show changes often depending on popular trends. Mesmerism, for instance, has taken a rise and fall in recent years. It is what lies beyond the veil that people are now morbidly interested in. Personally, I find it fascinating that even in a country driven by science, people still crave the supernatural. It's as if belief is wired into the core of humanity. Everyone, everywhere, no matter the age or the level of civilisation, cannot let go of this obsession with magic."

"People are pretty much the same wherever you go, when you get right down to it," Alan said. "Everyone is just running around all confused and looking for answers."

Hogarth gave a veiled smile at his friend's insight.

"Quite," he said. "Madame Masque has been with this particular troupe since the beginning, however. A testament to her skill. Everything else is, quite frankly, a warm-up for her. They have travelled the world to great acclaim, and now have settled here for the foreseeable future, it seems."

Alan gave a non-committal grunt. "The building was probably going cheap. Rats and woodworm thrown in free."

"Is there a reason that you're being especially grumpy tonight?" Hogarth asked, carefully keeping the sharp tone from his voice.

"No. I just find it's less effort than making myself seem happy."

"I'd hate for you to tire yourself on my behalf," Hogarth muttered.

Alan regarded his friend's sardonically raised eyebrow and heaved a sigh. "Just on edge, that's all," he said.

"For any particular reason?"

Alan looked round the room again, checking the faces of the other audience members that hung in the half-light. They weren't what he expected at all. Rather than the black-clad, pale-faced and oddly formed shapes of London's superstitious elite, many of whom he'd met, the audience was composed of middle-of-the-road people that walked the city by day and hunted for the entertaining spectacles by night.

"Honestly?" Alan said. "I just don't see the point. I appreciate what you're doing but I just get the feeling that I'm stuck with Slay. I can't see what this psychic would know that you don't."

"I think that was a compliment but I can't be sure. Is your friend with us?" Hogarth asked, searching the corners of his eyes as if he might catch Mister Slay unawares, even though he'd never seen the spectre himself.

"No," Alan replied. "I don't think he is. He doesn't like you much, Hogarth."

"Good," Hogarth replied dryly.

A waitress made her way over to them with a companionable smile and a tray tucked under one arm. She gave a brief bob, the pupal form of a curtsy, and addressed Alan.

"Doctor Hogarth?" she asked. Alan pointed to his friend wordlessly and with a flush of her cheeks the waitress turned to the Black man at his side. Hogarth gave her a polite smile. "Madame Masque has agreed to see you before the show. I'm to show you to her dressing room."

"Splendid. Thank you," Hogarth replied.

Eyed by the other audience members from behind whisper-concealing hands, they were led beside the stage and through the rich green curtain which Alan realised was just cheap material hung particularly well. The theatre's back corridors had changed little since its time as a tavern. Ill-fitting doors led off to old boarding rooms, now storage for the painted-board worlds of entertaining lies. Leading to a door like any other, the waitress motioned for them to approach and ducked away. Hogarth knocked lightly on the worn wood. An accent that sounded Hungarian to Alan's ear bid them enter.

Low lit with ancient gas lamps, the room contained a small table, cramped bunk, and little else. At the low table sat a figure in a high-necked and long-sleeved black satin. A mass of black tresses piled atop the psychic's head and Alan caught Romany features in her profile as she turned to place her hand mirror on the table beside her. As she stood in a hush of fabric, Hogarth made introductions:

"Alan, may I introduce Madame Masque—"

"Jessamine Maskeline," Alan chuckled as the woman's face slipped into shock. "As I live and breathe."

Jessamine let out a pleased gasp and pounced like a jungle cat. She threw her arms around Alan who returned the hug, and she grabbed his face to scrutinise his eyes.

"I don't believe it," she said in her warm, rolling accent. "Of all the people I could meet, in all the places I could meet them. James, you didn't tell me that your afflicted friend was this rapscallion."

"Oy!" Alan said with a laugh.

Jessamine slapped his face playfully.

"You know each other," Hogarth chuckled with a roll of his eyes. "Obviously."

2

"**T**HIS IS JUST a different kind of circus," Jessamine said. "After Grandmamma passed we took the circus across to Ireland. Our mandrake roots fell to the blight there. The circus fell apart without them. We had to do what we could to get by. I tried other circuses, of course. But it wasn't my acrobatics that they were interested in. When they found out that I had Grandmamma's gift…"

Alan nodded along as he sipped his tea. Hogarth decorated the wall beside him simply by leaning on it. Jessamine sat with her own steaming teacup in her hand.

"And now you've crossed my path again," she said with a sad smile.

"Like a bad penny," Alan said with only a hint of humour.

"What kind of trouble are you in this time?"

"Oh, the usual—"

Hogarth cut off whatever quip Alan was about to make.

"He is haunted, madame, by a dark spectre. A curse, I think, bound to his blood by a ritual blade."

"Your leg?" Jessamine asked. Alan shifted his weight, suddenly aware of the throb once more, and nodded. Jessamine probed further. "And this spirit has been with you ever since?"

"I knew him as a boy," Alan said. He averted his eyes as he spoke, taking in more of the room although there was little else to see. "Although I don't remember him, really. And then he killed my father. I evened the scales on that front and he tipped them back toward himself before taking off where I can't follow."

"An insidious character," Jessamine whispered. "Let me see what I can see." She held out her hand for his.

Sacrificing his hands to Jessamine's own, he could still feel the calluses of the trapeze artist she'd once been. Beside them, Hogarth hung his head in some manner of reverence, and Alan was sure that both of his friends stopped breathing because he could only hear his own like a tenacious draught running through an old house. It could have been a trick of an eye that had become so accustomed to the stable light of tesla technology, but he was certain that the gaslight dimmed of its own accord. Focussed on a point somewhere beyond their clasped hands, Jessamine's dark eyes oscillated slowly as if she were looking through a mirror to search the reflected room beyond. Alan, staring intently at her face, once doll-like and now matured, tried to read every twitch of her mouth and microscopic contraction of her eyes. The sound of his own breath started to annoy him, and he found himself breathing shallow, trying to reduce the rasp.

"I sense no spirit," Jessamine said, after a while.

"He's not here right now—" Alan started, but Hogarth cut him off with a click of his tongue.

Jessamine fell silent for an agonising moment. In that moment, Alan caught Hogarth's eye; the shaman's grandson, all grown into a doctor of men and magic, nodded gravely.

Jessamine continued: "You are right, James. This is a curse in the blood. You are surrounded by loss, Alan, like soot on a lantern's glass."

Alan retrieved his hands and rubbed his leg absent-mindedly as Jessamine's eyes refocused, regarding him with sadness.

"As we feared," Hogarth offered.

"I'm not getting rid of him, am I?" Alan said in a whisper.

Jessamine gave him a pitying smile that stabbed deeper than any cursed blade.

The three leapt out of their seats as something hammered at the door. They looked at each other, sharing an embarrassed chuckle as the door swung open to reveal a pale man dressed head to toe in black on black. The silver and emerald ring on his right forefinger was the only colour about him. With a rich and exuberant voice, he addressed the room.

"Madame Masque, I was unaware that you were taking private readings. My apologies. However, the curtain rises shortly."

"Gentleman, this is Herman Kohl," Jessamine announced, "the man responsible for all that you see tonight. Herman, these are good friends of mine, Alan Shaw and Doctor James Hogarth."

The man nodded to them, his broad chin wobbling.

"Thank you, Jessamine," Alan said with resignation. He made to leave but Jessamine pinned his arms with a hug. He reciprocated by patting the laces of her corset.

"Yes, thank you, Madame. Your expertise is appreciated whatever the outcome," Hogarth said, taking her hand lightly.

Herman, staring right through the newcomers, cleared his throat.

Alan tried to step away but Jessamine wouldn't let him.

"Come back. After the show, I mean. Won't you?" she asked. "Don't just run off. I'm not sure what we could do. Yet.

But we can try to wipe the soot from the glass, perhaps."

"Break a leg out there," Alan said, and followed Hogarth to the door.

3

THE THEATRE LIGHTS dimmed as Alan and Hogarth took their seats. A nervous susurration ran around the room. From somewhere in the fresh darkness came a nervous titter. In the old British tradition, someone else shushed them. Slowly, the stage lights rose to half illumination, just enough to make out the piebald figure of Herman Kohl stood centre stage, hands clasped before him and his head bowed.

"Ladies and Gentlemen–" he began in a slow, purposeful voice, nothing like his exuberant manner from only minutes before. He didn't move, addressing the ground before his feet more than the audience themselves, the shadows hanging heavy over his face. "–The Thirteenth Circle welcomes you to the Britannia Theatre. We admire your curiosity, and your bravery, and we aim to reward your stalwart souls with spectacles both arcane and spiritual." Kohl looked up and his pallor glowed in the half-light. "Heed this warning well. This evening is not entertainment. It is a spiritual exploration. What you are about to witness is not for the faint of heart or the weak of mind. I assure you that, if you are compelled to leave, you will be no less thought of." He paused again, drawing out the moment where someone might make an exit. In the dark, the crowd eyed each other, some craning their necks to spot the fearful. But no one moved. "Very well," Kohl growled, and the lights huffed out.

The sound of waxed rope on winches filled the dark. The curtain rose, revealing an even darker space behind. Alan waited for a spotlight that never came.

"May I present Mister Elliott Franz–" Kohl's voice came once more, right beside Alan's ear. He spun around but found no one behind him. He snorted at the trick. "–Master of levitation."

The gaslights rose slowly to reveal a thin, pale man in a well-made suit, fingers spread by his sides and a look of patient thought turned up to the theatre's now glowing chandelier. His glistening shoes hung a metre above the stage.

The crowd gasped and muttered.

Alan gave a grunt of mild amusement.

Hogarth gave him an I-told-you-so smile.

Elliott Franz was indeed a master of levitation. From the moment that he lowered to the stage, raising a polite hand for the audience to hold their applause, to the moment when an audience member was shown how to levitate a dark lacquered table with a brush of her fingertips, Alan had to try very hard not to become rapt. He leaned in his seat, craning his neck to regard the vault above the stage, peeking into the wings, scrutinising the air for pulleys and strings.

"Have you worked it out?" Hogarth whispered as Franz bowed and left the stage.

"Yup," Alan said with a wry smile that he hoped hid the lie. "Have you?"

The next act arrived in a wicker wheelchair pushed by an attendant, blankets across her knee and a black veil draped over grey hair. Stage light glinted from the garnets on her hairpins.

The old woman pulled back her veil to reveal a dark-skinned face, round and warm and set with heavy wrinkles. Her friendly eyes regarded every audience member in turn.

Surely she can't see all that way into the dark, Alan thought, just as her eyes met his. She held his gaze for a moment before turning her head away.

Kohl's voice ushered out of the dark: "Madame Bethan Roe. Seer."

Calling for volunteers from the audience, Madame Roe's attendant selected one slowly raised hand and bid them stand. Madame Roe dipped her chin at the man. His thin, dark moustache and hair oiled to within an inch of its life stood out against his yellowing complexion. There seemed nothing at all out of place about him, like a toy fresh from the box.

"A man of God," Madame Roe began in a Cajun accent, "often lost in thought. This contemplation leads to wisdom beyond your years, sir."

The audience member seemed pleased with that, and gave a thin smile to the room as he began to relax. But Madame Roe wasn't done.

"And yet, for all of your pondering, you fail to share your thoughts, even with your wife." Attention moved from the man whose face had grown taught, his breathing visible in the rise and fall of his waistcoat, to the woman sat by his side wearing a tilted blue hat with white feather. "She wonders if your thoughts ever turn to her."

With nothing else forthcoming, the attendant thanked the audience member who took his seat beside his wife. The room seemed forgotten for a moment as he reached for his wife's hand, kissing her palm gently and muttering something to her. She kissed him, all decorum lost in the twilight, and for the rest of the night they sat closer together.

With the other volunteers now changing their minds, Madame Roe bid everyone to close their eyes. Alan saw, by the dip of light beyond his eyelids, that the theatre had been pitched into darkness once more. Opening them, even he gasped.

Although the room was dark, there were flares of light, multicoloured auras that sat around each member of the audience. Each person had their own hue, blues and yellows and pinks. Hogarth gave off a grey glow, vivid and stable. And looking at his own hands, Alan made sparkler trails of red embers in the dark. As the house lights rose once more, banishing the auras, the stage was empty.

The crowd spoke in gasps and whispers as the low light hung pregnant with expectation. The scrape of a chair cut across the room, drawing glances from the audience. A broad shouldered man with a pursed mouth and narrow eyes made to leave, shooting a scathing look at the room in general.

"Poppycock," he spat, wearing a telltale pallor and a bead of sweat on his brow. The lady seated with him trailed behind as he left without a word, the woman avoiding gazes and muttering some apology too quiet to hear.

The lights dimmed again, redirecting attention to a small table and chair that had appeared in the short period of distraction. At its centre, a large chunk of crystal reflected the stage lights in a halo around itself.

Kohl's voice didn't come from the dark this time. Clearly the figure in black who swept from the wings, stars glistening in the train of her skirt and about her wrist, needed no introduction. Alan thought his ears might pop from the sudden vacuum caused by the audience's intake of breath as Jessamine took her seat, laying her hands on the table top, fingers spread and relaxed. She gave a sad smile, reflected into tiny mockeries in the chunk of quartz that made even Alan shiver.

"If anyone would speak to those we have lost, make yourself known to me," she said.

Shaken by what they had seen so far, no one seemed forthcoming. All bravery had been sucked out of them. "Please," Jessamine continued, "there is nothing to fear from beyond the veil tonight."

The room was slow to convince, it seemed, and Alan had to admit that although he knew a lot of people who had fallen over the years, he didn't want to chat with them in front of strangers. Gingerly, a hand rose, gloved in lace and quivering at the end of an elderly arm. The lady that it belonged to cleared her throat as Jessamine turned kind eyes on her.

"Who would you like to contact?" she asked.

A gentleman's handkerchief clutched in swollen knuckles, the lady started with a stutter: "My husband—"

Jessamine interrupted with a politely raised hand. That was all she needed.

Alan shuffled in his seat, placing his elbows on the table before him. He found himself gripping the cool glass of scotch but not taking a drink. Beside him, Hogarth's lips were taut with anticipation.

With eyes closed, Jessamine took a deep breath, her shoulders dropping into relaxation. After a moment, she turned her head slowly as if following a sound, then back the other way, offering her ear to the other side. Her lips twitched with a smile and she made to speak. But it wasn't Jessamine's voice that escaped her throat. Husky and uncertain, an undeniably male voice addressed the room.

"Hello? Can you hear me?"

Alan and Hogarth traded looks of wonder. When they turned back, the old woman stood at the foot of the stage.

"Yes," the woman said, a tear dripping from her chin. "I'm here. Alfred, I miss you, my love. I miss you every day."

"My Sally," Jessamine whispered. The voice, the spirit that she had conjured, seemed uncertain, surprised. "I—I need—"

"Yes, love? Tell me. Anything." The old widow was stretching across the stage now, her arms reaching across the boards toward Jessamine's feet.

Jessamine twitched. Although her head seemed locked in place, her eyes rolled downward, growing wide when they saw something in the quartz crystal; something that no one else could see. The widow Sally stepped back despite herself, hands clasped to her chest.

"I need—" the voice began again. But the tone had changed, becoming deeper, more urgent. "—justice."

A hundred eyes swivelled towards Sally, now alone in the middle of a theatre turned courtroom.

"I—don't know what he means," she said, turning on the spot like the courtroom accused. "Alfred was very ill. He passed in his sleep."

Jessamine spasmed, her upper body threw itself down onto the table with an echoing thud. The quartz leapt from the table, smashing to glitter on the boards. The audience recoiled, but no one moved. Alan's breath burnt in his chest as he held it. Both he and Hogarth exchanged looks again, this time uncertain if this was theatrics or real trouble brewing.

Jessamine hurled back in her chair, almost knocking herself over, arms shivering as they draped by her sides, head turned up to the ceiling, eyes wide and staring in panic. She let out a scream that shook the glasses and rattled the chandelier, cut short when she began to gag.

Alan was on his feet immediately and heading for the stage. The audience, the room, and even Hogarth faded to grey as his intent tunnelled toward his old friend. As he reached the stage's edge, Jessamine shuddered and heaved, trying desperately to breathe despite choking on something unseen. Another spasm jerked her entire body and the small table in front of her flew across the stage, bouncing inches from Alan and hurtling out into the audience where screams finally erupted. The sound of scraping chairs and tables, hurried feet, and petrified yells filled the air, but still Alan heard none of it as he clambered up onto the stage, scuttling toward Jessamine. Yet even Alan skidded to a halt, just out of arm's reach, when Jessamine's mouth slowly opened in a silent scream. He could see, now, the way her throat bulged from clavicle to jaw. As he watched, the velvet choker that she wore snapped and fell to the stage. From between her bared teeth, a muscular grey mass began to slither; not downward, but up, floating, a thick tendril of some unknown matter that stretched Jessamine's jaw to its limits in an effort to let it escape.

"Alan! Get back!" Hogarth's warning finally cut through the commotion.

Alan ignored him and advanced, trying to get to Jessamine although he had no idea what he would do once he got there.

The gelatinous tendril rose still higher from Jessamine's unprotesting jaw, the pockmarks and bulges along its length pulsing as it broadened. It could have been a trick of the eye, the low light and high shadow, but Alan swore he saw a rudimentary face fade in and out, like a man struggling to rise through tar. He tossed his head away as a cough of rich red dust filled the air. Hogarth stepped up beside him, letting his red-stained hand fall, muttering some hurried incantation.

The voice came again, sloughy and pained: "Justice…comes to the Thirteenth Circle."

The tendril burst like a balloon made of wet fog. Alan and

Hogarth covered their faces but it dissipated before splattering across them, unlike any material Alan had ever seen.

There was only Jessamine left now, hung in her chair like a marionette with the strings cut. The theatre fell silent, the audience lost to the streets. Alan heard a rasping pant and realised it was him. He darted forward, taking Jessamine awkwardly in his arms, brushing her tousled hair from her face. Her eyes stared upward, frozen at their widest, her mouth laced with remnants of the grey matter. Alan looked to Hogarth who stood solemnly a step or two away, at the storm-tossed theatre, and into the wings where Kohl stood frozen with Franz the levitator and Madame Roe's young assistant.

"Call a doctor, dammit," Alan roared at them. "Call a doctor!"

But by the glassy stare, the oozing grey liquid from her mouth, and the stillness of Jessamine's chest, they all knew it was too late.

4

I N THE BRITANNIA'S narrow corridor, Alan stood transfixed by the mote of grey matter that stained his cuff. He rubbed thoughtfully at the greasy spot and remembered wiping the same viscous fluid from the corner of Jessamine's mouth.

Constables wandered back and forth in pairs, muttering and sometimes giving him the side-eye. He didn't know any coppers out this way, but they had obviously heard of him. A lithe old sergeant with his helmet tucked under his arm approached with a polite cough, pulling Alan out of his morbid preoccupation.

"Mister Shaw? We haven't found anything, sir. Searched the place top to bottom. To be honest with you, we're not really sure what we're looking for." The Sergeant had an accent that Alan couldn't place. More and more accents arrived in London every day, it was hard to keep up.

"Neither am I, Sergeant," Alan admitted.

"As horrible as it is, I think we might have to chalk this one up to misadventure," the Sergeant said, hanging his head. "Damned shame. Young woman like that. Getting involved in this spooky work is nothing to be joked about."

"Spooky?" Alan said.

"Sorry, sir. *Spooc* is an old word for ghost in Dutch. Spooky, ghosty. You know?"

Alan managed a smile that he didn't feel.

"Spooky. Good word," he said.

The Sergeant said his goodbyes and made his way to the end of the corridor, collecting the constables there. It seemed the constabulary was done with the whole affair.

"Misadventure," Alan said to himself, and huffed.

From the door beside him Hogarth appeared, accompanied by the sobbing widow Sally who'd had her contact with her husband so violently snatched away.

"It's not her," Hogarth said with conviction. "The poor dear is beside herself. She had no idea what was going to happen."

"I figured not," Alan sighed. "Let's talk to the manager."

They found Herman in his dressing room sharing a bottle of whiskey with Franz the levitator.

"Any of that going spare?" Alan asked.

He was handed a glass and a slosh of not-quite-bottom-shelf whiskey. Hogarth gave him a look, carefully emotionless. Alan set the glass aside, untouched, even managing to hold in the sigh.

"We need to know anything that might help us fight this thing," Alan said, hitting the point so hard as to break the tip. "Anything at all."

With a slap of his thighs, Herman stood and began to slowly circle the room. His thespian manner had returned. No longer the sombre compere of the show, he spoke expressively, his hands seeming to massage the air; Shakespearean, theatric. Alan didn't trust it. Franz seemed rapt, though, following the manager's movements wherever they took him.

"A tragedy," Herman began, crestfallen, his voice heavy

with sorrow. "Madame Masque—Jessamine was the finest performer of her kind I've ever met—"

"Such a loss," Franz added with a sip of his whiskey.

"—a lost friend, a lost talent."

"So much misfortune."

Alan and Hogarth traced the verbal tennis from man to man as it continued.

"Yes, it is dangerous work, traversing the unknown. Bringing proof of the supernatural to the ignorant isn't without its hazards," Herman went on, massaging his brow as he perched on the small desk that served as his dressing table.

"Seattle all over again," Franz added.

Alan felt the entire room tense. Although no one had moved, no one had reacted, the air itself felt stiff.

"Why?" he asked "What else has happened?"

"Another loss," Herman said, finally looking at him. "Another friend taken by—"

"Give it a bloody rest," Alan snapped. He felt like flying across the room to throttle the theatrics out of the manager. Only the thought of such havoc disrespecting Jessamine's passing stopped him. He settled for steel coldness instead. "I'm not paying ticket prices for this. I want answers. The woman who died horrifically in front of us all, I knew since she was a girl. So don't test my already thin patience." Hogarth stepped forward to place a hand on his friend's arm but Alan ignored him.

Herman lost all colour in his face.

"I meant no disrespect," he said. His excessive chin shook and Alan was actually convinced, when Herman's voice broke, that he meant it. "Quite the opposite. But yes, we have lost another of our troupe recently. Joshua Taylor, our resident magician, took his own life in Seattle. What pain he must have been suffering to do such a thing, I cannot imagine."

"You will guide us through this, Herman. As you did in Seattle. The show will go on to greater heights," Franz offered along with a handkerchief.

Hogarth jumped in before Alan could as Herman dabbed at his eyes.

"I've never seen ectoplasm be so violently manifested. We're clearly dealing with a very potent spirit," he said. "Was there anything to suggest supernatural causes with your previous loss?"

"Nothing," Franz replied, letting Herman continue to sob quietly. "Joshua was a dour man, and too hard on himself, always. Some negative reviews from the Seattle elite got the best of him."

"WE WON'T LET this drop," Alan said. It came out half earnest and half a threat. "Whatever– *who*ever's responsible, you better believe I'll find them."

Hogarth gave a more companionable nod to the performers before following Alan out of the room. He had to trot to catch up as Alan was already moving at a fair clip toward the theatre's rear door, his cane rattling the boards as he went.

"They're full of it," Alan spat. "There's something else going on here. What the ghost said was personal."

They walked in silence for a moment, out into the city toward the nearest steam cab. Alan's last sight of Jessamine as an unmoving form beneath a gurney sheet played on a loop in his mind.

"You can contact it again, right?" Alan asked, giving Hogarth a resigned look.

"I can. But I don't think we should. My goofer dust wasn't

enough to save Jessamine, although it might have weakened it—"

"Fine. Then weaken it and I'll do what I do."

"You can't shoot a ghost, Alan," Hogarth said with dry scorn.

"You ever tried?"

The doctor opened his mouth to speak, realised what his answer was and who he was talking to, and decided to close it again.

"Didn't think so," Alan said. "Get more dust. We're doing it."

THE FLICKERING LIGHT from the parlour fireplace lit Hogarth, stripped to the waist, braces hanging by his sides. Red and white smears marked his upper body and face, making his pensive concentration seem laden with foreboding. He took a deep sigh and opened his hand toward the goofer dust circle around a strip of ectoplasm-stained cloth cut from Alan's cuff. Across the circle, Alan stood in the shadows by the wall, fidgeting with his revolver despite Hogarth's assurances that it would be of no use. Chester hung in the doorway, neither involved nor too far away if he was needed.

The fireplace flared, spitting embers into the room. Hogarth's voice was a low, melodic thrum. Although there was nothing to see, Alan felt certain that the air in the circle grew thicker. Hogarth shimmered like heat waves on a desert road. Sweat prickled the doctor's torso, his breath heavy but steady. His muttering grew more insistent, his outstretched hand tense. A log in the fire gave way, the crack resounding around the room. When Alan looked back, Hogarth's eyes were white from edge to edge, his teeth gritted in effort. Chester took a faltering step into the room, toward Hogarth. Hogarth seemed to sense his approach, shaking his head urgently without breaking concentration, and Chester paused a few steps away. Chester exchanged a glance with Alan, who tried to instil fortitude in the young man with a nod.

After a hanging moment, Hogarth whispered: "There's nothing there."

Alan stepped forward.

"It got away?" he asked.

"There's simply nothing there. No spirit to be found," Hogarth said. His eyes returned to their usual deep brown, his whole body sagging as the fire died, the air thinned, and he lowered his arm.

Alan stayed quiet, waiting for Hogarth to offer a solution. Chester stepped forward with a blanket and draped it around Hogarth's shivering shoulders.

"Thank you. I think I need to sit down," Hogarth said with a weak smile. He flopped into an armchair and tugged the blanket closer around him as Chester hovered nearby. "I'm not sure what to say, Alan. The veil was completely empty. The connection goes nowhere. I think this may be more complicated than we initially thought."

Alan snorted as he flopped down into an opposite chair. He stared into the dying fire where embers flickering like circus lights.

"Penny for them," Hogarth said, interrupting Alan's thoughts.

"My first shot is that it's Herman," Alan said. "I just don't trust him. But without some solid proof…I bring him in and he'd just get away with it."

"We'll find it," Hogarth said, earnestly. "You're doing the right thing by being patient."

"Don't get me wrong, if I was just a little more certain, he'd be riddled with holes already."

"Shouldn't you leave this stuff to the police, James?" Chester interjected, the longest sentence that Alan had ever heard him say.

"Usually I would, but what are they going to do against a rogue ghost?" Hogarth said. Chester *humph*ed but said nothing. "Alan, you will wait for me. That isn't a request. I'm coming with you." Hogarth shivered. "Just…tomorrow morning, eh?"

"Let's get some rest," said Alan. "There's nothing else we can do tonight."

Chester moved purposefully toward the door: "I'll set up the guest room."

LATER THAT NIGHT, Alan lay in the alien bed, comfortable, warm, surrounded by the smell of clean sheets in a dustless room. He tossed and turned, dragging his bad leg around with him, knotting the blankets with his writhing, and resorted to punching the pillows so that they had at least some lumps. He released a tired groan that turned into a chuckle. How backward he had become that a night in a rich bed had him wishing for some broken springs and tattered blankets to sleep in.

Beyond the room's lattice window the Bedlam pylon's guiding lights speared the sky along the Thames' opposite bank, lending a little light. He sat up, searching the darkest corners of the room, but everything was still. No traffic outside, no dark companions inside. A dull sensation rose in his chest. He rubbed it, wondering if it were possible to have indigestion without actually eating. He let out a surprised grunt as the sensation grew deeper, heavier, and his whole body began to sweat at once. The moisture disappeared from his mouth. His eyes felt like hot balls of sand. He gasped at the sudden rush of sensations, but his throat was too tight to make a sound, to breathe. Letting out a squeak as panic set in, he fought through the tangled blankets, stumbling to his feet, and almost fell toward the door. He burst out into the corridor with no idea where he was going, only that he had to get out, had to be somewhere other than that room, hallway, house. He was only dimly aware of a bedroom door swinging open as he hurtled past, Hogarth and Chester emerging, mouthing something that he couldn't hear.

The next thing he knew, he was on his knees on Whitehall Stairs, the slow churn of the Thames lapping against the lichen-coated stone, and cool, blessed breath leaking into him. The London skyline buzzed into focus, twinkling with electric lights, the spitting bray of London life coming to him on a sullen breeze.

He was alright. He could breathe.

"That was quite the display," Slay said. He sat on the stair's edge, kicking his ethereal feet out over the dark water.

Alan's shoulders heaved as a sob escaped him. He tried to speak, but his throat was still filled with barbed wire coils.

"What's wrong with you?" Slay smiled back over his shoulder at the old privateer.

The thud of footfalls on the pier behind him drew Alan's bleary eyes. Hogarth and Chester skidded to a halt in their pyjamas, uncertain of whether to approach Alan on his knees in the dark. Even the stoic Chester looked worried.

"Alan?" Hogarth began. "Are you alright?"

Alan tried to speak, but couldn't. Instead he shook his head and turned back to the river.

Slay was gone.

5

HE BRITANNIA THEATRE sulked in the morning rain, its door sealed by the police writ pasted over the seam. Alan shuffled further into his coat, ducking into an alleyway where the gutter pissed dirty rainwater in a violent gout, Hogarth close behind him.

"I expected a nice night at the theatre, perhaps to help a friend. I didn't anticipate a romp with murder and intrigue," Hogarth grumbled, straightening the raised collar of his coat for the hundredth time as rain tumbled from his top hat.

"If you'd known, you'd have still come along," Alan replied.

"Most likely. I was just having a moan. You seem to have so much fun doing it, I thought I'd give it a go."

They exchanged thin but warm smiles as they approached the theatre's rear door. Alan gave a knock.

"How are you feeling?" Hogarth said as they waited.

"Wet."

"You know what I meant."

"Tired and wet."

The door opened a crack to reveal Elliot Franz wrapped in a threadbare smoking jacket.

"Good morning, gentlemen. Can we help you?" Franz asked in his soft German accent.

Alan checked the levitator's feet. They were touching the ground for a change.

"We've come to talk to Herman," Alan said. "We've looked into the spirit that killed Jessamine."

"Ah." Franz looked genuinely saddened as he fussed with the tie on his robe. "How is the progress?"

"Unfortunately—" Hogarth began to say before Alan cut him off.

"Best if we talk directly to Herman, eh?"

"Of course, of course." Franz led the dripping men to the rear stairs and up to the dressing-cum-boarding rooms. At the darkly varnished door behind which they had questioned the manager the night before, he gave a knock and they waited.

"Is he out?" Alan asked when no answer came.

"No, I'm certain he's in. There were reporters outside earlier and Herman has no love for them at all. He's been taking refuge in his room all morning, I think," Franz replied, and knocked again. "We're all quite worried about our continued tenure here after the tragedy with Jessamine. But Herman has come through for us before. I have complete faith in him."

"Come through how exactly?" Hogarth asked.

Franz, clearly oblivious to the fact that the companions were grilling him, blabbed.

"When Joshua passed in Seattle, we thought that the news would break the show. But Herman turned it all around for us. The theatres were sold out for the rest of our tenure there. Every seat. He's a good manager."

Hogarth widened his eyes pointedly at Alan, who grinned darkly. That was the connection. That was what they needed.

Alan stepped forward, banging on the door and calling the manager's name.

Still no reply.

Without ceremony, Alan jammed the flat end of his cane into the jamb, splintering wood around the lock, and shouldered the door open.

"Herman Kohl, you dirty, murdering bastard, you're coming to the station—balls."

Alan stopped dead only one step into the room.

"Mein Gott," Franz stuttered as he leaned in to spy the tableau inside the manager's room.

Herman laid crab-like in the middle of the little room, spine bent backward in an eternal spasm, hands clawed, mouth gaping, eyes almost bulging from his head. A candle and its holder had been knocked to the floor, luckily snuffed out as it fell. The mirror above the makeshift dressing table had smashed, spraying shards all over the room. Alan circled the corpse, his feet crunching on the glass, methodical and emotionless, searching for signs of ectoplasm but finding none. Hogarth stopped, picking up a shard of mirror for inspection. He humphed loud enough to draw Alan's attention.

"Shattered. Surely someone would have heard it?"

"You'd think so," Alan said. He stooped, a glint of blue catching his eye from under Herman's arched back. "Hogarth. What do you make of this?"

He held up the blue glass bottle, unstoppered, a thick coating of wax around the rim. Upending the bottle, salt poured out onto his palm.

"A witch bottle," Hogarth said. "Herman was trying to catch the spirit."

Alan humphed. "This ghost is far from done. Franz–" he looked to the thin German who stood in the doorway, his mouth covered with a handkerchief as he stared down at his deceased manager in shocked silence. Alan vaguely remembered what it must be like to not be so used to scenes like this. But the previous night's events had killed any soft approach he might have still had in him. "–Franz! Gather everyone in the theatre."

"Should I...call the police?" the levitator asked, coming to his senses.

Alan and Hogarth swapped looks.

"Not just yet," Hogarth said. "I think this may be outside of their remit."

Franz scuttled off and Alan wasted no time taking Hogarth to one side.

"When this thing turns up, you should stay out of the way," he said.

"And what are you going to do without me? Sarcasm at it?" the Doctor replied.

"These people are more like you than me. The ghosts didn't aim for the people in the crowd, it didn't choose the widow. It's after the psychics and magicians. And we can't be certain that it won't take a swipe at you as well."

Hogarth narrowed his eyes.

"What's this really about? You didn't have a problem with me getting involved in a summoning last night."

Alan ran a hand down his face with a deep sigh. There was little time for discussion, and he just wished that Hogarth wouldn't be so damned insightful.

"Everywhere I go, people get hurt, James. I wish that I could blame it on Slay but it's been happening my whole life." Hogarth regarded him wordlessly, letting Alan fill the silence. "I've wondered if that's why I was orphaned. Maybe my parents knew that I'd be a hex on everyone around me."

"That's a bit of a stretch—" Hogarth began.

"I might have thought about it once or twice," Alan muttered, looking at Kohl's twisted corpse rather than at his friend. He only looked up when Hogarth grasped his shoulder.

"I assure you that if you were cursed in such a way, I'd know," said the Doctor.

"So everyone I know meets a grizzly end by fluke?" Alan scoffed.

"Or perhaps, and I mean no offence my dear friend, the situations that you find yourself in are a product of your choices. And people meet their own demise as a result of theirs."

Alan looked at his friend's hand still on his shoulder and patted it.

"I'm my own worst enemy. Is that your advice?"

Hogarth shrugged jovially, letting the revelation hang in the air.

6

"I SAW IT," Madame Roe said, her voice unwavering but her eyes sad. She looked from one person to the next, what remained of her troupe, then Alan and Hogarth, all in the half-light of the deserted tavern turned theatre. They might have been performing a séance, all sat around the circular table, if Alan weren't pacing out at the edge of the lamplight.

"You didn't think to mention a roving spirit?" Alan said. There was no malice there, only tiredness, but Madame Roe's attendant bristled nonetheless.

"For some, the spirit world is always visible. Shades move about all the time, unseen by most. There was no reason for Nana to suspect anything," he said, his accent matching the old seer's.

"Calm yourself, Remy," Madame Roe said, laying a hand on the young man's arm. "He meant nothing by it."

Hogarth leaned forward into the lamp light, resting his interlocked hands on the table.

"What exactly did you see, Madame?" he asked.

"I peered out of my room to see a shadow," the old woman drawled. "Coming from the direction of Herman's room. It disappeared in the dark, and I heard footfalls, the squeaking of a door."

"Are you sure it was a ghost?" Alan asked. "That sounds like a regular person to me."

"There was nothing regular about this one," Madame replied. "It had no aura, like a ghost. I could feel only the presence of death moving with it."

"Hogarth, could that be why you couldn't find it? It wasn't in the veil because it was wandering around here." Alan asked, satisfied with the response.

Hogarth sucked his teeth. "It seems feasible. We're clearly dealing with a spirit of particular force of conviction. Which brings me neatly to my next question. The spirit spoke of the Thirteenth Circle, of you all. And the search for justice." He eyed the remaining seers and magicians. "Make no mistake, Alan and I are not policemen. You can speak freely to us. With that in mind, what could your group have done to cause such a vicious spirit to seek justice from you?"

Franz was almost whimpering, the handkerchief now a permanent fixture over his mouth. It took everything Alan had not to step forward and snatch the damned thing from him.

"We dabble in the supernatural every day, all over the world," Madame Roe offered. "This spirit could have latched itself onto us at any point along the way. I've never seen a simple ghost with such power. Have you, Doctor Hogarth?"

"I have to admit that I haven't."

Madame Roe nodded as she continued: "I think this spirit may be of a more potent kind. The noises, the movement of objects and ectoplasm; I think we might have a poltergeist in our midst. A murderous one."

"That doesn't answer the question," Alan said, stepping into the lamplight.

"It's mad. Driven so by its death. Seeking justice from the

only people that it can communicate with," Franz muttered, his voice shaking and muffled by the handkerchief.

Alan looked to Hogarth who gave a half shrug.

"Then we best stop it," Alan said. "Hogarth, what do we need? I'll fetch it; you all stay together."

THE THEATRE'S CHAIRS, when sat in for short periods, could be quite comfortable. Leaning back, head propped against the wall and feet out in front, they were much less so. Alan shuffled his bottom, arms folded and eyes half closed. There would be no sleep tonight, but that was the part he was most used to. Hogarth had set himself up on the stage with a blanket. Franz slept in a chair, head laid in his arms on the table before him. Remy had dragged Madame Roe's dressing room cot onto the stage for her and slept on the floor beside. The sound of soft, sleepy breathing filled the room.

It always amazed Alan how people could sleep at a time like this. For him, insomnia came at every opportunity, especially when there was work left undone. But for others, it seemed like their only escape from a dark situation was the blessed relief of sleep. They clearly didn't have the nightmares that he had.

After struggling to his feet, he stretched and snatched up his cane to make his way to the sticky bar at the back of the room. He stretched over it to feel for whatever bottle came to hand first, catching sight of himself in the wall mirror behind the shelves and snorting his distaste for what he saw. Mussed hair, yesterday's stubble, clothes crumpled from rain and wear. He looked like hell. His head was banging again, his leg throbbed. He looked down at the bottle, hanging on the view for a moment, and then back at the room – the sleeping troupe,

Hogarth – and set the bottle back on the bar before storming out.

Wandering around the old building alone, he knew, was a bad idea. But the others had strength in numbers and he had to get away for a while. They'd been holed up all day, keeping watch. He actually felt the urge to walk for once rather than to sit and nurse his leg. He needed to stretch and clear his head. Moving through the old corridors, he could hear the rain still pounding outside and thought about heading out into it. But that would be too far away and even more foolhardy than he was willing to be. In a roundabout fashion, he made his way back to Jessamine's dressing room and broke the police seal to step inside.

Everything was very much as it had been. The absence of Jessamine herself was felt in the lack of perfume, dissipated by swarming police bodies. Flopping down onto the bunk, Alan thought of the first time he'd seen her, dangling over an immense drop in the big top, graceful and death-defying as she swung from the trapeze. He thought of the old woman who had given Jessamine her gift and her prediction: He would find love, but only once. And he'd been so confident that once would be all he'd need. The old woman was talented, that was for sure, and she'd passed it all on to Jessamine. Now their skills were lost forever. Alan took a small pin box from Jessamine's dressing table, turned it this way and that, and set it down. Next was the hand mirror: he turned it over as if he might find her image still recorded there. The glass was broken. His brow furrowed. Smashed and then placed back on the table? Had the coppers done that?

"Clumsy buggers," he said.

Then it hit him. The shattered mirror in Herman's room, Jessamine's hand mirror. And he remembered the huge mirror behind the theatre's bar.

He shot toward the door like a scalded cat. Hurtling down the corridors, he skidded on the waxed floor in the theatre doorway, bouncing off the jamb and into the room in a barely controlled stumble.

Franz floated in the theatre's vault, slowly spinning, a tendril of ectoplasm writhing from his straining throat, guttural chokes wracking him with violent convulsions. Alan's head snapped toward the bar's mirror to confirm his theory. With nothing to cast its reflection, a figure made of hanging smoke floated beyond the mirror's veneer, watching.

7

"**J**AMES!" ALAN YELLED, snapping Hogarth fully to consciousness.

The troupe and Hogarth woke with groans, yawns and rubbed eyes.

"Oh God," Hogarth gasped when he saw Franz dangling in the air and the grey pseudopod thrashing from his open mouth. Fumbling to retrieve the goofer dust from his jacket he yelled: "Bring him down!"

Alan cleared the space to the centre of the theatre in a few short hops. Standing on a chair and then a table until he was right underneath the floating performer, he swung his cane, hooking the T-bar handle into the high waistline of Franz's trousers and began to pull. It wasn't enough. Franz was buoyant, and every tug simply bounced him higher. Leaping, Alan grabbed the cane as high as he could, trying to use his own weight to his advantage.

The ectoplasm tendril thrashed, emitting a screech that shook the bar's glassware, the room filling with delicate, urgent chiming. Alan kicked his feet, willing himself heavier as his feet left the table top. The spirit dragged Franz higher.

"Help!" he shouted.

With Madame Roe watching wide-eyed from her cot, Remy and Hogarth darted toward him, the Cajun bear-hugging Alan's legs, Hogarth spreading the goofer dust in a circle at the table's foot.

Between them, Alan and Remy managed to drag Franz down, grabbing him and bodily holding him to the table. Alan couldn't help but notice that the levitator's struggles were growing weaker, the focus in his eyes slipping toward somewhere unseen by the living.

"James!" Alan barked.

"I'm done, I'm done!" the doctor replied, sealing the circle and beginning to mutter his incantation.

The tendril thrashed, beating Alan about the head and shoulders. He heard Remy grunt as he fell from the table, hitting the ground with a French curse that Alan hadn't heard in a long while. Alan managed to stand, arms wide to balance on the rocking table, and swung his cane in a two-handed swipe. The tendril moved, whether trying to avoid the strike or maddened by the intrusion on its assassination, but Alan's strike hit home, sliding through the ectoplasm like the thickest of porridge, breaking it off near the base with a wet *shplot*. The tendril broke into mucusy threads before evaporating completely. Alan dropped to his knees over the levitator whose eyes were half open, jaw slack, and gave him a resounding slap across the cheek.

The German screamed and wouldn't stop. Barking a laugh, Alan flopped back onto the ground, panting, where Hogarth caught him.

"Nice work," Alan said, patting the doctor on the cheek.

"Smacking it with a cane, eh? I can honestly say that I wouldn't have thought of that."

"Well you said shooting it wouldn't work. Remy, you ok?"

"A little bruised, but alive," came the voice from the other side of the table.

"Well done, all of you!" Madame Roe shouted.

MINUTES LATER THEY were together, Franz shivering and blanket-wrapped, Alan kicking his feet at the stage's edge. For once, he had a smile on his lips.

"Job well done, I reckon," he said.

Brandy bottle in one hand and glasses pinched in the other, Hogarth began handing them out. Franz took his in both hands as they still shook. Alan put his on the stage beside him, receiving a quizzical look from Hogarth which he ignored.

"So have we killed it then?" Alan asked. "Job done? I can go home to my bed?"

"Ah think that we only stopped it this once. Spirits aren't something that you can kill, as you mean it," Madame Roe said. Now back in her chair, she sat beside Franz, mothering him.

"What do we do, Nana?" Remy asked.

"We have to find out what business the spirit is seeking to complete. That is the only way."

"So let's go through this again. Who have you lot pissed off enough that they'd come back from the dead to kill you all?" Alan said.

Franz muttered something into his blanket.

"Eh?" Alan said.

"It was Joshua," the levitator whispered, taking another sip of brandy. "I saw him in the mirror. He was shouting, but I couldn't hear what he was saying. He screamed and screamed, and then—"

"The ectoplasm," said Alan. "So I ask again, what did you

lot do to him? It's truth or die, now. Because me and James aren't moving in here and fighting this thing every night. You can't afford us."

Madame Roe spoke up first: "Honestly, Mister Shaw. There is no reason that I know of for Joshua to hate us so."

Alan heaved a sigh, looking to Hogarth for answers. The doctor worked his mouth from left to right, thinking.

"I think that we're getting off course," Hogarth said. "Yes, the spirit is manifesting in a singularly violent way, but some things must remain true. Ghosts do not haunt people. As Joshua didn't even die on this continent, that means that he must be fixed to an object. Therefore, does anyone own an object that once belonged to the deceased?"

Remy spoke up first.

"Sure we do. Lots of it. When Joshua took his life, Herman wouldn't throw away any of his things in case we could use them again. It's all in storage in the basement. I moved the boxes in myself."

"What kind of psychic was he?" Alan asked. "A powerful one, I'm guessing."

"Not at all," Madame Roe replied. "He was a magician. An illusionist."

Hogarth humphed as realisation hit. "Of course he was. And what are an illusionist's most beloved tools?"

Alan chuckled, only a few seconds behind his friend. "Smoke and mirrors."

8

HOGARTH HANDED OUT what remained of his goofer dust to each person. Even Madame Roe, who demanded to be taken along, and Franz who begged to be left behind.

"And what will happen to you boys if I'm not there to look after you, eh?" the old seer asked.

"I could stay behind to look after Madame," Franz offered, weakly.

"We're all going. All together," Alan said.

By sheer force of habit, he checked his revolver was loaded, receiving an eye roll from Hogarth.

"It makes me feel better," Alan muttered.

Steeled and prepared as they could possibly be, the troupe and their companions set off with Remy leading the way.

"We will have to take the elevator down with Nana," he said, and began leading them to the deepest reaches of the theatre where the carpet gave way to naked floorboards that rocked and knocked under their feet, past the cellar door where Madame Roe couldn't go. As they passed it, Alan stopped beside the door for a moment.

"Alan? What is it?" Hogarth asked.

"Just thinking."

Reaching for the doorknob, he gently opened the door to reveal a dark stairway beyond. The door gave a sorrowful squeak. Alan's mouth stretched into a smile.

"What's so amusing?" Hogarth asked.

"I think we're going in the right direction, is all," he replied and kept walking.

The elevator's slatted wooden gate slid upward with an unsubtle rattle and sliding of pulleys. Remy guided Madame Roe in backwards and the others followed.

"This place is old, we'll have to lower ourselves," Remy explained, grabbing a pair of thick ropes at the wooden cage's rear. With Alan assisting, they yanked on the ropes, counterweights whizzing past in the shaft outside as they lowered foot by foot and hand over hand into the darkness beneath the theatre. When the gate slid open once more, they were faced with a gaping blackness.

"Well…" Hogarth whispered, letting it hang.

Alan humphed in answer.

Passing the handles of Madame Roe's wheelchair to Franz, Remy stepped into the darkness. After a moment there was a metallic grinding and soft amber lights pulsed above, growing brighter with each pulse and giving off a faint hum, revealing a long corridor between piled wooden crates. Remy gave the priming crank a few more turns before releasing it.

"This place isn't large. We should be able to find his things quickly. They will be at the back, I think," Remy said, leading the way.

Alan and Hogarth walked together at the rear of the group, squinting into the darkness that squeezed between crates, boxes and rolls of cloth.

"You think Joshua will try to get to Franz again?" Alan whispered to his companion.

"It's possible that it would want to finish the job before moving on to someone else."

"That's good."

"Yes, it will make him easier to protect."

"I was thinking it'd be easier to draw the ghost out."

"Are you insinuating that we use Franz as bait?"

"Of course not," Alan said. "I'm saying that's definitely the plan."

Alan gave a smile that Hogarth couldn't be certain was humour.

As old stone arches passed above and the faint smell of mould and damp grew around them, the companions crept their way through the cellar accompanied by the hiss of Madame Roe's wheels on the dirt. Ducking through an archway that might have once separated the tavern's keg room from some other storage area, they came to a series of tall, narrow boxes stacked beside each other, the kind that precious artwork in their frames might be transported within. The door-sized box fronts lay on the ground, some splintered, and packing straw was strewn everywhere. The boxes themselves were empty.

"Ah," Hogarth sighed.

"This is where the mirrors were," Remy said.

"Well, unless Joshua's ghost is handy with a crowbar, I think we're looking for someone very much alive," Alan said, roaming around the room. He peered behind boxes, picked up some straw and then tossed it again. "Which is handy. Because they're much easier to arrest. If we can find them."

"Arrest?" Hogarth asked pointedly.

"I always *intend* to arrest people. They're just never pleased about it. That's when the shooting starts," replied Alan.

Hogarth made an unconvinced sound.

"Joshua's mirrors could be used to control him in the afterlife, like any personal effects," Madame Roe offered.

"It's a lot of effort to go to," Alan said. "Whoever it is must really not like you."

As if on cue, the amber light from the cellar bulbs dimmed considerably, their humming dropping an octave. Remy swore in French.

"I should have primed them more," he said. "They only last so long."

"There's nothing more to find here, anyway," Hogarth added. "Let's head back before we're lost in the dark."

They all turned, heading through the archway one by one, when the lights gave one final hum and faded sadly into darkness.

"I think you jinxed us," Alan said to the shadows around him.

Hogarth's voice came out of the darkness beside him, a nice change from Slay's favourite trick.

"If I had jinxed you, you'd know about it."

"Everyone hold on to the person next to them," Madame Roe said. "Remy will guide us out."

Shuffling in the darkness, everyone was fairly confident that they had a hold of someone else. Just as they began to move, Alan interrupted them:

"Hold on. What's that?"

Although no one could see him point or gesture, they all began to look around. One by one they spotted what Alan had seen. On the far side of the densely dark space was the thinnest horizontal line of light at ground level.

Moving in the darkness, Alan cursed as his foot hit a discarded box lid, and cursed again when his cane slipped on another. With a frustrated sigh he dug in the depths of his coat for his old oil lighter and struck sparks from it, summoning the tiniest flame. With bare inches now lit around his hand, he fumbled his way to the cellar's back wall, the sliver of light coming from where it met the floor. Taking the lighter closer to the wall, he searched it inch by inch in the frustratingly small light source. Because of that, he found something that a cursory glance in the full light might have missed. He pulled on the slightly protruding stone and heaved on the wall, which slid aside with a little persuasion and a stoney grumble. From inside, lamplight poured along a short tunnel leading to an open space beyond where shadows moved.

Alan looked back over his shoulder for his companions, now bathed in secret light.

"It's an old smuggler's hole. I really love London," Alan whispered. "Madame, Remy, hold back here. Me and Hogarth will go in. Franz, you're coming with us."

The levitator's face fell a mile or more.

"Just kidding. Stay here," Alan said with a chuckle and ducked into the hidden aperture with Hogarth close behind.

They crept as quietly as they could, Alan tucking his cane under his arm and using the roughly hewn stone wall for support instead. At the end of the short tunnel the room did indeed open up into a smuggler's storage room. The circular space was bathed in the light of several old oil lamps, relics from when the hole was first used, and around the walls someone had stood the dead illusionist's mirrors in their black frames, creating a circle of reflected light. Someone stood at the room's centre, their form obscured by a billowing black cloak and hood as they stared into one of the mirrors where an ethereal figure made of green smoke writhed, coalescing and breaking apart, sometimes seeming like a man, other times like a trapped pea-souper with attitude.

"Joshua Taylor, I presume," Hogarth whispered.

Alan slid his revolver from its holster and turned to Hogarth, a question in his eyes. The Doctor nodded. They were ready. Taking a steadying breath, Alan stalked out into the room with the air of a Chief Inspector that he'd seen many times before.

"Don't move," he said, having fallen foul of magic users raising their hands before. "You're under arrest for the murder of Jessamine Maskeline, Herman Kohl, attempted murder of some other folks, and anything else I can bloody well think of."

The figure's spine snapped straight, their hood falling down around their shoulders. They were a foot shorter than Alan at least, their long dark hair twisted up and held in place with pins. The woman turned slowly and Alan saw a pale, middle-aged face with dark circles under each watery eye. She had the look of a baker about her, the kind of person who flushed when drinking gin and excused themselves to bed early.

"You can't stop me. I'm not done," she said. "Please let me finish."

Alan, taken aback, opened his mouth to speak and then didn't. His revolver drooped uncertainly in his hand. He looked back for Hogarth who appeared from the tunnel. Luckily, the doctor seemed less perturbed.

"Madame, my name is James Hogarth. I'm a doctor of anthropology and something of an amateur enthusiast in the occult arts. I think it prudent that you give us an explanation for all of this and perhaps we can put in a good word for you with the authorities."

The woman shook her head, a strand of hair falling from its pin. She stepped back toward the mirror behind her where the spirit thrashed. It coalesced, fists hammering on the inside of the glass, and let out a scream that no one heard.

"They deserve it. Justice. They killed my Joshua. Herman and his cronies. The first sniff of a bad review and Herman fired him just so they could keep their pockets lined. He was heartbroken. What else was he to do but end it all? And leave me all alone."

Alan and Hogarth gave each other side-eye as Widow Taylor turned to the mirror.

"He can't be free until they've all taken his place. Until they're all trapped like him."

"If Joshua's in the mirrors, and you've been using him to kill people, why smash them?" Alan asked.

Mrs Taylor turned to them then; her friendly little eyes turned dark, all bloodshot shadows.

"The gypsy bitch," she spat. "Thinks she knows it all. Following me around. Thinks she can stop me with her screaming and begging." And she gestured to two mirrors, both hung with thick black cloth. Despite himself, Alan drifted over, dread hammering in his chest, and he tore one curtain down.

9

EVEN NOW, AFTER all that Alan had seen, it was the little details that he could never ignore; the little ways that rules of nature broke or were adhered to, and how there seemed to be no rhyme or reason to it, only feeling and hard-earned wisdom. It was the pale ovals where Jessamine's palms pressed to the inside of the mirror that Alan noticed first. Second was the way that she looked so much more solid than Joshua's shredded smoke form. Jessamine hung in the liminal space of the mirror like a woman submerged, her hair and skirts tossed by some unnatural current. She spoke to him with a pained urgency that tore at Alan's heart, because he couldn't hear a word through the glass.

"Let her go," he said, tearing his eyes from Jessamine to the Widow Taylor.

The widow recoiled as if struck by his gaze. Even Hogarth took a sidestep as if Alan might explode.

"N—no," the widow said. "I have to trap them all. That's the only way he'll be free."

"Then you can join him," Alan said, bringing his revolver to bear on the widow.

"Alan!" Hogarth barked, stepping between the gun and its

target. "That won't help."

"Do you know that for sure?" Alan snarled.

"We need her to free Jessamine. Lower your weapon," said Hogarth, the usual imploring tone gone in favour of a direct order. "And that isn't how things are done. You know that. We have to arrest her."

So focussed were they on each other, that neither Alan nor Hogarth noticed Widow Taylor muttering to herself until it was too late. Joshua's spectre, thrashing silently in the mirror, slowed as if mesmerised, and faded from inside the frame. Alan spotted it first.

"Where'd he go?" he asked.

Hogarth looked around, checking the other mirrors: Jessamine, one still covered with a thick cloth, and three reflecting only himself, waiting for their captors to arrive. Slowly, one hand reached to his goofer dust pouch, as Alan's might toward his revolver.

"Keep your eyes open, Alan. He could manifest—" Hogarth gave a cough "—anywhere."

He coughed again and pressed his hand to the knot of indigestion that rose hot in his stomach. Realisation dawned, and he looked at Alan, who was looking back at him, worry written all over his face.

"James—" Alan began, but he was cut off as his friend doubled over in pain.

Hogarth coughed again, this time ending in a dry heave as his knees hit the old dirt floor. A thin trickle of spittle descended from his open mouth as he heaved again. With one hand clutched to his throat, Hogarth stretched out the other, shaking, and Alan caught it as he shot forward to catch his friend.

"What do I do?" Alan said, hurriedly.

Hogarth spasmed, throwing his head back with a choked off scream, his throat bulging down by the clavicle.

"*No!*" Alan yelled.

As Hogarth hung there, back arched almost double, silently screaming at the ceiling, Alan scrambled in his friend's pocket for the dust. Hogarth tumbled over backward, making a crab on the ground with elbows and heels, hands clawed in agony, tears streaming. Retrieving the dust, Alan began to make the circle, his hands shaking, dropping lumps of dust where Hogarth would have had one steady stream.

"It'll have to do," he muttered. "It has to."

Hogarth writhed as the ectoplasm finally appeared from between his bared teeth and Alan recognised the lumps that formed in it now, the rudimentary countenance of Joshua Taylor undulating and spreading, choking Hogarth to death.

Alan completed the goofer dust circle around his friend, all untidy wobbles but complete nonetheless. He still had a handful left. And then he stopped. The words. He didn't know the words. Hogarth would mutter in his Grandfather's dialect, words of control, of power. But Alan didn't know any. He wasn't the man one called for magic, or even thinking. He was a point of force applied to the right place for the most explosive outcome.

"Alright," he said half to himself, then raised his voice so that the dead might hear. "Listen up. Volkert, Adrienne, Rafferty, the Gargoyle, Jian Shi...Slay. Just a few of the villains who have regretted getting in my way. I'll do whatever it takes and I'm more stubborn than death. So, if you think for one second that I won't find you, that I won't make you pay no matter how far into the afterlife you run, then think again. He's my friend."

He blew into his hand, releasing the goofer dust into the

air above the circle. Swirling in a vortex previously unseen, it wrapped around the ectoplasm tendril before tightening, burning, caustic against the ethereal material. Joshua's ghost screeched as Alan spun, emptying his revolver into mirror after mirror with shatter after shatter, pausing only at the last one. Jessamine floated there, hands pressed to the glass with those pale little circles on her palms and fingertips. Alan faltered.

"Tell me this will free you," he said. "Please."

Floating back from the mirror's barrier, Jessamine straightened herself with a smile. With a wry wink, she held up a hand to say goodbye.

Alan felt the hammer hit home in the shudder of his arm, heard it in the ring of his ears, but he didn't see it. He couldn't look.

Behind him, Joshua's spirit splattered to pieces with a horrendous screech, the broken mirrors bursting inward in a torrent of shards. With his face turned away, Alan felt the glass stab through his coat. The fairy song of shattered glass coming to rest brought silence in its wake. Feeling pinpoints and slashes of blood well up wherever his clothes couldn't protect him, Alan finally turned back to the mirror's empty frame. Only the silver backing remained, reflecting a blurred impression of himself. Turning away, he found the circle where Hogarth's body lay slumped to the ground. Darting across the goofer dust circle, Alan skidded to his knees and dragged Hogarth's head and shoulders up onto his lap.

"Come on, mate," he said, slapping Hogarth's face lightly, leaving a goofer dust hand mark on the doctor's ashen skin. "Don't make me mouth to mouth you. Chester already hates me."

Hogarth's slack mouth stretched into a smile, his voice coming out rasping and accompanied by a wince.

"You said you'd do whatever it takes."

Alan burst out laughing.

"Trust you to have heard that," he said.

"This proves that not everyone you love dies," Hogarth said.

"We think highly of ourselves don't we?" Alan retorted.

"Don't be so coy. You're not as good at it as you think," Hogarth said, dragging himself to his feet with Alan's help.

Alan turned his smile away so Hogarth couldn't see, his gaze faltering on the empty frame where Jessamine had once been. Hogarth looked from mirror to broken mirror, scanning the sea of glittering shards that filled the room.

"That's about a century of bad luck," he said.

"What's new?" Alan said. His voice softened, although he still looked around the room, anywhere but at Hogarth. "I couldn't have done this without you."

"I know," Hogarth replied, dusting himself down.

"Come on," Alan said. "If we're lucky, Widow Taylor hasn't gotten far."

Heading out of the smuggler's hole in single file, Alan ducked back through the entrance and gave a huff of surprise.

"Blow me down," he said.

The remaining members of the Thirteenth Circle stood over the sprawled body of the Widow Taylor, snoring in her unconsciousness.

"Nice job, Remy," Alan said.

"It wasn't me," the Cajun replied.

Madame Roe piped in: "Franz levitated a box at her."

Alan turned his slack jaw to the levitator and corrected himself: "In that case, nice job, Franz."

"I was very scared. She startled me," the German replied.

Alan and Hogarth didn't look at each other in case laughter should sneak out.

10

WANDERING THROUGH TOWER Hamlets cemetery at midday was a sobering but not unpleasant experience. Every pathway felt like its own little world surrounded by trees of every kind, lined with memorials from monoliths to humble headstones. For those who cared to look, stone cherubs peered from the undergrowth, giving an otherworldly aspect to an otherwise morbid stroll. Alan's boots crunched on the gravel, echoed by Hogarth's beside him.

"To be driven from the thing that you love by other people's opinions is one of the coldest sensations a person can feel," Hogarth grumbled.

"Still bugging you is it?" Alan replied.

"Those critics didn't even know Joshua or his wife and yet they crushed the man from a distance, drove him to end his life, and affected everyone around him."

"People are shits," Alan said, displaying his awesome ability to boil any sentiment down to its smallest components.

"They certainly are," Hogarth sighed.

Alan regarded his friend for whom sighs were rare. He gave Hogarth a moment to share of his own volition before asking: "What is it, James?"

The doctor paused on the cemetery path and Alan stopped alongside. Hogarth shook his head.

"Of all that has happened in the past two days, one thing still burns me. And the annoying thing is that it isn't the first burn nor does it hurt any less for the frequency. I never get used to it."

"I reckon I owe you an ear or three after all you've done for me," Alan said. "Is it losing Jessamine? Because if it makes you feel better, I'm not...handling that well either."

Hogarth huffed a laugh that he clearly didn't feel.

"Danger and dying are par for the course, now. Just like they are for you. No, it's the waitress that I can't get out of my head."

Alan's eyebrows shot up. "Ummm. You've been thinking about her?"

"Oh not like that," Hogarth said, slapping Alan on the shoulder. "Not at all like that. It was how she looked right past me. Looked right at you instead. Do you know how often people look right past me when asking for someone with my name? Every day."

Alan wasn't sure what to say and so decided not to open his mouth.

"Do you know why I'm a doctor who works from his own home, Alan?" Hogarth looked up at Alan, sadness written all over his face. "Because they wouldn't let me be a professor. I can take my mother's name so that at least I look white on paper and that has helped me to get my doctorate from afar, but as soon as I walk into a room, I can no longer hide the fact that I'm a Black man. No one wants to take lectures from someone of my race. Just like no one expects a doctor with dark skin."

Alan opened his mouth to speak, but he couldn't think of

any words. His head was blank.

"It's alright," Hogarth said, patting Alan on the shoulder. "There's nothing you can say anyway. I'd just rather be dealing with the dead most days."

They walked further in silence, the scent of wild garlic almost overwhelming in the summer heat.

"It was a good service," Hogarth said after a moment.

"Don't you think that's an odd thing for people to say?" Alan replied.

"Yes, I suppose it is. But it saves having to come up with some other platitude in a moment where nothing you say is really of help."

Alan humphed. "I thought I might see Slay. He likes a good funeral. And rubbing it in."

"You haven't seen him lately?" Hogarth asked, now that the subject had arisen.

"Not while I've been staying with you and Chester over the last few days, no."

"Alan," Hogarth said, laying heavy on the pause. "You know that you can stay longer, don't you? If you like. There's no reason to go back to that draughty old place of yours."

"I know," Alan said. "But draughty as it is, it's mine. I might not have enough money to do it up nice like yours, but my adventures paid for that old place. Getting rid of it would be like finally letting go of them as well, you know?"

Hogarth nodded in understanding rather than agreement.

"And what if Slay returns once you're home?"

"I'm just going to have to live with him. Everything I try either fails or leads to disaster. As long as he's haunting me, he's haunting no one else. And..." Alan faltered into silence.

Hogarth let him have a moment, to see if he'd continue, but nothing seemed forthcoming without a little push.

"And?"

Alan sighed. "I'm starting to worry that if he goes there's just me left. And I'm not sure there's enough of me to be going on with."

Hogarth slowed to a stop like an old train losing steam. Alan continued on alone through the gravestones.

Extract from *The Illustrated Times*, Front Page, 3rd August, 1871.

Our fair capital saw a jamming of road traffic like no other today as a funeral for a visiting thespian drew in visitors from all over the country. Bow top caravans swarmed roads bringing cattle and foot traffic as the country's gypsy community descended in an early London Season in heretofore unseen numbers. Jessamine Maskeline, once of the famous Maskeline Family Circus and more recently of The Thirteenth Circle supernatural performance troupe, passed while on stage during a performance at the newly opened Britannia Theatre in Hoxton which witnesses have described as supernaturally petrifying. Ms Maskeline, also known as Madame Masque, was said to have been struck down by a spirit hell-bent on revenge. However, after a consultation with occult experts Professor James Hogarth and civilian consultant Alan Shaw, it has been ascertained that foul play was indeed involved from a previous member of the troupe disgruntled with her husband being released from employment with the troupe which unfortunately led to his untimely demise, and any supernatural involvement was simply expert theatrics on the perpetrator's part. The Britannia Theatre – the location of two deaths in as many days as Herman Kohl, The Thirteenth Circle's stage manager, also fell afoul of the perpetrator – is now considered cursed by the Hoxton locals thereabouts and will no doubt remain empty for some time as the living members of The Thirteenth Circle have left London in the wake of their crushing losses and put the building back up for sale.

Alan Shaw and the Atlantian Mechanism

1

April, 1872
London, England

LETTING OUT A grunt of pain, Alan threw up an arm to protect his face, already feeling the thin slither of blood running down his cheek. The sound of panicked fluttering filled his ears as a host of flapping bodies flew in tighter and tighter circles, blocking his sight, buffeting him with a strength he would have thought impossible. He tried to step back, to widen his stance as the storm of pigeons surged, knocking themselves out of the air in an effort to attack him. He arched his back and wheeled his arms as his foot stepped out onto nothing at all. He dared a look behind and downward, seeing only the overflowing gutter and a long drop to wet cobbles. Another stab of pain above his left eye, and he threw his arms up again, still wobbling, managing to stumble away from the roof's edge. He tried to see past the flock, through the swarming grey maelstrom of talon and beak, but they were everywhere. He dropped to a knee, pigeons closing in to fill the space he left. Somewhere beyond the storm of wings, he heard laughter; the great, booming sound of a threepenny panto villain.

Gritting his teeth, Alan slid an arm into his coat, taking a few blows to the head for his trouble. There, he found an old friend, the butt of his revolver, ready to shake hands. He didn't bother to draw it, but fired off three shots in quick succession, groaning as the bullets ripped more holes in his coat and shattered on the rooftop by his foot. The birds burst apart, startled, and he was left alone, kneeling, panting on the rain-slicked tiles. Wiping blood from his face, he set his sights on the laughing villain who stood at the rooftop's centre. In a long grey coat studded with old feathers and stained with white dribbles around the shoulders, he could have been one of London's pigeon-pestered statues come to life. The villain didn't flinch as one of the startled birds flew in and landed on his broad-brimmed hat with a calm coo. The rest of the flock fluttered to rest on the rooftop's edges, the chimney stack, the rocking tesla aerial, watching the humans with an emotionlessness that Alan would forever regard with paranoia.

"I have to say—" he panted "—that this is the worst plan I've ever come across. I hope you're a better actor than you are a villain, Beckett."

The villain laughed, throwing back his head, startling the pigeon who fluttered to a spot beside its brethren on the chimney. Alan groaned.

"And yet, two are dead and still more blood has been drawn," the villain yelled in a melodramatic bellow.

Alan struggled to his feet, then pulled a handkerchief from his pocket to apply it to the cut above his eye, trying to be nonchalant.

"Alright, I'll give you that one. I don't suppose we can just give it a rest, now? We've been out here all night, chasing around."

The villain ignored him.

"And it will work on the morrow," Beckett proclaimed,

pointing to the sky and then at Alan. "When the masses fill Trafalgar Square to celebrate the anniversary—"

Alan laughed, shaking his head. Beckett growled.

"Why!" The actor yelled, ripping off his hat and throwing it down. "Why must people heckle me when I'm performing my monologue? How am I expected to do my best work when I'm constantly interrupted?" He spun around, screaming out over London's weak watercolour morning, fists balled at his sides. "Rude! You're all rude. Do you hear me? I could be the finest Hamlet to grace the London stage, if only you'd let me get my damned lines out!"

Beckett turned to look over his shoulder and found Alan stood just behind him.

"It's not fair," the actor sniffled.

Alan smiled apologetically and lamped him.

KING STREET POLICE station was like any other cattle market in London. Constables dragged struggling criminals around disorganised desks toward iron pens where sullen faces stared out from between bars, waiting for the chop. To the room's rear, a glass partition kept the rabble and racket away from the Chief Inspector's office. Alan stepped up to the front desk, a crap-coated actor dangling from one hand. He hadn't even had to cuff him; Beckett had come all on his own.

"I need to hand in," Alan said, flashing his honorary badge to the thick ginger beard and brows behind the desk.

Wordlessly, the desk sergeant began to scribble in a ledger. After a second of relaying information in a bored fashion, the sergeant nodded to a constable who took Beckett off Alan's hands. Alan signed the ledger, but couldn't take his eyes off Beckett's back. Before the actor could disappear, Alan called out to him.

"Oy, Beckett."

The constable halted, letting the actor turn the puddles of his eyes toward Alan.

"You know where you're going I bet they've never even seen a play," he said.

Beckett's eyes lit up.

"Oh," he sniffed. "Do you think so?"

"And heckling is definitely not allowed," Alan added.

"A fresh audience," Beckett sighed. "I could perform a one-man show—"

The actor's voice trailed away as he was led toward the cells. Alan shook his head but allowed himself a smile.

LEANING HEAVILY ON the brickwork beside his front door to open the lock, Alan let himself in, wearily stripping off his coat and holster, and kicking his street-scuffed boots into the corner. Dropping his shoulders and stretching out his neck, he forced himself to relax, piece by piece, pushing the constant gnawing ache in his leg down a small dark hole at the back of his mind. Making fists with his toes on the thin carpet, he finally noticed the envelope waiting patiently on the hallway floor. The distance from his current vantage point to the ground seemed a mile away, and he decided that nothing arriving in the mail could be that urgent. He left it where it lay for another time. There was sleep to be had and anything else could wait. Scowling at the mountainous staircase that stood between him and his bed, he headed for the parlour instead. Afterward, he didn't remember crossing the room, sitting down, or grabbing the old blanket from the chair-back. He didn't remember his head resting on the wing of the chair or his eyes closing. But he must have slept, because he jerked awake, the inner monkey snapping out his limbs to grab for a nearby branch, only to find itself in a comfortable old armchair. Blinking bleary eyes at the clock on the mantle, he saw that only a few hours had passed.

He groaned.

The rap of knuckles on wood came again and Alan realised that he'd heard it the first time, too. A third time, louder, and he was struggling upright, heading for the front door. The knock came again, even louder, as he stalked toward it.

"Hold your bloody horses, will you?" he yelled.

The startled messenger leapt back almost into the road as Alan yanked open his front door. His face must have been especially threatening because the messenger's eyes simply widened as he shakily offered an envelope. Alan snatched it from the lad and fumbled in his pocket for a shilling, but the messenger had clearly decided the coin wasn't worth it and bolted.

He felt the presence of Slay over his shoulder.

"No rest for the wicked, old pal."

Alan pried open the envelope. Scanning the contents, he limped toward the kitchen.

Dear Alan,

I need your assistance. There has been a break-in at Professor Anchorage's rooms at the British Museum. I'll be at the museum by the time you receive this note. Meet me there as soon as possible.

Chief Inspector Jennings

Alan made his swiftest about-turn in years. Shoving on his boots and bundling other essentials into his arms, he slammed the door behind him and yelled for a steam cab.

2

A DISPLACED MONUMENT to another place and time, weaving the history of the world between its pillars like the loom of the fates: that's how Simon described the British Museum. As Alan stepped down from the carriage to regard the building behind its wrought iron fence, he could think only "warehouse".

After climbing the museum's steps as swiftly as his cane would allow, a uniformed copper directed him toward the rear of the huge building. Alan's sense of dread grew as he circled the museum, seeking out the tradesman's entrance where another pair of coppers gave him polite nods as they stepped aside. They were here in force. He remembered a trip to Egypt, and a tomb, and what that adventure had taken out of him. God only knew what manner of oddness was waiting in Anchorage's offices, tucked away in the catalogue rooms and storage units, well away from the respectable areas of the grand old institution who had no truck with myth and magic.

A murmur of voices drew Alan to the end of the alley where London detritus clotted in corners. A copper, hunched down, was scribbling on a pad and staring at the muddy alley floor.

"What have you found, constable?" Alan asked so sharply that he startled the copper who pushed his helmet back from his forehead and scratched his chin.

"Several sets of boot prints, Mister Shaw. That's about it."

"Unless the thieves had their names embossed on the soles, not much to go on," Alan offered, looking at the messy, scuffed footmarks. A set of tire tracks were of similar usefulness: generic, disappearing out of the alley into a street where the trail had been decimated by morning traffic. Still, the wide treads and distance between them told him there was a large vehicle to search for.

The copper followed Alan's eye line and sighed heavily.

"Now all we have to do is find one out of the hundreds of vehicles that crisscross London every day."

"Easy as pie," Alan said with a sigh.

The copper snorted in agreement as Alan moved on.

The rear entrance to Anchorage's rooms had been wrenched half off its hinges, the steel locking bar left in a misshapen mess. The thieves, if that's what they were, weren't the subtle kind. Alan scanned the roofs above as the museum closed in on the access alley on all sides, frowning at the boarded windows which stopped artefact-spoiling sunlight from getting inside. No chance that anyone saw anything from there. Stepping over the shattered entrance, he emerged in an undecorated workroom. Wooden crates with international shipping brands piled high, the floor dappled with packing straw. Moving around a stack, Alan came to the room's central area: an open space, where Anchorage could clean, study, and classify his findings; a door beyond the huge space led to the tiny office, a sure sign of the archaeologist's priorities if there ever was one.

A wooden plinth for observing larger objects from all sides

stood empty at the room's centre. Bustling between the workbenches which lined the walls, uniformed coppers scratched chins and made notes with shrugs and mutters. Near the centre of it all stood Chief Inspector Jennings, arms folded and brow furrowed at the room as if it were being purposefully obtuse. He ran a hand over his balding pate, stopping only when he felt a finger jab into his ribs from behind, and he spun around to find Alan smirking behind him.

"Bloody hell, Alan." Jennings said with a cigarette rasp. "People usually announce themselves before entering a crime scene."

"Are you classing me as people now, Jennings?"

Jennings' eyes narrowed, his greying moustache spreading into an upward curve that hinted at a smile beneath. "You'll always be a skinny street rat to me."

"That might be the nicest thing anyone's ever said to me. But you didn't ask me here to butter me up." Alan's pause was slight, but Jennings noted it. "Who's dead?"

"No one that we know of, thank God," Jennings replied. Alan visibly sagged with relief as the Chief Inspector continued: "I've had runners out looking for you since the early hours."

"I was on a rooftop. That's always the last place they look. You think they would've learned by now."

"I take it you found the villain?" Jennings asked, following Alan with his eyes as the privateer began to circle the room.

"I don't know how you can call him that with a straight face, but yes."

"And the deadly show he promised in his letters?"

"Pigeons trained to attack on command. He was going to swarm Trafalgar at the celebrations, killing the audience. Something about them cheering for metal men but they couldn't stay quiet for Shakespeare."

"Bonkers," Jennings said, without a hint of surprise.

Alan grunted his agreement.

"I brought you in because Professor Anchorage is missing, Alan. I know he's a friend of yours so thought you might want to look around and I'd rather you do it while I'm here than breaking in later and causing more fuss."

Alan paused halfway through rubbing his aching leg, his jaw visibly tense as Jennings talked.

"There has been a break in, as you can tell. Evidence of a scuffle." Jennings gestured to a small puddle of blood by the plinth with a pencil and motioned where droplets led off toward the shattered door. "Anchorage hasn't been seen since last night and didn't arrive at his usual time this morning."

Marking the blood as too little to be fatal – making him feel a little less anxious about his friend's fate – Alan made a non-committal sound.

Jennings lowered his voice, stepping closer as he indicated the nearby work tables and crates.

"Frankly, we don't know what half of this stuff is. The other half, we'd rather not know. I'm sure these crates have gone through customs in the proper manner. Nothing that the police would need to be involved with. Isn't that right?" Jennings gave Alan a serious look.

Alan barked an incredulous laugh.

Jennings nodded.

"That's what I thought. There's also this." Jennings held out an envelope with Alan's name hastily scrawled on it.

Alan scowled at it before taking it gingerly.

"You didn't open it?" Alan asked.

"I don't need to. You're going to tell me what it says," Jennings said, deadly serious.

Alan pulled a face but didn't argue as he ripped open the

envelope's end.

Alan,

Everything is fine. Don't get involved.

Anchorage.

"Hardly crammed with information," Alan said as he handed the letter to Jennings.

"Why wouldn't he want you involved?"

"Maybe he's trying to be subtle."

"Not exactly your forte," Jennings said with a laugh. "Unlike Anchorage, I'm more than happy to have your input here to figure out–" Jennings waved at the room at large. "–whatever this is. But please let's not have a repeat of the smuggling incident from the year before last? You *will* ask for help so that nothing has to burn down this time, won't you?"

Alan didn't answer. Partly from devilment, partly because, despite Anchorage's note, he was still looking around, eyeing the collection of objects on the workbench before him, screwing up his face with a mix of disappointment and confusion. Paper-tagged and set out in neat rows were fragments of machinery, the innards of clocks if Alan was any judge. Cogs and flywheels, rusted together into clumps and broken into pieces, some of them barely recognisable unless seen in relation to the rest. The opposite table was covered in curved sections of broken brass domes at one end and a collection of metallic rods at the other. This was far from the tribal statues and rubbings of ancient friezes that he had expected. It looked more like Anchorage had dredged the bottom of the Thames than dug up some ancient ruin.

He cast a glance back over his shoulder to Jennings who simply nodded.

"I was actually expecting something...weirder," Alan said. "This all seems a bit normal. No cryptic messages written in blood. No scrawled magic circles or claw marks on the floor. Nothing interesting at all." Alan circled the central plinth, eyeing the platform. A small amount of yellowish oil had pooled in the centre. "It's a bit boring. Anchorage could have had his bicycle on the plinth to oil the chain, cut his hand and gone out for a bandage."

"If it weren't for the broken rear door," Jennings reminded him.

"That must have taken some doing. Probably used a truck. Noisy. They were confident." Alan looked around, crossing his arms. "Who reported him missing?"

Jennings looked to a constable who flicked through his notepad.

"Doctor Tabitha Monroe, sir."

"Aha!" Alan shouted.

Jennings cocked an eyebrow at him.

"Who's she?" Alan demanded of the constable. "Because Anchorage works alone and is about as likely to have a woman in his life as I am to drink water. He's married to the mystery. He's never had a lady around for long enough that they'd learn his routine, never mind realise when it was broken."

The constable stuttered.

"S—she's with the Ministry of Analytical Engineering."

Alan's face screwed up in disbelief. "That Babbage lot? I can't believe that Anchorage would be hob-nobbing with one of them."

The constable rifled through his notebook hurriedly.

"Don't worry, constable. He doesn't expect an answer for that part," Jennings interjected, laying a hand on the copper's shoulder. "Carry on with your catalogue. Alan, if you will?"

Jennings led Alan toward the shattered door he'd entered through. "We'll do some chasing. You look like you're on your last legs. Perhaps you should sleep?"

Alan finally caught a whiff of himself: all-night sweat, gutters and gunpowder. But a bath would have to wait.

"I can't sleep knowing Anchorage is in trouble. I'll drop in on an old acquaintance. If something's been stolen, there's only one place in town where a thief might pawn something like Anchorage's kind of weird."

"I don't think I want to know." Jennings squeezed his shoulder gently. "Proceed face first and gun second, eh? We don't even know if anything's really wrong yet."

Alan snorted. "It's London, Jennings. Of course something's wrong."

Alan stepped back over the threshold, gave a nod to the copper who was now smoking a wrinkled hand-rolled cigarette, and headed along the alley.

"You look like trash, old pal. Maybe you should go lie down in the alley back there—"

Alan's hand shot up to silence Slay half way through his sentence.

"Not now. Just, not now. I need sleep, and to think, and to sleep some more."

Slay gave a huge yawn, stretching his arms wide.

"Couldn't you just lay down and sleep forever?"

Alan raised a bored eyebrow.

"Just trying to relate," Slay said with a chuckle, and he was gone.

With thoughts of his old friend wrapped up in god-only-knew what, faceless truck-driving thieves, and the haunting coo of murderous pigeons still echoing in his head, Alan stepped to the curb outside the museum and waved for a steam cab.

3

O UT OF THE traffic, a steam-driven old hulk swerved wildly toward Alan, causing riotous screeching and honking from the vehicles around it. Coming to a rattling stop, the carriage unleashed a cough of steam through which the driver leaned, eyes buried behind the shimmer of sunlight on goggle lenses. Tugging down the rag over his mouth to show a clean chin under a sooty nose, he said:

"Morning, Guv. Where can I take you?"

"East India Docks," Alan replied.

"I'm sorry to say you'll have to hoof it if you're headed toward the river today, sir. Everything between Fleet and the palace is closed off." The cabby flicked his head toward the traffic behind him. "Out of London's the only clear direction."

Alan rolled his eyes. As usual, his odd sleeping pattern had him convinced that it was still yesterday.

"The parade," he grumbled.

"That's right, Guv. Can I take you anywhere else?"

"Out of London does sound good," Alan thought aloud, "but a friend is counting on me."

The cabby gave a sympathetic whistle. "Well, I wish you luck, sir."

Alan gave the driver a wave as, with the toot of a steam whistle, the cab pulled away.

"Balls," Alan muttered, setting out the route toward the river in his head.

"That's going to be a long walk, old pal."

Following Slay's voice, Alan found the spectre standing beside him, arms folded, looking earnest. Alan set off towards the nearest monorail station, a fair walk to Trafalgar, with Slay catching up, hands in pockets against the chill he didn't feel.

"Why have you turned up all of a sudden?" Alan snipped.

"When you see one set of footprints in the sand, that was when you walked alone. When you see two, that was when I walked with you through your darkest hour."

"You've managed to commit blasphemy and cock it up all at once."

The spectre shrugged. "You get the gist."

"If you're going to be hanging around just stay quiet, will you? I don't need people seeing me talking to myself."

The streets were too full that morning and he knew that most people already thought him an eccentric, lying has-been without seeing him chatting away to no one at all.

By the time they had reached Shaftesbury Avenue, the familiar warning twinge of pain had returned to Alan's leg. He sighed heavily and rubbed it as he stared at the bumper-to-bumper vehicles choked with clouds of vapour, the air filled with impotent honks. For the sake of one day, for one celebration, the city of London had drawn to a frothing standstill.

"Don't you think it's a bit of a coincidence that the one day of the year you'd rather stay in bed, an old friend needs you to be out and about?" Slay said, never silent for long.

Alan stopped rubbing his leg for a second to stare at Slay.

"It's crappy timing, I'll give you that. But not everything is fate, Slay."

"No, no, no," Slay said with a chuckle. "Not fate. Chaos."

As the traffic jerked to another standstill, Alan gave a snort of derision and set off across the road, ducking between the shuddering chassis of trucks and automobiles.

"Don't give me that rubbish again," he said. "The universe doesn't care enough about little London, or littler me. There are no higher powers, no special attention. Chaos is a fluke just like luck and fate and all that stuff."

He gave a bark of surprise as a velocipede hurtled out of the steam and smoke, weaving its way through the traffic at break-neck speed. Alan stopped dead, just in time for the speeding vehicle to whip by.

"Bloody maniac," he shouted after the disappearing rider.

"If that makes you feel better," Slay said, dismissively. "But you know as well as I do that if something *can* go wrong, it *will*. You've been in so many situations where people and plans have come together in one place, all to the final result of causing chaos." Slay watched Alan as he set back off through the traffic, now eager to reach the opposite curb.

"Alright, if you're so clever," Alan whispered, as he reached the curb and stopped to breathe for a second. "Then why do people like me turn up? Why do we stop the monsters? Stop the chaos?"

Slay's grin stretched far too wide, nearly splitting his face in two. Ice water ran through Alan's veins.

"Oh Alan, you poor, deluded fellow. When has anything you've ever done not caused *more* chaos in the long run?"

Alan opened his mouth to reply, but no sound would come. He closed it again. Inky water rose up from his stomach to chill his heart. He swallowed hard, dispelling the knot in his throat long enough to speak.

"Why can't you just sod off?" he said.

Slay gave him a genuinely friendly smile, somehow worse than what came before.

"Because we're pals," he said.

Alan turned away, stomping off down the pavement, not caring if anyone heard or saw.

"We certainly are bloody not," he said.

The pavement became more and more crowded, bodies clustered as far as the eye could see, even more-so than usual. Over their heads, union flags waved. For once, the foot traffic was moving slower than Alan wanted. Anchorage and the thieves could be anywhere in the city. He was playing catch-up, feeling loose ends pulling away in all directions, leaving him to pounce after them like a dim-witted kitten.

Elbowing his way through the swarming pedestrians, he started to use his cane liberally to pry and shove. By the time he reached Leicester Square he was sweating; the pain in his leg had risen to a meaty throb, choking off sensation in his foot.

People ran like rainwater through the square, so many that he couldn't see his usual café across the way. More flags waved and the chatter rose to a level that drowned out the huff and honk of traffic behind him. There was nothing for it: he'd have to go with the crowd through Trafalgar.

Joining the jostling herd, Alan felt the rise of an affliction that came to him more and more regularly of late. He had once thought it reserved for old men, a sickness that seemed unavoidable as hair grew grey and teeth long. But it had come to him, now; he was spending more and more of the present thinking about the past. Or rather, obsessing. Missed opportunities, times when he should have thought rather than shot, stayed rather than ran. He had tried to snap himself out of it, drowning out the memories with a crackling gramophone or sloshing bottle but, no matter how he tried, his mind was thrown back more than it was cast forward. Slay didn't help, of course, taking every opportunity to remind Alan of his many blunders, but even when he didn't drift into the past, the past seemed to come looking for him.

He'd taken the pigeon murders case knowing that the parade loomed, knowing that he would either be too tired to attend after some all-night adventure or, if he didn't find the villain, distracted with the police elsewhere. Then serendipity had thrown the plight of a friend in his path and here he was, headed toward Trafalgar on the one day of the year when he wanted to avoid it, and every person in the city seemed to be on that same street, carrying him along toward a moment of his past that had long since turned sour. He hated it when Slay was right.

As he rounded the corner out of Leicester Square, he passed an old brick façade from which, as a boy, he had once escaped, been drawn back to, and vowed never to see again. Yet here he was, outside St Martin's workhouse, now a tesla plant tucked behind the National Gallery. Everything from his childhood had been repurposed, pasted over until it resembled nothing that it had once been, but Alan remembered what lay in the past and dreamed of wrecking balls.

Ejected from the crowd as it surged forward, he watched as people clustered elbow to elbow at a cordon of rainbow bunting that ran around Trafalgar Square. Above, some brave soul had strung yet more bright flags between Nelson and his lions. A banner hung over the National Gallery's façade:

Celebrating thirty years of automatons in the British Empire

Police were stationed at intervals to enforce the barriers, but they were smiling, nodding, passing pleasantries with the crowd. Somewhere in the square, a quartet competed with the rumble of voices and feet on pavement. For this one moment, every face seemed happy. Grinning urchins; servants allowed respite for a while to watch the parade; rouged ladies wreathed in pastel dresses and men with light summer jackets: it was as different as it was possible to be from a cold April night long ago when a misguided street kid had crept from shadow to shadow across the square, unaware that he carried the fate of an empire in a satchel over his shoulder.

Alan shook himself out of the memory.

Somewhere out there would be Simon and Lottie. Jasper was back from boarding school and Alan knew that even though the lad was growing into a proper young man, he'd never lost his fascination with machinery, the automatons in particular. Today's parade would be as exciting for Jasper as it was inescapable for Alan. Although it was unlikely they might spot him in the crowd, Alan hunched his shoulders a little, retreating into his coat. He didn't need to see his family today. Simon's worried eyebrows, Lottie's brief hugs of pity, and, worst of all, Jasper's look of adoration for his privateer uncle.

Usually a mere annoyance, Alan was aware of every single pigeon he saw. They seemed to be everywhere, even more than usual; every rooftop and lamppost was mobbed by dusty grey bodies. Alan couldn't help but see their unblinking marbles impassively surveying the crowd as the calculating, emotionless eyes of little feathered psychopaths. How many of them had been trained by Beckett? How many were out there, right now, waiting on the whistle that would never come? Alan tried not to think about it, but with every guttural coo, he gave a little shiver.

Moving on, tossed and spun by yet more people pouring into the square from side streets, Alan made his way with only Nelson's stoic gaze to guide him south. By the time he reached The Strand, he was panting heavily, aching all over, and pretty damned grumpy. With a grunt, he lifted the bunting and made to cross the road. A hand appeared at the end of a deep blue wool sleeve, barring his way.

"Sorry, sir, but you're too late. The parade's on its way and we're not to let anyone cross. Keeping everyone safe and all that," the copper rumbled with a conscientious smile.

Alan tensed his jaw. Along The Strand he could already see it approaching, a glint of sunlight on brass. Digging into his pocket, he flashed his badge.

"I'm on police business. I need to get to a monorail shuttle," he said.

The constable eyed the badge and shook his head. "Sorry, sir. Strict orders. You could talk to the Captain. He's stationed over in the square."

Alan eyed the route the constable suggested, back the way he'd come. It looked an awful long way from where he was barely standing, through an army of happy faces and cheery voices.

"I'll just wait."

"Here, sir," the constable dragged over a milk bottle crate and stacked another on top. "Take a seat, why don't you? You look like you could use it."

Although a geyser of pride erupted inside him, Alan gave the copper a curt nod and perched on the crates, tension draining out of his body as the weight shifted off his leg. Along the road, the flash of sunlight on metal grew closer. Alan could hear the brass band, usually a sound he enjoyed, but what it heralded filled him with dread. Leaning on the lamppost beside him, Slay grinned like a child at the approaching procession.

"Isn't this fun?" he said.

Alan shot him a look, causing Slay to giggle.

"This is why you're so giddy isn't it? You knew we'd end up here," Alan grumbled.

"I knew nothing of the sort." Slay feigned hurt feelings with an extension of his slick, red lower lip. From somewhere, he manifested a striped paper bag and began eating whatever wasn't inside. Alan groaned along with his stomach.

The music swelled as the marching band neared the turn into Trafalgar, waves of red on black twinkling with brass buttons and instruments, the music inspiring cheers from the crowd around him. Slay clapped along with everyone else and occasionally shouted "Spectacular!" or "Wonderful!"

Alan massaged his forehead, admiring his knees.

"Look, Alan. It's you," Slay whispered right by his ear.

Despite himself, Alan looked up.

Row upon row of automatons led back as far as the eye could see. First were the Mark Is with their barrel bodies and pill-shaped heads, standing head and shoulders above the people around them. Then the later series', more streamlined, more advanced, some wearing uniforms of the postal service or emblazoned with armed forces insignias, leading back and back along The Strand. But Alan barely saw them. It was the very first automaton – the parade leader – that held his attention. A Mark I automaton, gleaming as if still new; a red sash hung across its chassis, and on its shoulder sat a boy dressed in rags, dirty with the struggle of living: one lucky urchin boy plucked from the gutter as the parade passed by. An old tradition.

"Look at that. It warms the heart, I imagine," Slay said with a grin. Alan stayed quiet but Slay ploughed on. "It's a tribute to your bravery, of course. The urchin who saved the automatons. Who saved the empire! Where would we all be now if you'd delivered that satchel? This moment, when you rode all the way to Buckingham Palace on the shoulders of the very first automaton. The beginning of everything. Do you remember? I don't. I was being beaten half to death somewhere in Whitechapel."

"The start of it all," Alan muttered as the automaton rounded the corner into Trafalgar Square and out of sight. The crowd's cheering swelled, drowning him out. "The start of the automatons. And everything they've been used for since."

"The building of an empire!" Slay sang.

"Foundations built on bones," Alan said. "Just like me."

Camera bulbs went off nearby, Slay's face flashing nightmarish in the harsh pulses. A single voice rose over the cheering crowd, drawing Alan's attention back down The Strand, something like the cry of a seagull, soon joined by others of the flock. Screams. The copper gave Alan a worried look and set off in that direction, squeezing between the barrier and automatons who marched on unaware.

Taking the opportunity, Alan ducked the cordon but paused as he made to cross, deciding to follow the copper against the brass tide and his better judgement. The crowd were ignoring the automatons; the great machines in front continued to move while the back of the procession had come to a halt, the two halves separating like uncoupled train carriages. Someone tried to halt the front group as Alan walked by but the Mark I automatons were under sturdy orders and were slow to respond. Stepping out into the widening space between cordons and the two groups of automatons, Alan saw four coppers trying to corral a Mark I like a bucking stallion. The machine jerked its body at the hips, arms at inhuman angles, one leg fixed in place on the cobbles, the other making wild jerks that span it on the spot.

In true London style, the crowd went from screaming, through quiet amusement, to laughing as the coppers failed to bring the automaton to heel. Even Alan felt a chuckle rising in his throat. But that was short lived as smoke began to billow from the grille in the automaton's belly, the metal glowing red. The coppers started to move back, hands held up to ward off the heat, and the screaming started all over again. The crowd surged backward. More screams rang out as people were crushed against the buildings that lined The Strand. The sound of running feet ripped through the music coming from Trafalgar. The coppers who tried to order everyone away found their advice easily taken.

Only Alan moved forward. Dropping his cane, he shrugged off his coat and reversed it, making a long-sleeved apron for himself.

"Oy!" he yelled to a nearby copper. "Gimme a leg up, will you?"

Making a sling with his hands, the copper accepted Alan's boot, shoving him upward. In a moment, there was a privateer-shaped backpack hanging from the metal man.

Alan began to sweat immediately. The machine's inner insulation seemed completely unfit for the task of whatever was going on inside. Although his coat gave his body and arms some protection, he could feel the furnace's heat through his clothes, starting to blister the skin of his hands. Craning his neck, peering through the sweat that clogged his eyes, Alan found the small brass plate at the base of the automaton's skull.

"Automated unit Delta Eleven, cease all action and—" he ordered, but his words drew out into one long syllable as the automaton began to spin faster, jerking wildly. The world became a whirling blur. Slay, at the side of the road, clapped and laughed.

The automaton's head turned, shredding bearings as it was forced past its natural range of motion. The single glass eye regarded Alan, and he almost fooled himself that there was some understanding there, a recognition of the end, but he wasn't given time to think about it. Legs flying out behind him, gritting his teeth in an effort to hold on, Alan could feel his sweaty hands starting to slip on the automaton's brass body as it spun faster and faster.

"–release steam!" he finally managed.

But even the wording of the emergency deactivation protocol didn't help him. Alan hit the cobbles, only partly caught by the copper, and they scrambled away together. The copper made swift use of a streetside water pump, Alan jabbing his stinging hands into the blessed cool water.

Above the brass band and the racket of the frightened crowd rang the sound of a dull bell being struck over and over. The automaton beat at its metal body with one hand, tolling its own doom as one hip joint began to warp from the heat inside its body, bending, bending, tilting the machine backwards until it crashed to the ground in a twitching, glowing heap of scrap. A great whine issued from its chest, a high-pitched scream of overheated cogs trying desperately to rip themselves free, to keep turning although surely the automaton's innards were a molten mess. The screech drew out, and then faded, faded, until only the plink of heated metal was left.

Clinging to the skirts of curiosity, eager to see, eager to keep someone else between them and the wreckage, the crowd returned, awe overriding fear, drawing them into possible danger to relish the marvel.

The older Mark I automatons, who had marched on unaware, reached Trafalgar. The oblivious hordes beyond began to cheer and music sprung up anew. But where Alan stood there was only stillness and the muttering of the morbidly curious. He watched as, from the rear of the halted parade, Mark IV automatons appeared. Their proportions were more human, their brass heads oval with two glass eyes peering out. They stood and stared down at the stricken, burning machine which still twitched and jerked. And then, a few of the most advanced Mark Vs appeared, stepping forward, bending to tend to the fallen. Alan couldn't hide his shock.

"Are they supposed to be able to do that?" he asked the sweating copper who had helped him to the pump. His hands were sore, but not as badly burned as they had initially felt. He flexed his fingers, feeling the sting of tightened skin, but it was manageable.

"They get more advanced every year, sir. They realised that there weren't enough trained people to run around fixing all the broken ones, so they taught them to fix each other. It's cheaper that way. Good thing, too. This isn't the first auto to burn out this week."

Alan rolled his eyes. "This day just isn't going to get any easier, is it?"

From somewhere behind him, he heard Slay chuckle. "Chaos."

Fascinated by the actions of the Mark Vs, Alan stood a little longer as they patted out the flames of their fallen ancestor with metal hands. He made to move on, eager to chase down a clue to Anchorage's whereabouts but, as he crossed the once forbidden Strand, a small group of overalled men stepped out from between the halted automaton parade and his eye was caught once more.

Waving the Mark Vs aside, hitching the legs of his trousers so that he could crouch next to the burning wreckage, a man with a waistcoat and tie beneath overalls regarded the machine with pinched consternation. A pair of engineers in overalls stood behind with a trolley. Their superior reached a hand behind him and was handed a long metal probe with which he began lifting parts of the broken thing to peer underneath. After a moment, he motioned for the engineers to approach.

"Careful, gentlemen. It's still quite hot."

"Yes, Mister Miller," one of them uttered.

This was surely the Ministry for Analytical Engineering, eager to take away their failure on such an auspicious celebration day. Alan watched for a second as the automaton was hoisted onto the trolley, then ducked back into the crowd, finally making it across the road and limping on toward Trafalgar monorail station.

4

A T AN INCONSPICUOUS distance from East India Docks, a little shop on Poplar High Street bore the legend 'Wilhelm Sauer Pawnbroker' above its unassuming door. Opening it by just a crack, Alan inserted his cane upwards, stabbing the doorbell with the end and stopping it from announcing his arrival. He slipped inside.

Clocks, bicycles, sea-faring equipment, decorative vases, and dusty glass cabinets filled with trinkets clogged the space. If anything ever moved in there, Alan was yet to spot it. Of course, there was no need. This business's real money came from the objects that weren't on display. Circling a counter of wood and glass, Alan cursed the bead curtain as it complained at his passing through. The back room continued the aesthetic of dust and half-light with the addition of a small space for a table and chair, a sink that might have once been a colour other than mildew green, and a rear door which had been boarded over from the inside. Alan sucked his teeth at the little room, the perfect vision of poverty, and grabbed the chair-back. With a little effort, the chair tilted on its hind legs and the large trapdoor to which both table and chair were bolted lifted with the hiss of counterweights in the wall behind him. Most of the little room's floor lifted away to reveal wooden steps leading downward. Taking them sideways, Alan crept down. The cellar below held boxes of tea, bolts of silk, casks of ale, crates of wine and spirits, all smuggled, and all the best you could find in London. Alan ran a hand over one of the crates longingly as he passed through. Behind a wooden partition, the cellar opened up, ten times the size of the upper building's floor plan. Wooden cabinets lined the walls and made rows in the space between. Most of them held weaponry of diabolical and illegal design from all over the world, knives with helix blades, guns of such ridiculous size and stopping power that no sane person would design them. Alan regarded one in particular, a rifle of sorts, although surely two people – or perhaps a large automaton – would be needed to carry the damn thing. Hunting and killing a bear were all well and good but that rifle would have turned one to jam. He shook his head and moved on. Contraptions. Everywhere. Weapons that fired grappling lines and expanding harpoons for dirigible-to-dirigible interactions of the piratic kind, vambraces with wrist-activated blades or derringers, and one oversized rubber glove underwired for the passage of large amounts of voltage to an assailant or victim stood proud on a specially made stand. A folded gliding frame propped in one corner reminded him of the Grand Exhibition days. Not for the first time, Alan wondered how many things bought in this shop had been turned on him over the years. He thought it was probably a lot.

Further toward the back of the room he found a dumpling of a man placing a revolver with the bore of a shotgun into a cabinet.

Alan made sure to bark out his introduction: "*What* are you up to, Willie?"

The cabinets' doors rattled with the little man's scream and he spun around, pressing his back to the unit he had been tending to, sending various weapons tumbling to the ground around him with a clatter. Eyes wide and chins a-wobble, making his giant silver moustache shudder, he regarded Alan with a moment of panic that softly faded to post-adrenalin panting.

"Alan. Mein Gott, you could kill a man by sneaking up on him that way," the man said in a rich German accent. "Or get yourself killed. What if any of these weapons had been loaded?"

"Then you'd be the stupidest dealer in London, Willie."

"Please, Alan, my name is Wilhelm. Willie is the name for the man's tackle and you know it."

Alan smiled. "Not seeing much difference, yet."

Wilhelm laid a hand to his barrel chest and wafted the other as if dispelling an offensive smell. "You have no amount of gentleman in you, Alan, none at all, to speak to me in this way. Unless you are here to purchase another armoured jacket, I demand that you leave immediately."

"No thanks. I've just decided to stop getting shot instead. I'm here looking for something a little rarer."

The dealer's demeanour changed to exaggerated intrigue, all signs of offence now gone.

"Something for your collection, perhaps? Or are you willing to sell something? My offer still stands if you have the dagger that gave you that limp."

Alan shot the dealer a look and Wilhelm wilted beneath it.

"It's in safe keeping. And it'll never see the light of day again if I have anything to do with it, as you well know," Alan sneered.

The dealer raised both palms in contrition. "Did you have something particular in mind?"

Alan made a grand show of walking around the cabinets,

noting their contents, occasionally shooting Wilhelm a chastising look when a particularly dangerous item presented itself. The dealer simply shrugged and gave a wan smile.

"It would be something you've never seen before, I think. Unique. Probably come to your attention as recently as this morning. Very old, possibly a machine of some kind."

Wilhelm began to follow Alan as he rounded a cabinet, trailing after the taller man.

"Something that is particularly...fresh to the market, you might say?" Wilhelm asked as Alan tried to look disinterested. "And is the constabulary particularly interested in this item?"

"You could say that." Alan finally stopped his circuit, stopped the act, and fixed Wilhelm with a firm, friendly look. "But it's more of personal interest. Someone broke into the museum, Willie. Anchorage has gone missing."

"Oh, dear Alan," Wilhelm said, taking hold of Alan's coat sleeve for a moment. "You had only to say. I am still rather in Lorne's debt after not mentioning my endeavours regarding those ungentlemanly smugglers. You know that I will always offer all the assistance I have. We are friends, after all?"

Alan cracked a smile, but nodded a little.

"Sure we are, Willie. If we weren't, the police would have ransacked this place by now."

"And my livelihood would be at an end. No food for poor Wilhelm."

"Oh, they feed you in jail," Alan quipped.

Wilhelm visibly shuddered at the thought. "I'm afraid that at this moment I am unable to assist. I have had no such interaction with interesting items today. It's been rather quiet. Whoever stole Lorne's artefact hasn't tried to sell it to me. And that means—"

"They're not trying to sell it at all."

Wilhelm shrugged. "Most likely. Perhaps a private collector of some tenacity is interested in Lorne's work?"

"Any ideas?" Alan asked, grasping at the threads of his lead as they whipped away.

"Without more detail on the item, it would be remiss to speculate. There are many collectors in the city and many more come from all over the world to trade here. I am sorry, Alan. I will keep my ear to the ground, so to speak."

Alan ran a weary hand down his face. He felt Wilhelm's hand reach up to grasp his shoulder.

"Lorne is a tough old boot, as you might say. I'm certain that he is well. And that you will find him. You are the other boot."

Alan couldn't help but smile at the old German. "Thanks, Willie."

He made to leave, but snatched a bottle of something from a crate on his way out.

"I'm confiscating this!" he shouted back over his shoulder.

"Gah! You will have me reduced to ruin with your petty thefts!" Wilhelm shouted after him, but Alan pretended to be out of earshot.

5

EANING ON THE telegraph post overlooking the East India dock, Alan plucked a fat, greasy chip from the steaming newspaper wrap in his hand and, blowing on it first, popped it in his mouth. He thought about washing it down with a swig from the confiscated bottle but left it corked in his coat pocket instead. He needed a clear head while working. There was time for wallowing later. Taking another chip he wondered how often over the years he'd stoked his engine with fuel rather than getting the sleep he needed, and what he would actually do if he were to go on holiday like had heard of people doing. He came up blank.

With a flutter of hefty wings, a pelican the size of a carriage hit the pier beside him and began to scooch closer, eyes a-glitter with designs on Alan's chips. Alan swore at it to no effect then banged his cane on the ground by its feet. The pelican gargled at him and lumbered into the air. But he had been distracted too long and he felt the chips whipped from his hand in a flurry of muddy feathers. The seagull hit the dock a little further down and tucked in immediately, crushing half of the chips to paste with its ungainly feet.

"You little—" Alan began, but cut himself off. Wiping his

hands on his trousers, he grumbled at the bird. "I suppose you earned them, you scoundrel."

Belly only half full, Alan strolled back toward the monorail through a crowd of dockworkers, labouring automatons, and carts laden with steel and rivets all headed to or from some nearby shipyard.

A scream, like the voice of an old friend calling to Alan, rose over the clamour of the docks. A hundred weary dockworkers swung their heads in the sound's direction but their feet continued their course, undaunted. Alan made towards it, heading off the main road and along a row of terraced houses, limping as fast as he could, never one to ignore an unknown scream. A klaxon blared behind him and a fire truck came hurtling around the corner, ladder swinging above, firefighters hanging on like circus clowns. Alan whipped out his badge, waving both it and his cane. Hands reached down as he reached up, and the firefighters yanked him aboard while the truck barely slowed.

"Thanks," he said, looping his arm over the truck's ladder to hold on. "What's the crack?"

Goggles attached to the chinstrap of his helmet, a fireman turned a fly-like gaze on him.

"Auto gone mad, Gov. Again. Down by the school this time."

"Bloody hell," Alan gasped.

The fire truck took another corner at speed and screeched to a halt, almost jerking Alan off his feet. By the time he had taken in the crowd, the school yard with its red brick building beyond, the automaton mid-maddened dance, and then managed to climb down, the firemen were hard at work. One barked orders and two more advanced on the machine as it spun slowly on the spot, its glass eye roving, spitting embers from the red-hot grille in its belly. Alan pushed his way to the front of the crowd that was becoming less and less certain of their safety as the firemen took a hookpole and latched it onto the automaton at the neck. Another maintained a safe distance, hose in hand, and, with the harsh pop and whine of a compressor, water spewed forward to hit the automaton. Steam billowed as the other firemen used the water strike's momentum to drag the flailing automaton to the ground. Soon, the machine's thrashing calmed, the jerks of its limbs growing sleepy and the pop of swiftly cooling metal ringing a death knell that Alan had already heard once today. The whole effort took seconds, playing out like some dire street performance. The crowd began to disperse with the worst – and most interesting – of it over. Alan finally saw, at the windows of the school building, a hundred little faces pressed against the glass in fear and awe. This one had been very close indeed.

Alan scanned the mass of bodies, looking for something but uncertain of what. Some people broke away from the crowd, running toward the fearful little faces pouring out onto the school house's doorstep. A huddle of teachers nearby smoked cigarettes with shaking hands. Alan kept looking. And there it was, dotted throughout the crowd of soot and oil-stained people, attached to lingerers who watched the automaton's death with just a little too much interest. They all bore a tin badge that he recognised. The United Human Front, a familiar sight around London ever since the first automaton had marched out of Professor Normen's workshop. No matter how dirty their clothes got, those badges were always clean. He tried to think if he'd seen them on the Strand that morning as well, but dredging his memory brought up nothing.

Separating the crowd with a sweep of their arms, a pair of overalled engineers appeared, allowing a third man to step between them. Alan narrowed his eyes. He looked familiar, but it wasn't until he hitched the legs of his trousers to squat down by the newly burnt out automaton that Alan remembered why: the same fellow from the parade, here with his men and his trolley. He recognised the cut of the suit beneath the overalls, the high-nosed tone as he ordered his subordinates to pick up the automaton. As they replied, Alan was reminded of the name he'd heard earlier. Miller, and a 'mister' at that. Steeling himself for an interaction with a man of learning, Alan stepped forward.

"S'cuse me," he interjected. A not unpleasant scent of cologne and oil wafted from the man who met his gaze. "You're with the Ministry, aren't you?"

Pocketing a rag with which he'd wiped his hands, the engineer held one up in interruption. Alan couldn't help but notice that Miller's hands were extremely clean. The rag had been for show. "I've already told Mister Sledge that I have nothing to offer the press at this point. When I do, I'll be sure to alert him."

"I'm not a reporter." Alan extended his badge, actually enjoying it for the first time. "The name's Alan Shaw. I'm with the police."

The doctor's face visibly fell.

6

THE MINISTRY FOR Analytical Engineering's main entrance was right on The Strand, perfectly positioned so that the automaton parade would pass by their creator's doors. As he approached in the wake of Miller and the engineers, Alan found yet more United Human Fronters. These were congregated outside the Ministry doors, throwing refuse at the building. Old lettuces, rotten turnips and any number of brown and disgusting items flew through the air to splatter across the chests and pile around the stanchions of a pair of Mark Is holding a solemn guard outside the building. The UHF's chants, unchanged since Alan was a boy, echoed back from the Ministry's unflinching façade.

"Man over metal!"

"Blood and oil don't mix!"

Miller's engineers elbowed their way through the crowd, dragging the still-smoking carcass of the Mark I in their trolley. Alan turned to Miller, who was walking beside him.

"I thought the Fronters would have given up by now," he said, nodding toward the protestors.

"We get them all the time," Miller replied, unperturbed. "Those below the breadline spouting half-baked ideals. They think we're stepping on God's toes. How autos are any different from dirigibles or cabs, I have no idea. We'll go around the back, gentlemen," he added to his subordinates.

"It's been thirty bloody years," Alan said as he jammed his cane between a pair of protesters who tried to bar his way, wrenching them apart. "That's a long time to hold a grudge. Doesn't anyone care that those guards are being pelted?"

"Of course not," Miller called back to Alan as he walked on. "They're only machines, after all. They're not really guards, as such. More like purposeful targets. It gives the UHF something to vent their frustration toward. A fine idea as it stops them trying to actually get in. They're easily pleased."

"So, you just leave them out there?"

"The Mark Is are robust by design, Mister Shaw. They can withstand a lot."

Alan gestured to the burnt-out hulk they escorted. "Try telling him that."

As volleys of stones and refuse continued to fly overhead, a woman in a well-worn apron and oversized boots turned an enraged scowl in Alan's direction, opening her mouth to spit some anti-auto bile. She too wore the familiar badge on her blouse, a cog slashed through with red enamel "UHF" overlaid in bold letters. Alan swanned past the woman with such confidence and speed that she had no choice but to throw coarse words at his back.

Miller led them down a side street to the large gate which allowed vehicles through the Ministry's encircling wall. A flash of identification and they were inside, the gate opening just wide enough that they might slip through with the trolley.

Alan realised what a thin façade the front of the Ministry for Analytical Engineering building really was. Although appearing to rival London's most impressive museums and galleries in size, the building was thin, acting more like an elaborate stone fence around a vast open area of warehouses which took up the space where Alsatia had once stood. He had to admit that it was an improvement. Alsatia had been nothing more than an extension of the Thames' mud banks, collecting all manner of human refuse and dumping those that couldn't survive into the river. But the huddle of shacks, lean-tos and blind alleys was long gone, and behind the Ministry's high stone walls was filled with a different kind of activity: people and automatons, trucks and trolleys, rolling by on neat cobbles which had once been the deadliest knot of alleyways in London.

All the while, Alan kept his eyes peeled for anything especially out of the ordinary. The Ministry was always up to something if the stories were to be believed. Everything from having automaton servants used as spies in influential households to there being laboratories for the practice of technomancy in the basement. But to Alan it looked like any other lumber mill, dye works, or shipping yard in London.

Miller and his engineers led the way through a door beside a large segmented shutter that made up one wall of a warehouse. The interior was nothing like the grotty innards that Alan expected. A well-lit drafting table stood off to one side where rolls of paper were weighed down with chunks of metal. Machines for making other machines stood in rows against one wall. In the central space sat a wide wooden platform encircling a raised plinth, a frame over the whole thing resembling gallows. On it stood a man who Alan identified as an engineer by his overalls, and an automaton like Alan had never seen, naked as the day it was made.

"Welcome to my workshop, Mister Shaw," Miller said as if making some grand introduction. Alan couldn't really see what the fuss was about.

"Just Alan is fine," he replied with a thin smile that he didn't mean and looked around as the technicians dragged the cooling automaton carcass to the corner of the room and left it there. Miller gestured toward the drafting table where a pair of stools lay in wait and began to pour tea from an oversized flask. Alan perched himself gratefully and accepted a cup when offered.

"I was expecting this place to be fancier," Alan said, taking the tea.

"The work of building machines has always been done in warehouses and workshops. Automatons are no different. No use having expensive carpets if you're just going to spill oil on them," Miller said with a shrug.

Alan gestured to the platform where the second engineer tinkered inside the automaton's head.

"That fellow needs some work, does he?"

"He certainly does. That's Gregory, my assistant. The automaton is something of a work in progress as well," Miller jested. "A new labourer model that I've been tinkering with."

The assistant, Gregory, knelt to a large metal toolbox at his feet and took the opportunity to shoot a glance toward them before going back to his work. Brown eyes, brown hair, average build, unspectacular face; the kind of person who made up the ever-shifting backdrop of London. The only thing of interest was a dirty bandage wrapped around the assistant's hand.

"Dangerous job?" Alan said.

"An occupational hazard of working with machines, I'm afraid," said Miller, with a disarming smile. It became strained, held a little too long, and Alan let it hang. "What was it that you wanted to know about these broken down machines? I'm certain that everything we at the Ministry know of any relevance has been passed on to the authorities."

"Oh, I'm sure," Alan said. "But I've been right next to two of these broken down machines, today. I thought you might be able to give me an idea as to what's happening to them."

Miller gave a shrug and gestured to the defunct automaton still in its trolley.

"I'm afraid there isn't much to work with. Even if I was the man for the job," he said.

"You aren't?" Alan asked. Miller was a man in love with his own voice, that was easy to see. And Alan was happy to facilitate the bluster in the hopes of an insight.

"Digging through scrap isn't my forte," the engineer went on. "I'm a designer of new models. Newer, better, more efficient. Those old things are so clunky and oversized. I have no idea why we still use them." Miller gestured to the machine that Gregory tinkered with. "My new model can do everything that they can do, and more, without lumbering around the place filled with hot coals. A malfunction in the Mark Is is almost to be expected, at this point."

"Is it?" Alan asked with feigned naivety.

"Certainly," Miller continued. "Some of those units have been running with very little maintenance for almost thirty years. Day and night. And they weren't the most sophisticated machines to start with. Lord knows, I'm amazed that they've lasted this long."

"Well, when you put it that way," Alan said. Then, to follow up on his status as blather facilitator: "I don't suppose you know who I should talk to about a machine in the British Library, do you? Something that the Ministry might be looking to study?"

Alan watched the engineer perform an impressive facial waltz in just a few seconds. Shock, maybe even anger, through to innocent confusion. Alan had to stop himself giving a round of applause.

"That isn't my area of expertise either."

But you know something anyway, don't you? Alan thought. He carried on with the dumb trick.

"Blimey. It must be brilliant to be such a specialist. I'm more a Jack-of-all-trades, me. I tend to notice all kinds of things."

He missed Miller's retort as it was cut off by the warehouse's door swinging open.

"Ah, I am blessed with visitors, today." Miller interjected eagerly. "Alan, this is Doctor Monroe, one of our finest behavioural analysts."

That name. Alan knew that name. It took him a moment to remember that Monroe was the one who had reported Anchorage's disappearance that morning. The one who knew the professor well enough to note his absence. Despite the recognition, Alan tried to regard her without emotion. No need to tip her off just yet.

In high-waisted trousers and silk blouse, glasses perched atop her tightly wound brunette curls, Doctor Monroe froze in the doorway, her body stiff with held breath, eyes wide and fixed on Alan. She swallowed a mouthful of the apple she held in one hand, possibly a little early, and gave a polite cough as it went down the wrong way.

"Tabitha. Are you alright?" asked Miller.

"Just a goose walking over my grave," she said, her composure expertly regained.

"This is Mister Alan Shaw."

She knows exactly who I am, Alan thought. *Never mind a workshop, this lot belongs on stage.* He offered a hand without comment. The doctor exuded a haughty politeness as she shook his hand firmly, just once, then made to speak with Miller. But Alan wasn't done. She'd covered up her reaction so well, he wanted to poke at it some more.

"Monroe, Monroe. That rings a bell," he said with an innocent smile.

"I have no reason to be recognised, I assure you," was her curt reply. "Miller, I have your latest report. It looks promising but the load-bearing risk recognition is still a little low."

Alan wasn't going to let her get away that easily. This was the most fun he'd had in months.

"Oh, I'm sure you get up to all kinds of things–" he said, letting the sentence hang for a split second "–working with these incredible machines. I'm glad you're here, Doc. You might be able to help me."

Doctor Monroe moved her mouth as if there were still apple in there to be chewed. He looked from one to the other, Miller with his face now adopting a haughty indifference and Monroe looking as if Alan had caught her with her hand in the tea fund. He decided to throw her a bone. She'd been working with Anchorage, after all. The professor wasn't usually a bad judge of character.

"I was just asking Mister Miller what he thinks is going on with these automatons. Any insights?"

Doctor Monroe's eyes strayed to the chunk of melted metal in the trolley. Only because he was purposefully trying to read her did Alan see the twitch of an eyebrow, the slightest tightening of the lower lip.

"They certainly have quirks in their systems. Latent pieces of code that have been known to act strangely." Her eyes snapped back as she delivered a measured response. "We're obviously much more careful with later models. Perhaps I should have a look at it, just in case it's the A.E. that's the problem."

"So, they're just broken then?" Alan asked, turning his face back to Miller while keeping his peripheral attention on Monroe.

"All that heat is bound to affect their analytical engines eventually," Miller agreed. He looked confident, like he'd gotten away with something. Alan wanted to slap it out of him. But what had Jennings said?

Face first and gun second.

"Well, this sets my mind at rest," he said. "Thank you for your time, doctors. I'll report back to King Street and they can issue a bulletin advising that any Mark I owners have them serviced right away." He paused for a second and Mister Slay rose in his mind. What had the spectre said about chaos? Alan gave an innocent chuckle: "Funny though, it's pretty bad timing with the parade being today and these old models deciding to go boom. Nothing more dangerous than coincidences, I suppose. Good luck that you were available to attend, Miller. Both times. Especially with it not being your area of expertise."

Miller's jaw almost rattled with tension.

"Might I ask you something, Mister Shaw?" Miller said, all formality returning. "Tell me, are you actually a policeman?"

Alan could feel his silver badge burning a hole in his pocket.

"Not technically, no—"

"Then not at all, in fact," Miller said.

Alan ducked the verbal blow and came up fighting: "I have special considerations for my helping the police with their work."

"Work of a supernatural nature, if the newspapers are to be believed," Miller said, parrying the reply and striking out with his own.

"Sometimes, yes. Although I'm not a fan of the term, myself. The super is far more natural than people admit," Alan said, knowing that verbal jousting wasn't his strength. He couldn't keep this up much longer before he'd stumble over himself.

Miller raised his chin, offering his nasal hairs for inspection as he delivered the *coup de gras*: "Well, this is a house of science. Reason. Logic. Your *skills* seem ill-fitted to the setting, don't you think?"

Alan ground his teeth. He looked briefly to Tabitha, who was staring at Alan's knees in an attempt to avoid his gaze.

"Would one of you mind showing me out? I think I got a bit turned around on my way in," he said, knowing that retreat was best at this point even as much as he hated the idea.

"Would you be so kind, Tabitha?" Miller asked the Doctor. "Gregory will bring the broken machine for you. Although I'm quite convinced that everything inside has melted beyond usefulness."

Alan nodded a disgruntled goodbye and headed for the doors behind Doctor Monroe who apparently wasn't likely to wait for him. Gregory dragged the cart behind them.

Alan hadn't banked on Miller's quick retort, or that it would hit such a nerve. This was why he left the talking to other people. He paused on the threshold, turning back toward the engineer who was watching him leave. He could have said something, left with some offhand witticism hanging in the air. Instead, he smiled like Slay would smile, and left.

7

DOCTOR MONROE LED the way across the Ministry's work yard, effortlessly weaving through the chaos of innovation. Behind, Gregory dragged the laden trolley in silence. Canvas-covered trucks made wide circles between their arrival and departure; teams lifted and lowered on pulleys, crates and engines and tarpaulin-covered doodads shuttled back and forth on trolleys.

Alan tried not to sulk but couldn't help it. Miller had given his bottom a good spanking and he wasn't looking forward to talking to Doctor Monroe, either. Dealing with smart people was why he kept other smart people like Anchorage and Hogarth around. Gutters, blood and bullets didn't talk back.

Heading north across the courtyard they entered the rear of the main Ministry building. The inside was closer to Alan's expectations of a Ministry: dark wood from floor to ceiling, plaster mouldings and all. They traipsed along corridor after corridor lined with non-descript doors from behind which came the clack of typewriters. Alan found himself snapping his attention toward any whisper of distant conversation, so infrequent were voices heard in the Ministry. Although silent, workers swarmed the halls, some in suits, some in overalls or long brown work coats. Thoughts of an old duster he once had popped into Alan's head and he felt sad, just for a second. As expected, there were a lot of automatons about, mostly newer models with more human proportions, carrying, taking notes, or trailing after Ministry agents. All of them were clothed in some way. He wondered why, when it was so unnecessary. The same kind of people put bows on dogs, talked to irreverent cats, and played gramophones for their houseplants, Alan mused. Still, he understood the compulsion in the automatons' case. The machines were becoming harder and harder to tell from humans, and decency suggested clothes were appropriate.

Finally, they exited into a main hall. A pair of large oak doors muffled the chants of the UHF protest outside. In the centre of the hall's marble floor, a large hole had been cut and edged with wooden railings. In the void, too large to be on any single floor of the building, hung a huge, churning machine. Between a cubic steel frame held in place by chains, sectioned brass cylinders clicked back and forth covered in tiny pins that activated tines set inside larger cylinders which then span gyroscopically to another position and a new set of tines. The whole thing rotated in its frame, frequently changing the direction of its spins. Alan tried to watch it, to track the movement of even one small cylinder around the giant apparatus, and failed. He expected some kind of noise, like a furnace or a steam engine, but there was only the hush of well-oiled bearings and the clack of the pins. It was somehow haunting and inspiring; awful and awesome all at once. Without realising it, he had approached the railing to look closer at the impossible thing. A brass plaque before him read:

M.A.E

Commissioned on Her Majesty's request in the year 1857.
This, the greatest analytical engine in the world, was
completed in the year 1860.

"Where was I when all this was going on?" Alan said aloud. And then he realised the answer. He was as far from home as he could possibly be. And dead, as far as anyone knew.

"Magnificent isn't she?" Doctor Monroe said.

"She?" he asked, coming back to the present.

Monroe shrugged. "A silly tradition. Men insist that they name things they admire after women. That the objects tend to be easily controlled, silent, and servile contraptions is a pure coincidence. The exit is just over there."

Alan watched her. She was completely deadpan. Not a flicker of anger or injustice despite what she'd said and the truth of it. Behind them, Gregory stood like a patient mugger. Alan felt like he was standing next to a Tesla coil, so charged was the air.

"Actually, I wouldn't mind sticking around to see if you find anything out," he said.

The doctor's eyes became unfocused as she looked at him. He'd seen it before in privateers who wanted to face forward but pay attention to their peripheral vision. She was looking for Gregory's reaction, he was certain of it. Monroe nodded, eventually, and said: "Of course. This way."

She swanned on, outpacing him easily, purposefully. The assistant lurked behind. Along another corridor, he caught the door that the doctor didn't hold for him and followed her inside.

The workshop wasn't dissimilar to Anchorage's set up. A desk and a blackboard tightly wound with a sheet were the only real additions. That, and actual daylight from the windows to the rear of the room.

Alan nodded to the blackboard. "You don't use it?"

Doctor Monroe cast a glance over her shoulder as Gregory used a small winch to place the automaton on her work table.

"Thank you, Gregory, I won't be needing anything else," she said, rolling her sleeves. The assistant nodded and left. The door clicked to the jamb and she watched it for a few more seconds until the shadow beneath the door moved away. Then she continued, but in a voice slightly too loud, as if father were listening. "No, Mister Shaw. Chalk dust is extremely difficult to avoid and detrimental to the functioning of clockwork."

Alan nodded as if he understood, and eyed the door himself. As Monroe went to work, Alan circled the room, taking in the diagrams pinned to the walls, the rolls of blueprint paper, punch card programmes in a lacquered box. Ledgers left open showed rows of ones and zeros in neat, handwritten lines. On some of the other workbenches were analytical engines, smaller than he had ever seen. All the while, from the corner of his eye, he could see that Monroe was observing him from hers. That was until she became engrossed in the automaton's innards; then, it was as if Alan didn't exist. The doctor moved her hands across the machine, searching. She tried the furnace hatch, welded shut, then lifted an unresisting metal arm aside to peer inside the split brass chassis. Her deft, massaging movements were so gentle that Alan could have been fooled into thinking she was a different kind of doctor. And that was when it hit him. How much of an idiot he was. He had thought her cold, detached. But he saw the truth of it, now. Doctor Monroe's eyes purposefully projected impassivity; the pursing of her lips was from keeping them purposefully closed. Her tightly bundled hair and colourless, professional clothing, chilly observations, and deadpan delivery; everything was as much a façade as the Ministry's marble, all for the benefit of those who looked on and saw, god forbid, an intelligent, sensitive woman.

"You care about these machines, don't you?" Alan said, thinking aloud.

She shot him a look, the shock of his insight quickly masked with distaste at his impertinence.

"If you must stay and observe, please do so quietly. I'm trying to work, if you don't mind," she snapped. But it faded as she looked at him and saw no accusation in his insight: only interest and respect. She eyed the door through which the assistant had exited. "I love my work. I believe that if you create something, you should care for it."

Reaching into her tool box, she selected something akin to a small crowbar and set to work prising apart the melted plates of the automaton's body. She said something, barely audible over the sound of bending metal.

"What was that?" Alan stepped closer.

With a heavy sigh, Monroe took a hammer and started banging the automaton's chassis. As far as Alan could tell, it was completely purposeless. Then he understood why. Monroe eyed the door again.

"I said, I don't know where he is."

Closer still, Alan moved shoulder to shoulder with the doctor so they could hear each other despite the ringing hammer.

"Anchorage? What's going on? What was it that he brought back?" Alan said.

She banged louder. "I can't help you."

Avoiding eye contact, her eyes remained fixed on the hammer ringing down on bent and split brass.

"Can't or won't?" he whispered.

She ignored him.

Alan slammed his hand down on the hammer, letting out one final ring. The room fell quiet, his breathing like the ocean in the resulting silence.

"The former," she said in an earnest whisper. Shrugging him off, she began to clatter loudly once more, stirring the various metal pieces in a crate of spares while talking. "The Ministry is very, very careful about what goes on inside and what leaks out. We aren't allowed to engage in external research of any kind. The only reason that I haven't been dismissed for helping Lorne is because then they would have to admit that they have snooped on my work, and for educated men to find something of interest in a woman's research is far too embarrassing."

"I'm the most discreet person you'll ever meet, me," Alan lied. "What does Anchorage need a number cruncher for? At least tell me that."

The doctor sighed heavily. "A machine. A very old, very special machine that he found in the Mediterranean. But I don't know where he is now. Please believe me."

"He left a note telling me not to get involved," Alan said.

"Then maybe you shouldn't. Maybe he knows something that you don't."

"I think that *you* know something I don't."

"Most likely," Monroe jibed.

"That's not what I meant," Alan sneered in return.

"I know what you meant. What are you going to do? Beat it out of me?" Monroe waited for a moment, for some comeback, but Alan didn't have one. "I didn't think so. In which case, I'm very busy. If you'll excuse me."

Alan knew he was about to overstep, but that had never

stopped him before.

"If I find out that you're holding something back that will help me find him, Doctor Monroe, there'll be hell to pay," Alan whispered close to her ear. "Anchorage is a very good friend of mine. One of the few I have left. Nothing had better happen to him because you held back."

She turned slowly, and he saw the glistening of tears behind her eyes. Still, she didn't let a single one fall. She made to speak, but instead of a whimper her voice was steady and strong as she said:

"Get out."

Shrugging him away, she reclaimed the hammer, raining it down once more, its echoing ring bouncing back and forth across the lab, shaking windows and people alike.

8

LONDON HAD RETURNED to its usual ordered chaos as morning became afternoon. Alan sat beneath a café awning, watching the steam rise from a china cup and slowly massaging his thigh. His mind was in too many places at once, he knew. Anchorage, the automatons, clues and speculations. Threads spun out in the mad loom of his life and he was the Jenny, hurtling between them, trying desperately to tie them together.

The waiter, Charlie, came and went, removing the cold tea and replacing it with hot every time Alan didn't drink it.

Miller had told him absolutely nothing of use but Alan couldn't help thinking that the engineer had been practising a "not our fault" speech on him. Broken machines. Very old. Blah blah. Not to be blamed on the Ministry. No wonder they were picking up the Mark Is so swiftly when they went kaput. Monroe was tight-lipped but Alan didn't blame her. Her helping Anchorage would be the exact excuse the Ministry would need to oust her and there would be plenty of moustaches at the top for whom female scientists were something to be discouraged.

Alan heaved a sigh.

After a busy morning he had nothing to show in the way of Anchorage's whereabouts. The plinth in the professor's workshop kept coming back to him. Something had been stolen, he was certain of it. Maybe the machine that Monroe spoke of. Something big enough to need a truck to carry it away, and precious enough that Anchorage had bled to defend it. No common thief would even know where Anchorage's department was, never mind understand that what he kept there was valuable, and since Willie didn't know of it, it hadn't been stolen for swift profit.

"What have you gotten wrapped up in his time, old man?" Alan muttered.

As the sun skimmed overhead and began its long descent into darkness, Alan sat and pondered. The other shops around the square closed up, the crowds swelling and then thinning. He toyed with his teaspoon and tapped his cane. He shuffled in his seat and gave sighs in short, frustrated bursts. Still, no new ideas presented themselves. He was stumped. He wished desperately that Anchorage could be sat across the table from him, explaining everything in nice small words.

He was just about to lift his teacup for the first time when his hand froze. Where he lacked technical know-how, he excelled at leg work. And that meant knowing the right people to go to for what. This was a Ministry problem, he was sure of it. He needed insight from someone who wasn't affiliated but who knew them inside and out. A smile quirked across his mouth and the cup stayed untouched. Sliding a bank note beneath his teacup, Alan struggled to his feet, gathering cane and coat, and shot a wink to Charlie.

"Cracked it, have you sir?" the waiter asked.

"Not just yet, but I know someone with brains who can help. Thanks for the tea, Charlie."

"My pleasure, Mister Shaw."

Almost hopping across Leicester Square as he tackled coat and cane simultaneously, Alan was moving at a fair speed by the time he reached Piccadilly. It was a short stomp to Berkeley Square and the expansive town house that belonged to Captain and Mrs Harrigan. But it wasn't the Captain that Alan was hoping to find as he stepped beneath the pillars of the townhouse's porch. With his fingers firmly crossed, he rapped on the door with his cane.

It was a moment or two before there came the scissor-like sound of unlatching locks and the door swung open. As the butler looked Alan up and down with the interest of a marble bust, Alan realised something quite sad. He'd never actually been to this house before. The threat of wilfully being in Percy's presence was just too much to bear and so he'd always stayed away. He found himself sweating slightly under the butler's cool gaze.

"Is the lady of the house in?" he asked.

"Who might be asking?" the butler replied in an accent that implied the servant was much better educated than the visitor.

"I'm an old friend of hers. Alan Shaw?"

The butler's mouth pursed and when he said 'ah' Alan thought it was laden with an unspoken 'sod off'.

"The lady is not at home. Courtesy dictates that one should always send word prior to arrival. Perhaps that would help sir to arrive at a more convenient time," the butler sneered.

Alan thought about chinning the comb over right off the butler's head, but decided not to. Percy didn't need any more excuses for Helen to avoid Alan.

The butler reversed into the house like a cuckoo and was winding up to slam the door when he paused and Alan saw a pucker of annoyance in the man's face. Peeking over his shoulder, Alan watched the steam cab arrive at the curb and a vision in white and blue step out of the cab. From ruffled blouse to the ribboned bonnet pinned jauntily atop flowing blonde curls, Helen was the image of the finest gentry that London had to offer. Spotting her visitor, she hurtled across the pavement, leaving the steam cab door open and bags piled inside. Alan felt her smile approach like clouds parting over warm sunshine and he couldn't help but match her expression as Helen flung her arms around him.

"What a wonderful surprise!" Helen gasped. She looked deeply into Alan's face like few others were allowed to. "You look exhausted."

"I feel much better now," Alan replied.

She tapped his chest with a gloved hand. "Oh you. Geoffrey, would you mind collecting my bags? Thank you so much."

"Of course, madam." The butler stepped past them on the doorstep and went to work as Helen corralled Alan inside.

"He's a laugh a minute, isn't he?" Alan said as Helen began to remove the hatpin scaffolding holding her bonnet atop her head. Her hair fell down in a cascade and Alan couldn't help but let out a resigned sigh.

"Are you alright? Do you need to sit down?" Helen asked, her buoyant mood fading to concern.

"Oh. Yeah. Just my leg giving me gyp," he lied.

Taking his cane from him, she took his arm and guided him to the parlour, four times the size of Alan's own and lavish from wall to wall. It was impossible for him to see what the point of it all was, apart from the brand new Chesterfield suite which he died to break in with a series of sits and naps.

"Sit, sit," Helen said, forcing him down into an armchair

and taking another across from him. Alan couldn't help but look right through the woman in front of him to the girl he'd first met, humming like a cello with enthusiasm and excitement at every little thing.

Helen's face changed to friendly concern as she said, "I take it you have bad news."

"Why would you think that?" Alan asked.

"Because the only thing that would make you come here would be delivering some bad news in person."

"It's not like that at all. I just need some advice," he said with a laugh.

As quick as a tesla lamp, the light shot back into Helen's face. "Romantic advice?"

"Oh god, Helen. No."

She pouted at him as the maid brought tea, unbidden. "You need a good woman in your life, Alan. Why don't you let me organise a luncheon with one of my friends?"

Alan took the tea offered by the young maid who bobbed her knees before leaving.

"I can't think of anything worse," Alan said, setting his cup aside. "I need some advice about a case. It's Anchorage." Helen leaned even further forward, rapt as Alan continued. "He's disappeared."

"That's horrid. I'm so sorry," Helen said.

"It gets worse. Anchorage is wrapped up with the Ministry of Analytical Engineering. They want some machine that he's gotten hold of. But I've followed all the leads, questioned everyone, and I still have no idea where he is."

"I'm not sure I can help." Helen took his hands in hers. "I've been out of touch with the Ministry for an awfully long time. Everyone I knew, or rather those that father knew, have either retired or passed on. And even those were always reluctant to talk. You know how the Ministry are."

Alan sat back, rubbing his forehead with one hand and bracing the other on the chair arm. Half tense, half exhausted.

"I just need a clue. Something. Anything," he muttered.

Helen stared into her tea and the silence spooled out to fill the parlour. After a moment, she spoke with a sigh: "If the Ministry is involved, you can be certain that something underhanded will be going on."

"Have you heard about the Mark Is going haywire?" Alan asked.

Helen nodded in reply.

"Well they're definitely covering that up," he said. "But that's about it. Other than saving their own hides and being uppity toffs, that is."

Helen looked down into her tea and Alan saw the sorrow in the droop of her shoulders.

"After they stole my father's work and started a war with it, any other crime they're involved in could be considered petty," she said.

Alan stared into the empty fireplace and the years rolled back to another vista of cold ash where Delhi had once stood. Metal feet churning foreign soil. Tears held in the stern eyes of a beautiful rebel. He snapped his mind away from that, preferring to focus on the sadness that came from knowing that Professor Normen, Helen's father and the man who had given Babbage's analytical engine the ability to walk, was all but forgotten. The Ministry was happy to ignore the dead and his philosophy. Making tools for the betterment of humankind had been Normen's dream. The working people who he was trying to spare from dangerous and backbreaking labour hated him for it; the Ministry bastardised it and sent it to war. It had driven Normen to an early grave.

Alan broke his eyes away from the dead fire. He could see how it had all affected Helen. When someone felt emotion with such power as she did, he had no idea how she could trap it all behind that breezy nobility. So many people underestimated Helen, thinking of her as just some pretty face. But Alan knew how strong she was, how smart.

It suddenly hit him. There was one very smart person involved in this mess and, although she said she didn't know anything, Alan knew one thing about *her*: she cared for Anchorage with a power that rivalled Helen's own. Doctor Monroe didn't strike him as the type to sit back and let a friend be in danger any more than Alan himself would. She was too smart to trust Alan completely, too determined to sit back and let someone else handle the whole affair, and too eager for resolution to let him slow her down. Despite the cold shoulder she'd given him, she would be doing the thinking that he needed, right now, of that he was certain. He just had to steal her ideas. And that put him right back in his comfort zone again.

Sitting forward in his chair, he grabbed Helen's hands and kissed the knuckles.

"Helen, you're amazing," he said, and leapt to his feet, leaving her sat open-mouthed in her parlour.

He had to get back to the Ministry before Monroe left for the day.

9

THE LIGHTS IN the Ministry for Analytical Engineering's windows never seemed to go out, especially now that tesla coils supplied a wealth of energy to the building. As the sun descended to its daily death beyond the Empire's capital, Alan was left in an early evening gloom as he watched the Ministry's front doors and side street. Arcs of energy sputtered and crackled between coils and nodes up and down the street, lighting the early night in pulses of crystalline blue.

Engineers poured from the side street, trucks rumbled away into the dark, and mathematicians peered around the doors to make sure that the UHF had moved on before they trundled off home. Alan didn't see Doctor Monroe. She could have gone already, or be pulling an all-nighter. Stepping into a paper merchant's doorway across the street from the Ministry, he wrapped himself in shadows to wait.

"Are you going to be out here all night?" Slay asked.

"Hopefully not."

"You must be tired. Maybe just close your eyes for a moment."

"I'll sleep when I'm dead."

"Tease," Slay chuckled.

Although Alan refused to engage, Slay remained to pass comment on every little thing in order to drive Alan's annoyance as high as possible, evaporating only when Doctor Monroe closed the Ministry doors behind her and exited into the city. Allowing himself a smile, Alan pursued, taking the pain rather than letting his cane give him away with its tell-tale clack. The streets were quieter now, the crowds giving way to parade clean-up teams and a few evening strollers that he might hide behind if need be. He followed the doctor at a safe distance as she climbed to the Strand monorail station and entered the shuttle, and he leapt onto the next carriage along. He lost sight of the doctor for a moment as the ticket girl pestered him for change but managed to spot her again as she alighted at the Isle of Dogs platform. With a deft one-footed hop, he squeezed through the shuttle's door as it slid closed and continued his pursuit.

There's no way that she lives out here, he thought.

From his vantage point on the monorail platform, looking out across the Blackwall Dock as it stood back from the Thames, everything was dwarfed by a trio of iron-clad steamers that had been drawn out of the water for repairs. Standing four storeys above him, Alan imagined them falling domino-style into one another and realised that the dockworkers' hovels which clustered at their feet would be utterly crushed. By the light of hundreds of electric lantern strings, he could make out the hefty Mark I automatons that tended to the great winches and mechanisms that bound the ships in an upright position or held large sheets of steel in place while human workers in black glass masks welded them in place. Sparks flew in the shadow of the ships, fizzing as they fell to the murky Thames below. Now that light was so easy to generate, the night couldn't stop London's industry.

Alan realised that he'd let the view distract him and muttered a curse. The doctor had descended to street level and out of sight. He followed swiftly as he could, hopping down the platform steps and scanning the street. Among the hooting whistles of various dock yards around him, workers moved in droves between pub and work and home. The smell of the distant sea coming in off the river and the sound of clattering industry was just one more of London's many faces.

There, between two groups of oily dockworkers, he spotted the doctor moving swiftly through the crowd. She reached Manchester Road where it ran all around the Isle of Dogs, and approached a group of revellers outside a dockside tavern. They must have been there for a while or had a particular desire to be drunk quickly because the men and women in the group were in a tight circle, jigging with arms around each other and flaying the flesh off of an Irish folk tune. So, when the doctor snatched one of their coats from the railing beside them, they didn't even notice. Alan watched in amazement as Monroe swiftly let down her hair, tucking it beneath the raised collar of her new coat which she buttoned tightly around her good clothes and donned the cap that was stuffed in the coat's pocket.

"I'll be damned," Alan muttered.

In her new guise, she tagged onto a group of dockworkers who were laughing and jesting as they walked. They crossed the busy road, one of them giving the crossing guard automaton a kick on the shin as they went by, and made haste toward a pair of attached buildings on the river side, one roof slightly higher than the other. Both were sturdy and older than any other thereabouts, perched on the dock's edge to look out over the darkened water. Despite a lack of sign above the door, Alan knew this place by reputation. The Folly House pub had once been exactly what its name implied and was reputed to attract equally unusual patrons. Slightly behind the group, Monroe entered the old pub with only the slightest glance behind her, altogether too shifty.

Alan held his breath, but she didn't spot him. Making sure not to look around like a tourist, Alan continued on past the Folly House. He scanned faces and clothes and listened to snatches of conversation. Only one thing stood out. Around here, there were an awful lot of UHF badges pinned to coats, shirts and caps.

Heading toward a group of workers, he aimed himself toward a large man in overalls with leather knee patches. They collided, Alan bouncing off the man's firm labourer's bulk and almost to the floor.

"Watch where you're walking," the dockworker grumbled, brushing off his overalls as if it were Alan who was oil-encrusted.

Alan caught himself between cane and one knee, rising slowly, full of apologies. With a minotaur snort, the worker moved on. Alan waited a moment before sliding the pilfered UHF badge from his sleeve and attaching it to his coat with a satisfied smirk before ducking into The Folly House.

Every inch of the Folly House's innards was full; every stool and table were packed to bursting, every leaning spot was taken, and the bar was three deep with oil and smoke-soaked labourers. On every one of them, tell-tale shiny, was the UHF badge.

Alan fought his way through the host of London's labouring class and every head turned his way as he went. The deeper he elbowed his way to the bar, the more he realised how far away the exit was and how few bullets his revolver held should this go wrong. He also kept an eye out for Monroe, but in the mass of similar caps and coats, she was impossible to spot.

The barman, an unmemorable man with dark hair and eyes, was waiting for him when he arrived at the bar.

"Pint, please," Alan said.

The barman's eye slid up and down Alan's good coat, good waistcoat beneath, good boots, and silver tip to his cane. It hovered over the UHF badge on his lapel for a moment or two as Alan tried not to hold his breath. Never taking his eyes off of the old privateer, the barman reached under the counter, produced a pint pot, and filled it.

"Not seen you here before," the barman said in a cockney rasp.

"First time," Alan replied, offering payment.

The barman held up a hand.

"The Front drink free at the Folly."

"That seems like it might be hard to keep up with. So many of us in here." Alan could feel his own accent shifting back in time to when he was a boy, when the streets had taught him everything, and Simon was yet to teach him how to say his *th*s.

"We have an understanding benefactor who provides for the cause," the barman replied. Despite his words, his tone still implied hostility. "Nice to see some more rich folk joining in. Seems like they're all for servants they don't have to feed or pay a living wage."

"I've seen two autos go haywire just this morning. One nearly took down the crowd at the parade, another nearly exploded outside a school. They always made me uneasy but now they're outright dangerous." Alan took a companionable sip of his ale which tasted better than he expected. The benefactor was generous, indeed.

Seemingly convinced enough, the barman went to serve another patron. Alan folded down over his ale, making sure not to look around, meet any of the eyes trained on him, or risk being recognised. Still, he strained his ears for tidbits of conversation, and used the corner of his eye to watch for any blades or barrels extending in his direction. The general muttering in the room gradually changed pitch and, by the time he'd drunk his first pint and ordered another, he had the feeling that conversations had moved away from the new arrival and back to usual discussions.

A bell rang out – a single tone – as Alan sipped his fresh pint. The sound of wood scraping on flagstone filled the room as the Fronters stood in unison and made their steady way through the bar's rear door. Alan watched them all file in, just another phase of their lives spent moving from one place to another in droves, driven by a summoning bell. He followed, letting them lead him through a corridor and into the other side of the building. With windows boarded from the inside and the floor stripped back to dust and dirt, only sputtering oil lanterns on bare walls lit the room. With a throng of dark-clothed people filling the space, all facing a series of crates made into a platform at one end, Alan was reminded of the few cults that he'd been in the presence of. He found himself looking around for the insignia of a wolf eating a red sun and was extremely glad when he didn't find one.

After descending the piled brick stairs at the room's end, a fellow in similar clothing to the rest stepped onto the platform and held up a hand to quell the murmuring. His age was hard to determine; his voice sounded youthful, despite his salt and pepper hair and the deep wrinkles around his eyes and mouth from hard work and a lifetime of frowning over his troubles.

"Welcome, everyone," he said in a disarming, patient

Scottish accent. His wrinkles bunched as he gave a warm smile to the room. "Thank you for coming. I'm pleased to report that today's efforts have gone off without a hitch. Thanks to our benefactor's information on overheating the machines, we've shown the world how dangerous they are. Thank you to all who offered to be witnesses and approached the papers. No doubt the newssheets will be full of the story by tomorrow morning."

A general murmur of affirmation rippled through the room until the speaker held up a hand for them to fall silent once more.

"We've still a lot of work to do. You'll hear reports of a few more incidents over the coming days, so make sure to spread the word. Keep your eyes out for any autos left unattended. Other than that, keep up the honest work of flesh and blood."

Alan had seen worse and heard stranger; he certainly wasn't surprised to hear that the automatons going haywire were the result of human intervention, but he hadn't expected to drop into a conspiracy while following a lead on Anchorage. Wires crossed in his mind and possibilities fired off in all directions, defying connections. One thing that he was sure of: Monroe was deeper in the mess than he had thought.

Slay's cackle came to him and a single hissed word:

"Chaos."

Almost seeming to cheer on the spectre's whisper, the crowd of Fronters gave a round of applause as the speaker stepped down and retreated back up the stairs at the rear of the room.

Standing out like a sore thumb as the crowd swelled behind him, it was impossible for Doctor Monroe to miss Alan.

Her eyes widened while his narrowed.

"What do you say we step outside and chat?" Alan said,

managing to make it a threat.

Monroe opened and closed her mouth like a fish on a pier, moving only when Alan placed a hand on her shoulder and began to steer her toward the door. But it was his turn to stop dead and gawp when he saw the figure blocking the door. The face didn't ring a bell but the rag-wrapped hand brought the man's identity home in the end.

Miller's assistant gave a satanic smirk, backed by several burly Fronters.

Alan sighed.

"Balls."

10

THE UPPER FLOOR of the Folly House's meeting space was a disused loft filled with dust, rat droppings, remains of ancient pigeons and several deactivated Mark I automatons piled in a corner. Alan studied the brick walls, the joists and upright posts, and the dust cataracts on the windows to kill a little time. He had no doubt that the UHF leader would be along to monologue at them at some point.

The wicker seat that he found himself tied to was spectacularly uncomfortable and ropes burned into his wrists. Beside him, tied to her own chair with one leg too short so it rocked as she shifted her weight, Doctor Monroe seethed quietly. The situation was fairly dire, but Alan was managing to stay chipper. Humming a few bars of something he'd forgotten the words to drew tuts and annoyed huffs from his captive companion. The worst part was that the Fronter who took his revolver had also confiscated Wilhelm's bottle of contraband.

"How long are you going to give me the silent treatment?" he asked the doctor, as his chair creaked solidly, mockingly.

Monroe didn't answer quickly: "I have nothing to say to you."

"I apologised already," Alan said. "How was I supposed to

know you weren't in on it?"

"Actually, you didn't apologise. You just said 'oops'."

Alan gave a smirk to which Monroe replied with a frustrated exhalation.

"I thought you were in cahoots with the UHF. How was I to know?" he said.

"That leaping on me while surrounded by the United Human Front in the middle of their headquarters was a bad idea? Perhaps common sense?"

Alan's smirk slipped.

"I'll admit I can get a bit—"

"Impulsive? Brash? Thoughtless?" the doctor offered.

Silence fell. Somewhere outside, a whistle blew. Another shift over, another beginning. Although Alan couldn't see his watch, the rising moon beyond the dusty window told him that they had been there for quite some time already.

"You might as well tell me how Anchorage is wrapped up in this whole thing. Looks like we'll be here a while," he offered. "It'll pass the time, at least."

"What whole thing? I came here to investigate the automatons. It has nothing to do with Lorne. After you left, I studied the burnt out Mark I a little longer. Miller was quite right; there was almost nothing left of its analytical engine. However, that's of interest in itself. Between the insulation and the safety mechanisms built in to avoid overheating, the melted insides shouldn't have been able to happen at all."

Alan shrugged. "So—"

"*So* it was clearly tampered with in order for it to overheat. And that sounds like a half-baked Fronter plot if ever I heard one."

Alan smiled at her with the winning, charming smile that he hadn't used in a while.

"That's good detective work," he said.

"It's only application of logic and the careful consideration of variables," Monroe replied, unaffected by the smile.

"That sounds like a lot of hard thinking. People often tell me to try on patience for size. Never had much use for it, though. Find it gets in the way of doing stuff." Alan said as he struggled against his ropes again, just in case he could catch them off guard.

"People who thrive on chaos often say that," Monroe said.

Alan stiffened at the word. Slay, as always, coalesced in the shadows with a knowing smile.

"What's wrong?" Monroe asked. "Your face just fell a mile."

"Nothing. Something popped into my head."

"Something useful?"

"Rarely."

Slay mimed receiving a vicious wound.

With the shuck and click of a sliding bolt the attic's door opened. A familiar form in thick leather braces and work shirt sidled in almost apologetically.

"Sorry to keep you waiting," the UHF leader said in his pleasant Scottish lilt.

He dragged over a third orphan chair and sat down, regarding them both with a look of fatherly disappointment.

"Name's Campbell," he said politely. "I'm the closest thing we have to a spokesman around here."

"Alan. This is Doctor Monroe. I'd shake hands but…" and he wiggled his restraints.

"I know you're uncomfortable. Sorry." Campbell rubbed the grizzle on his chin. "What am I supposed to do with you two? I'm not in the habit of hurting people but I can't let you walk out. I can't keep you here, either. You've put me in quite the pickle."

Alan leapt to the point. "You've been sending automatons into crowds and overheating them and you don't expect someone to get hurt?"

"Figured it out then, have you? I don't hurt people if I can help it. That's not what the UHF is about. I always send my people along to keep an eye. They can step into the demonstrations if need be. They've been trained."

"By whom?" Monroe chipped in.

"Our benefactor, Miss," Campbell replied politely.

"Dare I ask what they're getting out of it?" the doctor asked.

Alan felt a little surplus to requirements.

"The same as all of us, Miss. A future where people need not fear the starvation of their families. One where machines haven't made men obsolete. One where craftsmanship, expertise and the work of a lifetime are still important."

Alan wanted to say something smart but he was finding it hard to disagree.

"The soft way isn't always the best way. You know that, too, I'll bet," Campbell added to Alan.

Alan had to admit it: "I do."

"Anyway, I just wanted to pop in and say hello. No need to be impolite just because we're on different ends of this thing. And as we recognised you, Mister Shaw, the ropes seemed like a fair precaution."

"I never had this problem when no one knew who I was," Alan quipped.

Campbell gave a polite chuckle. "The burden of fame. Try to rest. I'll talk over what's to be done about you with the benefactor. But fear not, I'll only do away with you if it's essential."

"I feel thoroughly reassured," Monroe said, dryly.

11

ALAN WOKE IN the night to a shuffling sound somewhere in the attic's shadows. Dusty moonlight filtered in, filling the room with a dream haze. Beside him, Doctor Monroe slept like a ragdoll tied to its nursery chair, head slumped to her chest, making little snoring noises. The scuffling came again and he recognised it. Footsteps. Reaching for his revolver, he remembered that not only had he been relieved of his gun but his hands were still bound and now very numb. Flexing his swollen wrists shot pins and needles up his arm and he held back a gasp at the prickling pain.

The sound of sliding metal filled the silent room and there was a thump as one of the deactivated automatons in the corner slumped to the ground like a drunkard, its leg stanchions sticking out into a pool of moonlight. Alan squinted into the darkness but all his years of delving in shadows couldn't help him make out any details.

Shuffle and slam. Another automaton fell beside the first and a glint of moonlight on metal highlighted a figure in the dark, narrow of shoulder, below average height and wearing some kind of metallic suit. The figure moved from automaton to automaton as Alan watched, sliding each one to the ground until they lay side by side, sharing a cot like Whitechapel urchins. Then, dragging a rat-chewed tarpaulin from the side of the room, the figure covered the automatons with the slow reverence of an undertaker and turned to leave. Moonlight glinted on a glass helmet rimmed with brass.

Despite himself, Alan whispered: "What in blazes—"

The figure's head snapped toward him, peeking into the moonlight, and Alan saw it more clearly. An automaton like nothing he'd ever seen, its chest and head were made from glass ovoids so that the complex clockwork inside could be seen whirring and clicking. Seeing Alan staring back at it, the automaton recoiled, taking steps back into the darkness, and slammed its heel against one of the fallen. The machine's arms pinwheeled as it lost its balance, releasing an accordion gasp. It hit the floor and, as Alan watched with his jaw dropped all the way to his chest, the machine rubbed its head in a perfect facsimile of human confusion.

The door slammed open, lantern light pouring in, silhouetting two burly Fronters.

Everything happened at once. The UHF men shouted a monosyllabic challenge, Alan tugged at his restraints, the machine reeled back in fright, and Monroe snapped awake. The doctor regarded the room blearily for a moment before spotting the automaton and beginning to scream. Not in fright, but demanding that the machine run.

Like a rabbit loosed before the dogs, the machine bolted for the window, the Fronters giving chase on reflex. Still, they were too slow and the window was already open. The daintily built machine slipped into the night as the henchmen fought each other for who would go after it first.

Doctor Monroe muttered to herself over and over as she struggled with renewed vigour at her restraints. "Oh no. Nonononono."

Alan bolted up from his chair, his bonds falling away as if they had never been tied. Taking the first thug by surprise, Alan's boot sent him through the window head first with a drawn out scream that ended with a splash. The second caught Alan's numb fist to the jaw but wouldn't go down so easily and traded a few neat blows to Alan's hasty guard before a kick to the knee and an elbow to the temple took the thug down.

"How?" Doctor Monroe said as Alan untied her, panting. "How did you get out?"

"You don't last long in this job if you can't slip a rope. But I didn't see the point in us escaping before we knew a bit more about what was going on. Then this happened and it seemed like the right moment. Shame, really, I was waiting for this benefactor fellow to show up."

Doctor Monroe went to stand and blinked her eyes violently, catching herself on the back of her chair. "Ugh. Dizzy."

"Take it easy," Alan said. "Your blood's in all the wrong places."

He limped toward the door – his cane another thing that he'd lost when taken captive – and leaned out. Monroe jumped out of her skin as Alan slammed the door and pressed his back to it.

"We're in bother. If you could think of a way out–" The door behind him shook in the frame and his heels skidded on the ground. Resetting his footing, anticipating another attempt by the Fronters outside, he added: "–anytime now would be grand."

Doctor Monroe looked around, eyes wild, head spinning, and spotted the automatons. She threw the tarpaulin aside and began to rummage around, moving from one metal man to the other.

Voices were rising outside and Alan could hear Campbell giving orders and encouragement to his fellows.

"Doc—" Alan began, but was cut off when the door shook again. "Gah! Hellfire. Hurry up."

Sparks flew in the corner of the room and Alan could see the doctor under-lit by a furnace's first light. The automaton at her feet shuddered and began to move as the pressure built up in its system and she gave it an order: "Automated unit Phi Three, commence action and—"

Alan let out a yell as the door behind him thumped, his feet slid, and the first gap appeared showing angry faces beyond. He closed his eyes, waiting for the inevitable trampling, knowing that to let go was a death sentence; to hold on was futile.

A metal hand slammed against the door above Alan's head and he looked up into the naive green eye of his saviour. With frustrated yells from the outside, the automaton pushed, pushed the door back, closing it to the jamb as questing fingers drew hurriedly back.

Monroe grabbed Alan's coat, dragging him toward the window.

"There was enough anthracite left over in them all to get one started," she said. "but he'll wind down pretty soon."

At the window, they looked down to the river below.

"That weird auto, you knew it didn't you? It knew you. In the dark, I thought it was a person," Alan said.

"We haven't decided if it is or isn't," the doctor replied. She pointed down to the river below. "But we'll never get to find out if we don't find a way down there."

"Oh, that's easy," he said, the moonlight coating his grin with manic shadows.

Grabbing Monroe by the hand, he jumped.

12

THE SHALLOWS OF the river Thames were like no other in the world. While the pumping stations further up the river redirected pollutants well enough, down by the Isle of Dogs where shipbuilding led to all manner of effluent, there was nothing to stop the collection of oil, rust, and industrial runoff in the river's nooks and crannies like the bay beside The Folly House.

Alan hit the river with his back, his coat taking some of the shock but stopping none of the cold tar water from grabbing at him, pulling him down to an uncertain riverbed where his boots kicked in the silt, sending him upward just in time for Doctor Monroe to hit the water, driving him down again. Sputtering, he surfaced and instinctively began to swim toward any kind of light, squinting through the ooze that coated his face and strayed into his mouth. Monroe could be heard gasping behind him, and then there was the sound of swimming. She overtook him easily, reached a small wooden dock across from The Folly House and dragged herself ashore. Alan struggled to kick, every thrust forward met by a painful burst. He was regretting every decision he'd ever made in life all over again when Monroe's hand came down on his shoulder and she hauled as he pushed, leaving them panting on the dock beside each other.

Monroe struggled for breath, spat what she hoped was only oil from her mouth, and used her first good breath to say the most important thing on her mind:

"You idiot."

"If I had a penny," Alan chuckled, spat, and scampered upright on his good leg to stand wavering there like an ink-soaked scarecrow.

"You can't possibly expect to get away with one good leg and no cane," Monroe spat, ducking her head under his arm and propelling them both forward.

"I'll have you know, I've been running away from things after being stabbed, shot, bitten, and cursed for most of my life. There's nothing that I can't shuffle away from at speed."

Still, he didn't fight off her assistance when she took his elbow.

As the moon took its lazy downward arc toward morning, the streets of the Isle of Dogs sparkled with tesla light on UHF badges, the pre-dawn air filled with hasty orders and muttered curses. Ducking behind a winch housing, Alan and the doctor waited for an opportune moment to move southward along Manchester Road, away from The Folly House and toward the shipyards proper where they could hopefully become lost in the morning murk. Their thick coating of oil and grease melted into the shadows so that, even with Alan slowing them down, they made good time and Alan was becoming confident that they had escaped until he heard a hiss from an alleyway across the road where the terraces came down toward the edge of the Isle.

Alan spun as best he could, peering into the dark, hand itching for a revolver that wasn't there, wishing for the comforting weight of his cane. Without either, he bunched his fists, the weapons that he could never leave home without.

A voice issued out of the darkness in a stage whisper:

"What are you doing here?"

Anchorage stepped out of the darkness wearing a worried smile. He was taller than Alan, of a robust build for an older gent, his hair completely silver. Alan had always marvelled at the archaeologist's athleticism. Far from the stuffy tweed wearers like Simon, Anchorage was as used to digging trenches as through old tomes, his globetrotting searches for lost civilisations keeping him young behind the eyes where other academics would be long since dead. Behind Anchorage, the unusual automaton stood like a young ward protected by their guardian.

"I'm supposed to be saving you," Alan replied.

"Well, this is a turn up for the books, then." Anchorage looked Doctor Monroe up and down, oil stained and miserable. "Tabitha. You have that singular look of misery that means you've met Alan."

"Let's move along, shall we?" Tabitha replied after a weighted moment.

Anchorage stepped out, taking Alan's arm to get the weight off of his leg, and they continued to scuttle between the shadows of Manchester Road with the odd automaton trailing behind, looking over its shoulder at the swarming firefly lanterns in the distance.

"My note expressly asked you not to get involved, didn't it?" Anchorage said.

"And you thought that would stop me?" Alan replied with a laugh.

"Saying it aloud, I realise my error," Anchorage admitted. "I should have known that a lever with 'do not pull' would only encourage you."

The trio of half-built steamers stood in the drydock like beached whales, three storeys high, their ribs on show. On the skeletal scaffolding around them lumbered haunting figures, tall and slow, embers burning low in their bellies: automatons working through the night.

Along the pier lit haphazardly by swinging lamps, Anchorage led them toward some tin sheds at the ships' feet that would be empty during the graveyard shift. Leading the small automaton by the hand, Monroe peered through windows and cracks in rickety doors while Anchorage slung Alan's arm over his shoulder like a wounded battlefield comrade. In time, they found an empty shed down by the water and piled in. Monroe flicked a wall switch and a single tired bulb gave a sad glow. Barricading the door and covering the single window as best they could with an oil cloth. Alan sat on an old metal drum gratefully, massaging his leg hard enough to bruise, breath heavy and head pounding.

Anchorage knelt by him, looking him over in the meagre light.

"I wasn't expecting to see you two tonight. But I'm glad I did," he said with a half-hearted chuckle. Monroe peered through a gap in their makeshift curtain, her face lit by a slither of lamplight ash she kept watch. She ducked back into the shadows as a swinging lantern light passed beyond the window. Beside her, the automaton hovered like a child. Anchorage smiled at the machine and said: "You've met Zoe, I presume."

"It's almost human. How did you do it?" Alan asked.

Anchorage gave a more heartfelt laugh. "No, no. Not me. I found her."

"Her? I didn't think you were the sentimental type, Anchorage."

"When I found her, there was a single word inscribed on her box. Zoe. Life, in ancient Greek," he added for Alan's sake. He turned a serious gaze on his old friend. "She is no mere automaton, Alan. I'm convinced that Zoe is the first artificial life ever created. Real life."

Monroe said something to Zoe in what must have been ancient Greek. The machine replied in tinny tones like a sentient music box, its glass head showing the complex workings inside, mechanisms designed to emulate spontaneous thought.

Alan looked the contraption over more closely. It wasn't as complex as the Mark Is in many ways. Its hands were fingerless metal mittens, and it wasn't built for strength or speed, only motion. Still, from what he had seen, the workings of its analytical engine were spectacularly complex.

"I think you'd better start at the beginning, Anchorage," he said.

With a sigh, Anchorage told his tale in hushed tones, Tabitha helping with details and chronology when he got it wrong.

"–I KNEW WE had been discovered, and so Tabitha and I decided that I should disappear with Zoe. It was the only way to keep her safe. Unfortunately, once Zoe spotted another automaton out in the world, she became quite consumed with wanting to converse with them." Anchorage said something in Ancient Greek and, although it was said with a fatherly smile, the automaton hung her head, contrite. "She has been the only one of her kind for as long as she has existed. Unfortunately, our own machines are built for function rather than conversation. Still, she feels a kinship with them. When we came across the UHF, she was determined to help the captured Mark Is despite my warnings."

"And I returned to work in the meantime," Tabitha said, "knowing that I must have been watched, been followed, by someone there. It isn't beyond the Ministry to watch their employees."

"Especially someone like Tabitha who threatens their androcentric monopoly," Anchorage added.

Alan looked between his companions.

"Well, we can't have that, can we?" he said, hoping that his reaction to the phrase was the right one.

The shed fell silent.

"So when I told you that I couldn't help, I meant it," Tabitha said to Alan. "He purposefully didn't tell me where he was going so that it could never be overheard. The fact that I followed the UHF's trail and Zoe happened to walk into the very room in which we were held captive is a very happy coincidence."

Alan humphed. He was as much a fan of coincidence as he was of fate and chaos.

"You seem to be struggling with something, Alan," Monroe said. "Which part of Lorne's story don't you believe?"

Anchorage chuckled. "Tell someone that you found an ancient research laboratory in a sub-aquatic rift in the Mediterranean Sea, and that there, among other things, you found a machine which is a very passable facsimile of human life, and they would be well within their rights to mull it over for a while. However..." Anchorage looked to Alan, who finally stopped his musing to smile back at his old friend.

"For us, it's just another Tuesday," Alan added. "It isn't that part that's bugging me. What I can't figure out is what to do with all this." He gestured to the world at large. Anchorage was safe and that was a weight off his mind, but there were still some thieves to find who knew far too much about a project that should have been secret, and a group of local terrorists who were trying to bring the city to a halt by crushing the public's faith in their automaton workers. "I see all this... coincidence and can't help but think that it fits together. It must do, somehow." He felt Slay's presence in the back of his mind, insisting on chaos when all Alan wanted was order, and added: "It has to."

"I don't see how it could possibly," Anchorage offered. "The thieves who tried to steal Zoe weren't United Human Front."

"And the Ministry is diametrically opposed to their efforts," Monroe said.

"Yet, here we are," Alan replied. "Autos everywhere. And on a day like today – yesterday – dammit. With the parade and all." He sighed heavily, forgetting to maintain his facade for Monroe. "It feels like I get older and the world goes faster. Targets get further away, villains harder to pick out. I'm getting slow."

Anchorage placed his hand on his friend's shoulder.

"That doesn't sound like the Alan I know," he said.

Alan pinched the bridge of his nose. "I don't think I've been him for a long time, my friend."

In the uneasy silence, Anchorage looked to Monroe for help but received only a mono-shoulder shrug. The young automaton looked between them all, clearly not understanding the words, but aware that a moment was being had. Monroe turned back to the window.

"Perhaps you've seen too many grand schemes over the years," Anchorage said to his old friend with a tone of consolation. "Some people just want to make a quick pound and eat a hot meal. Some people fear losing the work that would feed their children."

"This is London, Lorne. Everyone is up to something grand and diabolical," Monroe said, peeking out of the shed. "And I think that our someone might have just arrived."

Alan and Anchorage pressed themselves against the shed's little window, looking back along the pier toward the city where a truck idled, headlights lancing into the early morning fog that rolled in off the river. Doors slammed and three figures climbed out of the cab followed by many more from the truck's rear. Backlit by the headlights, the dawn light picking out their features, Alan's exasperation drew back to reveal glowing understanding. There, side by side, stood Miller with his hands buried deeply into his coat pockets, his assistant in dark docker's clothes, and Campbell. UHF members spread out along the pier behind them, lanterns and a few electric torches held high.

"I can certainly point you in the direction of a villain," Anchorage said. "The fellow with the bandage was the one who broke into my workshop. He tore the doors right off with his truck."

Alan's fog of coincidence and confusion burned away as the morning light began to rise outside the shed.

"All these years I've been chasing villains and it turns out, if I stand still long enough, they come to me," he quipped, his facade returned. "Patience, eh, Doc?"

Monroe snorted but Alan couldn't tell if it was derision or amusement.

"Looks like we've met the benefactor after all," she muttered. "Reducing confidence in the Mark Is so that he could replace them with his new worker model. And the Ministry found out about my work with Lorne and Zoe just in time. Her analytical engine would be invaluable to his work. I should have been more careful."

"You had no reason to be," Anchorage offered. "They spend so much time ignoring you, why would you ever suspect that they had you under surveillance?" He then translated the whole thing to Zoe who laid her arms around the doctor in comfort. Alan took a moment to marvel at the machine's show of empathy, before adding:

"Because they're idea-stealing, double-crossing, back stabbers? Still not your fault though, Doc."

"Shaw. Tabitha. Come on out," Miller bellowed. Alan guessed that there were enough UHF members to make secrecy unnecessary. "We know you're here. Let's not be at it all morning, we're all very busy."

"We can't let him get Zoe," Anchorage said hurriedly. "He'll take her apart."

"And we can't let him blow up any more Mark Is in the city, either," Monroe added.

Alan thought for a moment, long enough for Miller to lose patience.

"We know you're here somewhere. It's only a matter of time. Come out and we can continue our chat amicably," the engineer called out, but he also barked an order to some of his minions who began to scour the pier, breaking open sheds and searching inside. Beside him, Campbell looked uneasy as his followers swarmed forward.

"I don't think he knows you're here, Anchorage," Alan said. "And he never has to know. Doc, take Anchorage and Zoe and get them out of here. I'll distract them."

Anchorage made to protest but Monroe cut in:

"Alright, but how are you going to do that? You've no gun, you're lame, and you're vastly outnumbered."

Alan winced as he brought himself upright and headed for the door.

"With pure charisma," he said.

Even Anchorage was unable to quite contain the look of uncertainty. Monroe didn't even try.

"Fine," Alan said. "I'll just piss him off. Some friends you are."

"INTO THE LION'S den, old pal," Slay whispered as he walked beside Alan, his boots making no sound on the wooden pier. Headlights hung in the early morning fog, lanterns swinging like Will 'o Wisps in the murk which Alan swam through with a look of grim determination, using a rusty pipe as a walking stave. And all of this happening in the shadow of the colossal steamship and its scaffolding that rose between the old sheds like a half-eaten behemoth. "He has no reason to keep you alive, you know. He might just kill you right here and now, and Anchorage will be captured all the same."

"Nah," Alan scoffed. "There's one thing that people like Miller love to do more than anything else."

"You're counting on him taking the opportunity to gloat?"

"It worked with you," Alan shot back. Slay's face coiled like a cobra. "He won't kill me until he's had his say. Lovely morning, Miller! Hoped I wouldn't be seeing you again but here we are."

Miller's face was carefully blank, but Alan could see the tension in the engineer's pulsing neck vein. Beside him, Gregory glared through his eyebrows, the UHF badge shining on his chest. Alan tutted to himself.

"He was there the whole time, I bet. Watching. Blending in. You missed him," Slay whispered. "Sloppy,

sloppy."

"I'm glad you're here, Miller," Alan said with a forced smile. "Saves me coming to get you."

"For what? You were clueless," Miller sneered. "And you still are for that matter. You can't possibly understand the level of complexity at which I work."

"Well, it was pretty clever, I'll admit."

Miller's face cracked into a self-satisfied smile. "The Mark I model is woefully out of date. They need to be melted down. But this city is so cheap that they would never replace them until they posed a real danger. Thanks to my friends in the UHF, they have done just that."

Alan nodded along. "And your new model can step in."

Miller's smugness rose to dangerous levels.

"Precisely," he said.

Over the engineer's shoulder, Campbell's face went from patient obedience, through shock to anger.

Whoops, Alan thought, *looks like Campbell just learned something new.*

"And that must come with a lot of government funding," Alan said, ramming it home for Campbell who, by his thunderous grimace, was all caught up.

"Where is Tabitha?" Miller asked, unaware of the tide turning behind him.

Alan hoped he could pull off the sad dog look as he gazed out across the river where the mist was starting to break. It wouldn't be around much longer to hide Anchorage's escape.

"I was slowing her down. She could be anywhere by now," he lied.

Miller tutted. "No loyalty, that one. It will be her downfall."

She's loyal, alright. Just not to you, Alan thought. But he said: "I suppose you're right."

"No matter. If she knows what's good for her, she'll run far away and take on some quiet, womanly work," Miller added.

Alan thought of the female privateers, pilots, warriors and scientists he'd known and wondered what exactly women's work was supposed to be. If Miller meant running a household, he couldn't think of anything harder. Lottie had a will of iron and a steel rod running down her spine as far as he was concerned.

He's lucky none of them were here to hear that, he thought, and couldn't help but imagine Merry or Wai pummelling the hell out of a weeping Miller. Lottie still had her shotgun over the fireplace. A smile slipped onto his lips.

"Something amusing?" Miller snapped.

"I was just wondering how annoyed you were when you realised that the Ministry wasn't the first to make an analytical engine, and how much of the old automaton's technology you were going to pilfer and pretend was your own work."

Miller's face fell a mile. He looked to Gregory whose directionless malice now shadowed Miller's own surprise.

"I don't know what you're talking about," the engineer offered.

"You let this slip you by, did you? Greg certainly knew about it. Enough to tail Doc Monroe, break into the museum and steal what he found there. Or rather, he tried. Seems like the automaton was too much for him. Eh, Greg?"

Miller seethed quietly.

Behind Alan, a loud thud shook the pier's boards. He turned, keeping half an eye on Miller's men, and saw a large wrench sat on the planks. Craning upward, staring into the bones of the scaffolding against the backdrop of the iron steamer, he saw three figures shift in the early morning murk, and light hit the dark gold metal of Zoe as his companions climbed higher and higher. Beneath them swarmed darker forms, UHF members, lanterns cast aside to aid their climbing. They had been spotted after all.

"Balls," Alan remarked.

Miller's grin had returned as he stared upward.

"A distraction? How infantile," he said. "Gregory, do help the professor and doctor down. It would be an awful shame if they fell."

"You think that was a distraction?" Alan said with incredulity as he turned an evil grin on the engineer. "I haven't even started."

He swung his rusty pipe crutch in a wide arc, sending the Fronter to his right spinning into the mud banks below the pier, and clanking another into swift unconsciousness. Gregory advanced, and caught a steel pipe on the shin for his trouble. The next blow dropped him on his backside and Alan walked purposefully over the assistant's bandaged hand as he advanced toward Miller, the engineer bumping into the truck's grille in his haste to back up.

"Don't you dare," the engineer said. "You wouldn't."

His head snapped to the side, knees limp, body crumpling to the pier.

Campbell flexed his fist as he growled in his Scottish accent: "*I* bloody would."

He turned to Alan who was belting the consciousness out of some Fronters.

"Stop! Truce!" he shouted.

Alan froze, pipe raised high over his head. He let it drop onto a Fronter who was knelt gasping at his feet, clonking him on the head.

"Oops," Alan said.

"This doesn't mean that I agree with you," Campbell clarified.

"Oh, of course not," Alan replied.

"I just hate him a lot more than you."

"Got it. Can you call them off?" Alan said, looking up at where the black shapes were converging on Tabitha's trio and, further down the pier, another group were stuffing oily rags into barrels and setting them alight. If the escapees couldn't be caught, they'd be smoked out, it seemed.

"It doesn't work like that," the Scotsman replied. "Miller pays awfully well. I'm not their boss, just the spokesman."

"What's the point of that?" Alan asked.

"We're an actual democracy where people's individual opinions matter," Campbell replied in clipped tones.

"Pfft. When has that ever worked?" Alan said as a yell crashed down from above.

He almost broke his neck, snapping it up toward the shout. There was Anchorage, arms wide to block the Fronters as they advanced toward Zoe and, at the other side, facing off her own group of badge-wearers was Tabitha, but they closed in slowly, because she had just delivered a deft kick to one's arse and the rest seemed unenthusiastic about entering her reach.

With an exasperated huff, Alan set off. One foot stomped heavily, the other barely graced the pier's boards as he propelled himself forward in a lopsided skip. Where a wooden pallet held sacks of steel rivets, ropes had been tied off to a rail, holding counterweights in place until the next day's lifting. Alan eyed them for only a second before wrapping one around a hand and grabbing the trailing knot with the other.

"Are you mad?" It seemed Campbell had followed him this far.

Alan shot him a look and said: "Probably best not to think about it."

With a yank, the rope flew free, whipping into the hazy morning sky. A huge counterweight bag slammed into the pier beside Campbell, showering him with splinters and sand as it punched right through to the river below.

Alan still stood there, rope in hand, exchanging a glance with the Scotsman.

"Oops," he said. "Second time's the charm." And he yanked on another rope.

The sound of cable flying through the steel pulley and the whip of speeding scaffolding filled Alan's attention as, eyes watering and shoulder holding in its socket by luck alone, he hurtled upward. The powerful and possibly limb-shredding pulley wheel screamed as he flew toward it. Alan did the only thing he could do. He let go, catching the scaffolding right across the thighs as he tumbled forward without finesse to land on his arse on the boards.

After dragging himself to a stand with all kinds of bloody language on his mind, he ever so slowly limped his way toward his friends beyond the backs of the Fronters as they surged forward. Below, flames glowed through the voracious smoke that billowed upward, blurring edges and burning his eyes, the taste of charred wood and oil filling his mouth. Alan tried to breathe sparingly, but that only made the swimming in his head worse. Somewhere amid the smoke cloud Tabitha yelled out a threat that was cut off by a Fronter rugby tackling her around her middle. Zoe screamed like a gramophone and ran to protect her friend. All three tumbled, hitting the scaffolding's railing and releasing a large pulley that had been tied off. With its considerable weight behind it, the pulley swung, picking up momentum, slamming into the middle of Anchorage's back just as another Fronter knocked him off balance. Everything moved like a runaway zoetrope, except for Alan, who felt anchored to the spot as his old friend tumbled over the scaffolding's rail.

13

FOR ALL THE sickening heights that Alan had leaped across, hung from or been thrown over, he had never felt a lurch in his stomach like when Anchorage plummeted over the shipyard scaffolding. The automaton, Zoe, reached out for him, managing to cling to the professor's coat sleeve, but her efforts were a temporary delay at best. In her tinny tones she chimed loud enough to be called a scream, the syllables stunted but clearly calling Anchorage's name. Alan shook himself at the sound. Such a clear call of fear, of care, he could no longer deny what Anchorage and Doctor Monroe suspected; Zoe was no mere machine. But there would be no time to discuss it if Anchorage were committed to the fatal fall over which he now dangled.

Dragging himself forward with the assistance of the scaffolding's rail, Alan closed the gap between him and his friend. Tabitha was wrestling with a Fronter twice her height when Alan stomped by. Barely slowing, Alan kicked the giant's knee out from behind with a wet crunch, sending the hulk dropping to the boards with a pained scream and giving Tabitha a fairer fight. Rounding Zoe, he threw himself against the railing, grabbing Anchorage by the scruff of the neck and trying to haul him back. Zoe let out an urgent chime and Alan could see her servos and gears whirring in effort. Both of them still weren't enough. Anchorage slipped further with a jerk and the sound of tearing clothing cut across the clamour of the fighting.

"Let me go, both of you, or we'll all go over," Anchorage shouted, even though his eyes were wide with fear, his jaw tight with the prospect of his impending end.

"Not a bloody chance," Alan groaned, and held on even though he could feel himself toppling forward, his centre of gravity dangerously close to following his friend over the railing.

Hands grabbed Alan's coat from behind and he finally felt some backward motion. His feet touched ground and he was pulled back just as he and Zoe pulled on Anchorage, yanking the sweating professor over the railing and into a heap. Monroe cursed politely as Zoe rolled off of her.

"Third person's the charm," she groaned.

"Thank you all," Anchorage panted, staring up at the sky. "Very much appreciated."

They heard the clang of the fire engines first. Back toward the Isle, two sets of high voltage lamps speared the night, swerving their way. Below, Fronters darted like spiders to their skirting boards.

"Cavalry," Alan sighed, possibly the first time that he'd been happy to see the authorities in his life. Regarding the fire spreading along the pier below, catching a tool shed alight as it went, he laughed and nudged Anchorage. "Jennings is going to go berserk."

14

CLIMBING THE SWEEPING steps of the British Museum, Alan passed between the roman columns to the immense oak doors beyond.

The similarity between the museum's main hall and the vault of a cathedral was impossible to ignore, but the scientists who bustled inside would deny it at all costs. Mosaic floors, gothic walls and a glass ceiling represented the passage of time from ancient to contemporary. There seemed to be no one around, although Alan heard the echoing footsteps of an employee floating down from an upper hall and had to stop himself from looking for Slay. He headed toward the department of archaeology, or rather a small office tucked inside it that the archaeologists tried to forget about. The door to that forsaken room was nondescript, with an upper panel of frosted glass marked with:

Professor Lorne Anchorage
Head of Crypto-archaeology

"Head of? He's the only bloody member," Alan muttered as he slipped through the non-tradesman's entrance without stopping to knock.

Elsewhere, the museum housed its exhibits in glass cases or behind barriers so that the curious might see but definitely not touch a little piece of history. Here, artefacts whose existence they couldn't deny but also couldn't explain were kept on rickety metal shelves, in wooden crates fluffy with straw packaging, leant in corners and strung from the ceiling. Skulls, baubles, stone fragments and wooden whatsits of odd shape and purpose were covered in runes or wrapped in the skin of creatures that no longer existed. Giant eggs lay unhatched, sheaves of parchment undeciphered, rolls of tapestry depicted things not ready to be included in the historical or religious canon; it was all kept in Anchorage's tiny office.

Alan stood at the doorway for a second, taking it all in, feeling the weirdness of the world condensed into such a small space. This was the closest he ever felt to home outside of his own little collection of oddities. Further in, where the shelves ended, a dirty window cast half-light onto a small desk, a large free-standing globe and filing cabinets of all shapes, sizes and levels of decrepitude. Anchorage was up to his elbows in a drawer, muttering to himself. A brown leather suitcase beside the desk told Alan all he needed to know.

"Where to this time?" Alan asked.

Anchorage turned to greet him with a weak smile. "Good morning. I'm taking Zoe out of London. They'll have her in the dock and then open on a worktable in the shake of a lamb's tail if we stay here. I managed to convince the authorities and the Ministry to attempt a less invasive method of study first."

"And by convince you mean..."

Anchorage grinned. "Bribed them with telling Ernest about Miller and implicating them in a terrorist plot against the city."

They were still laughing when Zoe came in from the

workroom wearing a coat that Alan had last seen on Doctor Monroe, a small leather bag in her metal mitten and the doctor following close behind.

"We're all packed," Monroe said. "The most intact mechanism from Antikythera is in this bag. Zoe has offered to look after it."

The little automaton gave a whistle and waved to Alan who found himself waving back. He moved over to the large globe in the office's only spare corner and started looking for a latch to open it. Anchorage didn't even bother looking over his shoulder to see what Alan was doing but Tabitha was watching with a look of thinly veiled disdain.

"It isn't a drinks cabinet," she said.

Alan snorted as he continued to circle the room, trying not to seem disappointed.

"Seems like a waste of a good globe," he said.

"Ah!" Brandishing the file he had been looking for, Anchorage thumbed through, removing the odd page and setting it aside. "There are a pair of scientists in Vienna who are experimenting with a new kind of camera, one that can see through objects. I'm hoping that we can map Zoe's inner workings without having to take her apart."

Anchorage gave him a look that Alan thought he understood. This experiment was also far enough away from London that, if the Ministry should have a change of heart, it would be easier for Anchorage and Zoe to disappear.

"And you, Doc?" Alan asked.

"I'm staying here. They will only come up with some half-brained story to support their opinion of women in the Ministry if I leave. I have to stay and prove them wrong," Tabitha said.

"You've proved that more than enough by now," Alan said.

"You'd think so wouldn't you?" Tabitha huffed. "I plan to start by doing Miller's job better than he ever did."

Alan gave a devilish smirk. "I'll make sure the news reaches his cell."

Monroe actually chuckled.

The temperature in the room noticeably dropped as the three looked to each other, their smiles fading into companionable sadness. Astute as always, Monroe excused herself and led Zoe chiming and whistling back into the workroom. Alan waved to the little automaton as she disappeared. A pang rose in his chest, something he didn't recognise, but it felt like guilt, maybe sorrow. It didn't lessen when he turned to Anchorage who offered him a weak smile.

"I suppose I won't be seeing you for a long while," Alan said.

"No. I suppose not," the professor replied.

They nodded together for a while, lips taught and brows furrowed.

"Well then..." Alan rounded the desk, drawing close to his old friend and forcefully removed his hands from his coat pockets where he'd been fiddling with spent bullets and lint.

Anchorage's face turned to something like fear as Alan approached with a face as serious as Anchorage had ever seen it. He extended a hand to shake, or possibly to ward off his old friend, but Alan moved right past it and into Anchorage's personal space. Although his eyes were averted to some innocuous point at the side of the room, Alan swooped toward the professor and bound him in a fierce embrace. Anchorage retaliated with a pat on his friend's back which turned to reciprocation as the hug drew out a moment longer than he expected.

"Look after yourself," Alan muttered.

"Of—of course," Anchorage replied.

And as swiftly as he had advanced, Alan retreated right out of the office and the door clicked to the jamb.

DRAINED WASN'T THE right word to describe how Alan felt, but it was close. He kept thinking of himself like a bag of grain hung as a punching bag for the dockside brawlers. Hammered, his material worn thin in places, bleeding more and more of his filling with each hit.

He stepped out onto the street and hailed a steam cab. What he wanted was sleep, possibly food, and a steaming hot cup of very strong tea. He chuckled at that, climbing into the cab that drew beside him and barking a destination to the cabby. Not so long ago it would have been the bottle he thought about first. Now it was a hot cuppa. He shook his head as London whipped by outside the window.

"You really are knocking on, now."

Usually this would have been the perfect opportunity for Slay to chime in with some insult or other, but Alan remained unassailed all the way to Berkeley Square. Tossing the cabby some coin, he approached the door and knocked loudly. The same vulture of a butler answered.

"Wotcha," Alan blurted before the butler could caw some veiled insult. "Is her ladyship in?"

"Madame is taking breakfast in the conservatory—"

That was all he needed. With a rougher-than-necessary shoulder barge, Alan was inside and stalking at a fair pace toward the rear of the house where he hoped to god the conservatory was. Otherwise, he was about to look very stupid. He burst through the panelled glass doors with the butler ducking and diving behind him like a gull with only one good wing, trying to overtake Alan at every step. In the end he simply shouted over Alan's shoulder to announce him.

"Madame! Mister Shaw has arrived, once more uninvi—"

Alan shut the glass conservatory doors in the butler's face with a self-satisfied grin.

Helen dabbed the corner of her broad smile with her napkin and made as if to stand but Alan held out a hand to stop her.

"Don't get up," he said, and took the cast iron seat opposite her.

"You seem a little more like your old self this morning," Helen said, reaching across the table to pour Alan some tea. "I take it the case is going well?"

"All sorted," Alan said, gazing out through the terracotta pots and overlapping fronds of the conservatory's miniature jungle to the pristine lawn beyond the windows. "I thought you'd want to know that the Ministry was behind the whole thing. Trying to make the Mark Is look dangerous so they could replace them. Pretty boring when you get right down to it."

Helen nodded gravely. "Their greed never ends does it?"

"But the fellow responsible has been put away. Everything's moving in the right direction again. They even have a lady scientist running their research and development wing. They didn't have much choice in the end."

"Well, that's all turned out well, then," Helen said with a smile.

"Mostly," Alan replied.

They took a little breakfast together in the conservatory and drank tea until it was time for lunch, then they ate again and retired to the study to chat further. It was late afternoon by the time Alan made to leave and Helen reached across the occasional table covered in scone crumbs to put her hand on Alan's arm.

"Thank you for coming to see me, Alan," she said. "It really does mean a lot. You will come again, won't you?"

Alan looked at her confused for a second and smiled.

"Of course," he said, before kissing her hand and showing himself out, leaving Helen alone surrounded by wood panelling and dusty old books.

As he reached the door, the butler appeared like a wraith to open the door.

"Say," Alan said. "Where's Harrigan? Haven't seen him around lately."

The butler cast a look back over his shoulder, toward the study.

"Sir's responsibilities carry him far away and often for longer periods than we would like," he said. While his haughty demeanour didn't drop, it seemed to warm just a little. "Madame is frequently left to her own company."

Alan thought about turning around then, marching right back into the study and staying the rest of the day. He thought about ordering breakfast for himself at the Harrigan house every morning, and tea every evening. His mind raced with all the excuses that he could make to get Helen out of the house. And finally, he realised that he could do none of it. Because Helen was proud. And if she knew that Alan thought she was lonely or sad, she'd feel even worse for being a burden.

"Balls," he said.

"Indeed, sir," the butler replied.

"Listen, if she needs anything. Anything at all. If she gets too sad, or she gets ill, you come find me. I'll be visiting a bit more often."

The butler's face went taut with something approaching a

smile. "I will be keeping an eye on the post for your request to visit."

With a sigh and one last look toward the study, Alan headed out.

He walked home, marking the placement of all of his old friends on a map in his head, how the points moved away from him either geographically, socially or just mentally, and he wondered how it was that life could get so—

"Chaotic?" Slay said.

"And yet I can't seem to shake you at all," Alan replied.

"Life is chaos, old pal. Like peas on a drum, bouncing wherever the beat takes them. Some dance, some end up on the floor and roll out of sight. Still, we keep hammering away."

"Why do I feel like I'm the skin and someone else is holding the stick?" Alan asked.

Slay didn't seem to have an answer for that.

WHEN HE REACHED home, Alan went straight for the kitchen. Ignoring most of the cupboards so as not to disturb the spiders who built their civilisations there, Alan opened the only one that he thought of as his. There, a paper bag of sugar sat beside his only teaspoon and a cardboard carton of tea leaves. He began the mashing and boiling process, retrieving the milk from the refrigeration cabinet. The kettle was just beginning to whistle as a knock shook the front door. Alan regarded it suspiciously through the kitchen door and down the hallway. Removing the kettle from the hob with a sad lilting whistle that now reminded him of Zoe, he grabbed the revolver that he'd left on the dining table.

The knock came again, a little louder, and he stalked toward it.

"This better be a beautiful woman with a new leg or so help me god–" He yanked open the door and all the fight dropped out of him. "–Urm—do you actually have a new leg?"

Merry White stood on his doorstep, the flight goggles atop her head holding back her dark blonde chin-length waves. Alan took her in with a slack jaw. From her flight suit to her heavy duty boots, he swore that she hadn't changed a jot since he last saw her.

"Now then, you old sod," she said with a broad grin, her Northern accent just as warming to Alan's heart as ever. Her smile faded to confusion as Alan's jaw flapped without words. "You weren't expecting me were you? Do you still not check your bloody mail?"

Merry pushed past him and began searching the entrance hall. Alan followed her, spinning on the spot in silence, still half certain that he was imagining the whole thing. After a moment, Merry scooped to pick up the ignored envelope which had made its way into a corner in a series of door slammings and draughts. In one smooth motion she stripped the end from the envelope, flicked out the paper inside and handed it to him, exposing an official seal at the foot of the letter. Alan marvelled at the Letter of Marque; something he thought he'd never see again. That seal, this woman, his past made manifest in the entrance hall, it was a bit too much. He giggled.

"Pack your bags," Merry said with an excited grin. "We're off on a jaunt."

Letter of Marque delivered to Mister Alan Shaw on the 29th April 1972.

To those parties externally addressed,
With the receipt of this document, you are hereby

requested to attend upon work of the highest importance by this honourable office.

The matter in question is an investigation into reports of unexplained lights in the sky in and around the area of Witley, UK. There has also been a death from a mysterious cause connected with one such occurrence. The method of resolution will be left to your discretion.

According to our files on your previous exploits with this office, we think that this marque will be well suited to your expertise as will those of your partner in this matter, Meredith White, with whom you will be familiar. Await her arrival at your abode.

Yours faithfully,
Rook

Alan Shaw and the Ghostlight of Witley

1

May, 1872
Hyde Park, London

THERE WERE FEW things that still sparked childish excitement from Alan but one of them was Hyde Park pylon. Once the only place to dock an airship in the entire city, it was now one of many. Still, it had been Alan's first for so many things. His first Letter of Marque, his first adventure on an airship. He tried to brush away the memory of where it had taken him and instead focussed on the thrill of possibility that still filled the air above the park. The sight of the bulbous, circling zeppelins, the way that the propellers quivered the air, the promise of so many places that he could run to. And he had always longed to run away. His first dream had been to escape London and he had achieved it for a time. Now, as he looked up at the dirigibles and gliders and whirligigs, he felt that same exhilaration but something else as well, something far more disturbing. He didn't want to go. It had taken him some years but he'd come to the realisation that London was where he was supposed to be. No matter how far he ran or how well he hid, everything brought him back here. And there was another thing, illogical as he knew it to be: every time he'd left London something catastrophic had happened. His father had been murdered, he had lost the love of his life in the mountains of India, and unjustly killed a man. For someone who didn't believe in omens and portents, destiny and fate, the part of Alan who knew very well that the preternatural did exist feared that if he left, some fresh calamity would befall him.

Merry looked back at where Alan had faltered on the Hyde Park lawn between the roped off aisles filled with people from all over the world laden with baggage, children, and clutching tickets like little perforated lifelines.

"You alright?" Merry asked.

"Just thinking," he replied.

"Dangerous, that," Merry quipped and Alan made a show of smiling at her.

When he had needed a friend more than whiskey or sleep, Merry had flown into his life. And she had redeemed him. This time she needed him and despite his personal superstitions he'd be damned if he would let that debt go unpaid.

Merry led them to the foot of the pylon and flashed a booking slip to the operator who slid the steel doors closed behind them. First fiddling with his coat and scarf, he deftly navigated a series of levers that rotated the elevator's carriage in alignment with the correct docking branch above and they began to climb to the twang of well-oiled cables. London slipped away like a drowning child leaving only a bitter wind and the growing thunder of engines.

How the operators at the pylon's peak organised it all so that screaming metal death didn't crash down onto the city below was beyond Alan. But his faith in them was similar to his faith in Merry and her piloting skills. Neither had ever given him cause to doubt.

Reaching one of the pylon's lower branches, they alighted

from the elevator and were left alone on the steel gantry, hands gripping the railing. At the end of the gantry a glider waited with folded wings like a diving peregrine.

"You got a new glider?" Alan asked Merry as they drew near to the sleek machine.

"The old bird is still at home. She works fine for the desert but her bolts leak and welding moans when it's cold. She's a fair weather old girl, now."

"I know the feeling," Alan humphed.

The glider's side hatch, popped open and Merry ducked inside as she continued:

"This one is a little more England-proof but a tighter fit as well. No room to sleep in the back, not for two at any rate, so it's a good job we're not going far."

Alan followed her inside, noting the pared back design of the glider's insides, the lack of leather padding on the single rear bench, the sloping hull that would be easy to hit a head on. Merry strapped herself into the pilot's seat behind a console that looked flimsy to Alan's eyes. The old glider which had carried them around the world several times over had felt robust in its size and complexity. This new contraption had so few dials; the controls were a simple throttle and stick system, the sloping windows making it look like they were sat in a torpedo rather than a glider. Sitting himself in the co-pilot's chair, he reached underneath, grateful to find a little lever there, and slid himself as far back from the console as he could.

"You still scared of buttons?" Merry chuckled.

"We both know that you want me as far away from that console as I want to be, so less cheek," he replied.

With a smile, Merry started the launching sequence which had gone from stoking and cranking and calibrating to an ignition button that gave a sharp zap before a soft hum of energy tickled the soles of their feet.

"I'm all for progress," he said, squirming in his seat, "but these new electric engines are too damned quiet. You can't even tell if they're working."

"Let's find out," Merry said, and she yanked a lever.

The whole cockpit pitched violently forward as if the glider had spotted something tasty on the ground and as soon as Alan realised they were sliding forward, the glider had leapt free of its perch and was hurtling toward the Hyde Park lawn. He threw out his hands, pressing sweating palms against the bulkheads like a cat avoiding the bath as the ground swelled beneath them. Merry yanked back on the controls and the glider's wings jerked out into their full span, the nose pitching up, a throaty belch of engines dipping the tail behind them, their freefall shifting into a tree-scraping surge of flight that rattled Alan's teeth.

"Phew," Merry said with a devilish smirk.

Over the sea of slate and smoke, skimming between rooftops below and the bellies of circling airships that blocked the sun above, they passed beyond the London city limits and over the speeding meadows and drystone veins of the English countryside. Cauliflowers of sheep burst apart and cows eyed the speeding glider lazily.

"Flying over England is a nice change," Merry mused as she looked down at the cattle looking back. "African air is full of dust and sand. Emptying the filters is like tipping out your shoes after walking on the beach."

"Is that why you came home? Sand in the vents?" Alan asked so hard that he blunted the tip of the question.

Merry eyed him sidelong. "I just missed the green."

"Sure you didn't miss anything else?"

"If you mean you, then definitely bloody not," she said.

"Rook just has a sick sense of humour."

"Did he not have any jobs for you in Africa? The nearest one was all the way home?" Alan said, still kicking and screaming at the subject which might have been a castle wall for all Merry entertained it. He huffed. "Are we going to talk about it or not?"

"About what?" Merry asked, peering around the glider nonchalantly.

"The thing you're avoiding talking about."

Merry's mouth was taught, her squint seemed tighter than the morning sunshine called for.

"Ok," she said. "After you tell me who you were talking to last night. I could hear you through the wall."

She shot him a cocked eyebrow, daring him to deny it. It was like having his favourite gun turned on him. He fell quiet, unsure of how to share the insanity of Slay.

"I just talk to myself. Comes of living alone."

"Well we'll talk about the other thing when you're ready to talk about that as well," she said.

Alan shook his head. She had him.

"I'm guessing Rook sent you some directions," he said rather than letting Merry beat him into silence. "How long 'til we get there?"

"It'll only take an hour or so. There's an inn nearby where we should be able to get some food while we decide what to do. I thought we could make a loop of the place first," she said.

"Good idea. Once you're on the ground all those countryside towns look the damned same."

AS IT TURNED out, the small town of Witley wasn't spectacular from the air either. By lunchtime they had made a wide loop of both the town and its surrounding areas. Smothered on every side by woodland, Witley was trapped in a cul-de-sac of both nature and time. Thatched roofs were still the norm, and the same dirt roads that had been cut by cattle since the dawn of cows now saw the odd bicycle and even odder steam cab. The best part was that finding a place to land the glider was easy as pie with so many open meadows and swathes of scrub around the town. Soon they were traipsing through knee-high grass toward a tavern with a swinging sign, the only sure-fire symbol of hope in any century of English history.

Alan had lost count of how many White Harts he'd frequented over the years, matched only by the number of King's Heads and Red Dragons. But this one did have something extra special. Maybe it was the thatch, the way that it looked like the ground had been built around the ancient old place rather than the reverse, or the roaring fire under head-scratching eaves. The barman gave them a friendly smile and greeting as they entered, tossing a towel over his shoulder to give them his full attention. A woollen vest over a faded old necktie told them that he took his job as landlord possibly more seriously than he could afford.

"Visitors!" he said with a grin. "Always nice to see new faces around town. What can I get you?"

They took wobbly stools at the bar and the landlord took their hands in turn, shaking them with the big slab of meat he called a hand.

"Whatever's tapped?" Alan said, aiming the question toward Merry who nodded.

"Do you have anything on the hob?" she asked.

"Do we have anything on the hob!" the barman chuckled as he poured them an amber cider with a dribble of bubbles on top. "You bet we do. Only the best Mock Turtle Soup in

Surrey."

Alan wondered what might be mocking about it, but he didn't let on.

"We'll take two," he said.

The barman slid their ciders toward them and bustled away to prepare their food.

"Mock turtle soup," Merry repeated.

"Suppose it's hard to get serious turtle around here," Alan replied and picked up his tankard to clink it with Merry's. "To old times."

Merry rapped her tankard on his and spun in her seat to regard the room. "I've missed this. Africa is wonderful but there's nothing like coming home to a tavern and a pint."

"That's the difference between us, Merry. You get homesick and I've always been sick of home," Alan chuckled.

"You can't hate it that much. You stayed in the end," she said with a motherly tone.

Alan regarded the little floating bits in his cider and said: "Not by choice."

"Where else would you go?" Merry asked, cocking her head at him.

He didn't have an answer to that so he thought hard at his cider and let the question hang before saying: "So what's the plan? Spooky lights over the town. Ideas?"

"I suppose we ask around, keep an eye out, the usual."

The landlord returned with steaming ceramic bowls sprouting hefty chunks of bread from their deep brown liquid. Catching the end of their conversation, he handed them the soup with a look of faint worry.

"So that's what brings you," he said. "I doubted you were just passing through. Everyone nowadays goes straight to Guildford rather than here."

"You've seen them, these lights?" Merry asked.

"Many-a-time," the bartender replied sullenly. "Why don't you have your soup? We'll have a chat when you're nice and full."

There were chunks of something floating around in the soup; lumpy, spongy chunks that Alan couldn't identify. When he scooped one of them up with his slab of bread and slurped it down, he stopped caring what they were.

"This is the best soup I've tasted in ages," he said to the beaming landlord. "Promise you'll never tell me what's in it."

Locking his lips and throwing away the key, the landlord turned back to his work.

They had spent the better part of an hour in satisfied silence, their bowls wiped clean with the last of the bread and a second pint each. Alan sat with a faint smile on his face as he regarded the empty pub with a belly full of hot food and the edges of his mind feeling pleasantly fuzzy.

"We should probably find somewhere to stay," he said.

"You're more than welcome here, if it's a bed you need." The landlord chimed in. "Breakfast included of course."

Alan shrugged his indifference and Merry slid a banknote to solidify the deal.

"So these lights. Do they come every night?" Alan asked.

"No. Not every. But often enough that it has people worried." The landlord turned to them, leaning on the bar conspiratorially despite there being no one but them and the roaring fire to hear. "Now you listen to old Toby because I like you two and I wouldn't want to see anything happen to you. You want to take a look at the lights, that's fine. You stay right here and look west after sundown and maybe you'll catch a look. But stay here you must. Don't go wandering off into the woods that way. 'Specially not at night. And once you've had a look you head home nice and safe, alright? I don't want the death of nice visitors such as yourselves on my conscience, thankyouverymuch."

Alan gave the old landlord a smile that he actually meant. "Thanks for the warning, Toby, old mate."

Merry leaned in, as was their routine.

"Do you know what they are?" she asked, relying on the character of every barman she'd ever known to be unable to keep his mouth shut when it came to the gossip in his area. Toby was no more prepared than any other to brush off her prying.

"No one knows for sure. We all stay well enough away. We're not daft. And those who are don't live to tell the tale."

"The fellow who died? We heard about that," Merry said, referring to the glib mention in Rook's letter.

Toby nodded gravely.

"Just two nights past. That poor old frog, Jacque. Frenchman who runs the farm over the other side of the woods. Decided to take matters into his own hands and investigate. They found him in the woods next day."

The Privateers exchanged a hooded look of scepticism. This all sounded very much like the kind of local folklore that usually amounted to short sight and tall tales. Alan was ready to call this case an easy one and just enjoy the jaunt.

"Old fella was he?" Alan asked.

"He was a good old lad, sir," Toby said. "But I can hear your tone. Jacque didn't get lost in the woods like some bumbling old fart. When they found him– I shan't say in front of the miss. But it weren't natural how he went. Poor old frog."

"I wouldn't worry about that, Toby," Alan said. "We're privateers. Alan Shaw and Merry White. We've been sent to figure out what's going on."

Toby's jaw dropped and he looked between the two of them. "You're that orphan lad from that there London. Sorry miss, but your name doesn't ring a bell."

Merry rolled her eyes with a smile. "Living in his shadow, I am."

"So we've seen some pretty strange things," Alan said with a wink.

Toby leant over the bar, rapt. "I'll bet you have. Well in that case, tomorrow morning why don't I close up and take you to see the constable? You might be able to find Old Jacque's eyes. We never did."

The privateers exchanged a more serious look. Alan slid what remained of his cider back across the bar. He had a nasty feeling that he was going to need to have a clear head after all.

2

A QUAINT SPRING sunset washed Witley in shades of red. Sludgy shadows leaked from hedges and ditches to smother the village in rising night. Alan and Merry sat on the grass verge across from the White Hart on a blanket borrowed from Toby and waited to see something wondrous. They went through familiar old motions quietly, splitting some slightly stale bread and butter, passing paper packets of ham and cheese between them. Stars began to wink to life above and soon the sky was scattered with light. The warm glow of oil lamps from cottage windows did nothing to steal the starlight like tesla lamps did. Alan watched the stars for a while in silence while Merry chewed contentedly.

"For all the comforts of London it can never give you a sky like that," Alan said.

Merry made a sound of confirmation.

"You know what's funny, Merry?" Alan continued. "This is probably the closest thing I'll ever get to domestic bliss. Sat in a field in the middle of nowhere with a married woman." He laughed and shuffled his affected leg out straight. Speaking quietly, the silence playing out as he gathered his bravery, he said: "I missed my one shot at real happiness. Left her in India, just walked away. But I still think about her now and then."

"The woman you used to dream about?" Merry asked, suddenly more interested in the conversation.

"Still do," he said. "My dreams are like a scratched record. And when I'm awake I see ghosts." He chuckled with no feeling behind it and avoided meeting her eye. "You always said I was mad, Merry. I think you might be right. All the little slights and mistakes have driven me bonkers. I'm left in that ratty old house, checking corners for ghosts and arguing with myself because there's no one else to blame. Maybe I've been hit in the head too many times. Memories keep leaking out. And it's never the nice ones."

Merry put a hand on his and gave it a squeeze but he just kept on looking at the moon's lop-sided smirk.

"Why did you not send word, Al?" Merry asked. "After the wedding you just disappeared. No letter, no telegram. I heard about your dad through the bloody papers."

"I know," Alan muttered. But Merry wasn't done.

"If you'd have asked, I'd have come. We all would. Your friends. Your family."

"I know, Merry. I'm the only one stopping me. Stubbornness is just programmed into me."

"Bollocks," Merry chuckled. That snapped Alan's head back toward her. "You're not a bloody automaton, Alan. You're a person. Mistakes come with being one of those, you know. And sometimes things aren't even mistakes, sometimes things just…don't work out."

"Are we still talking about me?" he asked with a smile.

"I'll clock you one if you like," Merry said with a serious look.

"I'll be quiet."

"Is that who you were talking to the other night? Some old

ghost? Who was it?"

He could have broken his eyes away from her, looked back at the sky, checked the shadows for a spectre summoned by the mention of its name, but Alan kept on looking at his friend's earnest face like a little anchor to the better part of himself.

"Mister Slay. The one who killed Simon's father—"

"Your father," Merry corrected.

"—and gave me this limp." He rubbed his leg. "He...visited when I was healing and hasn't really left since."

There wasn't a shred of disbelief in her voice when Merry asked: "And you talk to him?"

"Sometimes." Alan said. His voice felt hot in his throat, like he was breathing sulphur.

Merry knew better than to talk when there was nothing to say and so she huddled a little closer to Alan until their shoulders touched and they sat together in silence as the air turned chilly and they had to wrap their coats around themselves.

There had been times over the course of his life when alcohol or opiates had shored up the ramshackle vessel that Alan called a body, overcoming injuries, keeping him moving, letting him continue in times of dire need where normal biology couldn't. It had led to differing results, sometimes just increasing the injuries in the long run when rest was ignored in favour of action, sometimes interesting hallucinations of sight and sound or a brief and pleasant narcotic dissociation. For a moment, as he sat on the grassy verge in Witley village with his friend by his side, he thought their cheese had perhaps gone off or the ham had been poisoned, because right before his eyes the sky started to bleed colours.

To the west of the town, just as Toby had said, it started as a single point of luminescence in the dark. Hot pink against the pale stars, it was difficult to see at first but it slowly grew brighter, banishing from the privateers' minds the thought that it could be airship lights, and continued to stretch from a point of light to an undulating halo of pink, then green, then electric blue over the course of a few minutes.

Tearing his eyes away, Alan spied back at the tavern and saw Toby in an upper window, the lights shifting on the glass, bathing the landlord in colour. All over the town, villagers stood in the dark, staring up from their vegetable patches while others had their curtains tightly closed against the lights, their houses cast into darkness as an antithesis to the spectacle.

The lights continued to billow outward, the halo expanding, shifting, as Alan turned back toward them. He couldn't help thinking that they reminded him of the Northern Lights that he'd seen from merchant ships as a boy, but he'd never heard of them appearing over England before.

"What do you think they are?" he said, but Merry didn't answer. From the corner of his eye he could see her looking up at the sky, rapt, but when he tried to turn to look at her, he found that he couldn't. He tried to say her name again but all that came out was the first letter as an elongated hum that he couldn't finish, and then the lights took Alan as well.

3

IN THE AFTERMATH of the phenomenon, the village came alive. Darkened windows were unhooded; lanterns were lit and carried out into the streets. The villagers of Witley gathered in muttering groups, casting wary glances up at the sky. Alan and Merry walked down the old dirt track into the village with Toby at their side. He had refused to let them go alone and they knew why when they walked past the first group of huddled villagers. Alan caught a snatch of the conversation and how swiftly it turned.

"Who's that then?"

"Never seem 'em before."

"Them's who landed the airship outside town earlier."

"They wearing any gold?"

"Look shifty to me."

Alan nodded to them jovially in an attempt to stop any thoughts of pyres or drownings. From the villager's scowls he didn't think he'd done well.

They managed to find a single village constable surrounded by the mob, turning on the spot as questions were catapulted toward him, clearly as lost as everyone else and sweating despite the evening's chill.

"Ridley, these folks are privateers—" Before Toby could finish, the constable swooped toward them.

"You're from the city?" Ridley begged. "You've come to help."

Alan produced his Letter of Marque. "That's right. We're here to find out what's going on and, if we can, fix it."

"See everyone! It's going to be fine," the constable shouted over his shoulder. "Just return to your homes and stay inside until morning." And when no one moved he added: "Please?"

That got some of them moving but, in true mob style, the angriest were the last to go. They were soon left with a single old widow, two burly poachers who were trying to hide the pheasants they held behind their backs, and the constable. The widow brandished her hand at the constable.

"Gone!" she barked, waving her hand. Something had worn a divot in her ring finger over time, something that was no longer there. "It's gone. The last thing I had of him. And Elizabeth's locket before it." She pointed to the sky. "They're here for our gold, I tell you. Every time they come, something else gets stolen."

"I know, Mrs Ramsey, I know," the constable placated.

"Who are?" Alan asked, interrupting her tirade. "Who's stealing your gold?"

"Sir, please don't encourage them," the constable said.

"Never ignore the locals," Alan said. "Not in my line of work."

The constable looked to Merry who backed Alan up by continuing the questioning in a softer tone: "What was taken, love? And what do you think it is that took it?"

The rage seemed to drain out of the old widow and left only sadness. "The woodfolk. Little people. Fairies. They took my wedding ring. They know!" she pointed to the poachers who visibly took a step backward. "They've seen the circles in the woods."

Merry turned to the sheepish looking fellows as the constable rolled his eyes and half turned away.

"It's just chat," one poacher said.

"Tavern stories," said the other.

"Then tell us," Alan replied. "If it doesn't matter, anyway."

The first poacher visibly swallowed and took a deep breath to speak. "Not many people will go into the woods because they're supposed to be full of fairies. You know, they take people away? We've seen the circles because we go...hunting there."

"Hunting. Right," Alan said. "Can show us these circles?"

The poachers exchanged looks and it was the second who spoke. "In the morning, maybe. We're not going in there tonight."

"Tomorrow it is, then," Alan said with a nod.

THE HUSHING BOUGHS and shifting sunlight through the trees almost washed away all thoughts of the previous night. Constable Ridley had come along with the poachers, Miles and Lenny, and they snaked their way from the village, the poachers leading the way from spot to spot to show the fairy circles that they had spoken of the previous night. Many were unspectacular, just loose rings of mushrooms or small stones. As they gathered around another, a deep hole in the bole of an ancient old oak, Merry inspected where silver coins that had been driven edge-first into the wood around the hole, presumably to stop anything fairy-like from escaping. The tip of each coin had been snapped off.

"Who owns these woods?" Alan asked as he looked around.

Lenny and Miles could have been twins for all he could tell the difference between them, so he had no idea which one answered.

"Well, it's complicated—"

Alan threw up a hand. "I don't care whose rabbits you're stealing. I just want to know who owns the land."

"It's an estate owned by the Chandlers. Now it is, anyway. This bit of land has been handed from toff to toff for centuries," Probably Miles said.

"Yep. It stretches from here to Old Jacque's place on the other side. One big house. Three big lakes and lots of woods," Constable Ridley offered, still beaded with sweat as the night before but now there were actual droplets running from his peaked hairline to his chin. He looked like he hadn't slept a wink. "But they rarely use it for anything. There isn't much left of the Chandlers, now. I reckon it'll get handed to someone else before long."

"Not much left of them?" Merry asked, returning from her inspection of the tree bole.

"Just old lady Chandler rattling around the big house," the constable replied, sounding out of breath.

"Are you alright, Ridley?" Alan asked. "You look off colour."

The constable wiped his brow and ran his sleeve along the waterfall of his top lip.

"I'm alright," he said. "Just a little out of sorts lately is all."

Alan humphed and turned to Merry. "Find anything?"

"Not really. The hole was just a hole," she replied. "Found the bottom a couple of feet down."

"Well it does happen occasionally," Alan replied.

"Not to us," she laughed.

The constable looked from one to the other. "You can't be

taking this fairy talk seriously."

"Not anymore," Alan said.

They wandered a little further together, the trees eventually breaking to reveal a wide lake surrounded by woods on every side. The lake was the same English grey as the sky, and a stiff wind made the water seem hassled, eager to be somewhere downwind. With the occasional stir of animals in the undergrowth behind them and the lap of water on the gravel shore, even with the braying of a mallard nearby it was one of the briefest moments of peace and quiet that Alan had experienced in a very long time.

"I could live here," he said to Merry who stood regarding the treeline, the lake, the sky.

"You'd be bored in a heartbeat and you know it," she replied.

He made a noncommittal hum.

"Over here's where we found old Jacque," Ridley said, leading them to a spot like any other down by the water. The sweating had slowed to a light shower but his skin had turned ashen pale as he regarded the spot where the old farmer had been found. He took a heavy sigh before adding: "Eyes popped like raspberries, his old cavalry helmet melted to his head, rifle and bayonet still in his hands as if he'd fought the Devil himself."

Alan crouched with difficulty to regard the ground while Merry studied the water, the trees, and finally the sky.

"Hmmm. Right," Alan said, unfazed by the description. He poked the smooth stones and sand with his finger, the lake water seeping up to fill it straight away. "And no one saw anything?"

"We all did. The lights was up in the sky," Probably Lenny offered. He'd been silent for the most part, looking into the woods or eyeing the water, jumping at every snap of twig.

"What's that?" Merry asked, pointing to a spot in the middle of the lake where a statue stood with the water lapping over its toes.

The poachers chuckled between themselves as the constable replied:

"That's one of Chandler's bright ideas. This whole estate is covered in follies and fancies. Weird buildings, odd towers, stupid statues. That's why they're broke." Every word seemed to drag too much breath from Ridley and as he finished his sentence, he puffed out his cheeks and bent over, hands on knees, to regard the ground. "Spent– all their money."

Alan bent beside the constable, a hand on his back, and regretted it. The constable threw up his breakfast, scrambled eggs splashing onto the shoreline. Ridley retched again and another offering to the ground spewed out.

"Bloody hell, Constable," Alan said. "You should have said if you weren't right."

"I think you should get yourself home," Merry said. "Can you take him, lads? We'll be fine out here now you've shown us the way. Why don't you tell everyone that we've found no fairies or anything like that and have them prepare to stay indoors tonight, just to be safe?"

"We'll do what we can, Miss," Miles replied, "But you know what they're like."

"Do your best, eh?" Merry replied with a wink.

As Ridley wretched again, this time producing nothing but spittle, the poachers took an arm each and carried him off toward the village at a snail's pace.

"I thought he was just..." Alan began, but he felt so bad for misjudging the constable that he faltered.

"A bit of a flop? So did I. Thought he was just turned sick

at the thought of the farmer. Looks like he's had some bad eggs," Merry replied. "I reckon we can handle a nice walk on our own, don't you?"

A STEADY STROLL took the privateers along the thin gravel beach which separated water from woods, accompanied only by the sounds of gentle nature. This was how they spent much of their time over the last couple of days since Merry had arrived on Alan's doorstep, not quite alone but happy in their silence together, punctuated by brief, companionable chat when a thought arose but neither forcing it to happen. This time it was Merry who broke in with such a thought.

"I'll admit it's an odd one and I'm not saying it isn't fun gallivanting around again but I was hoping—"

"For some explosions?" Alan said as Merry tailed off.

"Just one or two," she replied, an almost child-like pout on her lips that Alan remembered well.

"We'll have to settle for a nice safe mystery instead. This is more my speed these days," he replied with a chuckle.

"Give over. You'll never slow down and you know it."

"Running right 'til the end."

"You and me both, mate," Merry replied and turned her smile out to the glistening lake. "Although there might still be something in it. That old farmer didn't die from nothing at all."

"Something that mesmerises townsfolk, steals gold trinkets, and would kill the old man for spotting it."

Merry nodded thoughtfully. "But what *is* it?"

"Monster, probably. Like that troll in Paris."

"God, I hope not," Merry said, sticking out her tongue in disgust.

Alan had lost many moments in his life, only spotting them in hindsight. Moments when he was being a smartarse and should have kept his trap shut; moments of silence when he should have been talking. This felt like the latter.

"So how come you're out in the middle of the English nowhere with the smell of—" he sniffed the air, "—possibly cowshit but I'm not discounting pig, with some crotchety old fart you used to know?" he asked.

"Has your memory gone in your old age?" Merry replied.

"I don't mean the Marque. Or maybe I do. I mean, how come you're back into privateer work? We've both been avoiding talking about it. You had a cushy number flying sick folk around with Doctor Husband. But you're not there. You're here."

"And you want to talk about this now?" Merry said incredulously.

"Well we're not doing anything else." He gestured to the woods, the lake, and an abundance of overcast sky, all of it leaving plenty of room for a little conversation. "We can wait until someone else turns up and get them involved as well if you like. Maybe Toby."

"You're insufferable," Merry sighed.

"Yet, here you are. Suffering me."

Merry stopped walking and readjusted her goggle headband as if it were the most important thing in the world. When that was done she dropped her hands with a sigh, the sound of them slapping her thighs startling a nearby duck into flight.

"I just needed a change, that's all," she said. "Flying Lucian around is…quiet."

"Boring?"

"Yes. Fine. Boring," Merry snapped. She cleared her

throat, catching herself, and purposefully softened. "He's wonderful. But he wants a hardworking, quiet life. And I can't just be a-a side dressing to that."

"Side dressing?" Alan said with a snort of laughter.

"Yes, I feel like a bloody salad, Alan," she said, hands bunched by her sides. "Limp, cold, drizzled in something to try and make it more interesting. I was brought up in the air corps. I need steak. And chips."

"Makes perfect sense to me," Alan said with an earnest nod.

Merry's hands went slack, her shoulders drooped, and she laughed. "Aren't we a pair?"

"Like bookends," Alan said and offered her the crook of his elbow. "Back to back, holding up the world."

Merry took his arm with a chuckle and said: "Right. Bookends."

Rounding the lake's bend, they came into view of the house that Ridley had described and Alan knew that the constable had been right. The Chandlers had to be bonkers. Where the building had begun, it was impossible to tell. It could have been the immense building's Tudor style end with its exposed timbers and high peaked roofs, but Alan thought that section actually looked younger than the immense Georgian mansion to which it was attached on one side and which made up the central section of the insane building's facade. The emotionless observatory tower also attached to the Tudor dwelling was an eyesore and the twin domes of the mansion's other end looked more like they would have suited an extension of Notre Dame than an English manor. The host of oddly shaped chimneys and stone pavilions scattered around the gardens like bird seed led Alan to one conclusion:

"This fella didn't have his head screwed on right."

"Bloody hell. What an eyesore," Merry replied.

They wandered closer, picking out more odd details and flourishes as they went; crenulations fit for a castle stuck on to the central manor like an afterthought, the domes' copper roofs with their heavy coating of oxidised green. They were close to the building when their first true trial began. There had to be seven or eight doors to the place, and those were just the ones they could see. They had knocked on several and were banging on the mansion house's large oak set when a voice came from behind them.

"Can I help you?"

They turned to regard a middle-aged gentleman in head to toe tweed, hands in pockets and a confused look on his spectacled face. The glasses' thick lenses reflected the sunlight so that they cast shifting motes of light across his face and made it impossible to see his eyes behind them.

"We're privateers," Alan offered and displayed his Letter of Marque which the man ignored. "Alan Shaw and Merry White. Just wondered if we could ask you a few questions. Mister Chandler is it?"

The gentleman's face broke into a smile which, while warm, was rendered maniacal by the insect-like glow of his spectacles.

"What a rare delight to have visitors." Gesturing for them to follow, he led them toward the Tudor section of the house, moving like a heron, all spindly legs and elbows tucked tightly to his sides. It seemed that the occupants were as strange as their home.

4

THE CHANDLER MANSION hid a modern interior behind its many faux-ancient facades. Chandler led them through what looked like an inner city townhouse complete with wood panels and thick curtains, filled with furniture stacked and unused, vases poking from boxes, and things ready to be packed. The whole place seemed eerily outside of time and space, things plucked from previous eras without thought for the whole aesthetic. Chandler caught the privateers pondering and said with an embarrassed cough:

"I'm afraid that my father's projects have left very little of the family fortune. None, actually. We're having to sell a few knick-knacks to keep the place running. Auction houses in Guildford have shown keen interest in my father's…eclectic collection, and hopefully we'll be back on an even keel soon."

Alan and Merry nodded to each other behind his back, some of the oddness finally explained.

They were led past a sweeping regency period staircase that hung in a hall like ascending dinosaur bones and through a mismatched door at the hall's opposite end.

Penetrating from the ground floor all the way up to the eaves of the roof itself, surrounded by a mezzanine and with walls filled with crowded bookcases, Alan had seen smaller libraries than the Chandlers' study. He scanned the leather bound tomes, the open and unlit fireplace, the narrow lattice windows, and his mind felt like it was stretching into dimensions it wasn't designed to fill.

Merry's yell cut across the room, shattering the silence.

Alan spun around to where Merry stood, rooted to the spot, hands over her mouth, staring at the corner of the room. He followed her gaze and took a shocked step back with one hand on his revolver. A figure stood stock still like a noon shadow, facing the bookcase, its form hidden by the sweeping black mourning dress it wore.

"Oh my word," Chandler said. "I'm so sorry." He darted across the room to grasp the figure by the shoulders.

Alan scrunched up his face, his head turning away but his eyes fixed firmly on the figure as it was turned around, his imagination firing off in hideous directions. When the pleasant face of the old woman was revealed, he gave a steadying breath.

"Mother, you know not to wander around on your own. It's dangerous," Chandler sang to the woman who looked around the room, at the privateers, and finally at Chandler as if surprised to find herself there.

Merry puffed out her cheeks and rolled her eyes at Alan who gave a nervous laugh.

"Who are you? If I'd known you were coming, I'd have prepared tea," the widow said to Chandler.

"It's George, mother. I'm your son."

"You don't look like yourself, George," the widow said dreamily.

Chandler turned to Alan and Merry with a sheepish smile. "The spectacles often confuse her. Old age comes to us all, does it not? Why don't we all take a seat."

One by one they sat, with Chandler puppeteering his mother into an armchair. He looked from one face to the other almost apologetically. "I'm afraid mother has a muddled mind. She relives yesterdays over and over. Never too sure what she's doing today, though. It must be nice. I'm afraid the present can be rather boring."

"Today is turning out pretty interesting," Alan muttered.

Chandler let out a laugh in one short breath. "I suppose you're right. Mother can't really talk to you much. She drifts in and out but she's mostly out these days. Please make yourselves comfortable," he said. "I'll go and make some tea."

"I'll help," Merry said, jumping up.

"How kind," Chandler replied, holding open the library door and waving Merry through.

Finding himself alone with the widow Chandler who searched the air for something that even she seemed uncertain of, Alan decided to wander the shelves for a while rather than sit in rigid silence. He had reached a section on folklore and was drawing out a volume with a purple cover when he leapt out of his skin again.

"I wonder if I'm in any of these," the widow said, so close that her chin almost rested on Alan's shoulder. She reached past him, taking the book from his fingers and turned it this way and that.

"Nope. You're right here with me," Alan said politely.

"A pity. I would like to be a story," the widow said and slid the volume back in the wrong place.

"What would you be about?" Alan asked, easily slipping into the role of humouring her. But the widow simply walked away, sweeping her long black skirts through the room, and began to cluck and call for a pet which wasn't there.

To her back, Alan said: "So you see things too, eh? What a

pair. But you've got your boy, at least."

"She seems nice," the widow said, talking to Alan with the same tone as the invisible cat as if both were equally real to her.

Alan gave her a curious look. "Merry? The woman who was just here?"

"You should ask her to stay," the widow replied with a caring smile.

Alan opened his mouth to answer but the widow cut him off.

"We have so many rooms, George. And you have need of a wife. What should happen to the house if there are no more Chandlers left? Who would make this old place their home if not your children and theirs?"

"Bloody hell," Alan said. "You had me going there for a minute."

The widow returned to him, placing her hands on the sides of his face and her motherly smile dissolved into concern as she carefully read his eyes.

"Make sure you come back safely," she said.

Alan took her hands gently and removed them from his cheeks. "Don't worry, love. He'll be back in a mo."

"No," the widow said, the tears in her eyes bringing a lump to Alan's throat. "I don't think he will."

"SOME SAY THAT old houses have character," Chandler said as he led Merry through the entrance hall filled with boxes of heirlooms, past a cloth-wrapped grandfather clock like a penny dreadful spirit, and to the rear of the house where the corridors narrowed. This part of the house seemed purposefully gothic with the bare stone walls and pointed arch alcoves. Chandler senior had made sure that any servant using these passages would feel thrown back in time. The aesthetic continued through to a stone-floored kitchen outfitted with rough wooden work spaces and an ancient range capable of feeding hundreds.

"If that's true," he continued, "this old place must have multiple personalities. Built by a madman and haunted by a woman who has lost her mind, just little old me rambling around in it."

Merry thought she caught a hint of humour in Chandler's voice to cover the sadness of his family reduced to nothing in the space of a generation.

"It's a beautiful old place," she said.

He smiled at her graciously but they both knew a polite lie when they heard one.

Chandler clearly only ever used a small area of the kitchen for himself and his mother. There were certainly no servants that Merry could see. He pottered from shelf to stove, boiling water and steeping the tea before placing it all on a tray while Merry collected milk and sugar cubes from around the room at Chandler's direction. On their return, they found Alan lounging in a wingback chair, drumming his fingers, the widow haunting the edges of the room in swishes of black fabric.

"Mother, I've brought tea," Chandler announced.

With the cock of a head and a moment of bunched confusion on her face, the widow succumbed to this new reality and drifted over to take a seat with them.

"You were in the army then?" Alan asked.

Chandler looked shocked and paused in the middle of handing out teacups. "What makes you say that?"

"Your mother mentioned you going away and I guessed," Alan replied.

"Ah, I see. It was the navy actually."

With tea in hand and everyone settled in, Chandler sighed heavily and with eyes averted down at his teacup, he said: "Was there anything in particular that you want to ask me about? I'm afraid that there isn't much to draw the interest of privateers on the estate."

"We're investigating the lights in the sky," Merry replied. "Have you seen them?"

Chandler paused, cup in hand, and searched the air above his head for a memory. "No," he said finally. "I can't say that I have. I'm usually quite busy around the house." Alan and Merry had years of experience in carefully saying nothing and so, although they exchanged a look, they remained silent, letting Chandler go on. "Mother keeps odd hours nowadays, and so must I."

Alan humphed and changed tactics. The lights could be seen for miles around and the estate was even closer to them than The White Hart. "It must have been tough giving up a naval career for one in nursing."

"It wasn't as much of a sacrifice as you might think. I wasn't on track to the officer's mess. I was actually part of a small research retinue aboard a patrol vessel. We would perform research tasks based on the interests of the Royal Institute during any given week. Observation of arctic animals and whales, or ice floes and suchlike.

"Unfortunately our last patrol was cut short when we came across a Russian submersible. Perhaps they had been cut off for a long time, or they didn't get the message about the hostilities being over. I rather think that they wanted some kind of revenge and saw our ship as a way to even the score a little. In short, we were sunk and many of us captured. Luckily that didn't last long, although a few more of the crew were lost to the cold in captivity. Our freedom was negotiated for, the submersible crew were punished for risking a breakdown of the Paris Treaty, and we returned home. That was when I got news of father dying in my absence. So I returned home." Chandler took a deep breath and a sip of his tea.

"What about the death of the old farmer on your land? Know anything about that?" Merry asked, saccharine sweet.

Chandler's eyes grew wide, his tea pausing on the edge of his lips. "A death – my word, no. I had no idea. We're completely cut off from contact with the town. There are a lot of bad feelings between the locals and my father. He made an awful mess of the countryside, taking down hills and making lakes, building his little fancies all over the grounds. The local folk never did agree with it. They think there are fairies on this land, can you believe it? And that father had somehow angered them with his landscaping. Everything I need, I order from Guildford. I certainly hadn't heard about any death. No one said a thing."

Alan eyed their host while his brain whirred. Constable Ridley wasn't the sharpest and with no family of the Frenchman to ask questions, it was quite plausible that the old farmer had just been dealt with and nothing had gone any further. He looked at Chandler's hands, his glasses, his shoes where a walk on the beach had left a sandy tideline, and finally at the insane house. None of it really rang out as a murderer's set-up. The fact that Merry wasn't throwing questions at him, trying to catch him off guard, told him that she probably felt the same way.

"Who are you?" Widow Chandler interrupted. Standing up, her eyes flitted from one to the other and there was no recognition there at all. Her voice became harsh, her breath ragged. "Why are you in my home? Get out, all of you. Don't come back here without an invitation!"

Chandler shot up from his seat and tried to steady his mother by the shoulders.

"Mother, it's alright. Calm down. These are nice people," he said.

"I will not calm down. Not on the word of strangers in my house. Get out, I said!" the widow demanded and she began to struggle against Chandler's calm embrace.

He looked at them over his shoulder, a pleading look in his eyes.

"Perhaps you should go. She is easily exhausted by visitors," he said. "She needs her rest."

"Of course," Merry said, tapping Alan on the knee to get him moving. "We'll show ourselves out."

They retreated to the sound of Chandler talking in hushed tones to his mother. As they left the mansion behind and took a vague direction back to Witley, Alan couldn't help but feel like the jaunt had given them nothing but a cup of tea and a stroll.

"Any fresh ideas?" he asked.

Merry gave an uncertain hum. "'Fraid not. I guess we wait for tonight and see if it happens again."

5

"**A**RE YOU KIDDING?" Merry chuckled, turning the leather contraption back and forth in her hands. Adapted from horse tack, it was certainly robust.

"It was the best I could do on short notice, alright?" Alan said sullenly. He pulled his set of blinkers onto his head and began turning this way and that. With the broad leather visor in place, he was unable to see much at all from above or the sides. "I think the saddler did pretty well to make it fit our heads."

Merry burst out laughing somewhere beyond the leather barrier.

"You look a proper picture," she said. "But they should work."

"Crude but effective," Alan replied. "I'll let you make your own joke."

Both wearing their blinkers, they looked around the open field across from The White Stag, chuckling between themselves.

"Don't you two look a pair," Toby chuckled, startling them both. The privateers swung their heads around toward him and he broke into full laughter at the sight of them. "Do you think those things might work?"

"I'm hoping it will let us move around without being mesmerised. If we can keep from looking directly at the lights, that is," Alan said.

"Well I never would have come up with that," Toby answered, still holding in little chuckles.

"We're professionals," Merry said with a smile, and that set the barman off laughing again.

"Did everyone agree to stay indoors?" Alan asked.

Toby wiped a tear from his eye and managed to compose himself before saying: "It wasn't easy, but I think so."

"Thanks Toby. You stay indoors too, right?" Alan said. "Me and Merry need to get in position."

THE SUN DROPPED swiftly over the forests of Witley as the privateers trudged through the twilight foliage, marking their way with the fairy rings that the poachers had shown them that morning. By the time the sky had darkened to a dusky grey-blue, they were in a small clearing, scanning the sky for the first signs of emerging colour. Merry swung her binoculars back and forth; Alan turned in circles until his neck ached and he was dizzy. Both had their blinker devices hung from their belts, ready to apply as soon as they saw anything.

The cricket choir of dusk faded into the silence of midnight, punctuated only by an owl's infrequent hooting. In the undergrowth, small beasts went about their nightly scavenging, and still the privateers waited.

"It's not coming," Alan sighed.

Merry lowered her binoculars and rubbed her eyes. "Doesn't look like it. I suppose two nights in a row was a little much to expect."

"Toby seemed pretty certain that it came regularly."

"But without knowing what it is, we're looking for a pattern with only half the picture."

Alan humphed and perched himself on a fallen tree.

"Wait," Merry said, swinging her binoculars across the sky one last time. "There."

And there it was. A single pinprick of light that grew, expanded, the pale white of pure light giving way to waves of glowing pink.

The privateers grabbed for their blinkers, pulling them on and darting to their feet. Turning carefully from a patch of open sky to where they could see the faintest pink glow just beyond their blinkers, they set the expanding aurora to their right and then looked down at the ground.

"Ready?" Alan said.

"Ready."

And they were off, staring at the ground as they moved through the forest as fast as they could, using the very edges of the glow beyond their blinkers and a little guesswork to guide them as the colours shifted from pink to green. Merry was swifter, more sure-footed. Alan's cane slowed him down, causing him to trip and stumble on assassin roots in the dark. But soon they burst from the treeline, their feet crunching on the gravel of the lake's shoreline. Alan scanned the beach.

"We must be close," he said. "This is where they found Jacque."

"Alan. Don't look at the water," Merry gasped.

The entire lake from edge to edge reflected the auroras above, the shifting patterns made even more shimmering by the ripple of the water. To shield her eyes from the ethereal lights which shifted through turquoise to electric blue, Merry looked along the beach instead. Alan fought the urge to look up, an itch he was desperate to scratch. Instead, he stared actively down at his feet.

"There has to be something around here," he said. "Something causing it."

"Now we know it's over the lake, maybe we should come back in the light," Merry said. "There's no good searching when we can't even look for fear of getting mesmerised."

"What if it isn't here in the day? We didn't spot anything earlier—"

Alan's back arched violently, crackles of energy rippling through his hands and into his cane, sparking into the ground. The blast lifted him up onto his toes for a brief second of impossible ballerina-like grace before every muscle in his body went slack at once, slamming him into the ground with barely a groan.

Merry yelled his name and dropped to her knees beside Alan, her hands hovering in the air above him, opening and closing her fists, unsure whether to touch him or not, whether to risk the same fate in order to help. The crunch of boots on gravel drew her attention away from her friend to where a thin shadow stepped out of the forest. One of its hands crackled and popped with electricity, and as it stepped out into the light, the aurora's colours danced over its oily black body, reflecting them around itself. And in the large fly-like discs of its eyes, the mesmerising pink and green and blue eddies held Merry captive as it stepped toward her.

6

"SWAMP GAS?" CONSTABLE Ridley said with incredulity.

With the aurora faded for the night, the folk of Witley had taken to the streets once more in defiance of all advice. The privateers stood surrounded by lanterns and curious faces on all sides.

"Pure and simple," Alan replied. "Nothing to it and nothing to be done. Swamp gas rises and catches the light. Makes for some pretty colours but nothing to worry about at all. As long as everyone is careful and stays inside when the lights are up, they shouldn't give you any trouble."

The crowd murmured. Looks were exchanged.

"And you might want to check who *wasn't* mesmerised by the lights," Merry added. "Someone who kept their curtains closed is likely to be your thief, taking advantage of the trance to steal their neighbour's things."

The murmuring grew louder. The Whitley residents started eyeing each other in the dark, questioning, and a few started backing away from each other.

"What about Old Jacque?" Toby asked.

Alan paused for a second to think and finally said: "Freak

accident. Static from his gear and the lake water. Electrocuted himself."

Even Toby's face fell at that. "That seems a bit...unlikely. No offence," he said.

"We've seen stranger, believe me," Alan replied with a shrug.

Merry turned to address the townsfolk whose mutterings were beginning to rise.

"There are no fairies in the woods. And nothing sinister going on with the Chandlers. Other than them being a bit eccentric. Everyone can rest easy. Just go about your business and think nothing of it."

"And we'll be off, then," Alan said. Without another word, he shouldered his way through the bewildered crowd, gave Toby a companionable nod, and headed toward the glider with Merry in tow. He turned to her with a smile and said: "Job well done."

"Job well done," she echoed.

The glider was as much as they'd left it; the grass they had blown flat on landing had recovered itself so that the airship looked even more like a sleek animal hunched in the long grass.

Alan strapped himself into the co-pilot seat as Merry began her pre-flight checks. He stared out at the fields around them, the roofs of Witley peeking over the berm of the hill and the distant treeline beyond all bathed in moonlight. They would be home by the time the sun rose. He smiled to himself. He felt satisfied for the first time in as long as he could remember. He had done a good job and the mystery was solved. The only downside was this horrid ache in his back as if every muscle had gone into spasm while he slept, but even that was something to chuckle away. At least he'd lived this long, despite all odds, to get to a ripe age where aches and pains were a minor inconvenience of advancing years rather than coming after some heavy beating, explosion or high fall.

"Ready?" Merry asked.

"Ready for my own bed," he replied. "And it's always nice to receive Rook's money in the mail. Bills paid for a few months at the very least."

The tesla ignition zapped to life and the engines whirred up to speed. Gripping the controls, Merry paused, a look of consternation crossing her face as she gazed out of the window.

"Did we forget something?" she said.

"I don't think so," Alan replied and counted off his fingers. "Me, you, glider. Home."

Merry shook her head with a laugh. "I think I just had my first senior moment."

Alan barked a laugh. "There are many more where that came from, believe me."

As they were laughing, Toby's head rose above the hill's crest; he waved to them with both arms, drawing their attention, and they could see that he was laden with a pair of duffle bags, red in the face, and sweating.

The privateers exchanged looks.

"Did we just forget to pick up our kit?" Alan said.

"Told you we forgot something!" Merry answered. "Senior moment my arse."

Sliding open the glider's side door, they peered down to the beetroot-faced and panting Toby.

"Wotcha," Alan said. "Thanks for bringing our bags for us. Forget our heads if they weren't screwed on."

He reached down to the barman who took a step away. Still out of breath he said: "Would you just step down for a moment? I think something might be wrong."

"Wrong?" Merry asked. "Like what?"

"Just step down, if you don't mind," Toby said.

"But we're going home," Alan replied.

"Job well done," Merry added.

"Just for a second," Toby said, his breath finally catching up with him. He had a stern look on his face that Alan hadn't thought the friendly barman was even capable of making. "Please?"

The privateers paused on the glider's threshold, neither moving, barely breathing, staring down at the barman with the same confused look.

"You can't, can you?" Toby said.

Alan opened his mouth to contest but found it difficult to do so. He rubbed the ache in the small of his back with his fist.

"Bugger," Merry finally said. "We've been mesmerised haven't we?"

Toby smiled at her. "Good lass."

"I haven't been—" Alan began, and then caught himself rubbing his back again. "Bugger. I got bloody electrocuted."

"You both seemed so happy to be in the pub and relaxing and then you were so eager to be gone again," Toby said. "It just didn't seem right. Then there were your bags. One person forgetting their bag I can believe. But both of you? Not in a month of Sundays. I knew something had to be wrong."

Merry massaged her forehead. "Ugh. Headache."

"Me too," Alan said, closing one eye against a fresh migraine. He looked down at the ground where Toby stood with their things like a scruffy concierge and tried to will himself to jump down. When nothing happened, he settled for sitting on the door's edge, feet dangling over the ground which seemed an insurmountable distance away. "Toby, go tell everyone to stay inside. This thing isn't over."

TOBY RETURNED AT a dead run to find Alan stood a little way from the glider, vomiting into the tall grass, and Merry starfished in the field, holding on to the ground as if it might shake her off, eyes scrunched closed and breathing in long, slow draughts.

"Trouble!" Toby wheezed.

Alan held up a finger to the barman and vomited again.

"Oh, someone's going to be in trouble," he rasped when he was done. "Deep, deep trouble."

"I told Ridley what had happened to you and the idiot blabbed. Told the whole town that you were coming back. Well, they won't wait. They're headed to the Chandler place to sort this all out themselves."

"Sodding, bloody arse," Merry groaned and rolled over. After trying for a few moments to get to her feet, she gave up and crawled the short distance to the glider where Toby helped her climb in. Groaning and swaying to counteract the spinning of the earth around him, Alan made his way over, stopping to wretch one more time before clambering in behind her.

"I—I actually feel better," he said.

"Probably because we're back where we were told to be. The dizziness must be a punishment for fighting the mesmerism," Merry said, colour returning to her face as she settled into the pilot's seat.

"And we thought that Ridley was just ill. The creature must have had a go at him as well. This thing is smart. It knows that it can't get away with just killing a policeman and some privateers. It has to send us away, convince us that everything is fine. Toby," Alan added, "head home and stay inside, okay?"

The barman nodded and put some distance between him and the spinning turbines as the glider started to rock and rise off the ground.

"And Toby," Alan continued, shouting over the vibrating air. "Thanks mate."

The barman gave a wave as the glider lifted away with Alan standing in the doorway to feel the breeze against his clammy face. Unhooking the brass halo headset from beside the door and slipping it on, he addressed Merry through the headset:

"Can you remember anything, yet?"

"Bits and pieces," she said, her voice tinny and buzzing in his ear. "I remember you dropping and then this—this thing. Shiny black skin and big eyes. And then we were talking to the villagers."

"What the hell is this thing, Merry?"

"Maybe it lives in the lake. Maybe the Chandlers really did disturb something when they changed the landscape."

"Like a Jenny Greenteeth?"

"God, I hope not. If I find out they're real as well, I'll never swim again."

Witley dropped away below and the stars swelled above as the glider took a low run across the village. Alan hung out of the glider, hair whipping into his face and one hand braced on the glider's door. He scanned the silver-lit darkness below, searching breeze-stirred thatch and vegetable patches for signs of movement. But the village seemed silent, still.

"They're way ahead of us," he said.

"I'm heading for the Chandler place," she replied, and the glider swung around to head out over the forest.

"I'm getting a bad feeling here, Merry," Alan said.

Merry's headset popped and hissed as if she'd started to reply but had then fallen silent. Alan shuddered. It was a bad omen when even Merry couldn't think of anything positive to say. And sure enough, as the Surrey forest whipped away below, he saw what he had feared.

7

THE TREETOPS ROCKED and groaned as Merry blasted by, the glider's belly scraping the canopy at high speed, scattering sleeping birds into the night. It was impossible to miss the Chandler mansion, a flickering beacon in the dark. The villagers had beaten them there by a mile. As Merry made a pass over the mansion, the glider's tail swinging through billowing smoke and embers in a neat swoop, Alan heard her curse over the headset. The villagers stood in the mansion gardens, their faces bathed in roaring firelight. The timber structure of the mansion's Tudor section had gone up like kindling and flames already crept up the observatory tower's frame. At the top, Alan spotted a lone figure, hacking against the smoke, bent double and clinging to the tower's railing.

"Merry—" Alan began, stepping into a harness attached to the wall by a high-tensile reel.

"Seen him," Merry interrupted. "You ready?"

Locked into the harness, Alan checked his revolver in its shoulder holster and regarded his cane before setting it aside.

"Ready," he said, but the tone wasn't as confident as he'd intended.

Leaning out of the glider's door, he squinted against the

smoke that billowed around the glider's chassis and blocked any decent line of sight he had.

"This used to be fun," he said without any hint of believing it.

Despite himself, he checked over his shoulder, seeing Merry in the cockpit and checking the rear space for any shifting shadows. No sign of Slay. Small mercies. With a sigh and a wince, Alan hunkered down by the door, hanging on with one hand, and waited. Counteracting the wind speed and heat from the flames, Merry lowered the glider into the smoke. Alan buried his mouth and nose in the crook of his elbow, eyes now streaming but, as always, Merry was bang on target and the observatory tower's railing appeared just below him with a dark figure hunkered down beside it.

"Chandler!" Alan called out. "Get up!"

The figure didn't move.

"Balls," Alan muttered and jumped.

Giving off a high-pitched whine, the safety line spooled out behind him as Alan fell face-first through the air. With all thoughts of cursed limbs and haunting spectres lost in the adrenalin and thunder of the wind in his ears, he finally felt weightless for the briefest moment. But it didn't last. A rattle of pain went through his affected leg as he landed sharply beside Chandler.

Chandler stirred, peering up at Alan with a soot-coated face and streaming eyes.

"Where's your mother?" he shouted to Chandler over the glider's engines and crackling flames. Somewhere below came a sonorous creak that he didn't like the sound of.

Chandler lurched toward him, hanging from Alan's coat.

"I don't know. Get me out of here."

"Where might she be, Chandler? Her room? The study?"

"I don't know!" Chandler whined. "Please, you have to get me out of here."

"We're not going anywhere without your mother," Alan barked back.

Chandler jerked away, pressing his back to the railing, and Alan saw a glint of firelight on gunmetal. He slapped a hand to his holster, empty. Chandler thumbed back the revolver's hammer.

"Give me the headset and the wire. Don't try anything," Chandler snarled.

Alan slid off the headset first and then unclipped the safety wire. With one hand, Chandler clipped the wire to his own belt, all the while stepping back from Alan, keeping him in his sights.

"You should have left the old bag," Chandler shouted. "We could have gotten out of here together."

"You're not George Chandler are you?" Alan shouted back.

Chandler just smiled wryly, firelight flickering across his glasses, and tugged twice on the safety wire, activating the recoil and disappearing into the smoke.

Left alone on the top of the burning tower, Alan looked around himself, searching through the smoke for some way out. There he found Slay, like a photograph negative, affected neither by the smoke nor the light of the flames.

"Well. This looks dire," he hissed through a greasy smile.

"ALAN? TALK TO me. Where the hell did you go?" Merry craned around to peer through her window, trying to spot signs of movement in the smoke and flames. She tapped her headset for all the good it would do. "Alan! If you're ignoring me to be dramatic, I swear—"

"He can't hear you," Chandler said, and tossed Alan's headset onto the glider's control panel beside her.

Merry wheeled around, coming face to face with the yawning barrel of Alan's revolver.

"Chandler, are you mad? Where's Alan?"

"That really isn't your problem anymore," Chandler replied and gestured with the weapon. "Get us out of here."

"No," Merry snarled.

Chandler shook his head at her. "Please don't make this difficult. If you hurry, you can take me away and I'll let you come back for him. The sooner we leave, the sooner you can return."

Her teeth grinding together, Merry paused for a moment before turning around.

"There we go," Chandler said condescendingly.

Merry's hand snapped to the right, the glider pitching violently. Chandler fell against the cockpit wall, slamming his head on the bulkhead, and a shot rang out from the revolver, shattering the cockpit window. Smoke and embers billowed in and Merry jumped from the pilot seat and on top of Chandler. Both hands on the revolver, she wrestled this way and that, the barrel dodging from one side of her head to the other. Another shot cracked and the muzzle flash blinded her, her ears giving off a high-pitched whine. She felt the shoulder slam into her stomach, felt herself hit the ground and the air punch from her lungs. When she gasped, she tasted smoke and blood.

EVEN IN THE crumbling fiery chaos that surrounded Alan, the gunshots rang clear. He heard glass shatter, heard the shift in pitch and felt the wind change direction as the glider's turbines violently shifted direction. For just a moment, that cleared the smoke enough for him to get a view of the glider, wobbling drunkenly in the air. There was no way Merry was at the controls. The cabin swung toward him as the glider spun and he saw Chandler and Merry wrestling for the revolver.

"Merry!" Alan screamed, and he felt the railing bite into his stomach as he fought to be closer.

The glider continued to spin, its wings slanted to an ungainly angle. It drifted closer. The wing tip struck the tower's peak, ripping a ragged scar across the roof. Alan threw himself back as shrapnel and sparks filled the air, the glider's roaring turbine scything down toward him and blowing him backward head over heels. Alan dragged himself on his elbows across the platform, then turned in time to see the glider disappear back into the smoke. The pained whine of its engines faded away before a thunderous crash of grinding metal left him in stunned silence.

8

ALAN JERKED, GRABBING for the wall as the step he thought was below wasn't. Most of the smoke smothered the outside of the observation tower but the fire had crept inside and his descent toward the flames seemed both ill-advised and certainly deadly. But there was nowhere else to go. He peered over the iron stairwell's railing and saw that the timber it had been attached to below had already snapped, leaving a section listing away from the wall, dangling in the vault.

"That's a long way to jump," Slay said, peering down as well. "Maybe you should just take a seat and wait for the inevitable."

Alan didn't reply but Slay was impossible to ignore. It *was* a long way down. Even at his best it would have been a dicey move to try and leap across the gap toward a gnashing maw of red hot, twisted and splintered metal.

Pressing his back to the wall, Alan let out a cough and wiped his eyes on his sleeve. He peered up to where the observatory's platform creaked and groaned in the heat, and then over the stairwell's edge to the distant ground floor below and an open doorway that teased escape.

"Certain death in all directions," Slay said. "But don't worry. I'm here. Right 'til the end."

"Well you'll have to bloody wait," Alan grumbled.

Shoving off from the wall, making sure to set his good leg on the stairwell's edge for the best possible jump, Alan flew out into the tower's vault, and started to fall. Flames rippled below as he punched through plumes of smoke, embers snagging on his coat and hair, and the gnarled iron claw of the stairwell below reached up to grab him. His legs buckled as he landed, throwing him to his hands and knees on the hot metal. He rolled, his skin sizzling, smoke rising from his coat, and came to his feet clumsily at the stairwell's edge as it led down. Shooting a look back, he saw Slay's silhouette in the smoke, looking down at him with a chilling lack of expression. And then he fumbled his way down the rest of the stairs to the ground.

Chandler had left the door to the mansion open when he fled to the tower and Alan stumbled through into a corridor beyond. Flames licked at the walls on one side which must have been adjacent to the exterior, possibly even where the villagers had started the fire. Pressing himself to the opposite wall, he slid along it, the flames crisping his skin, reaching out with hungry tongues for a taste of him. He shoved on the first door that he came to and half fell through and down two steps to the kitchen. There were no flames there although smoke had crept in, and Alan had to run doubled over to stay below it. A discarded dishrag hung over a huge ceramic sink gave him an idea and he doused it under the tap, taking two mouthfuls of blessed fresh water before wrapping the rag around his face for what little help it might give.

Around the kitchen's island he found a servant's door that took him toward the rear of the building where the fire hadn't reached and he took grateful gulps of fresh air as he stumbled onward down the gothic stone corridor. A door at the furthest end opened onto the lavish entrance hall and he finally gained his bearings again.

The room was blisteringly hot and several of the straw-packed crates had burst into flame as well as the front doors to this section of the mansion. The villagers were clearly encircling the whole building, setting fires wherever they could. He went right and through the door to the study. The books were untouched so far, a short reprieve at best. But nothing else moved in the room. There was no sign of the widow. Back in the hallway, Alan eyed the sweeping stairway and followed it up to where smoke broiled on the ceiling and had begun to slither down the upper corridors. He sighed heavily through the dishrag mask that was already starting to dry out.

The stairwell banister smelled of acrid, heated varnish and Alan thought better of trying to use it to help him upward. Instead, he used his hands on the steps as much as his feet, ascending like a coughing dog, and took the sweeping mezzanine around to corridors that led off from the entrance hall.

Gasping under his mask, Alan tried to stay low but the tight corridor had filled with smoke far too quickly. He fumbled at doors and burst into empty room after empty room, fighting onward as the corridor changed from wooden panelling to more contemporary plaster, from the Tudor section of the building to the mansion house. Finally, he burst into a room where the smoke had crept underneath the door to curl around the ankles of Widow Chandler who sat perfectly still at the desk, oblivious to the catastrophe around her. Alan instantly saw why.

On the desk before her sat something that resembled a copper spinning top. Where a spinning top's handles would be was a small metal sphere that crackled with electricity. The contraption turned slowly, small holes in its upper surface gave off hissing gases that shifted through neon colours as they floated into the air. The widow's eyes were fixed, heavy lidded and unblinking.

Unceremoniously, Alan grabbed the widow by her shoulders and turned her away, swiping the spinning contraption from the desk for good measure. He shook her lightly, called her name, but she didn't respond.

"Give me a break," he whined. "I can't carry you as well as me."

A small vase on the desk held a single sprig of lander which had long since dried out. He tossed the dead plant aside and threw the trickle of water still in the vase into the widow's face.

She flinched, although her eyes stayed misty, and he tried again.

"Mrs Chandler. Your house is on fire. You have to stand up."

"George? Is that you?" the widow asked in a dreamy voice.

Alan felt his stomach lurch. Something about what he was about to do just didn't feel right. Knowing now that the man that had been living in her house wasn't George Chandler at all, but some imposter, and that he had been pretending to be the poor affected widow's son for god-only-knew how long, he just felt the guilt in advance of even speaking.

"Yes mother," he said, putting on the best accent he could. "It's me. I've come back and I need you to come with me. You're in danger but I can help you."

The widow blinked, her confusion fading into resignation as she once more regarded eyes she didn't recognise above the rag mask. Something down in Alan's heart wailed. He hadn't felt pity like that for anyone but himself since he was a boy.

"Please, Mother. We have to go," he said, trying to seem certain enough of the lie that Widow Chandler would accept this new reality, however briefly.

It was good enough. As he tugged on her hand, the widow drifted toward the door with him. He removed the rag from his face and tied it around hers, then led her out into the smoke. He was headed back the way he had come when a crash shook the house. The floorboards shook under their feet and the distant sound of shattering glass and ceramic told him that the main hall stairs had given in to the fire. He turned back, moving swiftly along the sooty black corridor. Sweeping down a spiral stone staircase, they found a smaller entrance hall with stone pillars that offered them another of the many front doors. Rattling the oak doors, Alan found them locked. He cursed, a heavy, devilish curse that he rarely used.

"George, please. There's no need for such language," the widow said.

He looked at her and couldn't help but laugh. She was so earnest, so refined, even in her madness.

"You're right. I'm sorry," he said, forgetting to change his accent.

The widow didn't seem to mind. "Perhaps you should get away from your father for a while. A growing boy needs his fresh air," she said, and drifted to the side of the door where heavy drapes hung like theatre curtains. There she found a large iron key which she handed to him. With a laugh, Alan fumbled at the door and they hurried out into the night air where a horde of angry villagers waited for them, silhouetted by the flames.

9

GRABBED UNDER HIS shoulders by strong hands, Alan was dragged coughing and spluttering to his feet. He swung around to clobber whoever it was but came face to face with the poachers, Lenny and Miles, their hands held up in surrender.

"Easy there, mate," Maybe Miles gasped.

Alan hacked a cough and gestured to Widow Chandler who sat on the ground, looking in awe and fear at the villagers advancing on them across the gardens.

"Look after Mrs Chandler," he said. "If anything happens to her there'll be hell to pay, you hear me?"

"Yup," Probably Lenny said.

"Loud and clear," Maybe Miles added.

Alan knelt by the widow's side. "These two men are here to help, Mrs Chandler. They'll look after you. No need to worry." And, turning back to the poachers, he added: "Get her to the White Hart."

The poachers might have said something in agreement but he didn't wait. Scanning around the gardens and the lake beyond, he spotted where the glider had crashed, a steaming shape sticking out of the water, and limped at speed toward it. Seconds later he was wading up to his thighs in the freezing cold lake, gasping as the water lapped up over his stomach and fighting on until he had to half walk and half swim to the sizzling wreck. He found the shattered cockpit window where water was pouring into the glider, flooding its insides.

"Merry!"

No answer.

Shattered glass tore at his trousers and snagged his sleeves as he clambered through the window. He splashed down into the cockpit, fighting to stand on the control panel, then the lopsided chairs, and finally swinging his way into the flooded rear compartment. The walls heavily dented, the lake bed now blocking what had been an open door, and nothing more. The climb back out was slower and he was out of breath by the time he had reached the top of the glider, holding on to the dented and twisted wing, using the height to search around.

That was when he spotted it, where the light of the moon and the flames reflected in the lake came together on the underside of the stone pier. A door hung open, hidden under the pier's overhang and impossible to see from the mansion. The frigid water slapped into Alan as he half dove and half slid into the lake. Hopping along the lake's bottom with his good leg and scrambling with his arms to stay afloat, he felt extremely glad that no one could see the ineffective flailing with which he dragged himself through the water. After dragging himself up onto the pier's hidden walkway, he took a second to catch his breath on all fours, dripping lake water in the dark, before fighting to his feet and ducking into the open door. Directly inside, a steel staircase spiralled down a stone throat coated with algae and stinking like an abandoned fish tank. He started downward, letting the stairs' rail take as much weight as he could, and soon found himself at the bottom of the shaft where a tunnel led off into the dark. Turned around by the spiral staircase he had lost all of his bearings. That was until he took his first steps into the tunnel itself and saw the dripping water that came through the tunnel's stone seams and pooled on the ground. It led out under the lake. Straining his ears, he thought he caught the sound of muffled struggling, the clang of something metallic. Chandler was down there, alright.

"What if Merry isn't with him?" came Slay's voice in the gloom. "What if she's floating somewhere else, forgotten and face down in the dark?"

Alan paused for a second, feeling a stab of pain in his leg that rattled up into his spine. Through gritted teeth he said: "Then he'll pay."

He couldn't see Slay's smile, but Alan felt the effects of it on the back of his neck as the hairs stood on end. With one hand on the slick wall, he limped as quietly and quickly as he could toward a faint light at the tunnel's other end, eventually coming to a brass portal, like those found on a submersible, which opened up to a larger room beyond. With a domed ceiling and walls made of reinforced glass, the circular chamber was the size of a ballroom. Around the walls stood control panels and scientific instrumentation that Alan instantly dismissed as something he likely wouldn't understand. At the room's centre a large donut-shaped contraption with a turbine at its centre reminded Alan instantly of the small brass machine in Widow Chandler's room. A hatch in the domed ceiling finally made sense, as did the lights above Witley. No monsters, then, only another madman for his list.

"If you had only done as you were told, we wouldn't be in this mess," he heard Chandler say, and the scientist stood up from behind the mesmerising drone, dusting his hands.

Then came Merry's voice. "If only you hadn't stolen a man's identity and taken a sick woman hostage—"

"Yes, well, I thought they were rich," Chandler said, matter-of-fact. "I was wrong. But it's of no consequence, now."

"The villagers aren't going to let you get away with this, Whatever-your-name-is. *I'm* not going to let you get away with it, either."

Chandler snorted. "They should be grateful that I've been content to just take their petty valuables but now the whole village will see the true power of mesmerism. I wonder if I can make them hold their breath until they expire," he said, thoughtfully, before turning back to Merry. "And you're hardly in a position to stop me. Tied up, your glider broken and your partner chargrilled. Just sit quietly and if you're lucky I'll only mesmerise you into forgetting all of this and send you on your way."

Merry snorted. "There's no way Alan's dead. When he goes it won't be in some house fire. The only way Alan will ever die is from some stupid decision he makes all by himself."

Alan couldn't help but chuckle as he stepped out of the tunnel, revealing himself.

"Ouch. That would hurt my feelings if I had any," he said. "Let's just end this, Chandler. We've all had a long day and there's no way you're getting out of here without a kicking."

Chandler wheeled around and Alan's eyes sprang wide. He had forgotten the revolver. Bringing his hands up for all the good it would do in fending off bullets, he twitched when he heard the hammer slam home. Once, twice, three times…four. But nothing happened. No gunfire clatter, no thundering pain, only an impotent click of metal on metal. Chandler stood shaking the revolver, spurts of lake water flying from the gun's muzzle. Alan laughed again, advancing across the room. But Chandler wasn't done. He flung the revolver end over end at Alan's head and this time hit his mark. The slam of metal into his forehead knocked Alan right off his feet.

His vision filled with fireworks, Alan rolled onto his belly and tried to stand but fell again as his hand was kicked out from under him and another boot slammed into his back. His whole world was swarming inkblots and ringing ears, clearing just in time to see Chandler in the opening to the tunnel. He aimed a remote at the flying contraption, jabbed a button, and disappeared into the gloom.

"Chuffing hell, Alan." Merry muttered as she kicked and struggled against her bonds. But she was cut off when the contraption she had been leant against whirred to life. She managed to tumble sideways, worming her way across the laboratory floor just as the machine's turbine reached top speed and it hurtled upward, uncontrolled, smashing into the portal above which had closed when Chandler bolted. The whole room shook, the glass walls vibrating with the impact. Where steel strips held the glass panels in place, spurts of water hissed into the room.

Alan shook his head, clearing his vision to see Merry unhook her bound hands from under her feet and begin working at the knots tying her boots together. In the work of a moment she was standing, hands still bound but able to help Alan to his feet at least.

"Come on, old man," she said, and started to drag him toward the tunnel.

"Tell no one," he muttered.

Shooting a look over his shoulder, Alan spotted what Merry had missed. The flying contraption, stuck against the ceiling with its turbines at full speed, wobbled like a spinning top and was starting to whirr downward. He shoved Merry as it scythed toward them at head height, him landing spread eagle on the ground and Merry landing head over heels in the exit tunnel. She glanced back, hair in her face, and made as if to come back for him but Alan waved her on.

"Don't be daft. Stay there," he barked.

Merry yelled his name and without even checking why, Alan rolled hard to one side. The contraption slammed down into the spot where he'd been lying, the turbine spitting sparks and shrapnel. He didn't even have time to scramble backward before it flipped like a coin and shot off again, hitting the wall hard enough to send cracks blossoming around the dome. Metal screamed, rivets popped, and spouts of high-pressure water burst into the room from all angles. Some latent system in the laboratory activated in response to the change in air pressure. The iris at the tunnel's entrance snapped shut as if it had seen enough, the lights winked out and the flying contraption destroyed one last control panel before the fight finally drained out of it and it came to rest. While Alan hadn't registered the pops and hisses and zaps of the laboratory's machinery when he entered, he felt their absence as the laboratory went dead. Darkness crashed down leaving only the faint green glow of the night through the lake above. Water poured in from the ceiling, already up to Alan's ankles as he scanned around the room for a way out, a lever, a button, something. His eyes only came to rest on the closed iris where the faint sound of Merry's pounding fists could be heard from the other side.

10

TRAPPED IN THE dome beneath the lake, surrounded by algae-tinted moonlight with freezing water gathering around his knees, Alan felt certain that this moment had slipped into the top five worst situations he'd found himself in. Still, he'd never broken anything that he couldn't escape from by breaking it some more. He just needed the right tools. Or rather the wrong ones.

Spotting an upturned locker by the wall, he grabbed for it in the hope of finding something useful. There were no crowbars or shovels inside, only a suit of shiny rubber, a pair of oversized glass lenses attached to the hood. Throwing the suit back and slamming the locker shut, Alan realised that he was no longer alone. Slay lurked, unfazed by the dire situation, grinning. Alan felt panic flutter in his chest. He made for the sealed iris as best he could. The water grabbed at him, dragging him backward as he strove forward. He reached the exit and pushed, hoping that the iris' panels might slide without power behind them. Pain shot through his leg as his fingers clawed between the brass panels. There was so little to hold on to. His hands were wet. The iris refused to budge. His breath was stolen from him with a gasping shudder as the freezing water finally reached his stomach. He heard the hot, excited panting of Slay over his shoulder and clamped his eyes shut, pressing his forehead to the iris, trying to put the sound out of his mind.

"This is how it ends, old pal," Slay whispered, so close that it might have been inside. "At least they won't have to bury you. I doubt they'll even find you when all this comes crashing down."

With the water draining heat and energy from his limbs, Alan shuddered in the dark, his throat too tight to make a sound, and he finally started to float. He rose swiftly and was soon pressed against the dome, fighting to stay in the air pocket between the water and the ceiling. But it was shrinking faster than he could paddle.

As his shoulders pressed to the dome's ceiling and he took his first mouthful of foul lake water, he thought of how quickly it had come, in the end. Not from a bullet or blade like he had expected, but without fanfare.

"Misadventure," he sputtered as he grabbed at the circular aperture in the ceiling with a precarious grip and hauled himself up a precious few inches. "That's what they'll say."

He tried to laugh in the dark. But there wasn't enough left in him. The cold reached his clavicle and his throat tightened for the last time. With a sound that might have been a whimper the water reached his face and he took a final, useless gasp.

"This was worth the wait," Slay whispered, appearing from the impenetrable black.

With the breath hot in his lungs, fighting the urge to open his mouth, to breathe out, Alan met eyes with the madman's spectre that floated before him, eyes red-rimmed and gruesomely wide.

Bubbles escaped Alan's mouth and he tried to cough some of them back in. He choked, the freezing cold lake reaching into him for the first time, and his insides started to burn. Eyes rolling in his head, he struggled with anything he had left, knowing there was nowhere to go. But that caused him to look up where a circle of pale light had appeared above.

He heard her voice as a sonorous moan distorted by the water. Merry's last words to him, stolen away by the lake. He tried to paddle, to reach upward, but there was nothing left with which to move his limbs. He was out of fuel and out of time.

Slay's chuckle drove a spasm through Alan's freezing muscles. "With salvation within earshot, you breathe your last."

And he did. Alan's body shook as the lake water plunged into him, the last pathetic bubbles of life escaping his lips.

Hands plunged into the water, grabbing hair and shirt collar. He choked on the air, spraying water out of his mouth as his head broke the surface. Water poured out of his ears and he could hear Merry again.

"Reach up, you idiot!" she scolded.

Cracking open an eye as he coughed and spluttered, he saw the silhouette of Merry's goggled head against the moonlight that poured down the tube. He kicked the one leg that would still respond, the other a frozen weight. Grabbing at his friend, his hands felt like they might be someone else's. But it didn't matter. It didn't matter that someone above hauled on the rope around Merry's waist, or that Alan was now adding weight. They were propelled up the tube as the lake finally found more room to flood and they were ejected onto the little cement island at the centre of the lake. Alan spluttered and gasped, dragging his eyes up to see the statue of Poseidon wielding his trident against the stars.

Merry was helped to her feet by Lenny the poacher as Miles wound the sodden rope around his arm, business-like.

"Thanks lads," she said. To Alan she said, "You owe everyone a pint, I reckon."

Alan let the insurmountable weight of his head turn toward her. He tried to smile, even a little, but he couldn't. All he could think about was that dark chamber, the water claiming his body, and the voice of Slay, threatening to be the last thing he ever heard.

11

WAKING IN THE White Hart the next morning threw Widow Chandler completely. She stared glassy eyed around the tavern, jumping at every swing of the door, asking Alan and Merry and Toby where her son was. The landlord took particular care with her, making sure she was fed and was taking tea as often as possible. Alan walked into the bar after a long sleep, familiar aches joined by some unfamiliar ones, and found her sitting by the tavern's bay window, gazing out across the fields. A little after lunch she stood up with something like resignation and walked out of the front door.

Standing in the field where Alan and Merry had first seen the lights, the widow looked out across the village for a long while. They all watched but gave her space as the tears shook her shoulders. Finally she sat on the grass in her mourning dress and watched the sun go down. That was when Merry went out to her with a blanket and they sat together in light chat. The woman who walked back into the White Hart was completely different.

"I want to thank you," she said to the Privateers and Toby. She looked at Merry who nodded her encouragement. When she raised her chin, they could see for the first time the woman beneath the mesmerism. "I feel—I have been away for too long." She looked down at the black lace sweeping around her feet and her face became grave. "I have been wearing this too long. My husband's house is gone and I won't miss it. You may judge me, but I won't miss him." She looked up at them and her eyes were firm but sparkling. "I will miss my son. But that is all gone now."

And that seemed to be it.

"We'll be taking the train back to London in the morning," Alan said. "You're welcome to come with us. It's a world away from this place."

"No," the widow replied. "Thank you. I want to stay here. I think the city might be a little too much to digest. And there will be solicitors to meet and sales of the land to make and…" she faltered for the first time.

"And we'll do it together," Toby chimed in. "Any help you need."

"Thank you, Toby," she said. As she looked between the privateers they could see by the pinch of her brow that she was trying desperately to commit as much to memory as she could. "Merry. Alan. Thank you all."

"I wish the result could have been better for you, Madame," Alan said.

"I think you can probably call me Mina." With a weak smile, the widow wandered away to sit quietly by the fire.

When the villagers arrived, squeezing en masse through the door, Alan panicked. He'd seen what these people could do in a large group when Chandler had tried to escape through the woods the previous night and had been hunted down in short order. But he soon dreaded it for an entirely different reason when the Witley folk began ordering drinks and meals from Toby, and curtly thanking Alan for it.

Alan shot a worried look toward his partner. "I didn't say I'd pay for the whole bloody village."

"Looks like word got around," Merry chuckled. "Better start exercising that billfold."

"This'll cost me everything Rook's paying," he whined.

Merry just patted him on the shoulder and ordered another pint before the money ran out.

ALAN POPPED THE chunk of stew-soaked bread into his mouth and licked the gravy from his fingers, chasing a dribble down his hand before it could escape. Even though the side of his face where his revolver had smashed into him ached and stung, he made a sound of joy in the back of his throat as he chewed. The White Hart was still bustling; the hatch through to the kitchen poured mouth-watering smells and Toby's curses as he burnt himself on the cooking range. Most of the Witley locals avoided Alan and Merry's eyes like scolded children. Alan managed to feel both at home and utterly out of place at the same time and so he focussed even harder on his food.

"I don't know how long I might stay," Merry said, staring down into a chipped tankard of Toby's weak cider.

"The room's yours," Alan replied with terse generosity as he dipped more bread into the stew and he ate it. "For as long as you like."

Merry smiled quietly.

The tavern grew quiet once more until only they were left at the bar. The rest of the villagers had returned to their homes to sleep through their first night in a long time without having to worry about lights in the sky. Only Chandler, who still refused to give his real name, would be sleeping rough in the tiny cell that Constable Ridley had been using as a storeroom.

Toby mopped his brow and frowned happily at all the tidying up he had left to do. After a moment or two, Mina began to gather tankards and crockery and take them into the kitchen where clattering could be heard.

"You've gone really odd after the lake," Merry said now that it was just them and the fire.

"Being nearly drowned will do that to you," Alan said, stirring the golden cider with his finger just to watch the bubbles go around.

"No, you've been on death's doorstep before and I've never seen you like this. I thought we could talk to each other, Al. About pretty much anything."

"We can," he said, trying to reassure her. He finally set his eyes on her and all the pretence fell away. "Sometimes you keep things from people so they don't worry about you. I don't want to be a burden."

Laying her hand on his, Merry fixed him with a look that she hoped was gentle and firm in equal measure. "You've been a burden since you first climbed into my glider. I've been carrying your useless arse for years. Why stop now?"

Alan tried to laugh but it came out as a forceful exhale. He avoided her gaze, preferring the slow spin of the bubbles.

"I really thought my time was up down there," he said, massaging his thigh. "And Slay was there again. I can't escape him. It doesn't matter what happens, the scales are tipped in his favour. All he has to do is wait. And every day I slide further toward him," he said with a flippant shrug that Merry saw right through to the cold resignation beneath. "I've never been scared of dying, Merry. You know that. But if the last thing I see, the last thing I hear, is Slay—"

He finally looked up to find pity in Merry's face and he had to look away again.

"I wish you'd got in touch," she said, gulping down the lump from her throat.

He gave her an incredulous look.

"You didn't want to ruin my happiness. I know," she added. "But it turns out I wasn't happy anyway." She drained her tankard and set it down. "Is he here right now? This Slay?"

Alan checked the shadows. "No. He comes and goes when he wants."

"Well let's just stick to the now, shall we? Toby?" The landlord's head appeared beyond the kitchen hatch. "Reckon we'll need another."

Extract from the *Guildford Tribune*, inside cover,
27th May 1872.

Reports of odd, colourful occurrences in the sky above Witley village have now been confirmed by official sources. The phenomenon, explained only by local superstition until recently, has now been given a far more satisfying explanation. Scientific research undertaken at the mansion of the locally reviled Chandler family was the culprit and has also been attributed as the cause or contributing factor in several deaths. The Chandler mansion, however, has been burnt to the ground and the lands surrounding it have been returned to local authority control as there are no surviving remnants of the Chandler family who wish to claim it. Council sources report that the land will likely be used for next year's annual Guildford Summer Fete.

Alan Shaw and the Wolves of London

1

July, 1872
London, England

"HANG ON, I'M coming," Alan called out through a yawn.

In the half-hop that he used around the house in order to take a break from his cane, Alan made his way to the front door. The knock came again. Polite, almost apologetic, and he grumbled under his breath: "Did no one ever tell you that patience is a bloody virtue?"

He opened the door to a London drenched in summer sweat. The heat beat down from an unusually clear sky to bounce from the cobbles in delicate waves. London's smell had real character in the summer. The river alone was a one-of-a-kind olfactory experience but when the sweat and the gutters mixed with Londoner's poesies and perfumes, the summer was a confusing season for the nose. Traffic of foot and tyre thundered back and forth, punctuated by lingerers and leaners which Alan scanned with the corner of his eye. No one seemed to be paying his front door any particular interest for a change. On the rooftops across the street he caught a movement, a shift of silhouette against the high sun. He looked up to see pigeons burst into the sky and snorted. Probably urchins scuffling around up there. Since the Sutton Hall orphans had found out that Alan's graphical adventures were true, and that London's favourite orphan-turned-hero lived right there on Berwick Street, word had gotten around, leading to a constant stream of little looky-loos.

Finally turning his full attention to the visitor who stood patiently on the doorstep, hands gripping her skirt, bonnet pinned at a jaunty angle atop straw-coloured curls, he wished he'd been paying attention all along. A furrowed brow tainted Helen Harrigan's smile.

"Am I disturbing you?" she asked.

"I'm happy to be disturbed if it's you," Alan said with a wink. His flirtation brought a little colour to Helen's cheeks and that was enough for him. "Come in."

"So sorry to bother you, Alan. But I wanted to talk to you about something quite urgent."

Despite himself, Alan let out a sigh. "Doesn't everyone?"

She looked at him quizzically for a second, her tight lips twitching with uncertainty.

"It's one of them questions. The ones that don't—" Alan continued.

"Rhetorical," Helen said, giving Alan a glance from toe to head and scrunching up her face. "You've had a long night, haven't you? You don't look well at all. I shouldn't have come," and she moved past him, toward the door.

"Me and Merry were chasing a fellow with spring-loaded boots across Whitechapel all night," he said, gently guiding her by the shoulders in a semi-circle. "Caught the bugger in the end, though. Why don't we sit down?"

"You had better before you fall," Helen said with a weak smile and headed toward the kitchen. "I need tea, quite badly.

Will Merry be joining us?"

"She's in the bath. We've not been back long."

Alan flopped into his armchair by the parlour mantelpiece and, after a minute or two, he took the cup that Helen offered him. She took her own to the chair across the fireplace and sat with it placed in her lap. Alan tried not to laugh but he couldn't put away all of the smile. She'd chosen the biggest mug he had. With a long crack down its centre, it dwarfed her hands and stood in stark contrast to her appearance of petite nobility.

"You're out of milk, I'm afraid," she said.

"Story of my life. So, what's going on?"

Helen flopped back in her chair, sparking Alan's memory of the ungainly child that she'd once been, moving in bursts of speed and sweeping arcs, all skirts and floppy limbs, a jellyfish of joy. A few warm embers burst in the dying hearth as Helen began to speak.

"I wanted you to be one of the first to know, as my oldest friend," she huffed as she stared into the hearth. "I'm sure that you've wondered why Percy and I have no children. We've had somewhat bad luck in that regard. Everyone else in our circle certainly has an opinion on it." Turning her gaze to Alan she saw only impassive patience. "How do you turn your face off like that? I wish I could do it." Alan gave her a slight smile but said nothing, forcing her to continue. "You know, when you're quiet it's rather unnerving."

"I'm just waiting for you to tell me what you came to tell me," he said. "Unless you want to talk about something else first? Work up to it?"

Helen sat forward in her chair and stared down into her cup.

"No, it just…makes me sad, is all. But I came to tell you

that we're going to be adopting a child. A boy. From Eleanor's orphanage. Even with Sutton Hall functional, she has so many little ones to care for and so little space. I thought, perhaps, that we could give one of them a better life. Parents." She looked up to find Alan leaning forward, elbows on knees, so that they leaned together like co-conspirators. "Like the Carpenters did for you."

Alan set aside his teacup and reached across to Helen, cupping her hands in his as a smile dawned on his face.

"I think it's a wonderful idea," he said.

"You do?"

"You'll be brilliant."

Helen surged forward into a hug, grabbing him around the neck and shoulders. He felt her tea spill onto his back but he laughed and wrapped his arms around her as well. And there they lingered.

"Oops," Merry said from the doorway. "Am I interrupting?"

Helen shot back as if she'd been electrocuted, sloshing more tea. She stuttered as she regarded Merry in her pyjamas and oversized smoking jacket. Without her goggles to hold back her hair, she looked odd.

"We've just had some good news," Alan replied, saving Helen from having to find her words. "Helen is adopting a boy from Lady Ottaway's."

Merry's face lit up with a broad smile. "That's wonderful! Helen, you'll make an amazing mum."

"Thank you so much, Merry. You're very sweet," Helen said with a blush.

"I'm going to make some tea," Merry said. "Anyone want one?"

"Please. I seem to have finished mine without realising," Helen said, handing Merry her cup.

Helen's naivety brought a warm smile to Alan's face as he eyed the tea stains on the carpet and felt the warm beverage soaking through the back of his shirt. As Merry left he called to her:

"We're out of milk!"

"Story of my life!" she called back.

"She's really lovely," Helen said, seriousness falling onto her face like a stage curtain. "Are you happy?"

Alan's confusion was momentary, but profound.

"Oh no, we're not—" he began. "Merry's married. But she's having a tough time and so she's staying with me, that's all. Wait, does everyone think—? Oh bloody hell."

"When you come back from an adventure with a woman in tow. Pretty, spunky, adventurous. People are going to talk, Alan."

"What's wrong now?" Merry said, returning to hand Helen her tea and keeping a cup of her own. She dragged over a chair and sat completing the circle around the fireplace.

"Everyone thinks we're knocking boots," Alan said.

Merry burst out laughing.

"Sod them," she said. "I don't care, do you?"

Alan turned sulkily to the fire. "Of course not."

"He does really," Merry said, winking at Helen who flushed and chuckled.

"Are you attending Jasper's party this evening?" Helen asked, turning on her socialite mode without losing a step.

"Yeah, we'll be there," Alan said, forlorn.

"Oh good! Merry, you must make Alan wear something appropriate, not his usual rags."

"As if I have any say in what this stubborn old—"

Alan groaned, resting his head on his hand, and was asleep before his friends said much more.

ACROSS FROM ALAN'S home on Berwick Street, with their back to the stone parapet, a figure swathed in loose black fabric waited out the day. The shadow from St Luke's church marked out the hours as the sun rose, blisteringly hot, pulling little waves from the slate rooftop. The figure sat and sweated themselves into a puddle. London had been described as inclement in hospitality and weather. They had dressed accordingly and been sorely caught off guard. A leather waterskin which could have lasted days lasted the morning.

Every now and then they shifted their weight, peering over the parapet at the house across the street, scanning the windows for any sight of the one they were here to shadow. Shaw had returned in the early hours with one woman only to be visited by another shortly after. The shadow scoffed. Shaw's reputation with women was clearly well earned.

Peering too long at Shaw as he stood on the doorstep, the shadow had been forced to duck, startling the pigeons which had become their only rooftop companions. They thought that would have been enough to gain Shaw's interest and they had prepared to retreat. But while his senses were keen as ever, his desire for the chase had lessened, it seemed, and the shadow was able to stay where it was, unassailed.

Like the grace of God, night eventually fell and the day's heat swiftly faded. Soon the shadow was tugging their clothing around themselves to fend off a night chill. One last check over the parapet found Shaw's residence in pitch darkness. Rushing from parapet to parapet, they checked the adjacent streets below, their viewpoint constantly blocked by alleyways and oddly shaped buildings higher or lower than their neighbours. They cursed the city and whoever built these hotchpotch dwellings.

They had to choose quickly. Where would he go? They

had to keep eyes on him if their plan was to work.

It hit them. The brother.

Scanning for the moon's glow beyond the swiftly gathering cloud cover, the shadow ascertained an eastward direction and took to the rooftops in a blur of shadows, vaulting stone balustrades and skidding along loose tiles. Where an alleyway passed like a chasm ahead, they leapt deftly and landed in a roll at the other side, stopping only briefly to catch their breath. A band of wide-eyed urchins stared out from under a makeshift shelter between two chimneys. The shadow held up a finger to the cloth mask across its face and ran on.

There, finally, in the street below, they spotted the retreating backs of Shaw and his companion and breathed a sigh as they slowed to a crouching stalk. From now on they would have to pay more attention. There was too much at stake to let him get away.

2

NIGHT CREPT IN to smother London from grates and gulleys, from the mud banks of the river and the ever-dark of the alleyways. Traffic thinned, crowds retreated home and silence gathered until only the faint hum of the tesla lamps remained. Used to cacophony over calm, Alan's ears rang in the quiet. He'd dressed up, under Merry's battery of scathing looks, in a fresh shirt and waistcoat, his trusted coat over it all. She'd even convinced him to leave his revolver at home. Merry had done her own thing, removing the sleeves from a velvet walking suit and coupling it with a long sleeved blouse and breeches. She had even tied back her hair with a band of ribbon to replace her goggles, managing to look elegantly practical in a way that few others could. Walking side by side with her in companionable silence, Alan felt at peace. And, because some things never changed, that made him nervous.

The way from Berwick Street to Hay Hill was unspectacular and Alan had walked it so many times that he could let his mind wander. It was the sound of slate scraping on slate that snapped him back into the moment. Whipping his eyes upward, scanning the lips of the rooftops, he had to squint past the tesla lamps and the lights still pouring from the upper floors of Savile Row's many tailors as they worked their way through the night. Shadows moved somewhere above, made indistinct by the light pollution.

"What's wrong?" Merry asked, not realising that Alan had stopped dead until she was a few paces down the pavement.

"I heard something. Up there."

Merry checked the rooftops, shielding her eyes from the light. "Rats, pigeons, urchins."

"I have a bad feeling," Alan said. "Like I'm being watched. I felt it earlier today, too."

"No, Alan," Merry said, sternly. She walked back to him and punched him on the arm. "Oy.

You are not imagining something's up to get you out of this party tonight. It's Jasper's birthday and you're going."

"It's not that at all—"

"Come on, you sly sod," she said, and kept walking, leaving Alan to trail after her, still casting glances over his shoulder.

They arrived on Hay Hill a few minutes later, Merry rapping on the old red door to be greeted by Lottie bearing her finest smile and a burst of party chatter from inside the house.

"You made it!" she said. "Lovely to see you, Merry. Alan— Alan?"

But his attention was elsewhere. Alan scanned the street, the alleys, and especially the rooftops of Hay Hill.

"He thinks we're being followed," Merry said, stepping inside.

Lottie leaned out of the doorway to scan the street herself.

"By whom?" she asked.

"Not sure. I just have a feeling," Alan replied.

"Well, your feelings are usually correct," Lottie said, matter-of-fact. "I'm sure they'll jump out at you when they're good and ready."

Alan humphed, taking one last look at the street before Lottie clicked the door closed behind them and led them into the hubbub of the party.

The Carpenters' parlour was elegantly decorated with paper streamers and fresh blue flowers in various vases. At Alan's first glance, the crowd seemed to be made up of the usual people: Simon's fellow science folk and their spouses, Lottie's friends, neighbours. He couldn't see Helen or Percy but Lady Ottaway was in her usual spot beside the fireplace. He gave her a jovial wave, a silent promise to be over as soon as he possibly could. Merry accompanied him to the alcohol and they dispensed themselves drinks.

"Uncle Alan!"

Turning with drink in hand, Alan was met by Simon's face from twenty years ago. Jasper was the double of his father, right down to the side parting and spectacles. He shared his father's intelligent glint but the broad smile and no-nonsense attitude was entirely Lottie's.

"Thank you so much for coming," Jasper said, grabbing Alan's hand and shaking it warmly in an adult fashion that made Alan smile. When he turned to Merry, Jasper didn't offer physical contact but gave a courteous greeting just the same. "Merry, thank you for coming as well. It's nice to see you."

Merry had no such problem with boundaries, however, and she advanced on the young man, kissing him on the cheek.

"Happy Birthday," she said.

Jasper showed once more that he was his father's son in the pulse of blood that rushed to his cheeks and stuttered delivery of his thanks.

"Steady on, Merry. You'll kill the lad outright," Alan chuckled.

"Your Uncle hasn't brought you a gift because he's a rotten sod," Merry told Jasper.

"Oh, I don't need gifts. I'm a little old for that, now," Jasper replied. "It's just nice to be back from school to celebrate with everyone this year."

"It's good to have you home. But Merry's wrong for once," Alan replied. Turning back to the table of alcohol, he leant right to the back and snatched a bottle of scotch before offering it to Jasper. "Your father's scotch is better than mine. Better take that up to your room and hide it for when you go back to school."

Jasper took the bottle, shaking his head at his Uncle.

"Alan! You can't give the lad a stolen bottle of scotch," Merry said, reaching for the bottle. But Jasper wouldn't let go.

"Anyone can buy a present. If it isn't brazenly stolen, it isn't really from Uncle Alan at all," Jasper laughed. To his uncle, he said: "Thank you so much. I'll go and hide it."

And he bustled away, the bottle concealed under his jacket.

"You're a terrible influence," Merry said.

With a grin, Alan made his way through the party.

Drinks flowed as the clock's pendulum sawed away the evening. Guests siphoned off until only a small group of the family's nearest and dearest remained, sitting or leaning around the Carpenters' parlour in a loose group. Alan sneaked sips of his whiskey to Jasper, bringing pink back to the lad's cheeks and knowing glares from Lottie. Alan and Merry chatted and reminisced, regaling their close group with tales of the adventures that they could actually talk about. In time, the conversation turned, inevitably, to Helen.

"It's a good thing that you're doing. Even more so than usual, I mean," Alan said to Lady Ottaway, his eyes elsewhere and face half buried in his glass to hide his uncomfortable sincerity.

"They are good people, and the world needs more of them. The children need to see that people like them exist. Even if they are few," Lady Ottaway replied. "It's a shame that so few children leave the orphanage before coming of age. It sours their souls, I think. And London is already so flooded with those."

Alan blinked at her brutal honesty. Silence wove its way through the group.

"Apologies. Gin makes me dour," Lady Ottaway said with a chuckle.

"The problem being that you're not actually wrong, Eleanor," Lottie said. "If only more good people—"

Alan didn't hear the rest. He was too busy eyeing the doorway at regular intervals and checking his wristwatch.

"Stop looking for her. You're far too obvious," Merry whispered.

"I'm not looking for her. She's just never late for a party. Ever. Simon, have you heard from Helen?"

"Actually, I haven't. Odd that she isn't here." Simon compared his pocket watch to the mantle clock in case something was amiss in his timepieces.

"It is odd," Lottie cut in. She looked to Alan with seriousness. "What did you say earlier about having a bad feeling?"

"I'm sure it's fine," he replied, unconvincingly.

"Of course they're fine," Simon said as a polite rap came from the front door. "See? That will be them, now."

Alan slid his drink onto an occasional table and followed.

"That's a copper's knock," he said mostly to himself, but it drew everyone in his wake into the hallway.

A familiar old sensation rushed through Alan as he watched

Simon open the door, waiting for some dark inevitability to reveal itself. He caught Merry giving him side-eye but he couldn't engage, so focussed was he on the constable on the doorstep, helmet tucked under one arm.

"Mister Carpenter?" the constable began. He had the carefully emotionless expression that Alan had come to expect before bad news. The copper eyed the amassed group of family and friends behind Simon. Clearly he hadn't wanted an audience for this. Every strand of Alan's being tightened. Hands bunched, pulse racing, his body prepared for familiar fight or flight. Only there was nowhere to go, and nothing to hit.

"Yes Constable, can I help you?" Simon replied.

The constable leant forward, lowering his voice.

"I have some bad news to report, sir. Could we speak in private?"

With a glance over his shoulder to his amassed family, Simon replied to the negative.

"Well then," the constable said, straightening himself physically and mentally. "I'm here on behalf of Mr Percy Harrigan–"

Alan felt Merry's hand slip into his and squeeze. He didn't reciprocate but didn't fight it off either.

"–there's been an unfortunate turn of events, sir. I'm afraid Mr and Mrs Harrigan have been the victims of an attack. Mr Harrigan is in a bad way but he's being well cared for in St James' hospital. He managed to give us your name—"

"And Mrs Harrigan?" Alan interrupted.

The constable gulped. "We're not entirely sure where Mrs Harrigan is but—"

"Aren't sure or have no idea? Out with it, Constable," Alan snapped. He felt Merry squeeze his hand again, steadying his anger, and Alan choked down his furious worry. Merry was right even when she didn't say anything. He continued with a more measured tone. "She's a very old friend. We need to know."

"She was taken, we think, sir. By the attackers. They left Mr Harrigan in a terrible state but he managed to reach help."

"Descriptions?" Alan asked.

"Most odd, sir. Mr Harrigan won't stop going on about wolves. We can't get much more out of him. He's on quite a lot of medication—" the constable replied.

"Did you come in a steam cab, Constable?" Alan asked.

"Ummm, yes, sir."

"Good. You can give me a lift to the hospital," Alan replied, turning to the rest of the group. Simon stood with his mouth half open; Lottie had wrapped an arm around him but there was a pinch of worry even in her stalwart brow. Jasper was pale; Lady Ottaway comforted him, swallowing him in her embrace, and the last of the child in him didn't fight it off. "I'll find out what's going on and report back. Just don't worry, alright?"

"I need to be back at the orphanage. When you find out what's happening, please let me know. I need to be with Thomas when news arrives," Lady Ottaway said.

Alan nodded, making the connection between the unknown name and Helen's news from earlier that day.

"And I'll come back here as soon as I can. Everyone just sit tight." And to Merry, he said: "You don't have to come."

"Just try and stop me," she said.

Seeing Lady Ottaway to a cab, they left the Carpenters huddled by the old red door and climbed into the compartment behind the constable who eased the steam cab into a shuddering motion, the tesla-charged steam engine making hums and huffs in equal measure. Alan sat quietly beside Merry who knew better than to try to engage him in conversation. He just stared straight ahead, to the cab's opposite seat, where a pale face he hadn't seen in weeks grinned with immoral glee.

THE SHADOW PEERED over the gutter and through the open curtains of the Carpenters' Hay Hill home. They watched the odd movements in the parlour as the drink flowed and food was passed around on little platters, exactly as they had expected. No one sat to eat together; every conversation seemed fleeting. Londoners were as easily bored with each other as they were with the countries they occupied. When enough food and air had been wasted, the party wound down.

The shadow's stomach gurgled but they were thankfully distracted as yet another steam cab pulled up outside the house.

How these people adore finding any way to avoid walking even a short distance, the shadow thought. *They arrive in cabs and leave in them, each over-dressed pig fatter than the last.*

But this one was different. Out stepped a policeman, putting on his helmet for even the short walk to the red front door before removing it again.

Tensing, the shadow ducked a little lower so that they were barely peeking over the gutter's edge. Surely this was it. A visit from a policeman so late at night must be the sign they had been waiting for. The shadow sighed with relief and to steady themselves. They had been watching, standing by, for more than a week for this moment. Now they had to steel themselves for the next stage. Tonight was the night when karma came to collect Shaw's old debt.

3

A STEAM CAB ride through midnight London was nothing new to Alan. The vacuous hush as the city slept, the sorrowful whistle of a lone street rat, the thud of rubber tyres on roads punctuated by the omnipresent chug and shunt of the engine. Merry stared out of the window, watching the city speed by, pensive and prepared for what might come. Alan scowled at his other companion, the spectre of Mister Slay that snarled a smile at him from the opposite seat. He had been blissfully silent of late. He didn't like Merry any more than he liked Hogarth and that kept him quiet other than in the wee dead hours of the morning when Alan caught a faint refrain of the madman's chuckle. Now he was back. If there was one thing that Slay could never resist, it was frolicking in the misery of others. But he said nothing, content to sit and grin, stirring the bile in Alan's stomach.

The cab drew to a halt. Alan and Merry spilled out onto the Knightsbridge pavement and rushed up the steps to the hospital without so much as a thank you to the constable. Corridors and bed-packed wards flashed by, wraith-like nurses drifted between them carrying hooded tesla will-o-wisps. Alan stopped dead in the doorway of an all-men's ward. Beds lined the walls on either side with moonlight coming in through the hospital's tall windows, the split panes casting shadowy crosses down on the patients.

It was both easy and difficult to spot Percy. Although there were many other patients wrapped in their linens or turned away, there was one body bandaged beyond recognition, an arm and the opposite leg held aloft by a pulley system, and Alan just knew that Percy was that medical mummy. Drawing close, he saw that Percy wasn't asleep at all. The eyes between the bandages were wide open, staring at the ceiling, glistening with tears and tense with pain. They swivelled toward Alan as he drew into Percy's eye line and the injured man's whole body grew even more tense.

"Percy," Alan started but he could find nothing comforting to say. "What the hell happened?"

From inside the bandages came a dry rasp that turned into pained exhalations.

"Wolves–" Percy muttered, and Alan saw beneath the bandages that Percy's lips were burst and bloody. "Took her." A groan escaped Percy loud enough to summon a nurse.

"Oh Percy, I'm so sorry…" Merry said, trailing off.

"What are you doing? You're not allowed in here this time of night," the nurse chastised them in a stage whisper.

"The man's in pain," Merry replied to her. "Get him something, quick."

The nurse saw that their expressions were of care rather than mischief and her heart softened.

"You can stay until I get back, then you'll have to go," she said, and darted to her duty.

"Percy," Alan said. "Did you know them? Is there a reason someone might want to do this to you? No time for pride. I need to know."

The slightest shake of a head drew agony across Percy's eyes. The purple fingers of his unrestrained hand slid across the sheets, toward the edge of the bed, toward Alan. Percy managed to squeeze out only: "Find her—"

"You have my word. For what it's worth to you," Alan said, and walked out.

Merry followed, looking back for only a moment at the man broken inside and out. She caught up with Alan as he stood on the pavement with an odd look on his face, nodding to himself.

"Penny for them," she said as she stepped up beside him.

"Just thinking," he said distantly.

"You think it's a ransom thing? Percy's navy pension would make for a tidy payment."

"Could be," Alan said, staring up at the tesla-tinged night and heaving a resigned breath. "There never seems to be any rest from it, does there? The chaos. It just keeps on coming."

Merry stepped in front of him, taking his cheeks in both hands, pulling his face down to look at her.

"We'll find her," she said.

His eyes were hard and sharp like shattered slate and she couldn't tell if her words soaked in at all.

"We should get back," he said. "Simon and Lottie will want to know what's going on."

It took a painful half jog to the cab station at Hyde Park Corner and an overpayment from Alan to get them back to Hay Hill in record time, travelling in silence the whole way. Alan's eyes were fixed on a point not far ahead of him, unblinking. As Merry watched him from the corner of her eye, she couldn't tell if he was nodding along with some internal thought process or it was the rocking of the cab.

The driver was told to wait and paid handsomely to idle in

the night's summer chill while the companions climbed the steps to the old red door which they found ajar.

Merry inhaled to say something but Alan didn't wait to find out what. Bursting through the door, he called his family's names.

Simon.

Lottie.

Jasper.

But there was no reply.

4

AS ALAN APPROACHED the Carpenter's door for the second time that night, it swung open to greet him. But Lottie wasn't there with some words of comforting determination. Nor Simon with a worried smile. Jasper's eyes, dull from sleep, didn't greet his uncle either. Nudged by the night breeze, the door swung open of its own accord to welcome Alan back to an empty house.

The Privateers didn't even look at each other. They burst in, Merry grabbing an umbrella to brandish against any villain that might remain inside, Alan screaming the names of his family as if on the edge of his last breath.

Stalking from room to room like a hound on the hunt, through empty spaces, past unused beds, it all passed in nightmare flashes for Alan. In every room stood Slay, sometimes in the corner, sometimes by the window, and his grin grew ever wider. Finally, Alan burst into the bathroom and found only his own reflection in the mirror. He looked at himself, pale and haggard, breath ragged, old and lost. His eye was drawn toward an old tin boat on the shelf. Simon's bathtime toy, passed to Jasper, and now an ornamental moment of the past.

Slay gasped over his shoulder. "How shocking. They're not all hiding on the toilet." And he cackled.

Alan drifted back down the stairs, right past Merry, and came to rest by the Carpenter's fireplace, head hung and breathing heavy.

"They're gone," he muttered. "They're all gone."

Merry eyed Alan as he stood in the middle of the room like an old rag hung out to dry. His cheeks seemed to have drawn in, his eyes turned misty. She tried to catch his attention but he just stared at a spot in the air by her side.

She had seen this before, in the darkness that followed his near death in Witley. But it hadn't been this bad. He'd still heard her, then. This time, any comforting words she shared just crashed over him without penetrating. How quickly he changed from the Alan she once knew to this barely breathing husk. Like the winding down of a turbine, all energy and hope lost in a moment to stop dead and cold. Worry for his family had flipped him toward madness faster than even his own demise had.

"You can go mad later," she said, and she shook him by the lapels of his coat. "Come on, you need to focus."

His eyes slid slowly toward her but remained distant.

Staying calm, doing her job and doing it well, Merry began to move around the room, dragging him along.

By one skirting board she found Lottie's shotgun, cracked open, chambers empty. She gestured to it. "Lottie didn't even get a shot off. Now that's hard to believe," Merry said, although it might as well have been to herself for all Alan replied. Near the parlour door a wet stain on the wall led her to glass shards at its foot. She ran a finger down the stain on the wall above it and sniffed her fingers before wafting them under Alan's nose. "And this is gin. I doubt either Lottie or Simon are the arguing-until-you-throw-something types. They tried to defend themselves. No furniture overturned," she continued, pointing it out for him. "Nothing stolen. And more importantly, no blood stains. Come on, Alan. Don't you dare shut down on me. Do what you're good at."

"Yes, Alan. Do what you're good at," Slay said from somewhere near his ear. "Lose all of the people that you love. All in one night."

Alan pinched the bridge of his nose but still didn't speak. A sick feeling welled up in Merry's stomach. These were people she loved, too. Every one of them had accepted her into their lives as whole-heartedly as they had Alan. Now she stood in their parlour without a clue, and her partner had decided to choose this moment to break the already thin seal around his sanity.

"Shut up," Alan said, and a sprig of hope sprouted Merry's chest even as she took a step away from him.

Alan finally focussed on her rather than on the empty air behind her, a huge relief to Merry who had been avoiding checking over her shoulder in case she actually saw something there. He reached out to her and grabbed her hand.

"Not you, Merry," he said. "Sorry. I wasn't talking to you."

"I know," Merry replied. She squeezed his hand. "He's not really here, you know. But we still are."

"Right." Alan started to look around the room, scanning fast. "Right. I noticed something. Where was it?"

He walked out of the room and Merry followed. After a moment of looking around as if he was seeing the Carpenter's hallway for the first time, Alan pointed to a piece of the stair banister where the wood had splintered in three deep, parallel slashes.

"Here," he said, still fighting the fog in his head from

closing in completely.

"That looks like—like claw marks," Merry said.

"And—and here–" Alan continued, picking up speed, turbines turning again.

Alan dipped to swipe up a fallen picture frame, the glass shattered across his smiling family. But it was the chunk of fur hanging from the corner that he pointed to. Merry plucked it and gave it a sniff.

"Smells fusty," Merry said.

"Like wet dog?" Alan asked with a cocked eyebrow. Merry nodded solemnly. He set the photo back in its place. "Claws and fur. Wolves that kidnap people."

"This is starting to look like our kind of strange, Al," Merry said.

Alan remained taciturn, as if every word said aloud took a toll.

Merry laid a hand on his arm as he stared down at the fractured picture.

"Alan. I think it's you," she said. "It's all people you know that are being taken."

"I thought the same," he said.

"Could it be something that you've pissed off before? And it brought friends? Percy said there was more than one." Merry grabbed him by the shoulders and looked him in the eye again, refocusing as she saw him slipping back into his head. "Oy. Don't wander off."

Reaching up to her hands on his shoulders, Alan squeezed them.

"We need help," he whispered, shaking his head clear. "Hogarth is out of town, Anchorage is in hiding. Let's go see Jennings."

IT WAS DANGEROUS to get so close but the shadow had to know what was going on. Too much hiding at a distance, too much guessing, could lead to them losing Shaw and everything falling apart. And so, when Shaw burst into the Carpenter's home with Merry White hot on his heels, the shadow moved toward the house rather than away, prowling up to a window to watch.

Shaw's lips were easy enough to read but his companion's accent made it more difficult. They were floundering, that was the only certain thing. The wolves had come as a surprise to Shaw. He seemed hollow behind the eyes, unfocussed and barely listening to his companion. This wasn't how the shadow remembered him at all.

The wolves will be disappointed, the shadow thought. *They've come for a man that no longer exists.*

The shadow threw itself against the house as the privateers came back out into the street and walked right past them, unaware of how closely they were scrutinised. Narrowing its eyes at their backs, the shadow decided that they would need to take matters into their own hands if Shaw couldn't solve this thing himself.

5

EVERY HELMETED HEAD snapped toward the door of King Street station when it slammed back, revealing Alan and Merry at full tilt.

"We need to see Jennings," Alan said to the night sergeant and barrelled behind the desk, ignoring the copper's protests.

Alan and Merry cut through the desks toward the glass partition beyond which he'd first met his future adoptive father and brother. Although he didn't know at the time, his life changed the second that Constable Jennings had kicked his little arse through the door into Chief Inspector Carpenter's office. And although he had sworn that day that he'd avoid coppers and police stations, it was this office that he returned to time and again when he needed help. First from his father, then from the constable turned friend, Jennings himself. But as Alan burst through the door to stand before the huge old desk in his casually arrogant way, he froze. The room sat unoccupied.

"Where is he?" Alan asked the sergeant.

"That's what I was trying to tell you, sir. He's not here," the sergeant said in his Irish drawl, a little out of breath from even a short jog. "He went home after you dropped off that spring-heeled nutter yesterday. But he didn't come back this morning. We sent people to his home but…"

Alan finally looked around the station proper and could see that even in the middle of the night, King Street station was a hive. Coppers everywhere, hollow eyed, sweaty, frayed and snapping at each other. Files upon files piled on the tables, the chairs, the floor.

"He's gone." Alan said with certainty.

"Do you think he made it home?" Merry asked.

"Honestly ma'am, we don't know," the Sergeant replied. "There's no signs of struggle at his home, no note. Nothing. We've been studying every person who might have a grudge against the Chief Inspector. But that's a long list."

Alan didn't say anything. He seethed, his breath shallow and fists bunched as he leaned heavily on the Chief Inspector's desk.

"This is happening too quickly," he said. "This thing is smart. Coordinated. I've seen every one of them in the past day. Each one is close to me."

"Sergeant, you shouldn't be looking for Jennings' enemies, you should be looking for Alan's. Get to it," Merry ordered, and the sergeant darted out, already shouting orders.

Merry spun around at the sound of shattering wood and glass behind her to find Alan staring out of the hole where the glass partition had once been. Jennings' battered old typewriter lay in the wreckage of an officer's desk on the other side surrounded by daggers of glass and scattered stationery. Alan stared at it as well, wide-eyed, as if he'd just seen the typewriter fly through the wall all by itself. The entire station froze, a hundred coppers gawking at him. Merry took a step back and felt her back hit the bookshelves.

"He was in the glass," Alan whispered. "That damned grin…"

And now it was worse because Slay was still there, only now a thousand little mouths grinned back at him from every shard that littered the ground. The next thing Alan knew, he was out on the street and unsure of how he got there. He came to a dead stop at the roadside, realising that he didn't know where to go or what to do next.

A hand rested tentatively on his shoulder and he half turned to see Merry on the verge of tears backed by a doorway full of staring uniforms.

"Alan—" she began.

"Stay away from me," he said, shrugging off her hand. "They might come for you next."

"This isn't the time to go off alone," Merry replied. "We should stick together."

"No, Merry." His voice softened. "I need to know that you, at least, are safe. Stay here. They'll look after you." And he stormed away, leaving Merry on the steps of King Street station, his heavy foot and cane ringing out into the night.

ALAN EVENTUALLY FOUND himself at his own front door without really meaning to. He stormed inside, rattling the walls and likely the neighbours in their beds with a slam of the door. In the kitchen he threw open the tea cupboard and reached past the box of leaves to another cardboard carton. Spilling the bullets from box to pocket, he stomped back toward the door to retrieve his revolver from its hook. There was one certain thing in his mind: he was going to shoot someone tonight. Possibly multiple times.

"It's just a party, Alan. You won't need your gun," he muttered, mocking Merry's northern accent.

Then he stopped with his hand on the doorknob. He

didn't know where to go. The few certainties he'd held had all run out.

"Ohdearohdearohdear," Slay chuckled, walking down the stairs from a pitch dark landing.

"Shut it. I've got no time for you," Alan snapped.

"Oh, but you must," Slay said. "You must *make* the time. Because you are lost and you are alone, and that is when your old pal Mister Slay comes to give you what you need. That's what I've been trying to tell you all night. But you always push me away." Slay pouted like a child, his bottom lip exposed in a pouch of visceral red in his otherwise ashen face.

Alan turned to his dark companion.

"What have you noticed that I haven't?" He closed the gap between them in a rush, coming nose to nose with Slay as the spectre leant down from the third step like a hanging willow bough. "What is it, damn you? My family's lives are at stake. If you were ever going to be useful, now's the time."

Slay's grin spread wide like a self-satisfied shark. "What did you miss? Only the whole point of your life, Alan." Slay leaned in and Alan felt the spectre's breath sure as the chill night breeze. "Again and again, I've told you. And still you don't listen. You bring misery to everyone that you gather around you like packing straw for your fragile ego. And now that they're being ripped," the spectre threw the word into the air with a high note, "away, what is left? You. Alone, fragile, talking to yourself in the dark."

Alan's angry brow lifted into worry.

"Yes," the ghost continued as he circled Alan like a swarm of gnats, no longer bothering to feign the act of walking, spreading his next word out in shattering syllables.

"I always end up here," Alan whispered. He looked around the old house, barely anything of himself in it. Just him at the bottom of the stairs that defeated him daily, and the old wisp of a madman's ghost.

"Yes," Slay said.

Alan muttered as if afraid of the words. "I don't know how but I brought this down on them."

Slay shuddered with delight.

"There's still one person to check on. Maybe I can still get ahead of them?" Alan said, the hope in his voice peeling back to reveal an uncertain question behind.

"Why can't you just accept that you bring nothing but pain and failure wherever you go?" Slay said with a caring tone.

"I do, Slay," Alan heaved a sigh. The thought of actually agreeing with Slay brought up some hardwired belligerence that he'd forgotten. Stubbornness flared right down in his core. "But I've tried running away to save those I love from being around me. It doesn't work. And walking away now isn't going to help Helen and Simon and everyone else."

Slay's lips were a hairline across his tense face. He said nothing.

Alan shook his hands like flicking off rainwater and massaged blood back into his cold and cramping fingers where his fists had been clenched.

"Maybe tomorrow I'll give up," he said, finally talking to himself rather than Slay. "But not tonight. If only because there's nothing else I can do, I need to keep going." Rallying every mote of the cold, hard stubbornness he could, he yanked open the door, leaving Slay to haunt the house alone.

"So close," Slay said as the door slammed.

Hitting the street, Alan headed east toward Soho Square. Lost in his fervour, he didn't see Merry peering out of the alley behind him.

Checking the pavement, the roofs, the shadows, Merry

made to follow. But a shadow behind her pulled free of the rest and a blade made itself known with a sharp prick at the small of her back.

"Don't move," the shadow said, their voice muffled by the cloth wrapped around their lower face.

Merry's lips tightened. She shook her head, disappointed in herself, and muttered:

"I hate it when he's right."

6

AS THE NIGHT rolled on even the most stalwart of cabbies had gone home rather than waste money on an idling engine. Alan stalked along the silent street, his cane clacking in the dark, wishing he'd learned to drive like Merry had told him to so many times.

It was a thankfully short walk to Bloomsbury and Alan walked it no longer assailed by Mister Slay. He had to get ahead of this thing, that much he knew. Whatever the wolves were, they had him right where they wanted him. As much as his panic-addled mind would allow, he scanned his memory for any furry, animalistic, wolf-like creatures he'd fought before but nothing in his rogue's gallery sparked recognition. Tentacles, yes. Hulking beasts from graveyards, sure. Undead tomb guardians, regularly. But nothing matched the pack of wolf-like creatures that Alan was imagining.

One thing he did know was that they were targeting anyone he'd been in contact with in the past day or so. At least, he hoped that his visit to Jennings was as far back as it all went. Either way, there was one person left that he had been in contact with that day, or rather yesterday now that the moon was past its zenith and hurtling through the darkest hours of the morning.

Finding himself outside the Bloomsbury orphanage, he knocked loud enough to vibrate the orphans right out of their beds. It was actually Connie who answered. He barely recognised her in bicycle bloomers and blouse, minus her characteristic layer of dirt and with the colourful rags removed from her hair in favour of strips of coloured dye. She peered around the doorway at Alan, sleep crusted in the corners of her eyes and her clothes crumpled in the rush to get dressed.

"I heard about Helen," she said. No hello, no surprise in her voice. "Have you found anything?"

Alan simply shook his head.

"You better come in." Connie widened the crack in the door for him to slip inside and yawned into the back of her hand. Locking the door behind him, she set aside the derringer that she had been holding behind the door, drawing a smile from Alan when he thought none could possibly be left.

"You know how to use that thing?" he asked.

"Good enough," she replied.

On the sweeping stairs that led to the bedrooms appeared orphan after orphan in their night clothes, hair mussed and some of them looking around as if they were still dreaming. Lady Ottaway appeared behind them all, wrapping the belt of her dressing gown around her. She looked down, saw Alan looking back up at her with a pale, grim expression and snapped to attention.

"You should all be in bed," she said to the orphans. "Go on, all of you. Back where it's warm."

There was a pause where no one moved, then Connie broke in.

"Oy!" she called up to them. "You heard lady Ottaway. Back to bed, you lot."

The first orphan trailed away to escape the weight of her glare and little pyjama'd bodies filtered past Lady Ottaway as she made her way down the stairs.

"Tea?" she asked.

"No time," Alan asked. He turned to Connie and said, "is everything locked tight?"

"Last thing I check every night," she replied.

"Do me a favour and double check?" he said. As Connie darted away without question he added: "And that goes for the attic, the basement and—and the bloody cat flap as well."

Connie nodded and disappeared.

"Alan," Lady Ottaway said with a worried tone. "I think you had better tell me what's going on."

Alan sighed. "I'll tell you what I know."

A few minutes later Lady Ottaway sat in her study chair with her long dressing gown wrapped tightly around her, one hand holding closed the collar at her neck, her slippers dangling out of the other end. Alan perched on the desk facing the door as they waited for Connie.

"That's everyone I've seen in the last day, all taken. I thought you might be next and God only knows what they'd do with the kids," he said.

"And you have no clue who these people are?" Lady Ottaway asked sternly.

"I don't think they're people. That's what I'm getting at," he replied.

She gave him a scolding look. "Alan, I know that you like to exaggerate about your adventures. It's all very entertaining. But this is no time for imaginative cartwheels."

"Lady Ottaway," he pointed to the ceiling, "on those kids' lives, everything I've ever told you is absolutely true. And I think that one of those stories that you find so hard to believe is coming here tonight. So whether you believe it or not—"

The double pop of Connie's derringer followed by a thud from above sent Alan darting out of the door. He and Lady Ottaway shot up the stairs side-by-side with the older woman outpacing him easily. She stopped on the landing, looking down both dark corridors for the source of the sound.

"It was above us," Alan said, staggering to his left and down one hallway. "This way."

They rounded the corner to see Connie propped against one wall, a dark figure looming over her, its shoulders heaving. From between the fingers of a talon-like hand pressed to its stomach, blood oozed onto the carpet.

"Gotcha," Alan said and, as the hooded head turned toward him to reveal a heavy brow with shadow-filled sockets and a long, wrinkled muzzle, he fired off three shots.

The wolf was faster. With a deft spin, it sidestepped into the open doorway beside it and disappeared. Screams erupted from inside as the orphans caught sight of the wolf for the first time. Alan gave chase, bursting into the room as the creature made it to the window and smashed right through, ripping the frame right out of the wall as it fell. Alan fired again, lighting up the row of petrified little faces in their bunks in the muzzle flash. He followed the bullet, looking down to an empty street below and only looked up when mortar hit the back of his head. He had two more shots and he used both of them, the bullets smashing through the rooftop parapet as the wolf disappeared over it.

The room fell into a heavy silence as he turned around. Little faces stared at him from behind their blankets, Lady Ottaway stood aghast in the middle of the room, and Connie rubbed her head where she had been slammed into the wall. Other than looking at him like he was a lunatic, everyone seemed alright.

"You just fired a gun in a house, in a room, full of children," Lady Ottaway spat, very carefully not raising her voice.

"Sorry," Alan said sheepishly.

"Downstairs. Now," she whispered.

There was no denying Lady Ottaway's order and he sloped past her. Connie hung back with Lady Ottaway, moving the children to double bunk in another room and locking the door to the room filled with broken glass and gun smoke. When she returned, she found Alan sitting in the study, reloading his revolver. He snapped it closed as she entered and put it away guiltily, then made to say something but Lady Ottaway waved him into silence.

"Are we still in danger?" she asked, coldly.

Alan swallowed before answering. "It would be stupid to come back wounded and knowing we've got guns. It'll slope off for now, I reckon."

"Then I'll inform the police and have them put on a guard. As for you, Alan, we'll be having words when this is all over. But for now, what do we do next?"

"I need to send Connie on an errand. She's still got contacts with the urchins around here. If it's using the rooftops, they must have seen something," Alan said.

Lady Ottaway's outburst rivalled the gunshots in volume.

"You want to send the girl after that creature in the dead of night with only other children for safety? Have you lost your mind?" Lady Ottaway advanced on him, hoisting him to his feet by his collar. "You can't *use* children. They're not bullets to be spent."

Alan grabbed her hands but found that he couldn't remove them. "Connie isn't some defenceless child," he replied. "She's a fighter, she's bloody dangerous. That thing should be *worried* with her on its trail."

"And what if it decides to remove the threat? Or cuts through those urchins as easily as it smashed through that window?"

Connie's voice pierced the argument from where she hovered by the door: "I don't mind going."

"I could give you my revolver," Alan offered.

"That does not improve the situation!" Lady Ottaway screamed in his face.

Alan gripped her hands gently, finally peeling them away through suggestion rather than force, and his heels reached the floor.

"Lady Ottaway. Eleanor. They have my family. What am I supposed to do?"

"We need to help," Connie added.

"Then help we shall. But sending children out into the night is not going to help anything. Sit," she barked at Alan. "And think."

Alan did the former, unsure of how the latter could possibly help. But all the villains of London seemed a mile away at that moment and Lady Ottaway's wrath was all too close.

MERRY SAT IN Alan's armchair by the fireplace piled with unscraped ashes, no hint of an ember left in the dark silver dunes. The shadow wandered around the room, eyeing the shelves filled with oddities, running a hand along the spines of Alan's adventures. The stranger's clothes seemed to billow like smoke and flow like oil around their body, making it impossible for Merry to get any decent read on who they were. What she thought was black she could now see was deepest blue. Their face and head were heavily swathed, their hands covered in gloves that came up to the forearm. The long curved blade which had been pressed to Merry's back lay dormant in a sash at the shadow's waist.

"Are you going to take me hostage as well, then? It'll be nice to see everyone else," Merry said.

The shadow ignored her for a moment as they slid a copy of Alan's graphical adventures from the shelf, turning it this way and that.

"You better put that back where you found it. He'll notice if one is out of place," Merry added, trying to get something, anything, back from the stranger.

After a moment of flicking through the pages, the volume was slid back in place.

"There's one missing," the shadow said.

Merry strained her ears for a hint of the stranger's accent, but it was too short a sentence, too muffled by the cloth.

"You don't wear a wolf mask like your buddies," Merry said. "Does that make you the leader? How come you came after me yourself? Should I be honoured or worried?"

The shadow turned to Merry and she finally saw a hint of the face beneath the cloth, albeit only a slash of brown skin and dark eyes.

"You're a clever one," the shadow said. "Poking around to see if I'll bite. But you haven't softened the dhal just yet."

Merry's ear finally latched onto the accent and she gasped before she even saw their face. The shadow tugged down their mask to reveal an Indian woman beneath. She smiled warmly, but it was tinted with cunning. Her ears were decorated with fine gold earrings, as were one nostril and one playfully cocked eyebrow. The edges of those deep brown eyes showed crow's feet, the long braid of jet black hair which fell from under her headwrap held strands of silver. Her large eyes narrowing with curiosity, the shadow said: "You're looking at me as if you know me."

Merry had to clear her throat of the surprise which had lodged there before she could speak.

"You're Rani aren't you? The freedom fighter," she said.

Rani tilted her gloved hand and back and forth. "Bandit, rebel, freedom fighter. It depends who you ask. He mentioned me, I take it."

Merry nodded. "And I looked you up. Curiosity."

Rani nodded her understanding. "Never a bad thing. For the same reason I know that you – can I call you Merry? – are a privateer of some renown. And that we have a mutual friend."

"Are you actively avoiding saying his name?" Merry asked.

"I'm not here for him, I'm here for the wolves." Rani said, turning back to the bookcase. "They are boys. Young and hot headed with grand ideas."

Merry stayed carefully quiet and Rani smiled at her knowingly before continuing.

"They're here to settle a debt that should have been forgotten about. But I don't want that to happen. Because somewhere between their bull-headed ideals and reality, death will come to some or all of them and we both know why. My country has lost too many young people on the errands of fools. I want them to come home before this gets out of hand."

Merry sucked air through her teeth. "It might be a bit late for that when Alan is involved. He'll be after blood."

"I thought he would pick up their trail faster, or they might reveal themselves," Rani said with a sigh. "But he isn't how I remember him, and they are more sly than I gave them credit for. But now I have you, Merry. Perhaps you can shout some sense into our friend's head and I can make them leave before he finds them."

"Why don't you just talk to him yourself?" Merry asked.

Rani shook her head with a jangle of jewellery. "I'm worried that my appearance might make things worse rather than better. He needs a clear head if he is to survive. They are already ahead of him in every way and from what I've seen, his mind is already—"

"He's been through a lot," Merry interjected.

"Haven't we all," Rani replied thoughtfully.

Getting to her feet, Merry sounded more certain of herself. "We need to get on their trail. We've got to beat Alan to them before one stupid boy kills the other."

"After you," Rani said with a smile and they headed for the door together.

7

O N THE TOP floor of the Bloomsbury Orphanage, a lattice window looked out over London. Alan stood there with the window thrown open, scanning the skyline for hooded figures on the prowl, wanting to avoid sitting in a room with a seething Lady Ottaway if possible. There was nowhere else to go, now. Everyone he knew was either taken already or safe as he could make them. In the absence of action, he felt the fear he'd been fighting all night well up and tip over the edge into anger. He slammed his hand down on his affected leg, a grunt bursting from his mouth to vanquish the threat of a quiver in his throat, the welling of a tear.

"Come on," he whispered to the city. "I've done so much for you. Give me one clue. Anything."

He startled at Connie's voice from behind him.

"Who are you talking to?" she asked as she shimmied up beside him to look out of the window as well.

Alan stepped back to give her space. "Just—the city, for a change. Reckoned it was worth a try."

"And what did it say?" Connie asked.

"Absolutely bloody nothing."

"I would have helped, you know, if—" she began.

"It's alright, kid," Alan interrupted. "You shouldn't be anywhere near this. And to be honest I'd rather you were here protecting the orphanage. You really have found your place, eh?"

Connie sighed and looked out of the window.

"It's smaller than having a whole city as your home," she said. "Less space to move and run. And there are some annoying rules. But I don't need to check every corner or shadow for danger anymore. And I know that Lady Ottaway will always be there for the little ones." After a pause, she added. "I know that's why you sent us here."

"I'm not exactly reliable," he said.

Connie looked at him incredulously with the same hyper-mobile facial expressions that had made him like her in the first place. "Being in one place all the time isn't the only way to be reliable."

"You've been visiting Lottie, haven't you?" Alan asked. "You sound like her."

"She makes good tea and a lot of sense," Connie said with a shrug. "Just look at tonight. What a mess. Your family have been taken by some hairy nutters and are being held god-only-knows-where. But I bet they're not scared. Not one of them. Because they know that you will be coming for them. They know that they can rely on you to bring them home safe. Lady Ottaway knows how to keep children safe in her own way. But I wouldn't want her scouring the city if I were kidnapped. I'd want you. And I bet Lottie and Simon and everyone else are all out there just waiting for you to turn up and take them home."

Alan felt his face constrict, his throat tighten as he regarded Connie's young face leaking world-worn confidence. He took a moment to reply so that his voice wouldn't quiver.

"Thanks Connie," he said thoughtfully. "These wolves

have been watching me. I know that for sure. So they must know I can't pay a ransom."

"It can't be about money," Connie interjected. "Surely they've seen your house."

"Thanks," Alan snorted.

"Sorry."

Alan humphed. "It can't be for leverage because they'd only need one person to make me do something for them. Why take everyone?" He thought for a moment. He couldn't help looping back to a certain fact so he repeated it. "They know me." And it clicked into place. "They know I always go to a friend when I'm in trouble. So they took them away. The list was pretty short, to be fair, and it ended here with Lady Ottaway. I'm such an idiot. They've been tiring me out. Running me ragged, getting me all wound up in my own head. Now the list is all neatly checked, they'll be coming to finish it off."

A smile crept across Alan's face and Connie took a reflexive sidestep as she saw mischief ooze from him. He turned to her with the first true smile she'd ever seen him make. Connie smiled back at him, still a little unsure.

"I've missed the whole point, Connie. Bloody hell. That's what Slay said. It's so annoying. He twists it all around and makes it about him and his chaos but it's always based in truth. Because that's how he has his fun."

"Urm…who?" Connie asked.

Alan's face fell. "No one. The point is, they want me, they'll come get me. They always do. I just need to let them find me."

Alan descended the stairs almost nonchalantly, leaving Connie alone on the landing. She heard the front door click closed and Lady Ottaway floated out into the hallway.

"Where is he going?" she asked.

Connie descended and sat on the third step with her arms folded on her knees.

"Buggered if I know," Connie replied, forgetting herself.

Lady Ottaway clicked her tongue. "Connie!"

"Sorry," the urchin replied on reflex.

BEING SHORTER BY a head, Merry had to jog to keep up as she and Rani cut through the London streets, avoiding open spaces and obvious routes where they might be easily spotted. So easily did Rani wrap the shadows around her that Merry had to keep checking if she was still there. Most reports on her new companion were about her ransacking British Empire trade routes in the hills and deep jungles of India but Merry was swiftly reminded that the bandit queen had grown up on the narrow streets of Delhi before it had been reduced to rubble. Rani might be a panther of a woman, but she had been born an alleycat and it showed.

"So when you say you know where they are, you mean you have a vague idea?" Merry asked.

Rani's mind was anchored on some point ahead, her focus so powerful that it barely fluctuated enough to answer Merry.

"More than vague. They will be down by the docks, close to the boats and an easy escape."

"These wolves have this all figured out," Merry replied, feeling a little like she was talking to herself.

"They should. I taught them."

Merry sighed. "Of course you did. And you're just going to saunter up and down the banks looking for them?"

Rani's eyes finally flicked toward Merry. "You have a better idea?"

"Usually," Merry replied with a bright smile.

Grabbing Rani's hand, Merry dragged the bandit queen south toward the Thames, slicing through the streets by alleys and shortcuts, jogging over the silent roads, ignoring the crossing automatons as their heads swivelled to regard them without comment. Soon they were crossing the broad avenue of The Strand and down narrow, algae-coated steps to a small pier overlooked by Charing Cross Station. Several small vessels bobbed next to the pier, covered by tarpaulins or stacked with boxes. Merry ignored them all. At the pier's furthest end, she spotted what they needed, a small river-skimmer with a motor at the rear. She leapt aboard and began flicking switches. By the time Rani had climbed aboard behind her, Merry yanked on the cord that primed the tesla dynamo and twisted the throttle. The boat leapt forward and out of the water, throwing Rani back over a slatted seat.

"Hold on," Merry said, busting a blood vessel to keep from laughing.

Rani glared.

They skimmed like a stone over the Thames, the engine whirring, wind ripping at their clothes. Rani's hood and scarf fell away to reveal a thin smile summoned by the dizzying speed. Deftly handling both velocity and steering strut, Merry carved their way along the river.

8

SKIRTING AROUND THE British Museum, Alan let his feet guide him so that he could keep his attention on his peripheral vision. They wanted him weak. They wanted him alone. And so, as he arrived at the centre of Bloomsbury Square, Alan stopped, leaned on his cane, and waited. The night was still and crisp. Although outwardly calm, his pulse thundered like hooves in his head.

"Alright. I'm alone, damn you," he whispered to himself. "Come on, you cowards."

He sighed heavily as the night spun out, weaving silence through the trees. The sigh turned to a yawn. Letting his shoulders drop, he bent slightly to rub at his leg then straightened and stretched his back with a few pops and clicks.

"If you wanted me knackered, you've done a good job. Why can they never come first thing in the morning after a good night's sleep?"

He turned, scanning the dark for a wolf's head grinning back at him. In the flicker of moonlight shadows through the square's trees he found only Slay stood like a monolith on the lawn, casting starlight shadows on the grass.

"Ugh. Thought I was done with you for the night," Alan said.

The spectre merely smiled.

A flicker of movement caught the corner of Alan's eye, drawing his attention to the shadows under one of the park's drooping willows. The figure stood perfectly still, so still that Alan thought there were two Slays for the briefest second. But the little moonlight and distant tesla glow allowed him to pick out more details to differentiate the newcomer; no pale face or impossibly wide grin, only a long, wrinkled muzzle peeking from beneath a hood which was no improvement at all. There were no visible holes, no blood soaking the wolf's loose black clothing. This wasn't the one that Connie had shot in the orphanage.

Alan turned slowly, letting the wolf know that it had been seen. It didn't move. The only movement was the rise and fall of its shoulders, the huffs of condensed night air and the slow bunching and releasing of its clawed hands. The night fell into the kind of stillness that only descended upon London in the very earliest hours of the morning when even the cabbies were asleep, the teslas at their lowest ebb, and those who stalked the alleyways had given up for the night. Man and beast hung in the darkness for a moment, watching each other. Alan felt that something was expected of him, but truth be told he felt glad to be standing still for a blessed moment. The wolf moved first, going from statue to greyhound, darting away into the night.

"It's a trap," Slay sing-songed in his ear.

"Good," Alan snapped, his breath fogging in the morning chill as he broke into a dead run, or the nearest he could manage, lurching through the park like a ghoul, ducking branches and dodging roots.

Exiting the undergrowth just in time to spot the wolf

disappear down a side street, Alan smiled to himself as he hopped-skipped onward. That alley was a dead end. He skidded to a halt, pressing his back to the building's corner, half to peek around, half to catch his breath. The wolf stood at the alley's end, looking for a way out. Alan gave what he hoped was a wolfish smile and stepped out to block the alley's exit.

"I guess you're not from round here, eh?" he called out, his voice echoing back from the stoic brick.

The wolf gave him a side glance and their shoulders rose and fell in a heavy sigh. With a burst of speed the figure grabbed a drainpipe and soared up the side of the building, digging its claws into the wall where handholds became too few, and stopping only to show their mask one more time, peering down over the guttering before disappearing.

"Balls," Alan muttered.

The wolf leapt the narrow space between rooftops, headed east, and Alan doubled back out of the alley, his neck craned to catch glimpses of the black-clad figure leaping effortlessly from rooftop to rooftop in the moonlight.

"Perhaps you should save your witticisms," Slay whispered. "You're going to need the extra breath."

Alan gave an annoyed grunt and started the chase, his legs shaking with the thud of the unforgiving pavement under his shoes. Where alleys presented themselves, he used in incomparable knowledge of the city to make short cuts, anything to shorten the wolf's lead. Coming to a panting stop, he grasped his knees where several streets met in an open area around St Giles church and its cemetery. Over it all, close enough to shake the old church as it passed, the monorail ran like a scar between the stars. The wolf leapt from the gutter of a nearby building, seeming to pause mid-air in defiance of gravity, and caught onto the underside of the monorail, swinging across the road before taking off across the roofs once more.

"Hellfire," Alan spat, and started to follow as best he could.

Electrical surges of pain pulsed through his leg, sapping the energy from the rest of his body. If the wolf was leading him into a trap it wouldn't get so far ahead that Alan couldn't follow. That meant it would be holding back a little, keeping him on the hook, and that gave him an opportunity.

Clocking the direction that it was moving, Alan opted to lose sight of the wolf, instead heading toward the monorail's platform steps at the south side of St Giles. Staring up at the stairway leading to a field of stars, Alan knew what he was about to endure. There was no armchair to default to this time and good rest was still a long way off.

He began to climb.

After the first few mountainous steps, sweat already seeped through his shirt. Icy pains shot down his throat with each drag of chill night air. Half way, his sweaty palm finally lost grip on his cane and it rattled down the steps. All he could do was watch it go, listen to the ringing of metal on metal. Finally, the cane clattered onto the pavement and all he could do was stare at it like some ocean floor relic. He could go back. But that would mean restarting his climb and any ground he had gained would be lost. Instead, using both hands on the stair's rail, he climbed hand over hand, focussing only on the next step. By the time he reached the platform high above the rooftops, he was on his knees. Sprawling forward, he dragged himself onto the platform and lay on his side against the railing.

Across the rooftops, the wolf was a jack-in-the-box silhouette, leaping back and forth, looking for him.

"Lost me, haven't you?" Alan wheezed. "Not so smart, now."

He tried to laugh but Slay had been annoyingly right, his breath was needed elsewhere. His cheeks, the air in his lungs, that damned leg, everything burned. Suddenly this seemed like the very worst idea he'd ever had.

He wished for Merry and her glider. He wished for the return of his youth, he wished that he'd never come home to London and met the devil who took his leg from him. In that moment, as his heart lurched along, the pain and the sorrow swelled into an exhausted sob. Legs akimbo, staring at the sky, he thought that if he died where he lay his corpse would at least make a fine mystery for someone else to solve. How the Protector of London came to be on a monorail platform in the middle of the night and how he had simply sat down and died.

"Bloody misadventure, obviously," he said.

"What a disappointing ending."

Hearing Slay's voice, Alan spotted the spectre perched on the platform's railing, feet swinging like a child. Clacking his dry tongue like a stick in a rabbit hole, Alan tutted.

"Can't you even let me die without criticising?"

"Of all the ways to go," the spectre continued. "Explosion, falling from a great height, a gunshot, a blade. I wanted to see the surprise on your face. See that cock-sure smirk fade away, for your life to be snatched away like you snatched mine. But, no. You have to be a disappointment. You have to just lay down and expire like forgotten milk."

Alan felt the hot sting in his eyes, felt the first tear trickle down his cheek. He felt his lips crack and his tongue swell, and every strand of his being seemed to be a dancing mote of agony.

"I'm just so tired," he said.

"And so dramatic," Slay droned.

The platform rumbled beneath Alan, a vibration like the pins and needles of his whole body waking up. As his breath dipped to a mere harrowing pant, he remembered that there had been a plan. The good idea that had sent him crawling up those God-forsaken stairs.

"Simon and Lottie–" he began, but Slay cut him off, rolling his hand as he reeled off the names.

"–and Jasper and Jennings and sweet Helen and blahblahblah."

"They need me," Alan said. Snaking his hand up the railing he found sweaty, infirm purchase on the metal bars.

"I assure you that they don't," Slay replied. "I bet Lottie has it all in hand, actually. I bet they're at home while you dither up here. It's a good job the afterlife is forever or I'd have wasted an awful lot of time on you."

Lights approached down the track, a pair of glowing white eyes that loomed at speed.

Jamming his good foot down with a resounding ring, Alan heaved himself up. His body felt like a depleted automaton, all his steam gone with just enough embers to lumber toward the platform's edge. The thin scar tissue in his thigh felt like it was ready to tear anew. A whimper escaped his lips and he snapped his mouth shut to cut it off.

"Suicide is it?" Slay said, a spike of glee in his dour demeanour. "One final splat. That's certainly better than the alternative, I suppose."

But Alan wasn't listening. Wiping his face on his sleeve, it was impossible to tell what was sweat and what was tears.

"I'll die later. I think I have time for one, last, stupid idea."

The air exploded with locomotive force and the platform lit up as light bounced from the monorail's speeding carriages. Slowing his breath with a long exhale, Alan let his eyes unfocus, felt the air batter against him, listened for the shift of the monorail's sound from high to low, and jumped.

MERRY RELEASED THE throttle and guided the river-skimmer silently along the centre of the Thames. The buildings on both banks were pitch dark with only a few blinking dots to advertise the ends of piers and aerials. Ahead of them, the horizon had become dusky blue with the threat of dawn. With the daylight the Thames would come to life, their stealth would be lost, and so would all hope of finding the wolves among thousands of workers and swarming vessels.

"There are a lot of docks in London." Merry whispered because it felt like the right thing to do. "Do you think you can narrow it down at all?"

Rani scanned the skyline, the water's edge, and finally said, "the north bank."

Merry wanted desperately to ask but thought better of it. Instead she gave just enough throttle to set them on course. The Tower of London loomed beside them and the eerie sound of disembodied birdsong drifted out over the river. Morning was definitely on its way.

Rani cocked her ear toward them in curiosity but quickly dismissed them. Merry bit her lip. All of this sneaking wasn't exactly what she was used to. Her palms itched, her forearm ached to squeeze the throttle, to hurtle toward the villains, engines aflame. Instead, she huffed in the dark.

Like the panther Merry compared her to, Rani ducked low in the boat. One hand gripped the boat's sides to help her balance, the other held out to Merry, patting the air. Merry cut the throttle. She slid off her seat and into the space next to Rani. The bandit queen pointed off toward the northern bank, to the crenulations of the tower itself where the first dawn light glinted on a silver mask.

As soon as Merry had spotted it, it seemed that the wolf spotted them. It leapt atop the wall as if it were on strings, darted along in silhouette, then it dropped and Merry lost it. She was breathing fast, eyes scanning, and she felt a pang of annoyance as she looked at Rani who hadn't moved and didn't seem to be breathing at all. Merry opened her mouth but Rani's outstretched hand finally came down to slowly rest on Merry's, silently begging for patience.

There it was again. Atop the encircling wall, the wolf reappeared briefly, completing an impossibly long jump and disappearing again.

"That's St Kath's Docks," Merry said and hammered the throttle.

They shot forward with a spray of grimy river water.

9

WITH A WET crunch something essential tore in Alan's shoulder, ripping a scream from his lips that was yanked away by the wind and speed of the monorail carriage. The wind grabbed onto his coat, filling the pockets with invisible rocks, dragging him back off the train. He hastily shrugged it off and it ripped free to disappear into the city below. Hooking his elbow through the carriage's door handle, Alan forced his feet down onto the steel coupling at the monorail's tail. The rushing air cooled his sweat to an icy sheen as he hugged the carriage wall. The last droplets of adrenaline and endorphins were wrung out of him and a laughter-sob rattled his ribs.

Wiping his tears against his shoulder, he blinked at the speeding London night. The familiar skyline hushed by in a flurry of inky slate and dormant chimneys, the fires below them all long since dead. Alan thought of all the sleeping heads that lay below, and wished as hard as he ever had to be one of them.

Leaning around the carriage's corner, he spied off to one side of the rail, scanning the night for any kind of movement. It was a burst of pigeons against the stars that drew his eye in the end. Their little black forms exploded from a rooftop nearby and, as Alan strained his eyes that way, he saw the wolf, moving slower now. Occasionally it would stop, look around, check over the side of a roof.

The sound of the monorail's rattling rhythm slowed and Alan knew that this was his one chance to drop to the rooftops without being ripped apart by the landing. Still, he waited. If he dropped too far from the wolf, he would still be unable to catch them. He needed it close. Drawing his revolver with his off hand, the other numb and useless, he held his aim as the carriage began to turn around the bend that it had slowed to address. Alan cracked off two shots, the rooftop slate near the wolf exploding into shards as far on the other side of the roof as he could make them. The wolf bolted first and looked around second, letting their instincts carry them away from danger. And that was exactly what Alan wanted. Another shot and the wolf sped up even further, hurtling across the rooftops toward Alan now, its route taking it right under the monorail.

Alan finally gave in to what his body had been crying out for all night and he went limp, collapsing from the monorail's rear coupling, falling. With his clothes tugging on the wind, the agony of weight through his leg relieved, and a thin buffer of hormones in his system, he took a deep sigh and a long, slow blink. Eyes adjusted to the wind and the dark, he trained his sights on the wolf as he hurtled toward it and twisted in the air like he hadn't done in an age or more. Slamming broadside into the sprinting wolf, they both bounced, tumbling together across the rooftop, only falling apart when a chimney stack got in their way. Alan skidded shoulder-first across the slate, coming to a stop a few feet from the wolf. With their face turned up to the sky, moonlight pouring into the deep crevasses of the moulding, Alan finally saw the mask for what it was. It was exquisitely made, possibly of silver, and where the wolf's hood had fallen in the tumble, he could see the comfortable leather straps that held it in place wrap around a head of pure black hair beneath. Somewhere at the back of Alan's mind, he noticed the detail and began sifting through his rogue's gallery. The wolf's height, fitness, hair colour. Nothing sprang to mind, possibly because his conscious thoughts were so highly focussed on crawling across the roof, closing the gap between them, making sure that his quarry couldn't run again.

Alan announced his approach with a clumsy right hook as he half fell on top of the wolf, and instantly regretted it as his knuckles hit the solid silver mask.

"Sodding thing," he snarled, and ripped the mask right off of his opponent's head, letting it clatter away across the tiles. Before he even tried to identify the face beneath, he punched it to balance some internal scorecard. Going for a second raw jab, he froze mid-slug when his opponent's watering eyes turned silently on him.

He was just a kid. Seventeen, perhaps. Full grown in stature but not in the shape of his chin and dapple of dark hair on his cheeks. Alan stared down into the large, dark eyes, scanned the brown skin for some recognition. The lad had a hardened look in his eye despite the tears and his few years. The wolves weren't monsters with supernatural abilities, just youths without fear.

"Who the hell are you, lad?" Alan asked.

But the wolf, stripped of his mask and beaten, simply looked off to one side, his attention not on Alan at all. Begrudgingly, Alan followed the youngster's eye line to where another wolf stepped out from behind a chimney stack. He looked around, left to right and over his shoulder as more wolves leapt from nearby rooftops or appeared over the parapet until there were assailants on every side.

"Now we're getting somewhere," Alan said.

The boy underneath him smiled up at Alan despite the bruises spreading across his face.

SHOVED THROUGH THE stone doorway, Alan barely managed to duck under the lintel and avoid another injury as he stumbled forward.

"Oy. Watch it," he said to the wolf behind him.

The silver mask remained motionless but the wolf extended a clawed metal finger, gesturing that he should keep moving. Alan audibly growled but did nothing as the other wolves poured in behind the first. The maths was simple enough for even him to understand. There were too many of them, seven in total, and he had only one good arm and one good leg. They had taken his revolver. He'd have to think rather than fight. He growled again.

The cellar that the wolves had made their base lay in the long forgotten foundations of St Katharine Docks. Stone arches held up the ceiling, separated by veins of ancient algae from which dark water oozed and dripped onto the uneven cobbles underfoot. Thick pipes ran helter-skelter through the space and Alan could see that the wolves had used them to hang ragged sheets, separating sleeping spaces where sodden bedrolls lay raised up on crates to escape the damp. For some reason that humanised the wolves far more than removing their masks. Alan could relate to anyone just wanting a dry place to sleep. On one of the bunks another wolf laid on their side, hands wrapped around their stomach. The one who had been shot. Lucky for them that Connie's derringer was only a peashooter. They'd likely be fine if not a little sore.

The prodding wolf led Alan on through another lower

archway and into a larger space beyond. Sewage pipe entrances yawned on three sides, long since disused and dry, but the bars meant for catching detritus were still in place and behind each set were Alan's friends and family, staring back at him from the gloom. Simon, Helen, Jennings and the rest, upon seeing Alan moved closer to the bars and into the faint lamplight that permeated the space. Simon made to speak first, but one of the wolves threw out a hand and hissed, bidding him to be silent.

"Don't you hush him," Lottie said. "What are you going to do if we aren't quiet, eh?"

The wolf leaned down so that they were eye-to-eye with Lottie through the bars.

"Pray you don't have to find out," the wolf rasped in a thick accent.

"Open this gate and we'll see what's what," Lottie growled, drawing a humph from the wolf before they moved on. Making sure to eye the wolf's back just in case they looked back, Lottie continued: "Alan, we're alright. No one is hurt."

Jasper edged forward between his parents. "Are you alright? Are you injured?"

"Nothing I can't handle," Alan replied.

Jennings sat in his off-duty clothes which struck Alan even more than the bruise on his friend's chin or the stubble around his moustache. Without his shiny buttons and dark blue wool, Jennings was almost unrecognisable.

"Evening, Jennings," Alan said.

"Alan. About time," Jennings replied as if they were chatting over any crime scene they had shared over the years. And that was all they needed.

It was Helen, her pale dress muddy right up to the waist, who made Alan finally stop dead despite the wolf prodding him. Alan shoved back with his shoulder and refused to move.

The wolf didn't try again.

"Percy's alright. No need to worry," was all he could think to say. Inside he felt a flurry of promises he wanted to make to Helen, to all of them. But a deeper part of him worried that he couldn't keep them.

"Thank you," she said. "We knew you'd come. Please be careful."

Sounding tired even to himself, Alan said, "got them right where I want them."

But he smiled only faintly as he was moved on.

He was proud of them all. Not one of them showed signs of bending under the hellish circumstances. Their confidence hit him like a cup of sweet, hot tea. He thought of all the whiskey and laudanum he'd shored himself up with over the years. All it took was a kind word from the right person to have the same effect. He laughed at himself. If Merry had only been there to add some scathing witticism his batteries might have been charged all the way.

Merry. She hadn't been captured. Leaving her behind had been the right thing to do after all.

Alan snapped back out of himself as he spotted movement in the gloom ahead. At the furthest end of the cellar, where odds and ends of furniture had been cobbled together in some dark replica of comfort, was a figure that Alan recognised as the leader type, elbows resting on a lopsided table. He was young, though probably older than the others if Alan was any judge. There was a distinct feeling of an urchin crew about the wolves, despite the expertly crafted masks and clawed gauntlets. Alan felt a pang of nausea rise in his stomach. Desperate and smart were a dangerous combination.

"You exceed your reputation, Alan," the leader said. And his looks and accent solidified Alan's theory. The wolves were from India, alright. And now that he spotted it, he could see the material of their clothes, their boots, the designs worked into their metal gauntlets, it was all distinctly Indian in style. "It wasn't easy to get you here."

"You should have just asked," Alan replied. "I had nothing else on tonight."

The leader's face gave a slight twitch that could have been the beginnings of a smile or annoyance.

Alan looked around the room, avoiding the eyes of his family behind their sewer pipe bars. He had to keep a clear head and seeing them like that, cold and wet and trapped, he would get angry. He couldn't let himself get angry when there was more than his own life at stake.

"If you're after ransom, you've chosen badly. I'm not rich. I can't pay for my family back. But I will be taking them out of here tonight," Alan said, letting the threat settle on the whole room.

"That's the man I came so far to see," the leader said. "The man I've heard so much about."

"Yeah, dead famous, me." Alan replied. "Let's cut to it. What do you want?"

"I've already got it." The leader pointed to Alan. "When we've done here, your family can leave. Unharmed. I only want you."

"You put Percy in the bloody infirmary," Alan replied.

"Didn't he shoot you once?" the leader said, now finally giving a tight lipped smile.

Alan humphed. The kid knew a lot about him, more than reading graphical adventures or newspaper articles would tell him. A proper villain, then, not just some wannabe.

"Are you still wondering who I am?" the leader asked. "I thought you would have it by now."

The leader stood, rounded the table, drawing closer to meet Alan eye-to-eye. Alan felt the cold grip of a claw on each elbow as the wolves held him in place but the leader interrupted:

"Let him go. We will meet as equals." The leader stepped closer still, surely knowing that he was in punching range but not caring or trying to seem that way. He looked Alan up and down.

Alan recoiled internally from the scrutiny but tried not to show it. With no coat, no gun, no cane, there was little of his Privateer persona left. He was just a man, past his best and ready for his bed. It felt like the wolves' leader saw exactly that.

The villain sighed. "I've been told so many times what a character you are. A hero thief like some old legend. Finally looking in your eyes, I see that it's all stories."

Alan had been insulted so many times that the barb just slid right off. But he couldn't help feeling on the back foot. Something was bugging him.

"Who's been talking me up so much? I should send them a thank you."

The leader shook his head in disgust. Alan could see the lad's hands twitching, itching to ball up and strike out. The kid was so angry at him, Alan almost felt bad for not knowing why.

"She isn't here. But I am," the leader said with certainty. He narrowed his eyes. "I wonder if you'll remember me. My name is Namish Bhat."

A gasp burst hot from Alan's throat and he fell back from the young man, bumping into one of the wolves behind him who grabbed him again by the elbows, holding him on his feet. He regained his wobbly legs with their help but bubbling nausea cramped his diaphragm, stealing the air from his lungs, denying him any words.

Finally, a relieved smile broke out on Namish's face.

"Yes," he said. "You remember my father. I was named after him."

Alan began to stutter something that never evolved into a full word.

Namish advanced, placing his hands on either side of Alan's face, staring deep into Alan's eyes, soaking in the horror of a decade of nightmares that poured out of him. "I have wondered my entire life how quickly you forgot us. How swiftly the faces of my family had slipped your mind."

Alan's eyes grew wide and in the hanging moment where Namish relished his captive's pain, he saw two things. Namish had taken more than his father's name. Alan could see the Raj in the face of his son. Alan felt the rumble of the crumbling temple under his feet, winced at the whistle and hammer of artillery outside the window. He smelled the jungle and fought desperately for the Raj's face to not rise in his mind, to not summon the look of shock and pain as Alan's bullet fatally wounded him at point blank range. But it was impossible because the face was right there in front of him, glaring back, and there would be no waking up this time.

Alan pulled his eyes away as a tear fell. He wished that he hadn't when he spotted Mister Slay in the cellar's shadows, shoulders heaving with excitement, spectral breath coming out of him in chilled pants. Alan screwed his eyes shut.

"Now, I see that you haven't forgotten them at all," Namish continued almost gratefully. "Good. They should be remembered."

"Please," Alan said. "Just...give me a moment."

Namish looked at his captive, how Alan's eyes scanned the empty corners of the room, how he hunched under the weight of his family's gaze on his back. With a brief refrain of pity playing across his face, Namish stepped away, moving back to the desk where he retrieved a long leather sheath from beneath the table.

"Perhaps you do remember Rani, then? She would no doubt have me say hello," Namish said companionably as he passed the sheath from hand to hand, the lantern light glinting from a silver handle that protruded from one end. "If I hadn't defied her by coming here, that is. She thinks I should forget about you and your transgressions against my family. She said that you were as much a victim of the British Empire as my parents, and my sister. That if you were a cruel man, an evil man, you would have left me to die with them."

Holding the sheathed weapon loosely by his side, Namish returned to the unprotesting Alan who had pressed the heels of his hands into his eyes. He took deep breaths, trying to push back the flooding imagery that usually came only in sleep.

"But we know different, don't we?" Namish continued. "We know that it is far more cruel for you to have taken me from them, to leave me in the hands of strangers, the only survivor, to mourn the loss of loved ones whose faces I barely remember. Do you know what that feels like? To forget the faces of those most important to you?" Namish pulled Alan's hands away and leant down to catch his eye. But Alan's attention was drawn past Namish. Over the young man's shoulder, Slay grinned.

"No, you are a cruel man, of that I'm certain. And I see that you know it too," Namish finished.

"You're here to settle a debt," Alan said, finally. His voice was hoarse but the shiver and stutter had gone.

"Fifteen years overdue," Namish confirmed.

Alan nodded slowly. "And you'll let them all go."

"You have my word," Namish said.

Alan nodded again. "Then I won't fight you."

From behind them came a clamour of voices. Simon, Lottie, Jasper, Jennings, and Helen. Alan heard bars rattle and curses fly. He heard pleading, some to him and some to Namish, to stop this, that some reparation could be made, but he couldn't tell who said what. And under it all, sure as he felt his own pulse, he heard the sound of Mister Slay's excited breath in his ear like the hush of a hungry sea. He felt a lump rise in his throat. Slay really would be there right until the end.

"Would you like to say anything to them?" Namish asked, breaking through to Alan. "Now is the time."

"Never was much good at that," Alan said, shaking his head. He could feel Slay in the chill sweat on the back of his neck, in the tight, ripping pain that came from the scar on his leg.

Namish drew an elegant sliver of pale steel from its leather sheath. "I tried to replicate some of my father's studies, although I can make nothing like his level of skill. The masks and claws, this blade," Namish said, his voice sad, uncertain. "It seemed fitting."

Slay was on top of Alan, now; he could feel the spectre crawling up onto his back, leaning over his shoulder with a neck too long and a grin too wide. He heard Slay's tongue slither along his teeth.

"For the little it's worth, I didn't murder your father. Not on purpose," Alan said.

"You forget that I was there," Namish said. "I heard your revolver with my own ears, saw the muzzle flash with my own eyes, watched the light drain from my father's eyes as he looked at me for the last time."

"I didn't say it was right. I just said that I didn't mean to."

Slay hissed in Alan's ear and he could hear the wet crackle

of saliva deep in the spectre's throat. "Too late, old pal. Too late to make amends. That dagger has your name on it. Enjoy your last few breaths."

Slay continued to chatter and spit as Namish lifted the blade level with Alan's heart, twisting his wrist and aligning his shoulders ready for the thrust. Alan looked down at the blade, then at the young man whose eyes were trained on the dagger's tip. He had frozen. Alan recognised the look on Namish's face, the force of will pounding at a wall of conscience.

"Oy," Alan said. Namish looked up at him. "This is justice as pure as it comes."

Between the two men, Slay's head snaked back and forth, from face to face, as understanding passed between them.

"No," Slay snarled. "You don't get to—"

"It's okay, kid," Alan said, ignoring the ghost. "Reckon we both need this."

Slowly taking Namish's hand in both of his, Alan moved the blade under his sternum, tilting it so that the upward thrust would pierce his heart.

"Like this," he said, managing to give an earnest smile as he squeezed Namish's hand. "I won't even feel it."

In the next room, the cellar door slammed back against the wall and chaos erupted. Voices rang out, metal clanged on metal, someone screamed Alan's name, Slay's rattle rose like a furnace's roar. The cavalry were coming.

Rani was a storm cloud passing through the room, her strikes like lightning flashes against the young wolves who pounced on her. She struck down the first with the flat of her curved blade, the second was taken to the ground by a whirling sweep of her leg. Merry was right behind. She kicked one wolf in the knee and rugby tackled another right out of the air as he tried to leap toward her. They slammed into one of the iron grates and Jennings grabbed the lad from inside, forcing him against the bars. Subdued, he couldn't fight Merry as she took his keys and tossed them to Simon through the bars. Grates rattled and keys clicked home as Merry took a kick to the stomach that dropped her gasping to her knees. For his trouble, the wolf received a right hook from the newly freed Jennings who then dragged Merry to her feet beside him. Simon and Jasper descended on a single wolf together but Lottie had grander ideas. With three short jerks she yanked a low hanging pipe free and held off the remaining wolves single-handedly, water spraying everywhere.

But none of it mattered.

Namish called for his wolves to stand down, but they were already down. Only a small and frantic unit of family and friends were left standing. Silence drifted down on the dockland cellar, broken only by the sound of dripping water.

Namish knelt beside Alan's sprawled form, tears streaking down his face as he cradled the man he had come to vanquish. Merry skidded to her knees beside them, clawing at Alan's shirt. Rani ripped off her mask, pressing the wadded cloth where blood oozed around the dagger in Alan's chest. Alan's hands found hers and their fingers knotted together in the blood. He stared at her fingers for a long moment in confusion then finally looked up into Rani's eyes. He let out a chuckle that turned to a cough. Blood laced his lips and Rani wiped it away with a gentle thumb. More faces surrounded him, his family all wanting to help but having no clue how.

Alan looked past them, blinking slowly as their voices faded to whispers. He searched the shadows of the cellar, felt around in his smoke-filled mind for the sing-song nightmare of the spectral lunatic. He waited for a final cackle, a final acerbic rhyme. He blinked, sending tears rolling down his face and, as the taste of blood boiled in his throat, he smiled.

Mister Slay was gone. And then, so was Alan.

Epilogue

Extract from *The Illustrated Times*, Front Page,
15th July 1872

*Today, London comes as close to a halt as the Heart of
The Empire ever might as we mourn the loss of a local
hero. Readers of the Illustrated Times will be familiar
with the name of Alan Shaw, once a lowly street urchin
who rose to become a privateer in Her Majesty's service,
civilian consultant for the Metropolitan Police, and who
has been the saviour of our fair capital on several
occasions. However, we must report with great sadness
that in the early hours of this morning, Alan Shaw was
slain while once more in pursuit of justice. The murderer,
of whom little is known, was said to be carrying out a
personal vendetta which led to several kidnappings. The
villain did not resist arrest once the score was settled.
Reports suggest that he begged to be placed under arrest by
Chief Inspector Humphrey Jennings who was one of those
kidnapped, and saved, by our hero. All but Mister Shaw
were returned safely.*

*The Illustrated Times would like to extend our
heartfelt condolences to Mister Shaw's family, friends, and
the city of London.*

*A funeral will proceed at Kensal Green cemetery on
Wednesday of this week for all who wish to attend.*

July 1872
Kensal Green cemetery, London

IT SEEMED ONLY fitting that smog should descend on Kensal Green on the morning of Alan's funeral, the sun giving only a source-less, diffuse light.

Merry stood alone in the fog. Despite the oversized coat that she had borrowed from Alan's wardrobe, she felt saturated to the bone, shivering from the inside out. Alan wouldn't have listened either. She looked to her side, where he had stood at the funerals of their privateer friends in the past and wished that she had one more chance to dig him in the ribs for some graveside quip. But there was no gallows humour that day.

People began to gather. Helen arrived with Lady Ottaway held tightly by the hand, Connie in their wake. The tall figure of Anchorage was accompanied by a woman, and a small hooded form that Merry couldn't make out. The priest droned through the ceremony, just a fly in Merry's ear. Soon mourners were stepping forward to take their final moment at the graveside, some in groups and others on their own, some laid flowers and others didn't. One lone figure knelt to the coffin, muttered something, and then walked away from the funeral altogether. A group of smaller shadows hung back by the trees and then scuttled off.

The conjoined mass of Simon, Lottie and Jasper huddled together like rooftop pigeons. Simon hadn't spoken in days. He ate, he drank, and he washed as he was told but speech still seemed too difficult. So it was Lottie who stepped behind the lectern at the head of the dark wood coffin. Jasper stayed with his father, gripping his arm tight in case Simon should wander off into the fog and never be seen again.

Lottie took a breath and her face hardened.

"Alan was a stray," she began, drawing wan smiles from the crowd with her deadpan delivery. "He never came when called, never arrived when expected, and was always late for a man with three faces on his wrist watch." A titter rippled around the people in the fog. "He was a horrid house guest, and a constant worry. The man never ironed his shirt. And we all loved him dearly." There wasn't a single waver in Lottie's voice. She stepped aside as strong and stern as she had arrived.

When it was his turn, Jennings gripped the edge of the lectern with bloody-knuckled hands. He spoke for the metropolitan police in an orderly and emotionless fashion, thanking Alan for his assistance on many cases through the years. He was supposed to step down, then. His job was done. But he didn't. He stood for a moment in silence, flexing the aching hands with which he had almost beaten Namish Bhat to death. Watching the light in Alan's eyes go out, the smile slip from his face, had been too much for Jennings. He paused, reliving the burst of wild retribution that saw him leaping atop the young Indian man, slamming his fists against the boy's blood-slick face, only stopping when Simon and Jasper dragged him away. Jennings hung his head as he spoke, feeling a yolk of guilt lay across his shoulders. He shouldn't have succumbed to revenge, and then again he should have succumbed more.

"Alan was my friend," he said. "I knew him longer than many of you here today, I knew where he came from and I was so immensely proud of the man he became. Even if he never really understood it. Part of me wishes I'd told him. Even though I'd have got nothing but some snide comment for my trouble. Still," he swallowed, "I hope he knew."

Jennings stepped down, making room for Anchorage. The two men shared consolatory shoulder pats on their way past each other.

Anchorage regaled them all with a tale of Egyptian tombs, leaving no detail out and not caring whether anyone believed the truth of it or not. Finally, he said with a smile:

"Alan's moral compass had a spinning needle. That's no secret. But if I could wish you to remember one thing about my dear old friend it's this: for a man with no blood relations, he protected those close to him as if they were family."

As he stepped down, a petite figure in a deep hood played an ancient lullaby which no one had heard before or would again in an odd mix of hums and whistles.

"Some are born with the burden of a strong spirit," Hogarth said when his turn came. Still dressed in his travelling clothes and with his airship ticket sticking out of his jacket pocket, he hadn't even had time to drop his bags before getting to the service and Chester stood nervously with the luggage while Hogarth spoke. "It can lead to great conflict and great purpose. I believe that our friend bore a mighty spirit. I once told Alan that and he told me I was bloody stupid." Hogarth smiled and shook his hung head. "He never saw himself as we saw him."

He stepped down, standing shoulder to shoulder with Chester, their hands brushing in the gloom.

The priest motioned to Merry, who had planned to say a few words herself, but she could only shake her head when the moment came. Pulling away from Lady Ottaway, Helen came over to rest her head on Merry's shoulder and grip her hand tight. Helen being taller by a head, it was uncomfortable but welcome.

The funeral drew to a close and people wandered away. Merry stayed. The gravediggers tried to move her on but she silently paid them off and waited a while longer.

"I keep thinking he's going to run in, all out of breath and covered in something disgusting," Merry said as a final shadow arrived.

"He could make an entrance out of a light breeze and a piece of string," Rani replied.

"He was an idiot."

"Yes. He was."

Rani's arm slid into Merry's. They stood together until the fog no longer hid them and weak sunlight caught the stale roof water and overflowing gutters of London, giving the capital a deceptive sparkle.

"Are you going home?" Merry asked.

"I might stay for a while. Namish is alone here now. He needs someone to support him until…We both know how the trial will end."

Merry pulled away from Rani to stare at her coldly. "And you're happy being a friend to Alan's murderer, are you? Patting his head on the way to the gallows?"

Rani's face grew tight around her eyes, the closest thing to grief Merry had seen her display.

"I'll help an orphan who has made a dire mistake and needs guidance," Rani said. "To honour an old friend who never got any."

Merry turned away. "It's not the same."

IN THE COMING days, the funeral continued in fits and starts as companions from across the years and across the globe made it to London to pay their respects. Lottie accepted visitors and

Merry put up those who needed places to stay in Alan's house. Still, Simon didn't speak. He accepted condolences with a weak smile, shook hands and received hugs, but it was Lottie who did the talking, Jasper who brought the tea and sandwiches. Slowly but surely the visitors petered out and all that was left were piles of letters, postcards, and vases of wilting flowers. Simon sat at his desk from dawn until dusk each day, replying personally to each with a steady hand. And when that was done, he heaved a sigh and called Lottie's name, the first sound he'd made other than sobbing in over a week. Darting into the room with concern written across her face Lottie stalled in the doorway as her husband gave her a tight lipped smile.

"Shall we have some tea?"

Lottie's relief leaked out through her smile and with a lilt of love in her voice she said, "I think we should."

Jasper helped his mother to bring in the tea tray and the Carpenters sat in front of the large fireplace. Simon laid a hand on his son's head and shed a tear as he saw Alan's chipped old cup steaming in Jasper's hands.

ALAN'S LIVING ROOM was filled with a quiet kind of bustle, exactly the kind that he would have hated. Merry sat in the window seat with a stack of Alan's graphical adventures beside her, thumbing through them one-by-one and occasionally tutting or snorting. Percy had managed to make his way in, leaving his wheelchair at the door, but the effort had exhausted the bandaged and bruised mess that he was, and he sat quietly in the second wingback chair. On the stool beside him sat a young boy happily picking his nose. Helen bustled around, helping the boxing and sorting efforts, but returning to fuss around Percy regularly. When she returned, the boy looked up, withdrawing the finger guiltily. Helen just beamed down at him and stroked his wild street haircut which would need to grow out before it could be tidied. Percy couldn't take his swollen and blackened eyes away from Alan's chair which sat vacant across from him.

"I don't know what would have become of me if I'd lost you, Helen," he said from behind his mask of bruises. He reached up, gripping Helen's hand and she squeezed back as she looked down at him.

This was a new Percy. There was something homely about her husband, now. They had a lot of time to sit together, to talk and read while he healed from the wolves' attack. And with the arrival of Thomas, it was as if everything had finally been drawn together for them, as it was always meant to be. Not even the other people in the room could hold him back from expressing his affection as he once would have.

"Let's not think about it, now," Helen said softly.

"Of course," Percy replied. "He said he'd bring you back safe and he did. That's all that matters."

Silence played out as they regarded the empty chair together. Finally, Percy spoke again.

"I just realised something."

Helen looked down at her family. "What's that?"

Percy chuckled, winced, and said in a rasping tone. "The blighter still managed to have the last word."

"How is your pain, dear?" Helen asked.

"Fine, fine," Percy replied, but the ruse was obvious.

Helen gripped his shoulder gently. "Come on. You need rest. And Thomas' eyelids are drooping as well."

"We should get him home, I suppose," Percy managed.

Helen rolled her eyes as she took her husband's weight for the short walk to the door. Addressing the room from under

Percy's arm, she said: "We must be off. But I hope to see you all before you go your various ways. Please do come and see us. Won't you?"

With various nods and waves, the Harrigans were gone.

Atop a stepladder, Anchorage turned back to his search through Alan's collection of oddities, passing them down to Zoe for packing in assorted crates and boxes. Somewhere in the house, Rani drifted from room to room marked only by the sound of footsteps on threadbare carpet.

"What's to become of this place?" Anchorage asked, hoping to break Merry from her silence for a moment.

"He willed it to Lady Ottaway. Furniture and all. Apart from the dangerous stuff that he wanted passed to you."

Anchorage eyed the graphical adventures piled by Merry's side. "And those?"

"I guess I'll put them in storage or something. I'd hate to throw them away," she replied, thumbing through a new issue.

"Maybe you should pass them on. Stories are for sharing, after all."

Merry hummed her agreement but made no suggestions.

Anchorage coughed as he disturbed a stockpile of dust at the back of a shelf. Retrieving a smooth river stone with interlocking spiral markings, he wiped it with his hand, and stared at it aghast.

"Look at this," he said. Only Zoe looked up from where she was carefully packing trinkets into wooden boxes. "Would you believe that I've been looking for this for over twenty years? And it was here all the time, just sitting on Alan's shelf like some common paperweight."

Zoe whistled.

"I'm sure he wouldn't mind you having it," Merry said half-heartedly.

"I'm amazed that none of this has caused serious problems," Anchorage said, wrapping the stone in a rag and handing it to Zoe. "Be especially careful with that one."

"That lying sod," Merry scoffed.

"That's a little harsh, Merry—" Anchorage began.

Merry stabbed her finger at one of the graphical adventures. "I saved him from that Maltese grotto. The pirates had him bang to rights and I saved him. Here he's got it the other way around."

Anchorage smirked. "Alan's grip on the truth was always rather fluid."

"I'll bloody slap him—"

Merry stopped short, swallowed, and then slowly closed the comic book, setting it aside. Anchorage came to her side, crouched beside her, and they held hands while the morning traffic honked and hawkers squawked outside. When Rani walked in, the old friends parted slowly. Merry wiped her nose on her sleeve and peered out of the window to avoid eye contact with Rani. Anchorage looked between them and cleared his throat awkwardly. Zoe gave an uncertain trill.

"Best be off," Anchorage said. "Lots to put into safe keeping. Some lead boxes to purchase just in case. Merry, I'll be in London for a little while longer. Please come see me."

Merry didn't turn. When she spoke, her voice sounded hollow bouncing back from the window pane. "I will."

"And Rani," Anchorage said, taking the bandit queen's hands in both of his, "it has been a pleasure to meet you despite such dire circumstances. I can see why Alan thought so highly of you. If you ever need anything—"

Rani cut him off with a smile. "Thank you, Lorne. But I doubt we'll meet again."

"Right. Of course," he said falteringly. And then, with

nothing more to say, he added. "Safe travels."

With whistles and shuffles, Anchorage and Zoe left only a bandit and a privateer in the rundown parlour.

Merry didn't turn away from the window but checked the corner of her eye when Rani sat hip to hip with her on the window seat. Merry ignored her, taking great interest in the foot traffic and the odd reporter who still buzzed around the place. When she glanced aside again, Rani was still looking at her, a soft and unreadable expression on her face. Merry snorted and looked away again. And she kept looking away until she couldn't anymore, until her throat strained against the tears and she thought it might burst.

In one purposeful movement, Merry spun on her bottom and wrapped her arms around Rani. The bandit queen hugged her back, wordlessly.

"How will you get home, when you go?" Merry asked quietly, her voice mostly muffled by the folds of Rani's clothing.

"By ship, I think. I can be home in a matter of weeks."

Merry sniffed, pulled away so that she could wipe her nose. "Would—wouldn't you rather fly?"

Rani's calm sadness broke into a broad smile. She nodded gently as she regarded her goggle-wearing friend.

One by one they all went their separate ways. The Harrigans returned home, feeling complete for the first time. Anchorage slid boxes of newly paper-tagged trinkets onto shelves already brimming with curiosities. The Carpenters chatted quietly by the fire that had once kept warm a pair of chuckling boys wrapped in oversized towels. Merry eased the controls of the glider, glancing over to where Rani sat with her bare feet up on the console.

IN THE OLD parlour where dust had once gathered like old memories in the nooks and corners, the sound of children playing on the floors above banished a sad silence. Connie entered with a group of orphans carrying cushions and blankets which they set around Alan's old fireplace. When they were all comfortable, Connie turned a new issue of The Graphical Adventures of Alan Shaw to the children so they could see the pictures and began to read.

Dear Reader

Thank you for reading *Grave Purpose*. If you enjoyed this book (or even if you didn't) please consider leaving a star rating or review online. Your feedback is important, and will help other readers to find the book and decide whether to read it, too.

About the Author

Craig Hallam's work spans Fantasy, Sci-Fi, Horror, and Mental Health non-fiction.

Since his debut in the British Fantasy Society journal in 2008, his tales have nestled between the pages of magazines and anthologies the world over. His Gothic Fantasy novel, *Greaveburn*, and Steampunk trilogy The *Adventures of Alan Shaw* have filled the imaginations of readers with their character-driven style and unusual plots.

His critically acclaimed non-fiction book on living with depression and anxiety, *Down Days*, hit #1 on the Amazon Bestseller list and has helped people all over the world to feel less alone with their mental health issues.

He continues to write in every genre imaginable and in the cracks between them, creating stories of real people in fantastic worlds.

Embrace The Weird!

craighallam.wordpress.com

Or tweet at him:
@craighallam84

More From This Author

Greaveburn

From the crumbling Belfry to the Citadel's stained-glass eye, across acres of cobbles streets and knotted alleyways that never see daylight, Greaveburn is a city with darkness at its core. Gothic spires battle for height, overlapping each other until the skyline is a jagged mass of thorns.

Under the cobbled streets lurk the Broken Folk, deformed rebels led by the hideously scarred Darrant, a man who once swore to protect the city. And in a darkened laboratory, the devious Professor Loosestrife builds a contraption known only as The Womb.

With Greaveburn being torn apart around her, can Abrasia avenge her father's murder before the Archduke's letter spells her doom?

Paperback ISBN: 978-1-908600-12-7
eBook ISBN: 978-1-908600-13-4

Not Before Bed

A collection of tales to tingle your spine and goose your bumps. Enter worlds filled with tentacle pods, bogeymen, dark gods; vamps zombies, werewolves, and things with no name. 'Not Before Bed' isn't just a title…it's a warning.

Paperback ISBN: 978-1-908600-34-9
eBook ISBN: 978-1-908600-35-6

Available from all major online and offline outlets.

9 781913 117191